WEBSTER

By Amanda Desiree

Published by Inkshares, Inc., Oakland, California
www.inkshares.com

Edited by Adam Gomolin
Cover design by Tim Barber, Dissect Designs
Interior design by Kevin G. Summers

ISBN: 9781950301621
e-ISBN: 9781950301652
LCCN: 2023939603

First edition

Printed in the United States of America

PART TWO

PART TWO

EXCERPT FROM
SMITHY: THE MILLENNIUM COMPENDIUM
BY REID BENNET, PHD

CHAPTER NINE: NEW START, NEW PROBLEMS

Defeated and distraught after the latest tragedy, Preis-Herald's researchers relinquished their work of fourteen months, their controversial headquarters, and their dreams of scientific greatness, separating to pursue individual, uncertain futures.

Nobody's future was less certain than their research subject's.

The dissolution of the Yale study ought to have ended Smithy's story. His name should have been lost in ignominy, relegated to an obscure historical footnote or a puzzling trivia question. Instead, his transfer to a new home launched a new and frightening phase in the saga that would eventually grip the world . . .

LETTER FROM RUBY CARDINI
TO TAMMY COHEN

August 7, 1975

. . . *While I'm grateful to Piers for allowing us to accompany him and Smithy to Fresno, I wish I hadn't seen what I saw. I'll try to give you an accurate picture of what happened without making you feel as dispirited as Jeff and I do.*

The Center for the Scientific Advancement of Man is the most aptly named organization I've ever seen: its sole purpose is to advance and enrich one Manfred Teague, AKA "Man—not Fred, not Manny—just <u>Man.</u>"

Dr. Teague is sixtyish, stocky, and florid-faced with pale eyes, thinning blond hair, and a little Van Dyke beard. He also has a god complex and an excessive taste for drink. If ever I thought Piers was arrogant, I did him a disservice.

When we entered the lobby of the visitor center, we were greeted by a giant portrait of Teague in formal attire standing astride a bearskin rug beneath a lion's head mounted over a fireplace. A dog lies supplicant at his feet while a chimp cowers in his arms and a large bird (a hawk, I think) perches on the mantelpiece behind him. I'm surprised he didn't force the artist to include a concubine with a bowl of grapes and a palm frond in the background. The work is called <u>Man and Beasts</u>, and it typifies Teague's worldview. His laboratory is Man's world, and he rules it entirely: animal subjects, research assistants, office staff.

Visitors.

Man met us without the least courtesy. Rather, he acted like we'd done something to offend him, although we were on time and had come at his invitation. He looked over Jeff and me once, briefly, then focused his attention on Piers. He never even shook our hands or asked our names.

Teague was even colder toward Smithy. You would think, having paid such a large sum to acquire him, Teague might show some excitement at seeing him. Instead, the first words out of his mouth were, "So, this is the little beast. Let's have a look at him." He then proceeded to thoroughly inspect his new toy, check his gums, feel his muscles, etc.

Poor Smithy cringed the whole time. He was so anxious, he was shivering. Jeff held him steady during the examination and groomed him to try to calm him. About halfway through the interview, Smithy signed, "Who are you?" but Teague didn't react. He didn't seem to care that his chimp wanted to talk to him, nor did he ask for a translation. Clearly Smithy's language abilities are what make him so valuable, so I'm puzzled as to why Teague never addressed them. He merely said Smithy looked healthy enough, even if he was too well-fed, and that he should eventually breed successfully. Then he led us outside to the cages.

Teague's chimps are actually well-off compared to some medical test subjects, though I grit my teeth as I write that. Unless they're actively participating in a trial, they don't have to live in a tiny box with bars in some darkened basement. They reside in twos and threes in large outdoor cages with small trees, climbing platforms, and ropes, almost like zoo enclosures. The campus includes about fifteen acres of fields and groves and a small man-made lake where the chimps are occasionally taken for walks. I hope Smithy gets lots of exercise. I can't imagine how he'll survive if he has to stay caged all the time.

The first attempt to put Smithy in a cage failed. Teague unlocked the door and told Jeff to toss him inside. Poor Jeff started to carry Smithy into the enclosure, and Smithy went wild. He tried to clamber over Jeff's back and escape. He thrashed and pulled at Jeff's hair and beard something awful, but Jeff never complained. He kept telling Smithy that everything would be all right, but I could hear tears in his voice. I'm sure Smithy did, too.

Finally, Piers took Smithy from Jeff and carried him into the enclosure himself. Smithy clung to Jeff so tightly, Piers struggled to peel him away. God forgive me, but I hoped in a dark part of my soul that Smithy would take a bite out of Piers.

Up in their branches, the other animals in the cage screeched and threw sticks (and other things) down on the new arrivals. I'm surprised our boy didn't have a heart attack. He hasn't seen any other chimps since he was born and had no idea what was happening except that he was in danger.

The whole time, the hair on Smithy's back and arms was standing straight up like porcupine quills.

Teague told Piers to leave Smithy there. I protested, arguing that Smithy, as an outsider, would be attacked. The bastard just laughed at me. "Kid, that's the law of the jungle. Your fancy little Lord Fauntleroy has to learn what he is and where he is. Getting bitten or scratched is a chimp initiation. He's got to find his place in the hierarchy." Then he showed me a cattle prod and said, "If things get out of hand."

Jeff went in the cage and helped disentangle Smithy from Piers. The poor little guy clung to them both. Jeff kept asking Smithy to let go, and, after about ten minutes, Smithy did. Teague stood by, toying with the cattle prod the whole time. I think Smithy sensed what would happen if he didn't behave.

When Piers and Jeff exited the cage, Smithy leapt for the door. Teague barely shut and locked it in time. Our poor boy hung on to the bars and cried, signing, "Out! Out!" over and over. Then he signed, "Sorry," like he thought we were leaving him there as punishment. It made me sick. The only reason I didn't cry was because I swore to myself I wouldn't lose it in front of Teague. I didn't want to give him the satisfaction of seeing me as a 'weak' or 'soft' little woman.

Teague told us to come back to the house and have some lunch, to leave Smithy to "get used to his new home."

When I looked back, Smithy had given up groveling at the door and retreated to a corner of the cage farthest from the other chimps—who were mercifully still in their places in the trees. He was rocking back and forth with his hands over his face, like maybe he thought it was all a bad dream he could wake from if he first rocked himself back to sleep.

I can't bear the thought of leaving him in that place. He must be so frightened. His friends are gone, his home is gone, his clothes are gone. He's been thrown in with a bunch of strange noisy monsters out to get him, and he has no idea why. No matter what he did at Trevor Hall, he doesn't deserve this. Throwing Smithy in the deep end and expecting him to swim isn't workable. Chimps can't swim.

The whole thing sickens me. Literally. I feel like I'm going to throw up any minute, and I haven't eaten anything since we boarded the plane.

4

Once we got to our hotel, I cried for over an hour. Jeff held me, and he cried, too.

Despite Teague's "clean break" philosophy, we mean to reason with him. Jeff and I have talked extensively, and we agree we're not willing to leave Smithy behind. We're going to appeal to Teague to take us on as researchers at his facility. It's not such a crazy idea. We have experience handling primates, and we practically have our degrees in hand. I could transfer my credits to the local university and finish up there, or petition Yale to let me take a yearlong sabbatical for more field experience. It won't be forever. Eventually, we will have to let Smithy go, but not like this. Not right now. We're going to stand by our boy as long as we can and help him adjust. Then we'll go home.

If Teague won't let us stay, we'll just have to kidnap Smithy.

Wish us luck!

Ruby

LETTER FROM RUBY CARDINI
TO TAMMY COHEN

August 10, 1975

Dear Tammy,

We've succeeded! Sort of.

Man has agreed to add us to his staff. Jeff is relieved. He was having nightmares about Smithy being in that place. Now we'll be able to keep an eye on him. Perhaps seeing a couple of friendly faces will buck him up enough to adapt to his new circumstances.

The downside is that now we'll be in that place. That's almost enough to give me nightmares. I keep telling myself it's jitters: I was reasonably prejudiced against CSAM at first because Man was taking Smithy from us. I was primed to see horrors everywhere, so naturally I found them, and in doing so, I overlooked the positives of the organization. CSAM has conducted some interesting and wide-ranging research. This could be a great opportunity. I must believe I'm doing the right thing.

I agree with what Jeff said on our first day here: "Smithy's our responsibility. He's like a defenseless child, our child! He depends on us. We can't cast him out like garbage. Even if he hurt our friends, we can't judge him without trying to understand why, and we'll never get that chance if we turn our backs on him like Piers. Piers's experiment is in ruins, so he's pissed. For him, Smithy was only a route to more accolades. For me, Smithy represents the best part of my life. It's because of Smithy that I met you."

He can be sweet, even when he's tearful or raging.

We'll start our new jobs in two weeks. That leaves us time to make some bare-bones preparations. Jeff will stay in California and look for a place for us to live. Meanwhile, I'm going back to Connecticut to arrange the move. I have to gather my things, sell off or give away what I can't take with me, and do the same for Jeff. He'll be back to oversee the packing of his camera equipment.

We've decided something else, too: we're in this together, and that means getting a license from the justice of the peace. I'm full of butterflies and tearful but triumphant at the same time. I expect CSAM to be the "worse," but I'll have a "better" to counter it.

I called my folks last night for the first time in over a year. I had thought to write but suddenly I wanted to tell my mother my news. When she answered, I hardly knew what to say after so long. Mom sounded surprised—and unsteady, once she knew it was me—but she stayed on the line. We had a long talk about all that's happened in my life and about Jeff and our plans. Vince had filled Mom in on more than I had expected, but of course neither of them knew about me pulling up stakes to move West. Mom cried over that, but I suppose that's natural upon learning your lately estranged daughter is moving thousands of miles away. I think she's happy, nevertheless.

My dad even got on the line for a bit. That was more nerve-wracking, but we stayed cordial. He's not happy that I'm going the secular route instead of marrying in the Church, but Jeff is a Methodist, so we couldn't have a Catholic celebration, anyway. I think Daddy's at least glad I won't be "living in sin" anymore. He started to warm up a little toward the end of the conversation. He even made a crack about grandchildren. Maybe he thinks getting married will get me to stop thinking about an advanced degree and turn me into Suzy Homemaker. We even talked about them coming out to New Haven for the wedding, but it's short notice. At least talking is a start.

I'd better wrap up and start packing because we have tons to do and not much time to finish it all. I'll wire you about the dates for our departure. Please come! I'd love to see you again before we leave.

Warm regards,
Ruby

ANNOUNCEMENT FROM
THE *NEW HAVEN REGISTER*

August 27, 1975

Kurt and Martha Dalton are pleased to announce the marriage of their son Jeffrey, age 25, to Ruby Veronica Cardini, age 22, of Scranton, PA. Miss Cardini is the daughter of Umberto and Patricia Cardini.

The couple wed in New Haven on August 26th. Both attended Yale University and met while collaborating on a research project. They move to California in September; Jeffrey will pursue a graduate degree at Fresno State University.

POSTCARD FROM RUBY DALTON
TO TAMMY COHEN

August 30, 1975
Front: Image of Santa Cruz Boardwalk;
Text: "Santa Cruz, California"

We made it! We're honeymooning in Santa Cruz, about halfway between CSAM and my darling new in-laws. My older, married SIL Angie has offered to help me set up "house," though our new apt hasn't space for much beyond a murphy bed and coffee table.

I finally got to walk on a "real" beach! It was magical. We found more magic at the Mystery Spot, a natural wonder where gravity is askew, water runs backward, and people appear to shrink or grow depending on where they stand. We skipped the Winchester House though; we've had enough of haunted houses.

Please visit us soon!

xoxo

Ruby & Jeff

EXCERPT FROM
SMITHY: THE MILLENNIUM COMPENDIUM
BY REID BENNET, PHD

CHAPTER TEN: PHASE TWO

. . . Manfred "Man" Teague was already infamous among his peers. After Smithy arrived at CSAM, Man's reputation grew more controversial.

While he was long regarded as a controlling, unpredictable firebrand, most people were unaware of Teague's deep-seated paranoia, or that he spied on his employees throughout the facility. Hidden recorders gathered audio. "Security cameras" were conspicuously placed in laboratories and the animal quarters, but cameras were also secreted in the break room and the offices of Drs. Edgar Torrance and Janet Fairbanks.

Lawsuits inevitably brought these recordings to light. The ensuing transcripts shed additional insight into the experiences of the Daltons, their fellow researchers, and the chimps.

CLOSED-CIRCUIT FOOTAGE

Date: September 3, 1975
Location: Corridor D, Research Animal Quarters

The concrete-walled, windowless space is arranged like a kennel. Animals are stacked in twenty-one sturdy chain-linked cages three levels high. Each cage is roughly five-by-five-by-six feet. The room is devoid of natural light; overhead fluorescent fixtures provide the only illumination. Each cage contains a macaque, capuchin monkey, or chimp.

A stout blond woman wearing a dark sweater, plaid skirt, and tights, weighs food on a scale near the sink on the left side of the room. She fills a series of plastic trays. The door to her left opens and a black woman wearing jeans and a T-shirt enters, followed by Ruby.

Taniesha says, " . . . only a few on the ward right now. Later I can show you the ones outside."

Marianne looks up from the trays, puts her hands on her hips, and asks, "Is she allowed in here?"

Taniesha says, "Man said to show her around, so I figured I'd introduce her to some of our subjects."

Ruby says, "Hi, Marianne."

Marianne doesn't respond and returns to her work.

Taniesha crosses to the opposite end of the room, away from Marianne. She points out the cages, and says, "Our little guys, the capuchins and the macaques, don't have real names. We go by the codes on their ID bracelets. See: MONKEY #IA689."

Ruby asks, "Why's that?

Taniesha says, "Ah . . .they don't tend to be as hardy as the apes. But we still give them nicknames. I call this one Bozo. All that hair sticking up looks to me like a clown's wig. The chimps get proper names. Right now, we've got twenty-four; twenty-five with yours. Only twelve are in trials currently." Taniesha points to the highest cages and says, "The one on the left is Bashful. Next to him is Kidd, as in Captain. Then Woolly, Nero, Fred, Bill, Gef—"

Ruby says, "Like my husband! Are they all males?"

Marianne points directly behind her to two chimps on the lower level and says, "Those are Camille and Violetta. Dr. Pankhurst named them. He's not here anymore."

Ruby asks, "Why?"

Marianne says, "He was an opera buff. He named them after tragic heroines."

Taniesha says, "I don't think she was asking about the chimps, Marianne. Pankhurst wanted more latitude to pursue his inquiries. He said Man was too overbearing. It's a shame; he was cool. Even if he did always blast opera music."

Taniesha pauses in front of one cage. The chimp inside fidgets listlessly with a corn husk and watches the two women with suspicion. Taniesha says, "Man's particularly proud of this one."

Ruby asks, "Any special reason?"

Taniesha says coldly, "He *acquired* her all by himself."

Ruby watches her questioningly.

Taniesha adds, "In Africa. Man goes there pretty often. He calls it his 'shopping trip.' He usually brings back new specimens, but mostly I think he goes for sport. Rosalie here served both purposes."

Ruby asks, "How do you mean?"

Taniesha says flatly, "He likes to hunt, as you may've guessed. Rosalie and her mother were minding their own business one day when Man was out hunting. He shot and killed her mother. Said she was gonna attack. Took the baby girl home to experiment on her."

Ruby, visibly shocked, says, "My God!"

Taniesha turns from the cage to face her, expression wooden. "Exactly."

Ruby asks, "Did he—? Does—? How do these animals come to be here? Has he *acquired* any others that way?"

Taniesha says, "Not with his own hands, but that's common practice among animal traders, regardless of what the governments might say. Of course, some chimps are bred stateside, like this one." She steps in front of the next cage, and the ape inside stares back. "This lady is Eleanor. Man named her."

Ruby asks, "For the Queen?"

Taniesha says, "For Eleanor Roosevelt. That's who he says she looks like."

Ruby says, "Oh." She gazes at the chimp's wrinkled face and says, "Hello, Madame Eleanor. You've got a cool namesake."

Eleanor turns her back.

Ruby says, "Hmmm. She's not very sociable."

Taniesha says, "She's on meds. I'm not allowed to say what kind."

Marianne says, "You don't know that!"

Taniesha says, "OK, fine. Eleanor's in a double-blind trial, but her symptoms of moodiness and withdrawal are more in line with the drug than the placebo."

Ruby says, "Am I allowed to know what kind of trials are going on?

Taniesha says, "Sure. We've got three active drug trials and one more in the red-tape phase. A mobility study. An aggression study—seeing what colors or noises or combinations thereof are most noxious. Some off-the-wall stuff, but you get used to it . . . " She hesitates in front of a row of empty cages. "Ahhh . . . it looks like one study is in progress now. Victoria—we say *Old Vic* 'cause she's been around the longest—should be in here. The other chimps in our collection are Wendy, Ajax, Muriel, Rocky, Nando, Grandee, Ted, Philip, Fanny, Belle, Old Kate—she's right behind Old Vic in the matron department—and Mr. Splitfoot. He's got the devil in him; we have to keep him and Nero separated."

Ruby whistles and says, "Wow. That's a lot to remember."

Marianne snickers, and Ruby glances back at her.

Taniesha pats her shoulder and says, "You won't be working with them all at once. You've got time to learn their names. And you will. They'll become familiar, and they'll grow on you. Unfortunately."

Ruby asks, "Why do you say it like that?"

Taniesha looks somber and says, "Some of the trials we do here are hard on the apes. Sometimes they leave marks. Or worse. Kidd used to play all the time, just like a kid. He'd spin in circles when he was out in the big cages or anywhere he had room; put his hand on the ground and push himself till he got dizzy. But he went through a trial . . . I can't even remember what it was now . . . "

Marianne washes her hands at the sink and calls, "Meningitis."

Taniesha says, "Yeah, complications from the disease they injected him with to test the vaccine cost him the mobility of his arm. Now he can't

14

swing—and he certainly can't spin. You hate to see that kind of thing happen, but you can't do anything about it."

Marianne says, "Better it happens to an ape than some poor kid. We do important work here."

Taniesha says grimly, "Yeah. Well, that's all for corridor D. Corridor E—for *external*—refers to the outer enclosures, if you hear anybody mention that. Now I'll take you back to C . . . "

She opens the door and leads Ruby out.

Ruby pauses at the threshold to glance back at the cages. Her gaze travels over the imprisoned animals, then she shuts the door.

Marianne turns off the faucet and loads the trays into the refrigerator.

CLOSED-CIRCUIT FOOTAGE

Date: September 8, 1975
Location: Corridor B, Lab B

Ruby and Taniesha, each wearing a work apron, stand in a corner, whispering inaudibly. Ruby slouches, hands in her pockets, but both women jump to attention as the lab door opens. Ruby squeals as Smithy, on a leash, runs inside with open arms. He stops short, jerked backward by Man, who enters the room behind him.

Man orders, "Heel!"

Smithy struggles, prying at the collar around his neck.

Ruby kneels and signs to him, "Stop. Be good."

Smithy whines.

Man jerks the leash again and says, "None of that! Now do you see why I don't want him to have anything to do with you? You get him worked up."

Ruby stands and puts her hands behind her back in a submissive pose. She says, "Sorry, sir. I expect he's just excited. He probably didn't know I was still here. I'm sure he'll calm down momentarily."

Man says, "He'll expect you to treat him like a little prince. He'll start whining and begging you for favors." Man points to Taniesha. "Don't you allow it!"

Taniesha shakes her head and promises, "I won't."

Man says, "I'm expecting you to keep an eye on both of them." He points to Ruby. "I don't want her spoiling him! You're going to be managing this chimp for the coming series of trials,

Taniesha. We'll see how he takes direction from one of his African cousins. You monitor him the first week and make him heed you. This one is a little higher maintenance than most. You see, he apparently can talk. But I'll let that one"— again pointing at Ruby—"explain all that to you. No coddling, girls! I mean it. Now, I have an eleven thirty meeting down the hall, and I want absolutely no disturbances. Keep it down in here. I'll be seeing you later."

Man tosses the lead to Taniesha and leaves. Smithy stays in place, cowed, watching the door close. He looks up at Taniesha and trembles.

Ruby hisses, "Ass!"

Taniesha says, "Two more years and I get my degree. Just two more years, and I'm done."

Ruby asks, "How do you stand it? Don't you ever want to punch him in the face?"

Taniesha says, "Only every day."

The girls laugh.

Ruby approaches Smithy at last. He throws his arms around her legs, and Ruby comforts him.

Taniesha watches, letting the leash hang loose. She asks, "What's this about your chimp talking?"

Ruby says, "Oh, I thought everyone knew."

Taniesha shakes her head.

Ruby continues. "Smithy's always lived exclusively with people. He uses sign language to communicate with us. I think he sees himself as human. His skills are remarkable. He knows more signs than any other simian in a language study to date. At one point, we measured him learning twelve new signs a week, and he retained them all over a week later. He's hungry for new words. If you don't teach him the sign for something he wants to know, he'll make up his own sign for it and teach it to you."

The chimp looks up at Ruby and bats his eyelashes.

Ruby laughs. "Yes, we're talking about you, Smithy. He's vain, too."

Taniesha says, "Wait . . . I think I read about this chimp in *Time*. No, that animal was called Webster."

Ruby says, "Yes, Webster's his official name, but everyone on the project called him Smithy. He likes that name best."

Smithy signs to Taniesha, "Who are you?"

Taniesha asks, "What was that?"

Ruby says, "'What's your name?'"

Taniesha says, "It's Taniesha, Smithy." She holds out her hand. Smithy stares at it, then up at her face.

Ruby says, "He wants to know your sign. See, within the Deaf community, people choose a distinct sign that represents something meaningful about themselves. It's faster than trying to finger-spell your name. If you're a musician, for example, you might combine the sign for playing an instrument with the first letter of your name: say, the letter T and 'guitar.'"

Smithy again signs, "Who are you?"

Ruby asks, "So, who do you want to be, Taniesha? How do you want to identify yourself to Smithy?"

Taniesha says, "Ahhh. I don't play any instruments. I've got a tattoo of a rose on my left shoulder, and my right ear is pierced three times."

Ruby says, "OK. Smithy, this is our new friend, Taniesha." She signs, "Friend," puts the T-sign over her left shoulder, and pinches her right earlobe. "Go on, just like this." She repeats the sign.

Taniesha copies Ruby. She says, "Taniesha, Taniesha, I'm Taniesha."

Ruby says, "This sign means 'friend.'" She links her index fingers together.

Taniesha mimics it, repeating, "Taniesha. I'm your friend." She signs her name and 'friend.' Smithy glances from one woman to the other. She asks, "Is he getting it?"

Ruby says, "Be patient. Sometimes he plays dumb. Let's do something else." She turns her back on Smithy. "So, like I said, Smithy was raised as a human and ate human meals: burgers, spaghetti, p-i-z-z-a. What do you feed the chimps here?"

Smithy's ears twitch, and he makes the sign for 'play.'

Taniesha says, "Well, the Man provides a healthy, balanced diet for his subjects. It's probably not too tasty, though: a mash of grains and lentils supplemented with leafy greens and fruit. Sometimes at supper, there's also some kind of meat."

Smithy signs 'play' more rapidly. Taniesha notices and asks, "What's he—"

Ruby interrupts. "Do the chimps ever get special treats? Say, on their birthday or after completing a difficult trial?"

Taniesha says, "No-o, no birthdays. We do reward them with food sometimes, maybe a banana or an apple. If your boy has a sweet tooth—"

Smithy signs, "Play Taniesha."

Taniesha exclaims, "Hey! He said my name!"

Ruby speaks and signs, "Good boy! What do you want to play?"

Taniesha imitates the sign. "That means 'play'?"

Ruby says, "Uh-huh."

Smithy signs, "Tickle." He runs to a corner and hops up on a chair. He signs, "Taniesha tickle."

Ruby says, "He wants you to play tag. If you catch him, you tickle him."

Taniesha says, "I'm not chasing him around the lab. If Man comes back in—"

Ruby says, "Man's in an important meeting. Besides, Smithy will let you catch him so he can be tickled."

Smithy signs, "Play," and runs to the opposite corner.

Ruby says, "Go for it! You'll get to know each other this way."

Taniesha runs after Smithy. He runs back to the other corner. She chases Smithy around the room while Ruby watches. Finally, Smithy jumps onto a chair and Taniesha corners him. Smithy whimpers.

Taniesha says, "It's OK. I'm a friend." She signs, "Friend."

Smithy slaps her arm, and she recoils. "Ow!"

Smithy pulls at Taniesha's shirt tail and sniffs at the material.

Ruby says, "It's OK. He's just playing."

Taniesha looks at Ruby for a long moment, then cautiously reaches out to Smithy. He pulls back.

She signs, "Friend," and offers her hand again. Smithy seizes it and tugs on her fingers, examining them. Taniesha scratches Smithy behind the ears with her other hand. Smithy hoots and she scratches his back. Taniesha starts to tickle Smithy and he squeals. Smithy slips past Taniesha and jumps into Ruby's arms.

Ruby says, "That's a good start."

Taniesha says, "He ran away from me."

Ruby says, "But he let you pet him. And he didn't bite you."

Taniesha says, "You didn't say he bites."

Ruby says, "Because you'd have been nervous. Smithy can sense fear. This way, you got to play a nice game instead. See, Smithy? Now you've made a new friend."

Taniesha approaches; he watches her closely. She pats Smithy's back; he submits.

"Now," Ruby asks, "what else can you tell me about their meal plans?"

LETTER FROM RUBY DALTON
TO TAMMY COHEN

September 19, 1975

. . . For a minor private research lab, CSAM is surprisingly large, comprising a learning center where the doctors occasionally lecture to CSUF and the laboratory complex where the research occurs.

The latter is where I'll be spending most of my time. It features a well-lighted reception area and an atrium with a fountain (Corridor A). Farther back and farther down (to save surface space, Man had the land excavated so the hallway slopes down, and parts of the facility are underground) is a row of offices and lab rooms (Corridor B); the doctors each have their own office (Man's is twice as large as the other two, with a view of the fields).

The rest of the staff congregates in a central office space with desks, typewriters, and a mimeograph machine (Corridor C). Nobody gets a private desk; each assistant takes whichever seat is available during their shift. This area is subsurface, so we have no view. We do have a little kitchenette/break room, very modern, with a microwave, refrigerator, and too-bright lighting.

The last section (Corridor D) houses the animals actively participating in a study. This area looks like a dog pound with cages stacked one atop another. The animals within have barely enough space to stand at full height or turn around. Fortunately, a sanitary drainage system prevents the animals on the bottom level from being showered by the waste from their upper neighbors. Some labs overlook those logistics. Nevertheless, it's a brutal, barren prison. The inmates shiver, shudder, and stare at you with wondering, accusing eyes, questioning what they've done to deserve this exile—and what horrors you plan to inflict on them next.

The rest of the campus is open and landscaped. The external primate housing (Corridor E) consists of naturalistic enclosures with trees and rocks, located a quarter-mile from the laboratories. Remarkably, these cages aren't overstuffed; I haven't seen more than five animals in an enclosure at one time. Beyond is open terrain: trees, a man-made lagoon, and some terraced gardens for growing crops to help feed the animals. From time to time, researchers take the animals out on leashes to walk, run, and climb for exercise. The groundskeeper lives in a trailer among the cages so he can attend to the animals' needs promptly. He's an interesting character, but more about him later.

Man owns two dozen chimps, twenty capuchin monkeys, six spider monkeys, and thirty macaques. Eventually, I'll work with them all on various research projects, but for now, I'm assigned to the chimps, which is what I most wanted.

You know, I thought working with Smithy for the past year made me "experienced," but I've never been around _real_ chimpanzees. It's like they're a different species altogether and Smithy is an odd hybrid we created—something between humankind and the animal kingdom.

Real chimps are foreign and more than a little frightening. They're so loud. And aggressive. They push and bite each other to show dominance or protect their daily rations. Smithy's worst tantrums at Trevor Hall would be standard behavior here. You probably wouldn't be surprised by how readily they smear and fling their feces at one another, but it made me recoil. Man liked that.

At first, I was surprised he granted my request to work with the chimps because he's not a generous man, but now I believe he wasn't doing me any favors. I think he gave me this position because he wants me to see what Smithy is up against—and what he expects Smithy will become now that he's removed from genteel human society.

Man's chimps vary widely in age and mental capacity. The oldest has been with the facility since its inception twelve years ago; the most recent acquisition before Smithy has been here eight months. None has any experience with signing, but I'll encourage Man to introduce them to it. When and if I manage to gain any clout in this place.

Most animals are used in medical testing and sometimes end up incapacitated—or dead. Man is always eager to increase his supply against future losses. That's why he bought Smithy.

It chills me to hear Man speak so cavalierly about "attrition." I don't think I could administer a drug or perform a procedure I knew would irreparably harm a chimp, even if my job depended on it. God forbid Man ever orders me to do something that would harm Smithy directly. He's twisted enough to do it.

Man's never once shown me courtesy. He won't even address me by name: I'm "Girl," or "Hey, you." Yesterday, he shoved a stack of hand-written notes at me to transcribe and barked, "Now!" It wouldn't cost him a thing to be civil to me. He'd still be the big shot.

Fortunately, the other people who work here seem more humane.

My favorite person so far is Taniesha Jones, a part-time lab assistant about our age. She's a graduate student at CSUF, where Jeff is trying to get some final classes. Taniesha's been working for the Man for almost two years. She's smart, focused, and efficient; yet, Man is horrid to her. He's constantly cracking awful jokes about her skin color. He's rude to all the women, from what I've seen, but Taniesha gets the worst of it because she's black. After seeing what she endures, I'm ashamed of pitying myself. Part of me wants to urge her to quit and find a new job where she'll get more respect, but my selfish side doesn't want her to leave me behind in this dump.

The other junior female researchers, both full-time, are Marianne Foster and Eileen Fenn.

Marianne is a snooty twenty-year-old who lords over me the fact that she's younger and yet knows so much more than me. (In my defense, I'm new; once I learn the routines, I should be able to keep up with her). Marianne's been here four years already, longer than any other assistant. She's either a prodigy, or she started volunteering in high school. (Apparently, most people leave here after a year.) She analyzes the quantitative research findings. It's impressive how she can crank through the numbers, and she fully understands her importance. Still, Marianne isn't coddled by any means. Man treats her like an appliance. I don't think she's after respect, though. Marianne feeds on drama and is the resident instigator.

I made a grave error early on. Marianne asked, innocently, if I thought Man was crude. Taniesha and I had already bonded over our shared disgust. I thought Marianne was doing that, too. You know: "Us girls need to stick together." I expressed my dismay over how he treats Taniesha, and how he's belittled me. Piers's objectification was disquieting, but Man's attitude is much more demeaning. I also expressed concern for the animal subjects. She listened, asked questions, and clucked her tongue. I failed to notice that Marianne didn't share any war stories of her own.

The next day, Man called me into his office. He told me that I wasn't a princess in a mansion but an employee in his lab—a job for which I had begged. As long as he pays my salary, he can talk to me "any damn way" he pleases, and he doesn't "give a crap" if I like it or not. "If you want to cry, get the hell out now and find some fruit who'll make a fuss over you. As long as you're taking my money, you'll do what I tell you, when and how I tell you. And you can keep your damn opinions to yourself, or you'll be out on your (expletive) ass along with that grubby husband of yours."

Surprise: "that fat bitch" (Jeff's new appellation for her) is a stool pigeon as well as a stats whiz, and one who had no problem smiling in my tear-streaked face as I stumbled out of Man's office, stifling sobs.

Meanwhile, Eileen, who is thirtysomething and shy, keeps her head down, focused on her work. She only tells me what I need to know.

CSAM's two male researchers, Isaac Morgan (part-time) and Keith Brenneman (full-time), have been here less than a year. Isaac's cool—he says hello, speaks when spoken to, and is ready to help—but Keith has let Man's crudeness rub off on him. The first day we worked together, he kept hitting on me. The fact that I'm married didn't seem to bother him, and he acted like it shouldn't bother me, either. Ugh!

Two full-fledged doctors work under Man's authority: Edgar Torrance and Janet Fairbanks. I was astonished that Man had a woman in a position of authority. However, that doesn't mean Man is at all enlightened. Fairbanks hangs on his every word and constantly kisses up to him. She acts like he's doing her a favor by letting her work with him (or rather, as Taniesha says, letting her do the bulk of the research so Man can claim credit). I'd suspect Fairbanks was smitten with him if that weren't so stomach-churning.

Dr. Torrance seems all right. He treats the researchers with dignity, but he cares nothing for the well-being of the research animals. To him, they're objects, just parts in his design, a means to an end. That attitude's not uncommon in this field, but it still saddens me.

Neither Jeff nor I have seen Smithy in days. Though we're working here to be closer to him, we're at Man's mercy as to whether we actually can.

We haven't even seen much of each other. I'm on a swing shift, getting called in at all hours so I get exposed to various aspects of the facility, while Jeff officially works the graveyard shift so he can take classes during the day. We've been little more than roommates saying "hi" and "bye" as we pass in and out of the apartment, occasionally nabbing a nap together or sharing a meal on the go. I'm praying this is our initiation by fire and not how our lives will play out at CSAM.

I was ~~surprised~~ dismayed when Jeff told me he wanted to get a master's degree from Fresno State. He was so close to finishing his PhD! I asked why he didn't consider transferring to a bigger university with a doctoral program or completing his degree long-distance.

"Berkeley's the nearest likely university, and that's too far. Besides, where else could provide the resources for a primate study? I'd rather get the master's here. Most of my credits will transfer, it'll be quick, and with an MAS, I can become an adjunct professor at the college."

He made sense, but I still think it's a step down. It's like Jeff is starting over. Still, he insists he <u>wants</u> to do this. I guess I should get on board.

Jeff came home from work this morning in a tizzy. He was ranting against the janitor, Brad Vollmer.

"Janitor" maybe isn't the right term, but I'm not sure what else to call him. Plant manager? Caretaker? In addition to acting as on-site handyman, Brad cleans cages, sterilizes equipment, and feeds and exercises the animals. He's a round-the-clock jack-of-all-trades. Man seems to trust him, which would normally make me suspicious, except I don't get a bad vibe from Brad the way my skin quivered when I met Teague. He's a little odd and scruffy-looking with long hair and a patchy goatee, but otherwise, he seems harmless.

Jeff might disagree about that. His beef today had to do with how much leeway Brad has to remove the animals from their cages.

Dr. Fairbanks reported to me yesterday that Smithy's been rejecting his food (I don't blame him; the vitamin-fortified slop looks like dog food and probably tastes like mud) and seems lethargic. When I repeated this to Jeff, he panicked. We've both read of chimpanzees who go into a depression and die, either from self-starvation or what's commonly called "a broken heart." We don't want that to happen to our boy.

So, at the end of his shift, Jeff dropped by Brad's trailer to ask how Smithy's been acting and if we need to be concerned. As luck would have it, Brad had Smithy with him in the trailer.

<u>*They were smoking a joint together!*</u>

Jeff watched them for a minute to make sure of what he was seeing. He said Brad was showing Smithy how to draw the smoke and blow it out, then he handed the joint to Smithy and encouraged him to do the same. That's when Jeff spoke up. Smithy was delighted to see him again, and they hugged and groomed and got reacquainted before Jeff lit into Brad about the marijuana. Instead of being fazed, Brad was cheerful and had an excuse.

"Your chimp's been real down lately. He won't eat or sleep or play or try to get to know the other apes. At night, he cries or runs around and tries to break out. He's in a bad place, man. I thought I'd bring him in for a visit and a toke. That always mellows me out when I'm upset. I figured it'd help Smithy, too. And it'll get him to eat again!"

Jeff told me all this while I got dressed, imitating Brad's voice and posture. He mimics average people just as well as celebrities. I suppose I can't fault Brad's motives as much as I can complain about his judgment. His explanation had bizarre, internal logic. But what Jeff repeated to me of what Brad said next was both surprising and beautiful:

"Smithy's just like us, you know. Chimps think and feel, too. They have the same mind and heart and soul as we do, so why shouldn't they enjoy the same pleasures in life? He deserves that much."

Now, Jeff is concerned about Brad working with Smithy and possibly making him sicker by exposing him to drugs, but for the first time since coming to CSAM, I feel hopeful. I know the marijuana wasn't good for Smithy, but I have a feeling Brad Vollmer will be. He's the first person to show a genuine interest in Smithy for his own sake.

I'll drop by the trailer the next time I get a free moment. Maybe I'll be lucky enough to reunite with Smithy, too. If not, I'll at least spend a little time getting to know Brad, seeing what sort of ally he can be. Heaven knows we need all the help we can get.

DIARY OF RUBY DALTON

September 19, 1975

Working at CSAM is an exhausting eggshell walk. Just this morning, as I was settling in, Taniesha and I were having a friendly exchange: Happy Friday, how are you, etc. We started chatting about the big news that "Tania" was finally caught. Her story has always sounded weird to me. I think she's a bored rich girl who watched <u>Bonnie and Clyde</u> *too many times, but Taniesha believes she was brainwashed. She was explaining to me how it could be done just as Man cruised through the office.*

He threw a stack of papers on my desk with such force, I had to raise my hands to block the pages from sliding into my lap. "Is this a lab or a coffee klatsch?" he shouted. "I hope someone is paying you to gossip. <u>My</u> *employees* <u>work</u>*!"*

I felt so embarrassed. We weren't slacking off; we had just sat down. I worried I might have somehow got Taniesha in trouble, but she reassured me.

"He does that all the time. You exist. You're in his path. And you need this job, so he knows you'll suck up whatever he throws at you."

I dread seeing what Man will do to me, knowing how desperate I am to remain near Smithy. I can't just quit if I don't like my situation, because it would mean abandoning him. I've got to remind myself how Taniesha has it worse here than anyone else, and she endures. If she can take it, I can take it. I must!

LETTER FROM RUBY DALTON
TO TAMMY COHEN

September 30, 1975

Dear Tammy,

I devoured your last letter. I'm so eager for any news of the world beyond concrete walls, fluorescent lighting, primate vitals, and constant criticism. You're my vicarious lifeline through next summer. At least Jeff has some place to go besides work and home. If I had the energy for a hobby, I'd take one up. After being glued to a desk for ten hours a day, I'm too soul-weary to do more than dream of having a real life. At least I can plan for something better someday. Smithy doesn't even have that luxury.

I can't guess what the most traumatic transition for him has been: dislocation from Trevor Hall, sudden silence after a lifetime of language, culture shock, abuse. Man reduced Smithy to his primal state as soon as he got here: shoes, pants, shirt, and toys were all confiscated, and poor Smithy was dumped naked and defenseless into a cage filled with strange, hairy, toothy creatures who looked like him and smelled like him but were nothing like him to his mind because the only company he's ever known is human.

Man refuses to accept that Smithy has been socialized as a human. He thought the clothes were an affectation, "a circus act," and worthless to our overall goal of teaching him language. OK, wearing clothes didn't affect Smithy's ability to sign, but it made him more human-like and endeared him to us. It was for our benefit rather than his.

Without clothes, he looks like an animal. Surrounded by apes, he's clearly an ape, whereas before, surrounded by people, we could fool ourselves into thinking he was an odd-looking little person who really did belong to us. Nevertheless, Smithy isn't like the others. He doesn't understand dominance displays. When another chimp gets in his face and screams at him, he doesn't know he's supposed to bow. He panics.

He asks for food, like we taught him, and he's puzzled when nobody responds. Before, he was always reinforced for making the right signs. Now all the rules are changed and he's not himself anymore. Smithy looks like a chimp, people here treat him like a chimp, but he's not truly a chimp. He's some mutation, too human to be caged, too wild to be housed. He was special in our world, but here, he's a freak.

Jeff said, "We didn't do him any favors. We raised him to rise above himself because we thought it would be cool to have a chimp that talked and acted like a human. That was our hubris. The world doesn't need a talking chimp. It doesn't need a chimp who can eat with a fork or use 'Please' and 'Thank you' any more than it needs a chimp that can tap dance. The world doesn't know what to make of him. Teague doesn't want his vocabulary comprehension; he wants his body to experiment on. Smithy doesn't belong here! Not in this facility, not anywhere. Nobody will appreciate him. He's an outcast. He isn't going to make it here, Ruby. I feel it.

"And it's our fault. We did this to him. We estranged him. We took him from ignorance to knowledge. That's _our_ sin. But _Smithy's_ the one getting punished. He trusted us and look where we led him."

We thought we were doing something wonderful. We thought Smithy's life would be grand. How could we have been so stupid? Did Smithy ever seem like he was benefiting from our language lessons? Did he ask for them?

Smithy blames us. I can tell. Sometimes, I stand within view of the cages, and he glowers at me. I can hear him thinking, 'Damn you for marooning me in my own flesh! Damn you for corrupting me!' Smithy knows we've let him down, and he wants to punish us for the weeks of being chased around his enclosure, of being bitten and pinched, of having his food stolen, of being left to flounder.

I sneaked out to check on him during my break yesterday afternoon. I thought he'd feel better knowing I was keeping an eye out for him. When I reached his enclosure, the other chimps were chasing and hooting at each other. Smithy was alone, curled up under a tree. His cage-mates don't know me yet, and they still act territorial when I'm around. As usual, they ran to shake the bars of the cage and screech at me. This big fat brat called Nero even threw some dirt at me. Smithy saw me coming and unfolded from his fetal position. I saw recognition in his eyes and thought he was glad to see me. I waved. Smithy made eye contact and began to screech and hoot. He went to a pile of feces in the corner and threw some of it in my direction! It was a deliberate imitation. It looked obscene.

All the chimps went into a frenzy, racing back and forth, creating a cacophony like hell during rush hour. Smithy looked me in the eyes again and screamed at me, like he was saying, 'Is this how you want me to act now? You want me to be an animal, huh? How am I doing?'"

I ran back into the building and spent the rest of lunch crying in the ladies' room. It sickened me to see our Smithy so degraded, even if he was playacting. I don't want to watch him devolve into a beast. But I don't see any other future for him as long as he lives here.

But now that he is here, I've got to stay, too. What would happen to Smithy if I left? Who else would take care of him? Who would love him for who he is instead of treating him like a dumb research animal? Sure, Brad can slip him some extra food and sign a little with him, but Jeff and I are the only ones who can give him a sense of dignity. We remember what he was and what he can be again.

I owe it to Smithy to stick with this brain-deadening, soul-crushing job for as long as I can—even if it means putting my own happiness on hold. After everything we've done to him, I can't desert him. I may go downhill with him, but I can offer moral support on the way . . .

PRIVATE INTERVIEW BETWEEN
REID BENNET AND CELIA ARMENDARIZ
CIRCA 1989

Reid Bennet: *It's well known you launched your career through campus radio; how did you get your first show?*

Celia Armendariz: I pestered the head of the communications department, Mr. Templeman. I had a ham radio set when I was a kid, and I'd pretend I was a DJ. I played records I liked and talked about current events, asked questions. Anybody who was on the frequency at that time could respond or even request songs. It was great. As the middle child in a large family, it was easy to get lost. I enjoyed having people listening to me for once. I knew I wanted to get into broadcasting. I knew I'd be good at it, but Mr. Templeman wasn't convinced. First, I tried to reason with him about how progressive it would be for the school, told him about my background, even sat him down and gave him an audition, but he still wasn't sold. I kept pushing and pushing until I finally wore him down.

RB: *That was a big deal, wasn't it? The first campus show hosted by a woman.*

CA: Indeed, but it was past time for it.

RB: *Were you proud to achieve this milestone?*

CA: Yes and no. Yes, I got my way and got a show, and I was the first woman to get one, but they gave me the lousiest slot. Midnight till three a.m.! That's the Witching Hour.

Laughs.

So, that's what I was going to call the show, at first, but I decided it might sound Satanic, give people the wrong idea. I went with *Whispers in the Dark* instead. Lucky for me, lots of college students wanted a friendly voice in the background while they were up late cramming for tests. A fair amount of people in the community were night owls, too, so I built a following. Yeah, occasionally callers would razz me or make crude come-ons, but I also had regulars checking in. I'd talk about issues I cared about, get other people to care about them, too. Still, I didn't hit my stride until '79 with the trial.

RB: *Before that, had you considered profiling CSAM? Maybe interviewing people who worked there, since it was part of the community?*

CA: No. It wasn't a big deal to students, just a research lab affiliated with the campus.

RB: *Did you hear about the things that went on there?*

CA: Sure. People who worked there complained all the time about how Manfred Teague was a pain in the ass. He couldn't keep anybody for long. Even though CSAM paid slightly more than on-campus work, it still wasn't worth putting up with his tantrums. The animals were feisty, too. One of them, I think they called him Lucifer—

RB: *Mr. Splitfoot.*

CA: That's it. He bit off a finger or two.

RB: *Did you hear any other stories about what went on in the lab?*

CA: You mean the weird stuff? Now and then, a word or two, but I didn't think much of it at first. I had bigger concerns, bigger ideas. I was talking up national and international questions. CSAM, as messed up and melodramatic as it was, just wasn't on my radar. Not until it was on *everybody's* radar . . .

CLOSED-CIRCUIT FOOTAGE

Date: October 8, 1975
Location: Corridor C

A ring of people stands inside a large office space. Five desks are visible in the shot. Two desks have typewriters. Papers are scattered over a third. A white lab coat is draped behind the chair of the fourth desk. Jeff stands in the back of the group, leaning against the fifth desk, his hands in his pockets.

Man enters the room, leading Smithy on a leash. Ruby edges closer to the center of the circle and cranes her neck to look at Smithy. Brad, a lanky young man with shoulder-length hair, a patchy goatee, and sideburns, wearing ripped jeans and a stained T-shirt, stands closest to Man; a calm expression on his face. He watches Smithy closely but doesn't approach him. The chimp waddles awkwardly around the circle.

Smithy approaches, then passes the people standing in the circle: Marianne, wearing her usual skirt and sweater; Isaac, a short, youthful man with curly brown hair, striped T-shirt, and jeans; Keith, a stocky man with dark hair, sideburns, a thin mustache, polo shirt, and slacks; Eileen, a skinny red-head in a peach jumpsuit; Taniesha, who wears a long-sleeved black top and dark jeans; Dr. Edgar Torrance, a bespectacled Asian man wearing a lab coat; and Dr. Janet Fairbanks, a plump brunette woman with glasses, a tweed suit, and a lab coat.

Man says, "OK, boys and girls, here he is! Step up and meet the wonder chimp! Give him your hand. If he doesn't bite it off, maybe you'll be the lucky stiff who ends up working with him."

Jeff scowls at Man and folds his arms. Ruby says, "Smithy has already met several of the people here, including Brad and Taniesha, and he hasn't harmed any of them."

Man says, "That's right. Taniesha, you and Smithy are old buddies. Come forward! Say 'Howdy!' to your long-lost cousin."

Taniesha tosses her head at the insult but steps forward. Man continues. "See if he'll let you take his blood pressure."

Dr. Fairbanks hands Taniesha a sphygmomanometer. She sticks it in her pocket and approaches Smithy with both hands raised and open. She signs as she speaks. "Hello, Smithy! Remember me? I'm Taniesha."

Isaac looks interested and asks, "Did he teach you to sign that?"

Ruby says, "I did."

Man warns, "You keep out of this!" He points to Jeff. "You, too! This animal is useless to me if he won't cooperate with the staff at large."

Smithy eyes Taniesha warily. His body tenses. She comes closer and he snaps at her, waving his arms to ward her off. Taniesha recoils. Man pulls back on the leash and brandishes the cattle prod. He says, in a singsong voice, "Looks like someone wants the prod . . . "

Taniesha looks around the circle and says, "He wasn't like this when I worked with him yesterday. He behaved just fine. We played and I tickled him and everything."

She turns back to Smithy, "Hey, Smithy!" She signs, "Tickle," then says, "Wanna play?"

Smithy swipes at her menacingly. The other researchers draw back. Marianne covers her face.

Brad looks around the room and points at one of the desks. He says, "Hey, Taniesha, there's a lab coat on the back of that chair. Put it on."

She looks at him, confused.

Brad continues. "Try it and see what he does."

Dr. Torrance asks, "Why? Is the chimp more likely to respect authority?"

Taniesha picks up the coat, shrugs it on, then turns back to face Smithy. "Is this better? Can we talk now?"

Smithy cocks his head and looks up at her. His stance remains defensive, but he doesn't growl. Taniesha cautiously approaches him. He pulls back when she stretches out her hand.

Taniesha signs, "Friend."

Smithy grabs her arm. The crowd gasps. Ruby starts forward, but Jeff holds her back. Taniesha presses her lips together but stands still.

Smithy pulls at her coat sleeve, sniffs it, then signs, "Tickle foot." He pulls her hand down to his left foot. Everyone applauds. Taniesha smiles, relieved, and tickles Smithy.

Man says, "Nice trick, but you're only half way there. I gave you an assignment, remember?"

Taniesha says, "I know. OK, Smithy, I need something from you now. Give me your arm." She pulls at his arm and Smithy allows her to take it. Taniesha fixes the cuff on his arm and puffs it up, still tickling him with her free hand. Smithy keeps still until the job is done. Everyone claps again.

Slowly, Isaac approaches him, then Keith, and the rest. They hold out their hands, letting Smithy touch or study them. Jeff and Ruby look at each other and smile. Man looks on, tapping the unused cattle prod against the floor restlessly.

LETTER FROM RUBY DALTON
TO TAMMY COHEN

October 8, 1975

. . . *Finally, Man admitted that Smithy was fit to go out in public and assigned him to a study. Smithy will be part of a trial to test a food supplement designed to help people with a low-calorie diet (e.g., soldiers, lost hikers, starving Biafrans) keep on weight. It's a blind study, so I don't know if Smithy's food will include the relevant stuff or not. Still, I'd much rather have a chubby Smithy than a Smithy riddled with smallpox.*

Jeff says that after we've been here a while and proven our worth—and proven Smithy is more gentleman than maniac—we can push to have him entered in cognitive trials, or possibly a new language study. In the meantime, we'll continue to sign with him when we see him, and we'll encourage Taniesha, Brad, and anyone else we can convince to sign with him, too, so his language skills won't atrophy.

Taniesha's been skittish since Man alluded to the attacks. "You let me play with Smithy! You told me to give him my hand! He could have ripped my whole arm off!" she said.

I pointed out that nothing had happened, and they'd had fun playing together, but Taniesha remained unconvinced.

"You can take your own chances and let me make up my own mind," she said.

I trust she'll come around. The more she sees of Smithy, the more she'll relax.

As for Brad, one other thing happened today that I should mention . . .

CLOSED-CIRCUIT FOOTAGE

Date: October 8, 1975
Location: Kitchenette/Break Room

Ruby stands at the counter making a sandwich. Brad enters the room behind her, leans against the counter, and asks, "Feeling better? Smithy didn't run amok and climb the Empire State Building or break anyone's back."

Ruby says, "I'm glad we didn't have to see anything like that, but I think Man was disappointed." She looks up at Brad. "Thank you for your help. That was a good idea you had, with the lab coat. I'm not sure why it made a difference, but—"

Brad says, "You wanna know how I knew to do that? Taniesha said she didn't have a problem with Smithy yesterday. Well, yesterday, Taniesha was wearing a yellow blouse with flowers on it. Today, she's wearing a black sweater. See, I've been watching Smithy closely and I've noticed some things."

Ruby says, "Oh?"

Brad says, "Yeah. He doesn't like people who wear dark clothes. Have you noticed that?"

Ruby says, "Can't say that I have."

Brad says, "I mean, he always growls at Phil and Bob when they come around on patrol, and at the mailman, too. Every time he sees that dark figure coming up the walk to the mailboxes, Smithy snarls and hoots and even throws stuff out of his cage. I thought it was a territorial thing, but he doesn't make a peep when the milkman delivers."

Ruby says, "The milkman brings yummy foodstuff. The mailman always brings bills. I would snarl at the mailman, too."

Brad says, "Except the other day, after his shift ended, Phil came over to my office to bum a joint." Ruby scowls and opens her mouth, but Brad silences her with a hand gesture. "He was off-duty and just wearing some jeans and a white T-shirt instead of his security uniform. Smithy was with me, and he just looked at Phil and then went back to his dinner. He recognized Phil, but he didn't mind him this time. I think it's 'cause he wasn't wearing that dark uniform. Smithy didn't stop snarling at Taniesha until she covered up her dark clothes with the white coat. Then he calmed right down. You really never noticed that when you were living with him?"

Ruby looks down at her sandwich and clenches the butter knife.

She says, "No, I never did."

Brad asks, "Can you think of any reason why he would act up that way?"

Ruby says, "No, I can't."

Brad shrugs and says, "Anyway, it was a thought. I'm gonna keep my eyes peeled, see what else I notice. Enjoy that sandwich!"

He exits the kitchenette. Ruby finishes assembling her sandwich, but her movements are slow and her expression preoccupied.

CLOSED-CIRCUIT FOOTAGE

Date: October 8, 1975
Location: Corridor C, Main Office

Ruby and Jeff collect papers and notebooks from a desk. Jeff puts on his coat and helps Ruby into hers.

Ruby asks, "Can I ask you a weird question?"

Jeff says, "I suppose."

She says, "On the day Wanda was attacked, do you remember what she was wearing?"

Jeff withdraws; his posture tenses and he says, "It wasn't on my mind. I was more focused on how long it was taking to get to the hospital." He rubs his eyes. "I looked at the medics and out the windows, and I glanced at her from time to time to make sure she hadn't passed out . . . or bled out. She was wearing a dark sweater . . . black or dark blue, I think?"

Ruby clutches at the collar of her jacket and presses her books against her chest.

Dismayed, she says, "Really?"

Jeff says, "I had these crazy thoughts about how bloody her clothes were going to be. I was kinda afraid the nursing staff would see her and think I was an ax murderer or something. I saw all the blood running down the side of her face. It had soaked through the towel even before we'd left the house . . . and it ran down her neck onto her sweater. But you couldn't see any blood on the sweater itself. It blended in with the dark material. It looked like her clothes were damp. Why do you want to know this?"

Ruby turns and walks toward the labs.

She says, "I—Brad has a crazy theory. I wanted to check it out."

Jeff follows beside her and asks, "What is it?"

Ruby says slowly, "He's noticed that Smithy is hostile to people who wear dark clothes."

Jeff asks, "And?"

Ruby says, "I told him I wasn't sure why that would be."

Jeff says, "Ruby, are you thinking that bitch—"

They pass down the hall and out of range.

DIARY OF RUBY CARDINI

October 8, 1975

. . . Jeff stayed quiet during the drive home. I thought he was brooding over the accident, and I regretted spoiling what had been a good day. Back in the apartment, Jeff flopped down on the couch and stared down at his hands for a long time before calling me to sit by him. I was prepared for him to tell me off for reviving bad memories, but instead he told me about a totally different set of memories.

"Maybe I should have mentioned it before, but we were all upset at the time, and I didn't want to make you feel worse. And then we came here, so it seemed like it didn't matter."

He broke off as if reconsidering. "Remember when you asked me to set up 'Smithy Street' so you could watch it again before we left Newport? Well, after you finished, I decided to watch some of our other footage. I was feeling sentimental. I wanted to look back at better days. But I saw a pattern.

"I looked at one of our early lessons, when I was quizzing Smithy about furniture. I saw him point to a lamp and sign, 'Who is that?' At the time he did it, I just corrected his grammar. But seeing it again shook me because of everything that had happened since. Why did he ask 'who' instead of 'what?' He did it three more times after that, Ruby, and he referred to one of the windows as a woman. That was during our first month.

"Next, I looked at one of Wanda's cooking episodes, and there was Smithy, looking all around the kitchen instead of at her. Like he was watching something moving, but nothing was showing on the film. Nothing we could see.

43

"In June, we taught him colors, and that lava lamp tipped over. I watched it three times. Smithy never touched that cord; it went over by itself.

"Or maybe something we couldn't see pushed it.

"Then I put on the orientation film. Nothing happened for the longest time—until we went through the closed-up section. Smithy was gaping up at something on the stairs, fascinated. He wouldn't look away. Wanda had to pick him up and carry him for the rest of the tour, and he was fussing and looking around the whole time. Even when we got back downstairs, he wouldn't quit looking around. And Maisie wouldn't quit barking."

Jeff rubbed his hands back and forth over his thighs. "She was there the whole time, Ruby. From our first day in Trevor Hall, she was watching him. And Smithy was the only one who knew."

My stomach squeezed and I had to put my head down to the scuffed-up coffee table. We'd all speculated on how much longer Smithy had been aware of the ghost than us. I had figured back to the night of the first fire. Or back to the night Smithy almost choked on the knob that came off his furniture.

Certainly, while Tammy was grieving her grandmother and dressed all in black. When Smithy shunned her. Because she looked too much like the thing that hovered around him. Because she was dressed like Taniesha today.

But I never suspected that spook was lurking in the background since the start of the experiment! We'd been optimistic and full of pep. Was she watching me when I explored the house on my own? Or did she only come out once Smithy showed up?

Jeff patted my hand, and I looked up. His lips wobbled a little and the skin around his eyes was stretched too tightly, but his face was trying to smile. "But that's all over now, honey. We've left the house. We're free. Not . . . I mean, things aren't great here and Smithy . . . none of us has a whole lot of freedom right now. But we're safe. We can start over. Trevor Hall and its ghosts are staying put."

That's something I'll have to remember the next time Man starts wielding his cattle prod or Marianne tries to start more gossip. At least we slipped the ghost.

LETTER FROM RUBY DALTON
TO TAMMY COHEN

October 20, 1975

Dear Tammy,

I apologize for not writing sooner. Most days, I'm too exhausted to pick up a pen. I'll write a little bit each day until I've caught you up.

After two months at CSAM, Jeff and I have each been appointed new, 4/12 shifts. We have one free day that overlaps and about five hours per day/night together the rest of the week. I call that progress. Perhaps Man is finally willing to treat us with some respect.

We're adapting quickly. I've been forcing myself to show no preference to any animal (not to a chimp over a macaque, and not to Smithy over any other subject) so I can prove what a disinterested researcher I am. Isaac and Eileen have accepted me. So have Dr. Torrance and Dr. Fairbanks. They chat with me in the break room, but they haven't invited me to call them by their first names. Maybe Piers was an anomaly.

Fortunately, I don't see much of Keith; we're working different shifts for now. Marianne still drops snide remarks here and there, but I suspect that's her style. I keep telling myself we only have to work together; we're not married, and we don't have to be best buddies. I can be civil to her as long as she doesn't actively obstruct or undercut me.

I've continued to hit it off with Taniesha and Brad. Taniesha even asked me to go shopping with her this weekend to pick out a dress for her cousin's wedding. It feels good to have a friend in my new home!

As glad as I am to have met her, I'm even more grateful for Brad. He's much more than a zookeeper or plant manager. He may not have the same educational foundation as some of the others who work here, but he works as hard as any assistant and participates in every study.

In some ways, his work is tougher and more important than data collection and analysis because he's caring for each animal, body and soul. That Brad even believes these research animals have souls whereas Dr. Torrance sees them as furry test tubes is wonderful. I respect him for the dignity he's willing to accord our animals, and I celebrate him for what he's done with Smithy.

Ever since our arrival, Brad has taken a strong interest in Smithy's abilities. Outside of my early conversations with Taniesha, he's the only person who's asked about Smithy's signing. He's noticed which gestures Smithy makes most often. The other day he asked me, "What does it mean when he does this? And this?" His mimicking wasn't clean, but I could still read the signs. And it seems that Smithy's top phrases are "please," "out," "sorry," "food," "hug," and "go home."

I taught Brad a few words pertaining to feeding and grooming, and he practiced them with me for a few minutes. I thought that would be the end, but when I stopped by his trailer a couple of days later, I saw that he had made little drawings of the signs I had demonstrated and tacked them up on a bulletin board to study them. (They looked better than my old flash cards.) And he had more signs to ask me about.

Smithy's a regular chatterbox with him. Brad is the person he sees most frequently, so that makes sense. I'm so glad they've built a rapport! I was concerned about Smithy's skills lapsing in this isolated, impersonal environment, but that won't happen as long as at least one person can reach out to him. We won't be able to immerse him like we did at Trevor Hall, but we won't leave him stranded.

Jeff has calmed down since the pot incident. He's no longer worried Brad is going to kill Smithy. But he still doesn't quite grasp how valuable Brad is.

Brad isn't one of us. He doesn't have an academic background. I have to keep reminding Jeff that that's exactly what makes Brad special. If you tell him Smithy can talk, he'll talk to Smithy. He won't fire back at you with linguistic theories or talk about reinforcing a conditioned response. He doesn't question or doubt. He accepts Smithy at face value for who he is, not for what he might represent to science.

Brad genuinely _likes_ Smithy, and Smithy can tell. He seems drawn to Brad. I think he trusts him. Smithy needs Brad as much as he used to need us. Maybe even more, because Brad can be with him much more often than Jeff and I can.

Knowing Smithy has a friend makes me feel as if I have one, too.

EXCERPT FROM "DUMB ANIMAL? PREIS-HERALD RECANTS STANCE ON WEBSTER'S LANGUAGE SKILLS"

TIME MAGAZINE, October 27, 1975

Popular psychologist Piers Preis-Herald emerges from a professional sabbatical into the pages of this month's issue of Science with incendiary claims. Once a major champion of primate language studies, which he helped pioneer with a longitudinal study of Webster the chimpanzee, Preis-Herald now repudiates his own research.

"Webster never learned to use or decode language. He is not a 'signing chimpanzee.' I was wrong."

In poring over his many articles from the past three years, one asks how this astonishing collection of data could be read as anything but an endorsement of cross-species communication. With new hindsight, Preis-Herald admits he was hasty.

"I've spent the months since we disbanded the study carefully re-reading every note and journal entry and scrutinizing every frame of film footage. This time, I saw what I did not want to see before."

One standard for language use is that the subject freely utilizes language in a way that is understood by others. Yet, Preis-Herald says much of Webster's language production lacked clarity. "If you transcribe his signs exactly, you will frequently see combinations such as, 'Webster orange give good.' Yet, the trainers charged with recording his language production might report that Webster signed, 'Give me one of those tasty oranges, please.' They extrapolate from the most minimal data and fill in the blanks with their own projections of what Webster must want or think."

A startling eighty-five percent of the dual records (cases where both films and journals of the same incident exist for comparison analysis) follow this pattern. However, Preis-Herald concedes that his student researchers did not willingly embellish their records. "I doubt any of them were self-aware enough to notice what they were doing. It's natural to form order from chaos."

Further, when multiple observers recorded observations, often each person had a varying interpretation of what the chimp conveyed. "The example I gave might be processed by one student as 'Give Webster a good orange' and by another as 'Webster wants to give me an orange because I am a good person.' The fluid arrangement of signs muddled the interpretation of Webster's communications.

"What most piqued my interest about the study was the use of syntax by non-human animals." Syntax describes a set of arbitrary, man-made rules for how words are ordered and employed (e.g., Are adjectives placed before or after the noun? Can you dangle a participle at the end of a sentence?). Preis-Herald initially speculated that ape intelligence was sophisticated enough to observe rules of syntax, but Webster never manifested any.

"Webster's signs emerged in haphazard order," Preis-Herald says. "He could not be counted on to use the same arrangement twice. 'Give me an orange' would variously be rendered as, 'Orange Webster give' or 'Give orange Webster,' regardless of which order was reinforced."

Preis-Herald's Canadian colleague, Robert La Fontaine, has expressed similar frustration in his own observations of his research animals.

Another hallmark of language use is that the subject produces language voluntarily. Preis-Herald notes that over seventy percent of Webster's so-called language production was elicited in response to an interaction generated by one of Webster's keepers. "It's as though he were observing the Victorian dictum, 'Speak not unless you are spoken to.'"

Again, Preis-Herald avoids suggesting that his team coached Webster's responses. "The questions were straightforward enough. All Webster had to do was regurgitate the signs in his signature random order to appear as if he were responding to a prompt. I doubt now whether he ever understood a single sign."

Such criticism—especially from the study's own creator—would have seemed like heresy a short time ago, when Preis-Herald regularly graced the media (including the pages of *Time*) with glowing updates about Webster's progress. The study launched in 1973, amid great fanfare, and quickly became a milestone for its methodology as well as its unorthodox subject matter. In Newport, Rhode Island, Preis-Herald assembled a diverse team of graduate and undergraduate students and took the rare step of appointing female researchers as proxies. It was an ambitious endeavor in every aspect.

Perhaps too ambitious.

"My students were brilliant people. Each brought something unique and valuable to the study. Each also brought an extraordinary degree of optimism to the table." Preis-Herald acknowledges, "They wanted to believe in the success of our project. They wanted to believe they were destined for greatness. They believed so strongly that they created a self-fulfilling prophecy, fueled by the desire for wonder.

"The hope that they would transcend the limits of man's knowledge manifested in two delusions: first, that Webster was able to communicate using human language, and second, that they experienced a brush with the uncanny."

Preis-Herald's assistants saw "enormous significance" in a range of minor household accidents and odd noises, some of which may have been perpetrated by a mischievous chimp.

"The mishaps became exaggerated and conflated with local superstitions about the old property, causing a great deal of hysteria. It's incredible to think how such disparate, intelligent people nevertheless became susceptible to believing the most outlandish things. Unfortunately, that includes Webster's so-called talent. In its ardor and desire for a more meaningful world, [my team] saw his behavior as reflective of higher understanding."

Preis-Herald counts himself among the susceptible. "I first gained professional repute for my work on persuasion. With Webster, I persuaded myself that he was something greater than the sum of his output."

But he asserts that the year in Newport was not a total loss. "Webster's greatest scientific contribution ultimately lies not in what he can tell us about the Great Apes' ability to communicate, but in what he tells us about ourselves."

In scientific research, chimpanzees often serve as a simulacrum for human beings. No exception is Webster, who mirrors mankind's desires and dreams. "There are important lessons to unpack about man's desire for something beyond our mundane existence. How do we create meaning from suggestion? What do we value? What do we believe and why? These are rich topics for discourse." So rich that Preis-Herald admits he is considering writing a book about the Webster study within the context of human fallibility . . .

LETTER FROM RUBY DALTON
TO TAMMY COHEN

October 28, 1975

. . . *I went back and re-read it thinking it was a fraud, that Robert LaFontaine or some other critic had falsified it. But the prose sounded enough like Piers. When I finished reading, I was furious. I knew Piers was bitter, but I never imagined he would utterly betray Smithy so! That quisling!*

Jeff has a slew of other names for him that I won't reprint. Suffice to say our walls are blushing, and since they were thin to start, I'm expecting the neighbors to file a complaint.

"The ass**** is gunning for Smithy!" he declared. "He blames Smithy for wrecking his reputation so now he's going to wreck what's left of Smithy's. Piers couldn't establish Smithy's legitimacy and he wants to keep anyone else from achieving success where he failed. This bull**** is poison! Nobody will want to work with Smithy now! Even if they see signs of his ability, they'll be discouraged from writing about it because other scientists will just think they're 'susceptible'!"

I might think Jeff were exaggerating if Piers had stuck to publishing his doubts in an academic journal with rarefied readership. Putting them in Time, *where every housewife and schoolchild in America will see it, is scorching the earth.*

Doesn't Piers realize he's trashing his own career by denouncing his research? Does he think recanting and apologizing is how to win his way back into the establishment's good graces? Are his peers supposed to think he can be trusted with grants again? What about this apostasy suggests trustworthiness?

He's gutted primate language studies for who knows how many years to come! If Smithy is now portrayed as a high-profile failure, nobody will care to draw attention (or ridicule) to a new investigation. Even Osage will be suspect now.

Good God—is *that* what Piers was planning? He's driven a knife into La Fontaine's research with his vitriol about ours. What a bastard!

I can't help wondering what Wanda must think of this. She gave her life to this research, and now Piers says it was all for nothing. Do you suppose he told her what he was planning to write?

Jeff has tried a couple of times to reach Eric on the phone, but with the time difference, he hasn't been able to catch him. He's angry and has the idea that if we who conducted the research collaborate to write an article of our own, challenging Piers's assertions, we can salvage Smithy's credibility. I don't know about that. Piers has tarred us thoroughly. He's practically got us believing in pixies. It's worth a try, though. I don't want to submit to this narrative.

Will you join us in issuing a pro-Smithy statement?[1] You wrote the most convincing arguments in your memoranda. If anyone can push Piers to the wall, it's you, Tammy. Please, will you lend us your voice? We need all the support we can get.

Smithy needs it . . .

---

1 A rebuttal to Preis-Herald's article was submitted to *Science* in November 1975, but was rejected for publication. References in the editor's correspondence indicate that Dalton and Dalton were the primary authors of the piece with Cohen and Kaninchen contributing. Though no draft of the submission can be located, one can assume the lost article served as a template for the arguments at trial.

CLOSED-CIRCUIT FOOTAGE

Date: November 1, 1975
Location: Corridor D, Research Animal Quarters

Taniesha and Marianne enter the animals' quarters. Marianne says, " . . . the hepatitis vaccine trials. Man wants chimps five years old and younger. We need to see whether the vaccine is suitable for children."

Taniesha remarks, "That's harsh. Those babies are gonna be marked for life. If they live long enough."

Smithy bangs on the door of his cage.

Marianne says, "These trials will allow us to see the longitudinal results of treatment. And if the vaccine doesn't work, we can—"

Smithy's screeching drowns out further speech.

Marianne complains, "What is his problem? Hey, Smithy, calm down!"

Taniesha approaches his cage and says, "Yeah, Smithy, you're too old for this study. You don't have to worry."

Smithy signs, "Dark woman."

Marianne asks, "What's that? Did he just call you *the black woman*? That's what it means when he covers his eyes, right?"

Taniesha remarks, "Oh, hell no! No, Smithy, I'm *Taniesha*." She slaps her left shoulder and pulls her right earlobe, then says, "Say *Taniesha*."

Marianne says, "It's not like he means anything personal by it."

Smithy screams loudly.

Marianne continues, "God! Let's pick our subjects and get out of here; I can't stand that racket."

Taniesha repeatedly signs her name as Marianne checks cages and makes notes. She says, "*Taniesha. Taniesha.* Go on, practice it. I don't want to see any more of this *black woman* nonsense."

The researchers exit Corridor D. Smithy continues to sign and rattle the cage. A shadow flickers across the door. Smithy retreats to the back of his cage and covers his eyes.

DIARY OF RUBY DALTON

November 13, 1975

For once, today was decent—largely thanks to Brad.

He took Smithy outside for the second time this week; I hope Man doesn't notice his favoritism. I saw Brad heading into Corridor D as I arrived for my shift. The first thing I noticed was the oversized T-shirt that he swam in rather than wore.

He grinned and waved. "I'm gettin' ready to take Smithy out for a picnic. Want to come?" I would have loved to join, but it wasn't my choice. Brad kept wheedling though, suggesting I meet them on my break.

Fortunately, Dr. Fairbanks didn't object to my request for a break. Once in the cool air and sunlight, I headed toward the lake where Brad likes to take his charges. Our timing was perfect; I spotted them coming over the rise.

This time, Brad was wearing a tank top, and his large T-shirt hung off a smiling Smithy. They'd had to tie the thing at his waist so he wouldn't trip over it. Smithy also wore an old A's cap, bill turned backward, at an angle. He looked so comfortable, outdoors and free and wearing clothes again.

Brad winked. "Betcha didn't know Goodwill sold chimp chic." (He pronounced it "chick.") "We oughta have a fashion show for you and Jeff."

The thought of Smithy strutting down a catwalk in oversize castoffs made me laugh. I felt a twinge in my jaw muscle and realized how long it had been since I'd even smiled. It felt unfamiliar, like trying to remember the words to a song that was popular in high school.

I asked Smithy about his wardrobe. He identified "red shirt" and "hat." I also asked what they'd had for lunch. Smithy signed, "milk," "sandwiches," "oranges," "cookies," and something else I couldn't recognize

(Smithy curled his fingers like an O and put them to his lips). Brad got flustered when I asked him about it and said he was trying to teach Smithy a few new things, but he didn't explain further. I couldn't find anything resembling that sign in my battered ASL dictionary.

After a few minutes of "conversation," the three of us returned to the facility. Brad made Smithy step behind a tree and take his clothes off. Smithy sulked but cooperated. No one else was in sight as Brad led him back to his cage, so their secret stayed safe. Jeff was thrilled when I told him about it. He hopes to picnic with them Sunday, provided it doesn't rain.

I feel embarrassed now over how leery I was of Brad when I first arrived at CSAM. It was partly because of his drugs and partly because he was so nosy about Smithy. Now I appreciate how genuinely interested he is in the little guy.

If I'm entirely truthful, I was also being snobby. I spent last year in a rarefied atmosphere (a Newport mansion, for heaven's sake!) among educated, intellectual people. Brad's no dummy, but he's not the sort of person I'm used to socializing with. When Isaac suggested we invite him to join "the team" for lunch the other day, Keith vetoed and jokingly referred to Brad as "a commoner," implying he's not one of us, though Brad works harder than anybody else on staff to do everything Man needs.

Brad admitted he quit community college after a few weeks, but I believe it was from boredom, not inability. Anytime Brad gets interested in a subject, he'll teach it to himself. His signing is improving steadily because he applies himself so much. He even reads the notes and reports of CSAM's studies so he can understand what we're doing. A "common" custodian wouldn't do that; his tasks don't require it. Brad cares about what goes on here.

Furthermore, Brad has "common" sense, an important and refreshing quality in this swamp of egos. He's got an instinctive understanding of people, and he's flexible enough to get along with everyone, from Drs. Torrance and Fairbanks to Keith and Marianne. They're none of them best buddies, but Brad avoids antagonizing anybody. That native intelligence is better than book learning. I wish I had some.

In other news, I received a letter from Eric. He's trying to talk the IRB into approving language studies with pygmy chimpanzees: "They're *nearly as intelligent as humans, and they're more docile than common chimps, so they should be safer to work with."*

Sadly no one is biting. True, animal studies are expensive, but I suspect Piers has had a chilling effect on the field. La Fontaine is still working, but he's climbing up by grinding Smithy into the mud. He agrees with Piers's criticisms as they pertain to our study. Of course, he's free of such biases and Osage is a genius. Blech!

I enjoy hearing from my old friends. Old?! Yes, they already feel distant even though we were still together a few months ago. To think we were once a family!

I mustn't let myself mope. I'm making new friends. Things will get better. They must!

VIDEO FOOTAGE: "20/20" INTERVIEW WITH TANIESHA JONES

Broadcast Date: April 6, 1989
Location: Home

Taniesha sits in a chair on a shaded porch. A strand of red bougainvillea wraps around the pillar behind her chair. She wears a collared, green button-down blouse tucked into tailored dark pants. Her hair is in dreadlocks, held back from her face by a gold headband. Gold hoop earrings adorn her ears. She wears minimal make-up. She starts to speak.

"Smithy didn't like women much; lots of men at that time didn't. I think he was afraid of us. He'd cooperate with me during feedings or in a trial, but we were never buddies. Not like him and Brad.

"They really loved each other. Any time Brad was in the room, Smithy would light up. It was like seeing a little kid when his mommy comes to pick him up from daycare. And Brad doted on him. He always found ways to be around Smithy. It didn't matter who was running the study; Brad would get involved, too.

"Unlike the rest of us, who picked up one or two of Smithy's most common signs, Brad actively studied sign language. He'd sit up at night with an ASL book or watch film strips from the library, and he spent a lot of time with Ruby and Jeff Dalton, who had previously worked with Smithy and already knew a chunk of the language. Brad committed to meeting Smithy on his own terms and making sure he felt understood. Maybe that's why Smithy took to him so well.

"I used to tell him, when I thought he was being careless, that Smithy was a wild animal, not a pet. I'd say, 'You've gotta be careful, Brad. You never know what he's gonna do.' He'd already attacked two caretakers before, so the rest of us gave Smithy plenty of space unless we *had to* work with him.

"Brad waved off all my warnings. 'Nothing will happen. We're buddies.'

"But he did get hurt in the end. I just didn't realize how badly he'd be torn up."

HOME VIDEO FOOTAGE

Date: November 16, 1975
Location: An open field

Smithy and Brad, shirtless and wearing a floppy hat, sit on a blanket in a grassy field. Behind them is an ornamental lake. Brad pretends to put his hat on Smithy's head. He pulls it away at the last minute, but Smithy grabs it back and plops it on his own head. Brad tugs it down over Smithy's eyes and starts tickling him.

The camera cuts to Smithy sitting between Jeff and Brad. Jeff points to the camera, directing Smithy's attention. Smithy glances at it, then away. Brad lights a homemade joint and offers Smithy a Twinkie. Smithy crams it into his mouth.

Jeff says, "Nobody's going to take it from you, Smithy." He signs, "Slow."

Brad says, "He's excited. He misses good food."

Jeff says, "*Good* food? Don't let Ruby hear you say that."

Smithy watches the smoke trail from Brad's mouth. Brad holds out the joint so Smithy can see it. The chimp reaches for it, but Brad holds it out of reach. He signs, "What do you want?" Smithy pinches his thumb and first two fingers together in an 'O' and presses his fingertips to his lips repeatedly.

Brad asks, "What's the magic word?" Smithy signs, "Please." Brad passes him the joint.

Jeff watches the exchange and asks, "Are you sure that's OK? He might try to eat it . . ."

Brad says, "Nah, he knows better by now. 'Sides, it smells kind of funky. Who'd want to eat a joint? No matter how hungry it makes you."

Smithy blows smoke rhythmically. He purses his lips at Jeff, then turns and blows smoke into Brad's face. Brad nods in approval.

Jeff says, "I still can't believe you taught him to do that."

Brad says, "Yep. Well, he watched me long enough. He figured out how to roll 'em and smoke 'em on his own. I just taught him how to ask for a joint." He repeats the gesture with the three fingers. Jeff mimics Brad, and Smithy offers him the joint. Jeff looks surprised; then laughs.

Brad continues, "I taught him manners, too. He didn't like to share before. I told him, 'Hey, buddy, show a little kindness. The world's a mean place, but you don't have to be.'"

Jeff takes a puff, then passes the joint to Brad. Brad smokes it, then gives it back to Smithy.

Jeff says, "Don't let Ruby know about this, either."

Brad says, "She already saw him make the sign, but she doesn't know what it means. You won't tell?"

Jeff shakes his head. "Never!" He watches Smithy and Brad pass their joint back and forth.

Brad says, "I teach him other stuff, too; whatever he asks about. Like, he asked about this lake. He called it a 'beach' at first, so I taught him 'lake' instead. Some words I make up if I don't know 'em. If Smithy doesn't beat me to it. You know he comes up with his own signs? When we were first getting to know each other and I didn't know a thing about sign language, he started teaching me. He kept doing this—" Brad signs.

Jeff says, "Who are you?"

Brad says, "Yeah, and I didn't answer, so he named me himself." He scratches his chin, spreads his hands, then makes fists with his thumbs and pinkies protruding and wiggles them. "That's me: beard, let me out, let's go have some fun."

Smithy jumps up and runs to the nearest tree. He signs, "Up," and begins to climb. Brad laughs, gets to his feet, and says, "Let the fun begin." He runs to the tree and pretends to climb up after Smithy. The chimp screeches and climbs higher.

Jeff says, "Smithy needs to be in a language program. It's great that you talk to him, but he needs to go back to school. Think what he could do with real guidance. If Man noticed him creating signs and teaching you . . . Hey, maybe we could get Smithy to teach the other apes language!"

Brad shakes his head and says, "Hey, school's out, man. Come play with us!" Brad signs, "Jeff play."

Smithy signs, "Jeff chase," then leaps off the low branch and tears around the lake shore. Jeff rises and moves toward the camera. The picture cuts off.

UNEDITED INTERVIEW
WITH ISAAC MORGAN[2]
CIRCA 1991

Brad Vollmer was always kind of a weird dude. He was high all the time. I never saw him smoking, but he was always too cheerful. No way anybody working for the Man could smile that much! It was Brad who finally brought Smithy around.

Smithy'd run around the cage all day, trying to get away from bigger chimps who screamed at him, took his food, and threw crap at him. Kind of like chimp hazing. His nerves must've been shot. Sometimes you'd see him shivering even though it wasn't cold. He lost weight. Lost hair. He wouldn't take food. You'd give him something, and he'd chatter and shake his hands at you. I thought he was throwing a tantrum, y'know, but later I found out he was making signs, telling us what he wanted. Our food wasn't what he was used to, I guess, so he didn't eat it.

One evening, I was taking one of the animals back to Corridor E, and I went by Smithy's cage. He was in a corner, hunched over and rocking, looking like the saddest thing in the world. Then Brad came out of his trailer and sat down on the ground right in front of the cage and did the same thing. He slouched over and hung his head, so his hair was covering his face. He wrapped his arms around his legs and started rocking, like Smithy. At first, I thought he was making fun of

---

2 Material from this interview originally appeared in *Crossing the Communication Divide: Smithy and the World Beyond* by Colin Frye and Debbie Lawrence; the unabridged interview appears here courtesy of the authors.

him. I thought it was wacky, even for Brad, and kind of mean. But that was his way of getting close to Smithy.

Nowadays, we have all this research. We like people who are like us. When people copy us, we like them more. Brad was copying Smithy to get his attention, to show that he understood.

After a minute or two, the chimp looked up and saw this human curled up and crying like him. And he got curious. He started watching Brad, but Brad didn't look up. Then Smithy reached out and poked at his arm. I was about to say to Brad, "You're too close, back up!" But he slowly unwound and brushed his hair back and looked at Smithy. He didn't poke back, didn't say anything. They just looked at each other. I lost track of how much time went by, but eventually Smithy got up and moved to another corner of the cage, and Brad got up and left.

After that, I went by the enclosure more often on my breaks and I'd see Brad there. Usually, he and Smithy sat and looked at each other through the bars. Once, Brad brought his lunch and ate it in front of Smithy. He pointed to what he was eating and pointed to Smithy until Smithy finally got some food from his own tray and ate with him. Nobody else had been able to make him eat. All Brad did was show him how it was done.

And Smithy talked to Brad! Brad pointed to his food and Smithy made signs. Brad told me later he had no idea what Smithy was saying. "He could've been naming the food or he could've been telling me how it all tasted. I watched so I could remember what he was doing for later." Brad started carrying around books about sign language, but I think he learned most of it from Smithy himself. He talked to him most.

Eventually, Smithy got used to the rest of us. I wouldn't say he liked us all, but he *tolerated* us, y'know? Brad was his favorite, though.

After a month or two, Smithy got assigned to his first trial. He ended up in the control group of a nutritional study. No cognitive skills were required. It was way below his potential. Anyway, the trial ended after ninety days, and he was released back into the subject pool. I mean, sent back out to the enclosures. I figured Smithy would've settled down by that point, but the problems started right up again. Only this time, Smithy wasn't the victim. And once he started gambling, everything went to hell . . .

NOTES BY EILEEN FENN
January 22, 1976

Disturbance recorded in Enclosure 2 this morning. (Predicted hierarchy of inhabitants: Nero, Moses, Woolly, Smithy.)

Each chimp received a serving of whole-grain loaf and fruit. B.V. instructed to give some chimps bananas and some chimps melons at random to see how they respond to unequal treatment. (Per E.T.: unequal availability of more desirable fruit, *i.e.*, cantaloupe, will stimulate competition/aggression.)

On previous observation, Nero received a banana but took melon from Smithy by force and coerced Moses and Woolly into yielding through dominance display. Therefore, I predicted Nero to force compliance from Woolly and Smithy.

Observations via monitor: Food distributed @ 0700. Melon: Nero, Woolly, Smithy. Banana: Moses. Nero stood upright, bared teeth, pounded chest. Typical dominance display. Smithy retreated to SE corner; Woolly remained crouching over melon. Nero abruptly stopped chest pounding, started screaming. Moses screaming, too, baring teeth. Woolly abandoned melon. Nero, Moses threw fruit to Smithy. Nero, Moses, Woolly together retreated to NW corner. Smithy took all fruit up tree; sat/ate ten mins. Nero, Moses, Woolly remained agitated thirty mins. Remained apart from Smithy for remainder of observation period.

Per B.V., Smithy signed to cage-mates to yield their fruit. I witnessed no display from Smithy. No standard dominance behaviors. No vocalizations.

Why release fruit to him?

NOTES BY JANET FAIRBANKS
January 31, 1976

Accumulated observations of Webster indicate increasing, atypical dominance. Given reports of aggressive behavior in his previous environment, evidence suggests subject is entering early-onset adolescence.

Man advises introducing Webster to a female. Allowing them to mingle and socialize at this stage will foster breeding when adolescence manifests in full. Relocation scheduled for Tuesday.

NOTES BY JANET FAIRBANKS
February 3, 1976

Today marked the first attempt to introduce Webster to a 6-yo female, Rosalie. Since arriving, he has either been kept exclusively with male chimps or housed alone. This was his first exposure to the opposite sex.

Webster was removed from Enclosure 2 yesterday and placed in currently vacant Enclosure 5. After a night and a day to adjust to his new accommodations, Rosalie joined him. The goal was to let the chimps share a meal and encourage them to play or solve a puzzle task together. This did not occur.

Upon entering the cage, Rosalie displayed agitation and emitted high-pitched screeches. She stiffened and refused to move any farther into the enclosure than the gate. Webster retreated behind a tree and observed the newcomer. He whimpered but neither demonstrated hostility nor approached Rosalie.

Rosalie attempted to exit the enclosure. She rattled the gate and screeched. When I refused to open the cage, she climbed the sides, searching for a gap. Webster observed her from behind the tree. When Rosalie had reached the cage ceiling and clung suspended from it, he advanced into the open space and attempted to climb up the wall after her. Rosalie observed his approach, and her distress increased. She crawled across the ceiling to avoid him. When Webster pursued her, Rosalie dropped to the ground and ran to the gate. She shook the gate more forcefully. Webster remained at the top of the cage, watching her.

Rosalie continued to scream and attempted to force her way out of the cage for over an hour before Man approved her removal. I returned Rosalie to Enclosure 4, where she seated herself in a corner and remained impassive for the remainder of the night. She did not eat at suppertime nor interact with her cage-mates. Violetta and

Camille both avoided her. Closed-circuit footage shows Rosalie sitting and rocking while staring out of the cage for about four hours before finally lying down to sleep.

Closed-circuit footage shows no atypical behavior from Webster during the same period. Occasionally, he formed gestures that could be interpreted as signs. Webster appeared to signal Brad Vollmer when supper was served (according to the American Sign Language Dictionary, this sign means "out/go out"). When Taniesha Jones passed the enclosure, Webster made the sign for "hello" and a patented sign Ms. Jones claims is her name.

He formulated other signs without people present. Several times he made the sign for "go out" and covered his eyes. Ruby Dalton reports this sign variously indicates "sleep" or the color black, depending on the context.

I am unable to explain the antipathy between the apes. We will attempt a second introduction between Webster and Rosalie later this week.

NOTES BY JANET FAIRBANKS
February 6, 1976

Day 2 of the attempted introduction between Rosalie and Webster again failed. This time, the encounter occurred outside the enclosure on neutral ground. Taniesha Jones was instructed to walk Webster before breakfast while I walked Rosalie. At 0645, we rendezvoused beneath a grove of trees.

I observed Rosalie's hackles rise as Webster and Ms. Jones crested the hill. Once he was in sight, Rosalie ran to me and clung to my legs. Webster sat back on his haunches and watched her. His lips curled back; if I were inclined to anthropomorphize, I would call it a sneer. It was not an inviting display, but it lacked obvious aggression.

Ms. Jones and I switched leashes, and she groomed the young female from a distance while I engaged Webster. We walked, I offered him peanuts, and I groomed him. He permitted it, but I felt tension in his body when I touched him, and I was conscious of his acute attention to everything I did. Wary surveillance is not uncommon when animals first meet or enter a new situation. I do not think it sufficient to explain Rosalie's apparent terror of Webster.

We returned both chimps to Enclosure 5 without incident. Webster repeatedly glanced at Rosalie but did not touch her; she refused to acknowledge him. The gate of Enclosure 5 was open, and Brad Vollmer had already placed food inside to entice the chimps. Webster entered unhesitatingly, but Rosalie balked. I repeatedly instructed her to enter the enclosure, and when she refused, I sent Ms. Jones for the cattle prod.

Upon seeing the device, Rosalie entered the cage with a submissive posture. She refused to approach the food. Ms. Jones gestured to Webster, and he approached Rosalie, offering a loaf. Rosalie retreated, snarling. Ms. Jones then instructed Webster through a combination of verbal orders and gestures to leave the food on the ground and move to the opposite side of the cage. Given space, Rosalie quickly ate the food, then retreated.

I dismissed Ms. Jones and continued to observe the chimps' progress on the monitors. The apes kept to separate sides of the enclosure. Webster engaged in typical tasks (eating, climbing), whereas Rosalie maintained a defensive crouch and observed her cage-mate. This went on for about twenty mins, after which, I turned my attention to reviewing data.

At 0813, the microphones picked up loud, agitated chattering from Enclosure 5. On the monitor, I watched Rosalie throwing dirt and sticks at Webster. The male chimp initially tried to protect himself by covering his eyes, but as the assault continued, he started throwing the detritus back at Rosalie. I hastened to the enclosure to avert a full-scale attack.

Vollmer was already there, calling to Webster (whom he addressed as "Smithy") and gesturing for him to desist. Webster ceased throwing projectiles at Rosalie but remained agitated. He rattled the gate and repeatedly made the sign for "out." Rosalie, meanwhile, retreated to the far side of the cage, shaking and banging her head against the enclosure. She covered her eyes and would not look at me when I addressed her. I instructed Vollmer to remove Rosalie from the cage and subdue Webster by whatever means necessary.

Vollmer signed to Webster to step back, and he gained entry to the cage. They continued to gesture to each other, then Webster retreated to the tree and Brad collected Rosalie, physically carrying her out of the enclosure. He gave her to me; she was trembling and appeared to be in shock. I removed her to my lab for study.

Rosalie displays lowered body temperature, dilated pupils, trembling, accelerated heart rate. However, she is uninjured and otherwise healthy. She is currently isolating in the medical ward for the next forty-eight hours.

A review of the closed-circuit footage shows Rosalie initiated the attack. She appears to take fright while Webster is swinging from a tree and throws dirt at him. As before, he does not display hostility until provoked.

I recommend terminating the socialization process. Perhaps we can reintroduce him to a different female in the summer.

NOTES FROM JANET FAIRBANKS
February 8, 1976

I witnessed Webster signing today during the afternoon feeding. When I approached Enclosure 5, the chimp displayed great excitement by jumping up and down and shaking the wire barrier. As I administered food and water, he gestured, and I again observed the sign signifying "black/sleep" (covering both eyes with both palms) and another I am told denotes "woman" (thumb touched to chin, lowered to chest). As I am a white woman, I conclude these signs are either produced at random or they are the result of overgeneralization, and Webster does not fully understand the signifiers he displays. This incident undermines the Daltons' claims in favor of the animal's linguistic skills.

Incidentally, I recommend obtaining some heat lamps for the animals. The space around Enclosure 3 feels positively arctic.

home the above wrote me a note, telling me to let me Smithy back to the club. Maybe he traced to the darkness in a way that conveyed his eagerness. Neither Sidney nor me at the time at the time of the problem so that could be wreck my faculties for its skirmishes and when he carried back on still.

NOTES BY KEITH BRANNEMAN
February 11, 1976

Noted aggression in Enclosure 2 on the CC cameras this evening. The other males have been edgy since Smithy was returned yesterday afternoon—manifested restlessness, lack of appetite, and massing on the opposite side of the enclosure as if conferring or backing each other up.

I couldn't identify what triggered the incident, but I heard loud growling and hooting from the speakers and looked up in time to see Woolly, Moses, and Nero flinging down branches and seed pods from the trees where they'd taken refuge. Smithy remained at the base of the tree, trying to fend off the attack. He was making hand gestures and seemed to be trying to communicate with his attackers.

Brad knows some sign language and says Smithy was telling them to, "Stop, go away, go to sleep." He claims Smithy was attempting to reason with the others instead of fighting back. Smithy kept signing, but the other apes don't sign, so it did no good.

Eventually, Smithy gave up negotiating and climbed the tree to confront his attackers. They retreated to the highest branch, then climbed onto the ceiling. Smithy stayed in the tree and screamed, pounded his chest, and threw leaves. It was a general dominance display. He turned in all directions of the cage instead of facing the other chimps directly.

One by one, the other males dropped to the ground, turned their backs to the tree, and covered their eyes. They did not calm down until Brad took Smithy out of the cage and back to his trailer. Smithy was worked up, too. Brad said Smithy wouldn't sleep and kept walking around the trailer all night, turning on lights.

Note: I think we need an electrician to check the lights around the enclosure. They kept flickering when I was trying to mediate the chimp fight. I also saw the lights dimming on the CC tapes just before the dispute broke out. Jeff once told me Smithy is afraid of the dark. Maybe he reacted to the darkness in a way that unsettled his cage-mates. Neither Dalton was on site at the time of the problem, so they could not weigh in. I will ask Jeff to check the tapes when he comes back on shift.

LETTER FROM RUBY DALTON
TO TAMMY COHEN

February 13, 1976

Dear Tammy,

I'm steamed! Smithy has been removed from the general population of apes and exiled to "Sick Bay," a solitary cage removed from the other animals for quarantining illness. He's not sick, but he's been identified as a "hazard" to the other chimps, so he's got to live by himself for who knows how long until Man decides to reintroduce him to society.

He's done nothing wrong. In fact, he's demonstrated admirable self-control. Over the past several weeks, poor Smithy has taken a beating from the other males in his enclosure and even from an older female Man assigned to be his playmate. Smithy didn't start any fight, and he didn't immediately fight back. The other apes just don't like him. They never have. They know he's different.

It would be better if they ostracized him, but because they got physical with one another, Man got involved. He's reviewed the CC tapes of the chimps' interactions and can't find a trigger, but the common denominator is Smithy, so Man's blaming him for his own victimization. He was content to lock Smithy in a cage full of animals as long as he was the one being bullied. Now that Smithy has somehow gained the upper hand, he's been banished to solitary confinement.

Dr. Fairbanks says it's a cautionary measure. They're concerned about the "sudden, inexplicable aggression between parties" and want to "separate out the risk factors" to "isolate and treat the problem." But I wouldn't bet on them rotating out chimps to see who the real "risk factor" is. Nero hasn't been kicked out of the enclosure yet.

Bottom line: They suspect Smithy of foul play or fraud or something. They think it's impossible he could have gained status by virtue of his own skills.

Man has also forbidden Smithy all but the barest human interaction. Brad isn't even allowed to bring him food or clean his cage; Man is doing that all himself—with cattle prod in hand. I expect he's watching the cameras throughout the day, waiting to catch Smithy flying into a psychotic rage. Instead, reports show he's losing his appetite, losing his hair, and slowly wasting away from misery. Again.

Dr. T saw him on the monitor. He told me Smithy was pacing around his cage, striking the bars and motioning with his hands. "Chimps in isolation usually shut down completely. Yours is keeping active." I think he meant to make me feel better, but instead I wanted to cry. Is Smithy losing his mind all alone in there? Is he talking to himself? Asking for help from anyone who might be watching? I wish I could see for myself what he's saying.

Remember how easily he used to escape from his room? For months, I've been wishing Smithy would turn back into Houdini, flee his persecutors, and defy Man. But whatever ability Smithy used at Trevor Hall has deserted him.

Marianne gleefully shared the juicy gossip that Man made a long-distance call to chew Piers out for trying to "sabotage" CSAM. Man's side of the conversation (which must have been pretty damn loud considering how thick the walls are in this complex), included phrases like "breach of contract," "fraud," and "time bomb." Maybe Marianne stood outside Man's office with a stethoscope to the door to pick all that up.

I hate this situation. I'm praying Man's grudge against Smithy doesn't kill him and that Smithy can be better integrated into the facility once released from chimp jail . . .

EXCERPT FROM
SMITHY: THE MILLENNIUM COMPENDIUM
BY REID BENNET

Smithy's exile lasted until the end of February. Over two weeks of observation, neither Man Teague nor Janet Fairbanks detected evidence of an aggressive demeanor. Teague allowed his staff to resume feeding and walking Smithy on February 25, and then finally re-introduced him into the general population by moving him to Enclosure 3 with Grandee and Bashful on March 4. No further incidents of intimidation or physical harm were recorded. Whatever had provoked Smithy remained unexplained.

Though working conditions at CSAM had always been far from ideal, Ruby Dalton's diary of the ensuing months indicates just how remarkably tumultuous the environment was even before crisis struck:

April 8, 1976

. . . Eileen's resigned. Man snapped at her Tuesday about some notes she turned in that he claimed were "piss poor." He yelled over her when she tried to answer his questions, though he only in got two f-bombs. Eileen took the dressing-down stoically, but she spent a long time in the bathroom after he'd gone. I wonder if she was crying.

I wish I'd gotten to know Eileen better. If I'd tried harder to befriend her, maybe she would have stuck around. Although, it's vain to imagine I had the power to root her in place. Nobody else seems to care she's left. We gave her no send-off.

At least Jeff and I won't be the new kids on the block anymore, once he replaces her.

April 21, 1976

Today we welcomed our newest colleague, Megan Turner, to CSAM. Megan wants lab experience to improve her chances of getting into grad school next year. "Andy Jackson says she won't last to the end of the year," Brad bet. Taniesha gives her four months; Isaac six.

August 9, 1976

Megan quit today. She was packing to leave as I came on shift. I thought she was simply cleaning up for the day, but when I asked how she was, she said, "I've had it with that son of a bitch. I had a boyfriend once who shouted at me and called me names. Never again!" Megan's so sweet; I can't imagine what she must have done to displease Man.

August 17, 1976

Man announced recent graduate, Mallory Wyatt, will join Dr Fairbanks's team on Monday. Isaac turned to me and whispered, "Six months?" I say three.

October 27, 1976

Exit Mallory.

I was typing my notes when Man roared for her to come to his office. She sprang from her desk, pad and pencil in hand. Man bellowed for her again when Mallory was only halfway down the hall; I guess she wasn't moving fast enough. I couldn't make out what he said to her, but I could hear him screaming all the way down the hall.

At last, Mallory came back, quivering. She told me, "Ruby, it's been nice working with you, but I'm leaving now." I'm not clear if she quit or if Man fired her; I was afraid to ask. I suspect she's a casualty of Man's anger at Jeff and me. And Smithy. Man's been in a foul temper ever since those damn rumors began circulating. He probably wanted to scream at somebody, and Mallory was a convenient target.

She lasted just over two months; I wonder if I can collect from Isaac.

Predictably, one wonders whether inherent instability in the organization begat the accusations and attacks that followed, or if the high turnover and emotionality demonstrated that the sinister forces allegedly afoot were already stretching tendrils into CSAM's midst. The Trevor Hall study, by contrast, appears far more functional, despite uneven leadership, daily hassles, and a shorter duration. Perhaps, given Smithy as a common factor, each distinct environment was destined to self-destruct in its own way . . .

VIDEO FOOTAGE: "20/20" INTERVIEW WITH TANIESHA JONES

Broadcast Date: April 6, 1989

At one point, you were assigned to study gambling behavior in apes, weren't you?

Taniesha laughs.

I've been waiting for you to ask. Everyone wants to know about that study. It was designed by Edgar Torrance, a senior researcher at CSAM, and involved three phases. First, the animal subjects would learn the value of tokens—"money." Second, they'd practice wagering money to earn rewards and learn the concept of risk. Finally, successful learners were rotated into a double-blind drug trial; selected chimps were injected with a chemical that was supposed to suppress their risk-taking behavior . . .

UNEDITED INTERVIEW
WITH ISAAC MORGAN
CIRCA 1991

The whole reason that study came about was because
the doctor who developed the anti-gambling drug
was having trouble with the university review
board. He wanted to test it on human subjects
and advertise at Gamblers Anonymous, but the
board had all these reservations, y' know: Was
the drug really safe? Was it ethical to withhold
it from the control group? And, oh yeah, the
manipulation depended on activity that was illegal
in California.

This doctor was an old college buddy of Ed
Torrance's. He offered his pal access to CSAM's
subjects. There's nothing illegal about *chimps*
gambling, and primates often sub for humans in
drug testing.

The drug was the most important part of the
study, but we had to build up to it by teaching
the chimps how to gamble and the value of money.
Then we could see how much they risked, or if
they adjusted their strategy, or if the drug got
them to quit cold turkey.

The pre-study sample included Smithy, Violetta,
Bashful, Woolly, Moses, and Eleanor . . .

VIDEO FOOTAGE: "20/20" INTERVIEW WITH TANIESHA JONES

Broadcast Date: April 6, 1989

. . . Ruby and I were in the kitchen. It was
rare for us to be on break together. Man knew
we were friends and deliberately screwed up our
schedules so we couldn't interact much. He liked
to experiment with people same as with chimps to
see how we'd react to unpredictability.

Torrance came in to refill his coffee and casually
mentioned a new study he was starting. He asked
if I wanted to work with him. I was assigned to
Fairbanks's project at the time, but she had
multiple part-timers assisting, so I agreed. I
wanted steadier employment and the opportunity to
build a stronger platform for myself within CSAM.
Torrance wasn't as backward as Man. He didn't
think women existed to serve and look pretty.
He'd give a leg up to anyone who had potential
and kept their head screwed on straight. He'd
worked with Marianne many times and even let her
share writing credit. At that time, I wanted to
get my name into print more than anything.

Torrance described his design and how he was
going to start by teaching all his apes the value
of money. He made a joke about how long it would
take because he was still trying to get his kids
to understand. Then Ruby piped up: "Smithy knows
how tokens work. He's used them before in Rhode
Island."

Torrance turned to her, polite but very
interested. His ears tuned like antennae, and he

82

said, "Oh, really? How long did it take you to make that lesson stick?"

Ruby said, "Not long. He'd be a good model to have in your study to show the others how tokens work. And he could be your baseline for how they should respond."

"Perfect!" Torrance said. "You're hired, too."

LETTER FROM RUBY DALTON
TO TAMMY COHEN

May 20, 1976

Dear Tammy,

I did it, Tammy! I finally got Smithy enrolled in a study where he'll be safe and engaged! It's projected to run at least six months, more likely a full year. Unless Smithy flames out (which he won't; it's perfect for him!), we won't have to worry about him for a good long time.

Dr. Torrance's new project, in part, will explore primate understanding of monetary worth. I mentioned Smithy's success with our token economy, and he said Smithy is an ideal candidate for the study.

This study is ideal for me, too. It will be my first opportunity to actually conduct research here! No mere mimeographing or transcribing reports. I'll oversee manipulation and record my observations. I feel like I'm being reborn.

We (Dr. T, Taniesha, Isaac, and I) met with Man yesterday to formally present our goals. His scowl grew deeper the more Dr. T talked. Every second, I swear, a new crease popped out on Man's forehead or slithered around his eyes. Still, he didn't say a word. I couldn't figure out what his objections would be, but I knew some were coming.

Finally, after Dr. T outlined his time frame (phase 1 will start next month and hopefully wrap by September) and proposed his subjects, Man cocked an eyebrow and squinted at us. He looked at Torrance, but I knew his comments were meant for me.

"You want to put Webster in a program to teach chimps to use money. But he already knows how tokens work, you say. Then you can't teach him anything new! He's a ringer! He'll throw off all your data! You won't know what he's learned from you and what he remembers from before. Why waste time and resources? That's bullshit."

I wanted to cry. The perfect opportunity for Smithy was sliding through my fingers.

Dr. T saved it. "I might agree with you if I were teaching finances, though I probably still would want to use Webster as a control to monitor the success of the sample's comprehension. However, the purpose of this study isn't really to show apes how tokens work; we want to see what they do with the tokens after they've learned, whether they gamble or not. So long as Webster knows tokens have value, he'll perform as we need."

Man's lower lip popped out like a fat slug sticking its head out of a shell. He fixed his beady eyes on me. I felt my stomach twist, but I forced myself to keep a straight face. "And her," he started. "I specifically said I didn't want her coddling that ape, yet you defy me and recruit her—"

Dr. T came to my aid then! "Ruby's participation is vital, too. She's taught apes how to use tokens; I expect to profit by her knowledge."

The slug drew back from Man's teeth but the eyes continued probing me, blaming me. I know he thinks I'm trying to wrangle special favors, manipulating his researchers to do it.

Aloud, he said, "I see." Just two words, like ice plunking into a glass. Then he jumped to another topic, and I could breathe again, knowing Smithy and I were both safe.

Jeff was thrilled when I told him. He wasn't crazy about Man bossing me around, though. Jeff gave me a huge hug and didn't stop smiling for the rest of the evening. When we embraced, I could feel all the tension in Jeff's back and shoulders melt away. I didn't realize until that moment how much of his anxiety has been for Smithy's welfare. With school, work, our new life in Fresno, I thought he had too much on his plate, but that one colossal problem has overshadowed everything else.

When we came here, I didn't expect us to end up as Smithy's protectors first and foremost. We're both sorry he's not enrolled in a language study, but at least this work will be stimulating. The suppressant drug at the end shouldn't have any negative effects. I see nothing but promise ahead . . .

LETTER FROM RUBY DALTON
TO TAMMY COHEN

June 5, 1976

Jeff finally has his MA in psychological research!

I used one of my sick days so I could watch him claim his diploma. My in-laws drove down for the ceremony, too. They smiled throughout the convocation and congratulated Jeff profusely afterward, but I couldn't help thinking it was not the big moment they'd imagined while he was at Yale. Yet, if the day felt anticlimactic, they still treated it as a holiday.

I tried to take a photo of Jeff accepting his certificate, but from our perch at Ratcliffe Stadium, we could only see little lines of graduates on the field. Afterward, though, I got several shots of Jeff with his diploma and mortarboard, including a candid one of Angie dousing him with confetti.

My in-laws stayed overnight at a hotel in town; our little apartment is too tiny to hold any guests. Even Angie declined to sleep on the couch when we offered it. We did some sightseeing (what there is to see of Fresno besides vineyards and orchards) and shared a late lunch at Farrell's before Jeff's folks hit the road. We both enjoyed seeing them again.

When we were alone, I asked Jeff if he was proud of his accomplishment. "No, I'm just glad it's over with," he said. So am I.

Our coworkers also celebrated with us. The day before graduation, a "congratulations" card showed up on Jeff's desk at CSAM. Megan, the new girl, had everyone (except Man) sign it. She and Brad even inked Smithy's finger and had him "write" a "message" on the back.

Now that our guests have gone and the parties are over, I can feel the hesitation before the next chapter in our life begins. Who knows yet what that will be? Jeff is displaying more ambivalence than I'd expected.

I teased him a little last night before we went to bed: "Now that your classes are over, don't get too used to having extra time on your hands."

"No," he said quickly. "I've already asked Man to give me more hours. He did."

That startled me. I'd thought Jeff would be pounding the pavement trying to find a teaching position before the new school year.

"I want to spend more time with Smithy now. I can sub come September and get a feel for how I want to run my own classroom. Then, next year—either in spring or next fall—I'll see about finding long-term employment." Again, I was surprised. Jeff had never mentioned delaying his job search.

I suppose, now that the new study is about to begin, Jeff is curious to see how Smithy reacts to psychological manipulation. The project shouldn't take a full year, so even if Jeff wants to stick around for its duration, he should still be a free agent in time for the '76-'77 school year.

In the meantime, Jeff and I can enjoy some extra hours together during the week. Until I enroll in classes myself, that is . . .

NOTES BY EDGAR TORRANCE
Study #478; Phase 1; Session 1 – June 24, 1976

The first introduction of tokens proceeded satisfactorily. Four chimps participated in the initial meeting: Violetta, Moses, Webster, and Eleanor. A separate session for the remaining participants (Woolly, Nero, Bashful, Old Vic) will occur this evening.

Isaac and Ruby assisted. Per Ruby's suggestion, we began the session by modeling the use of tokens to the chimps. The tokens are oversized poker chips painted gold ($5) or silver ($1) to indicate different value. Isaac showed the chips to the animal subjects and allowed them to handle the tokens. Moses attempted to eat one and Eleanor clapped her tokens together and pounded them on the floor to make noise. Woolly studied the tokens closely but did not manipulate them in any way. Webster did not touch or examine the tokens.

Next, we practiced exchanging tokens for goods to demonstrate their value. Ruby brought out a tray of food, which she kept out of the chimps' reach. Isaac handed her a silver token in exchange for a set of apple slices. Two silver tokens purchased additional apple slices. When Isaac attempted to purchase a whole cantaloupe melon with a silver token, Ruby refused to give it to him. I then traded a gold token for the fruit. We conducted three more such trials to show that tokens could be redeemed for traditional primary reinforcers.

Next, we assigned the chimps a simple task to perform, whereby they could receive tokens and redeem them. The chimps were given a modified Tower of Hanoi and instructed via demonstration to pile a set of rings onto a pole in a particular sequence. The first to accomplish this received $6 in tokens (one gold token and one silver token). Second place received four silver tokens, third place received three silver tokens, and last place received two silver tokens.

Many chimps expressed irritation through vocalizations and display upon receiving token rewards. Violetta threw her two tokens away and attempted to seize the fruit platter, but Isaac prevented her. Moses also threw his three tokens across the room and pounded the floor. Eleanor made noisemakers of her tokens as before, but repeatedly looked at the fruit as if to indicate her true preference.

Webster, by contrast, and by virtue of his prior experience, presented his four tokens to Ruby and motioned with his hand. She translated that he was asking her to give him the cantaloupe. However, he did not have enough tokens for this purchase.

Ruby attempted to communicate to the ape via signs that he could have the apple but not the melon. He persisted in requesting the melon, and she requested more tokens. Webster expressed frustration. As he turned from Ruby, the fur on his back bristled and his teeth displayed.

Webster crossed the room to where the discarded tokens lay and collected them. I discouraged Isaac from intervening and allowed Webster to present the illicitly collected tokens for redemption. This time, Ruby accepted all eight tokens in return for a melon and three servings of apples.

The chimps next engaged in more verbal display. Evidently, they realized they had been cheated out of their fruit. Violetta approached Ruby and clutched at the different fruits, but Ruby refused to yield any. Moses approached Webster and tried to take his fruit by shoving the smaller chimp away. However, Webster resisted by kicking him. Moses crossed to the spot where he had thrown his tokens and paced around as if looking for them. He crossed his arms and turned his back on Webster. Eleanor appeared distressed by the confrontation, but though she clutched her tokens to her chest, she did not seem to grasp their value as she did not attempt to exchange them.

Our next step would have presented a more challenging task for which the chimps might be more motivated to cash in their tokens for an edible reward. Before we could proceed, however, Webster approached Eleanor. He stood over her and made a sign, which Ruby translated as "Give me." Eleanor stared at him and backed away but did not engage in confrontation. Suddenly she screeched, leapt in the air, and began to jump around the room. Several moments passed while Isaac and I tried to calm her down. Ruby, suspecting a diversion, guarded the food.

Once Eleanor was again restrained, we observed that she had one silver token left. The gold five-piece was in Webster's hand, and he immediately redeemed it for another melon. Neither of us saw Eleanor drop this token, nor did we observe Webster taking it from her. Ruby claims he performed many such sleight-of-hand tricks while in her care in Providence (sic).

Regardless of how he accomplished it, Webster's determination to acquire all the tokens transmitted itself effectively to his peers. For the remaining trials, all chimps guarded their tokens carefully. After observing Webster, they also quickly adapted to the practice of redeeming tokens for more appetizing rewards.

This first group still shows a marked preference for primary reinforcers, but it now recognizes that tokens have value. I believe Webster's inclusion has helped in teaching these lessons. His modeling, as well as his mercenary attempts to steal from his fellows, has accelerated the teaching process tremendously.

DIARY OF RUBY DALTON

July 4, 1976

Happy 200th birthday, America!

I ought to feel more festive than I do. It's Sunday, and Jeff and I are together. We grilled hot dogs on the communal grill in the apartment's courtyard (we had to start them at 10:00 a.m. before the rest of the tenants descended). We then took a walk around the neighborhood and watched other families having cookouts, playing games, and enjoying a good time. There was a shindig downtown, but the crowd was bigger than we anticipated, so we didn't stay long.

This day was so different from how we spent our holiday last year. Instead of watching fireworks on the water, we ended up watching a nationally televised broadcast of festivities in DC. The fireworks looked much less impressive in B&W. The night was so much quieter than what I expected.

Of course, tonight differed importantly from last year in other ways. No emergencies. No police interviews. No worries. I wonder what Tammy is doing. Maybe she's watching fireworks over Liberty Island. And Gail; what is she thinking of tonight?

Is anyone watching festivities from Trevor Hall, I wonder?

NOTES BY TANIESHA JONES
July 12, 1976

After nearly two weeks of exposure to tokens and repeated practice exercises, all chimps in the sample have reached proficiency as judged by at least three experimenters according to the criteria described in Appendix D. Per Ruby, Smithy reached this level after only three days; however, he was the sole chimp in his preliminary study and had five instructors attending him.

Although the chimps recognize the value of tokens, can differentiate between denominations, and are skilled at trading tokens for other rewards, they have not yet developed the art of saving. With one exception,** all chimps redeem their tokens for food as soon as they earn them. This bodes poorly for Phase 2 (the gambling manipulation) because the players must have a stock of tokens to wager.

Walter Mischel has written that the ability to delay gratification is essential to predicting future success in life (1958; 1970). With this premise, I predict that all the chimps in our study are at risk for developing a high gambling addiction. If they can't control themselves enough to build up their bank, they are unlikely to resist the temptation to wager for big gains.

**Smithy deliberately sets out to amass tokens, which he then redeems for high-value prizes, unlike the other chimps, who cash out for low-value prizes.

I'm concerned by how ruthless he is in acquiring tokens. Smithy intimidates his peers into surrendering tokens against their will. He never uses violence or visible threat. Instead, he stares intently at the chimp he means to rob; sometimes Smithy will sign to them.

I've translated "give me" and "hurry" most frequently. He also will cover his eyes; Ruby explained this is a proprietary sign that can either mean "sleep" or "dark." I cannot determine the sign's context within the assigned activity. Isaac suggested it's a rough way to communicate, "I'm gonna punch your lights out if you don't give me your lunch money." I disagree. To reiterate, Smithy has never initiated aggression against another chimp, so they have little reason to expect force. Secondly, some of the chimps have started adopting the sign themselves.

This afternoon, Smithy advanced on Moses, who had just been awarded three tokens. Smithy stared at him and began to whimper but did not posture or sign. Instead, Moses became agitated, covered his eyes, threw his tokens at Smithy's feet, and covered his eyes again. Once Smithy collected the tokens, Moses relaxed. Isaac reported that Violetta also covered her eyes yesterday when Smithy asked her to surrender her tokens.

This behavior merits further observation. I think it's worthwhile to develop a sign language program. Clearly, the non-signing chimps are assigning meaning to Smithy's signs, even if it's not a literal meaning. We should see where this leads.

DIARY OF RUBY DALTON

September 12, 1976

Back from celebrating Jeff's birthday three days late. Since we haven't done anything special for him these past two years, I wanted to make up for it tonight with a dinner-and-a-movie date. Jeff wanted to go back to Farrell's, which was fine by me. The restaurant served him an enormous, free sundae for his birthday. He managed to eat the whole thing; I was hoping I'd have to "help" him.

For the movie, Jeff opted to see The Omen. *He'd heard enough about it from the guys at work to whet his appetite when it first came out, but he'd never had the opportunity to catch it. We found a second-run theater that was still playing it. Jeff was delighted.*

I was less enthusiastic. I've never been a horror fan. I don't like gore, and I'd heard a guy gets his head cut off in this film. Still, the movie had a good cast. How can you go wrong with Atticus Finch?

The story of Satan's spawn on Earth wasn't as gruesome as I'd feared. Even when the corrupt priest got impaled, you couldn't see much blood. It was more atmospheric than in-your-face. I felt myself getting pulled into the story against my better judgment.

Until Lee Remick took Damien to the zoo. Where they were attacked by baboons. I saw the shrieking beasts swarm the car, and my body tensed as if I were about to be ripped to shreds. The scene wasn't arranged to put the characters in real danger. The actors were in a car, for heaven's sake. I knew it was staged, but knowing isn't the same as feeling. All I could think was how alike chimpanzees and baboons are. And what would I do if our chimpanzees came after me that way?

The scene was over in about two minutes, but the tension didn't leave me when their car left the animal park. I seriously worried about the burger and fries and all the popcorn and soda in my stomach.

Then came the critical scene when you no longer had to wonder if the cherub-faced boy, who the Thorn family was sheltering, was the victim of coincidence or mistaken identity. That was the moment Damien tried to kill his foster mother.

I excused myself to the bathroom and stayed there for twenty, maybe thirty minutes. First, I put cold water on my face, then I locked myself in a stall and tried to stabilize my breathing. It didn't work, though, because I'd recognized the true horror of the movie.

It's not the devil that scares everyone, though the audience may think that. It's the idea that the child you've raised and loved as your own isn't the innocent you thought and never was. He can rise up and smite you as casually as if he were playing a game. No matter how good a person you are or how fine your intentions, dark forces can still align against you and destroy you.

Finally, I heard a strange woman calling my name. One of the usherettes had come looking for me at Jeff's request. I washed my face and rejoined Jeff in the lobby. He was genuinely concerned. "I'm sorry, Ruby. I didn't know you still took all this religious business so seriously. You haven't been to church in ages."

I didn't want to explain that it wasn't the Antichrist that frightened me. I thought I would sound stupid. I encouraged him to go back in and finish the movie, but Jeff insisted we both go home. I think Keith already told him how the thing ends. Even so, I felt like I'd ruined Jeff's birthday evening. I made it up to him when we got home, and he said he was glad we'd come back early, but some guilt still lingers.

So does some of the horror. That's why I'm up writing while Jeff's snoring. I know when I fall asleep, I'll dream of chimps on tricycles chasing me through Trevor Hall. And a figure in black, directing it all from the oculus.

VIDEO FOOTAGE: "20/20" INTERVIEW WITH TANIESHA JONES

Broadcast Date: April 6, 1989

Man didn't like being circumvented one bit. He allowed Torrance to run the experiment, but only temporarily. As Phase 1 was winding down, Man stepped in and yanked the study away from him, telling Dr. T that he needed him to finish running a vaccine trial, since pathology was his specialty. That reassignment was trumped up so Man could take over the project, of course. He wasn't satisfied with taking the reins; he had to boot Torrance altogether to punish him for overruling his judgment.

I kept waiting for Man to cut Ruby, too, but he left her alone. "He likes making me squirm," she joked. "He wants me to creep around on eggshells, wondering if I'll be next."

That was right around the time the bombshell came out of Newport . . .

LETTER FROM TAMMY COHEN
TO THE DALTONS

October 7, 1976

Ruby & Jeff,
  I thought you should see this right away. As you know, I've stayed in touch with Hope from the Meyer School. She sent me the enclosed and I wanted to apprise you ASAP.
  Call me when you can!

"DARK LADY OF TREVOR HALL
TERRIFIED TALKING APE"
BY PATRICIA HARTIGAN

THE NEWPORT DAILY NEWS
OCTOBER 6, 1976

A chill fills the air, and it isn't entirely due to the autumn weather. Halloween is just around the corner! It's the scariest time of the year. From Mercy Brown to the *Palatine*, Rhode Island offers many frights. One of the creepiest lurks in our own backyard.

Trevor Hall, a stately but decrepit Victorian manor, sits back from Bellevue Avenue in the shadows of copper beech trees. Those trees helped create one of Newport's most enduring ghosts.

According to local legend, at the turn of the last century, a servant fell from the rooftop of Trevor Hall under mysterious circumstances and impaled herself on one the trees surrounding the mansion. Since then, the figure of a woman in black has been said to prowl the Hall. She has been spotted on the stairs and in the corridors. Her voice has been heard in the night. Her shadow intimidates generations who grew up knowing to stay away from Trevor Hall.

Reports of the Dark Lady predominated in the 1920s and '30s, when the Hall operated as the Bradley Finishing School for Young Ladies, and later as a coed boarding school. Regaling one another with nighttime tales of her malignant appearances was a popular student pastime, and *"The ghost stole my homework"* became an oft-heard excuse.

More recently, the Dark Lady allegedly plagued Trevor Hall's latest and most famous resident: Smithy the signing chimpanzee. Also called Webster, this animal gained worldwide fame and local renown for his supposed mastery of American Sign Language, until lead researcher Piers Preis-Herald issued a retraction last year.

What Preis-Herald never told the public is that his team noted some very strange behavior from the chimp over the course of the study. Smithy was frequently observed to sign when no other person was in the room. According to a source involved in the project, Smithy complained often of a "dark lady," whom no one else could see, and he refused to go to sleep because of something "bad" in his room. Over time, Smithy also turned aggressive without provocation, most infamously mutilating his keeper, Wanda Karlewitz [sic]. Did the "dark lady" finally drive him over the edge?

OUT OF CONTROL

Though Smithy's freak-outs were unknown to the general public until now, they were as familiar to local residents as Trevor Hall's ghoulish reputation.

Mrs. Denis Belancourt is the owner of Herbert Terrace, the property closest to Trevor Hall. During the year of Smithy's occupancy, she had multiple harrowing encounters with the ape.

"He escaped his keepers all the time. Those kids were powerless to control him. Twice he came onto our property. He almost got into a fight with our dog, Rudy. I was terrified for Rudy's safety because

I'd heard the chimp had killed one of the students' pets during a tantrum.

"Another time, I was home by myself with a migraine. My husband and Rudy had gone to the beach, and I was lying down to rest when I heard noises on the terrace below. When I looked out the window, the ape was dancing in the fountain! I shouted down to him, but he didn't acknowledge me, so I went next door to get the students to remove him. I wasn't about to confront him myself."

Even when Smithy stayed within the confines of Trevor Hall, the neighbors suffered the consequences of his misbehavior. "The fire alarm was always going off, and the fire department was constantly going up to investigate his mischief. You would hear screams at all hours of the night and day," Mrs. Belancourt recalls. "It sounded like something from a horror movie. I could never be sure if it was the ape screaming or one of the students. I told my husband, 'He's going to kill one of them one day.'"

That day nearly came on July 4, 1975, when a young girl working on the project violently interrupted a party at Herbert Terrace to report that Smithy had two of her friends cornered on the roof and was preparing to attack them.

"Denis and several of our guests went to their aid. I didn't want him to go because I didn't know if he would come back. Fortunately, the chimp had calmed down by the time Denis arrived, and then the police came. They said the chimp snapped while everyone was watching fireworks and nearly pushed one of the students to her death. It was a terrible tragedy, but all the same, I have to wonder what those kids were thinking. Surely, all the noise and flashing lights were bound to aggravate the animal!"

However, Mrs. Belancourt does not fault the students in charge of Smithy for his misdeeds. "They were a bunch of kids. I think most of them were on their own for the first time when they came here. They were alone in that big house, day in and day out, with a little time bomb that they dressed like a doll and fawned over like a baby. I blame their professor. Dr. Preis-Herald was all over the television and radio programs to talk up his experiment [and] seldom put in an appearance at the house. I know, because I often waited for him to turn up so I could give him a piece of my mind. What was he thinking, leaving his students—and this neighborhood—at the mercy of that ape? He ought to be ashamed of himself!"

When asked if she had ever witnessed supernatural activity at the house, Mrs. Belancourt denied any personal experience, adding, "We don't believe in ghosts." However, other sources claim they were aware of supernatural interference in Preis-Herald's experiment.

Shaun Hendricks became close friends with a member of the team who confided that he had seen the ghost in broad daylight. He got really shaky when describing it. He said it looked like a woman, but it had no face. And he admitted the ape had seen it, too.

Fred Patterson vividly recalls the day Smithy's keepers came to his house for help. "My roommate was a history buff and collected a lot of material about Trevor Hall. When they heard that, they showed up at our door, begging him to tell them what he knew about the ghost." At that point, the researchers related a chilling catalog of household accidents: mysterious fires in the night, windows and doors inexplicably unlocking, items disappearing. "One night, they got up and found Smithy choking to death. One of the guys had to give him CPR to save his life. And that all happened in the first month they moved in."

THE RECORDS REVEAL?

Lore is more detailed than records, and the exact identity of the Dark Lady remains in the shadows. The favorite contenders are Trevor Hall's original housekeeper, Imogene Rockwell, who is known to have died there (though sources disagree as to how), and a nameless visiting parlormaid, who allegedly lost her balance during a servants' party on the rooftop.

Another possibility is a young teacher from the Bradley Finishing School. Overwhelmed in her first position and pining for home, the instructor started a fire in the boys' wing of the house, tales say, then committed suicide in her room in the opposite wing while everyone else was distracted. Thus, she expressed her hatred of Trevor Hall and her own sorrow in one stroke. A 1929 fire did temporarily force pupils and teachers out of the Hall for several days—days when the arsonist's body would have been left undiscovered. Could her soul be bound to the house as punishment for her dual transgressions?

Historian Reid Bennet scoffs at this account. "No evidence whatsoever exists that a teacher ever died while in the Bradleys' employ, let alone that one committed suicide." Bennet dismisses the suggestion that the death was hushed up to protect the school's reputation—and enrollment. "It's most likely the story was made up *post hoc* to provide a logical framework for the supposed haunting: the fiery outbreaks, the female figure, et cetera. It's remarkable how flexible this ghost is. She seems to embody all the aspects of tragic womanhood: jilted lover, jealous lover, romantic rival, lonely girl. People imagine her to be just about anything they want her to be.

Bennet acknowledges ghosts are exciting, offering hints of something beyond this mundane world, but he suggests they also play a more pragmatic role.

"Ghosts are embedded in the collective psyche. Therefore, it becomes convenient, when one falls on hard times, to blame one's troubles on a ghost. Everyone can sympathize with a plague of spooks. I'm not surprised that sightings of the so-called 'Dark Lady' peaked during the Depression just as the Bradley School began sliding toward insolvency. Likewise, when Preis-Herald began to lose control of his experiment, he and his team blamed the ghost. She makes a useful scapegoat, whoever she may be."

Trevor Hall is still on the market and has been, in the language of Victorian ghost stories, "untenanted" for over a year. Christine Belancourt and her family still occupy Herbert Terrace and enjoy their newfound peace and quiet. Piers Preis-Herald is still on the faculty at Yale, though his research team has long since scattered to follow their own pursuits. Smithy currently resides at the Center for the Scientific Advancement of Man in California.

As for the Dark Lady, nobody has reported seeing her since the chimp's departure, but who knows when—or where—she may pop up next.

LETTER FROM RUBY DALTON
TO TAMMY COHEN

October 9, 1976

. . . *Man paced around and around his desk and punched the corner every time he lapped it. At last, he paused to pound the surface with both fists. "Do you think I'm stupid? Is this why your boss sent you?" He snatched up a newspaper that had been spread over the desk and waved it in my face. I recoiled, half-thinking he was going to smack me across the face with the periodical. Jeff must have had the same thought because he quickly maneuvered me behind him.*

Man's body stiffened suddenly, like he'd been thunderstruck. "You knew about this all along! Goddamn you! I let you and your damned Trojan ape into this facility! I'm going to skin that Limey shit and wear his tanned hide to my next press interview! You must all think I'm a f***ing moron!"

Jeff and I stared at each other, then Jeff spoke up. "Excuse me, sir, but we have no idea what you're talking about. What are we supposed to know?"

Man slapped the newspaper on the desk and jerked Jeff forward by the shoulder; he practically bent him over the desk to make him read it. "Take a look at that, Mr. Know-Nothing!" I crept forward and stood beside my husband so I could see it, too. You know what it said.

"Did you all escape from the booby hatch?" Man ripped the paper from Jeff's hands before we finished reading it. Then he rolled it into a club and brandished it in both our faces. I was sure the newsprint was going to tattoo my nose and I cringed behind Jeff.

"What kind of freaks did Piers send me? Damaged goods and a couple of lunatic kids! Do you believe in the Easter Bunny, too?" He smacked the paper against his flat palm, loud enough to make me jump. "Where did this shit come from?" Smack! "Which one of you started it?" Smack!

We both insisted, truthfully, that neither of us had ever seen anything ghostly.

"And your chimp? What did he 'tell' you he saw?"

"Nothing." Jeff bit his lip and started over. "He, ah, never told us straight out that he saw anything unusual. And we've never even taught him the concept of 'ghost.' Only sometimes he would . . . do odd things or . . . or make signs that, uh, didn't fit the context—and we would joke that he was talking to the ghost."

Man heard what Jeff was trying not to say between the pauses. "You mean this magic WonderChimp is insane? This great communicator you've been praising to the skies _babbled_? And you rationalized it by turning to some spook shit? _And_ you've been trying for months to sell me on starting a chimp language program! Try snake oil next time!"

Jeff protested, "_Some_ people in the house believed in ghosts—"

"But not _you_, of course. _You're_ too rational." Man sneered.

Jeff maintained a straight face. "I'm agnostic. I saw things I couldn't explain but I didn't jump to conclusions."

"And you, missy? Quit hiding behind Romeo! What's your excuse? Have you seen any ghosts since you got here?"

"No, sir," I replied. "I'm shocked by that article. It's clearly yellow journalism intended to capitalize on Halloween."

"She made it all up, then? Your ape never cried about going to bed? Never complained about any dark woman?" Our silence dragged too long. Man cursed and hurled the paper across the room, where it cracked against the wall and disintegrated into a pile of loose leaves.

"You're trying to ruin me! You don't think I have enough trouble without this fairy-tale crap? Managing a major facility doesn't fill enough of my time? You think I'm not satisfied reading research papers and data sheets and writing grant proposals and trying to think up ways to keep you ingrates gainfully employed? You think I want to turn tables, too? You think I want every New Age nutcase in the nation crawling here to worship the magic monkey when I'm engaged in scientific inquiry?" Jeff and I huddled together, shoulder-to-shoulder, and kept our mouths shut against what were obviously rhetorical questions.

Man threw open the door; the knob slamming into the wall sounded like the crack of doom. "Get the hell out!"

Jeff flinched.

"You mean, permanently?" I squeaked.

"One more word out of either of you, and you go into the f***ing street! Just get the f*** out of my office!" His voice careened off the walls and ricocheted down the hallway. Jeff grabbed my hand and hauled me away. I looked down at my blurring sneakers so I wouldn't have to see the staring, gaping faces of my colleagues, peeking out of their own labs to see what transgression we'd committed.

"Why now?" Jeff lamented. "Why, when we're building a new life for ourselves, and Smithy is finally settling into place, does all this bull-shit come back to haunt us? Literally! It's like that bitch followed us here."

I told him not to say that. I felt like he was tempting fate. Even though we're thousands of miles from Trevor Hall, I still look over my shoulder whenever something odd happens and wonder if it was a coincidence. A couple of things have recently happened with Smithy that knotted my stomach. If we were still in Newport . . .

But we're not. And I don't want any of that talk starting again.

"And where does Reid get off denouncing the ghost?" Jeff continued. "He's the one who told us that story in the first place. Now he's acting like it was our idea?"

Some people will say anything to get their name into a newspaper, I suppose. But calling him a "historian" does give his version an air of credibility.

Jeff wanted to take me home so we could both stay out of Man's sight, but I wanted to go back to my lab. I didn't want to give Man the least reason to fire me, and walking out of a session would definitely qualify. Jeff was perturbed—mostly because he was afraid he wouldn't be around to protect me if Man came around wanting trouble—but I assured him I could call on Brad if necessary. "Dr. T and Isaac won't let him beat me, either," I reassured. So, he left—but to get drunk, not to go home and sleep, and I went back to my apes wearing an early Halloween mask: a rigid smile.

Mallory rapped on the door a short time later and asked if I was OK. I kept my grin in place—though my voice was shaking—and assured her there had just been a misunderstanding. I thanked her for her con-cern. I was less thankful when Marianne barged into the lab shortly afterward without warning. Woolly almost slipped past her into the hall-way, but I tackled him. I'm afraid I applied too much force squeezing his arms together to compensate for not being able to put my hands around Marianne's neck.

"Oh, my goodness, Ruby, what awful racket! You poor thing! What happened? You're all shaken up. Here; let's sit down a minute. Tell me how I can help you. I've been around a long time; I've got some pull with Man. Maybe I can fix things up between you, if you'll tell me what happened."

I told her (again and again) that everything was fine, there was no trouble, I didn't need any help. I continued my work as if Marianne weren't even in the room. I refused to look at her, much less acknowledge her questions. Finally, she left, perturbed.

Brad came in next. If I were going to confide in anybody, it would be him. But I didn't want him to know about all the mess in our past. I didn't want him wondering about Smithy's sanity, too. Mainly, I was ashamed: of the public nature of the blow-out with Man, the accusa-tions, the ridiculousness of scientists discussing ghosts in the first place. My adrenaline was wearing off and exhaustion setting in. Brad saw this and kindly reminded me he had an open door, then left.

By the end of the day, Marianne was broadcasting the substance of Man's latest long-distance call to Piers. "He said, 'I bet you've been rubbing your hands and gloating about how you put one over on Man Teague, promising me I was getting a deal! Well, I'm onto you! Don't think you can pass me your failures like some damn chain letter! I'll tell everyone about you and your madhouse of assistants! The academic community will find out what happens when you trust Preis-Herald, and you'll end up swimming in the same bullshit you tried to shovel onto me!'"

She embellished new threats into each telling, glancing at me every time. Did she expect me to defend Piers? Was I supposed to explain what the fight was about? I left her to it. The girl is a born storyteller.

Brad's decided Man is mad at Piers and taking it out on Jeff and me by association. He's mostly worried about Smithy landing in his cross-hairs next. And so am I.

I didn't see Man again for the rest of the day, and nobody served me with a pink slip. I plan to return tomorrow as if I still have a job. If Man wants to put me on the street, he can, but God forbid he evict Smithy! At this point, I imagine the next stop for him would be a roadside zoo.

Send us good thoughts—and please send us anything more you hear about this "Dark Lady" drivel. The more we know about what's being said, the better we can prepare. I hope!

Your comrade in arms,

Ruby

DIARY OF RUBY DALTON

The word is out. Everyone in the lab talks like they've read the article. Did Marianne mimeograph copies and pass them out as an early Halloween treat?

Brad knows everything now. He kept grinning at me while we waited for our morning coffee to brew. At last, he said, "I finally understand why Smithy doesn't like the color black." I didn't want to encourage him so I only grunted, but to Brad it must have sounded like, 'Go on.'

"Why didn't you tell me Smithy's in touch with the other side? That's totally boss! We should do something with that in the lab. Make him guess those cards with all the shapes on 'em."

I told him it wasn't "boss" at all, that it was scary not knowing what was going on around us. Smithy couldn't clearly explain what he was experiencing; we couldn't be sure we could trust what he appeared to be telling us. I pleaded with Brad not to discuss Smithy's "powers," both to avoid Man's wrath and to spare Jeff the aggravation.

Except <u>Jeff</u> was the one who gave Brad the scoop. He even told him what Eric saw and all about Smithy's "dark woman" signs. Brad was cool with it, according to Jeff. He says Brad whistled a lot and acted <u>proud</u> of Smithy.

Personally, I don't see what good dredging up the old craziness will do. "I wanted him on our side," Jeff explained when I asked what he'd been thinking. "Brad won't talk. He knows those stories could hurt Smithy. Plus, he's been a big help to us. I thought he should know everything, since he's on Smithy's support team."

Actually, Dr. Torrance has been the MVP on Smithy's team. He confronted Man in a private meeting (no easy feat) and <u>told</u> him it was imperative Smithy remain at CSAM. He insisted that Smithy's *familiarity with tokens provides a vital model for the other chimps and advances the study in a crucial way. "Whatever he may have done in the past, he's serving science now. Whether or not he saw ghosts in that house, in this study, he's an ideal subject. Cutting him loose would be an insurmountable setback."*

Or so goes Marianne's account of the meeting.

I could hang a medal on Dr. T for that! I don't know how Man disciplined him for daring to oppose him, but Ed decided it was worthwhile.

Amazingly, Dr. T still has his job and Smithy still has his place at CSAM. Jeff and I have been put "on probation" (i.e., our work hours have been cut). Man has decided we're "a contagion" and might spread madness and fantasy throughout his advanced research lab. He's sworn to watch us more carefully before he decides if we can be trusted to work full time again. At the first sign of instability or "treachery," we'll be "lining up outside the charity ward." I don't know why he thinks Piers is out to get him or why we would be spying for him.

This is probably the best outcome we could hope to get. Yes, we'll have to eat ramen noodles for a few weeks to make up for our tinier paychecks. I may even need to pick up a part-time job to cover the gap until Jeff manages to get a teaching gig. I keep telling him it's not too early to apply for spring semester. On the bright side, we'll finally have more time to spend together.

RADIO SHOW
WHISPERS IN THE DARK

Broadcast Date: October 13, 1976

Celia: So, get this—an East Coast newspaper is claiming that one of CSAM's chimpanzees, Smithy, who knows sign language, can use that language to talk to ghosts! Supposedly, he talked to ghosts when he lived in Rhode Island, and it freaked out his trainers. Isn't that incredible?

And totally unfair!

I mean, who is a chimp going to talk to in the Great Beyond? Marilyn Monroe? Jim Morrison?

Celia laughs

That kind of power should go to someone who knows how to use it properly. So, tell me: If you could talk to someone dead, who would it be? Line 1, you're on . . . .

LETTER FROM TAMMY COHEN
TO RUBY DALTON

October 14, 1976

Dear Ruby,

I'm truly sorry for all the crap you and Jeff have had to take. Maybe Man will get so worked up one day that he'll die of apoplexy, and you can be free.

October only has a couple more weeks to go. Once Halloween is over, ghostly fancy will turn to thoughts of Christmas shopping, and this nonsense will blow over. Besides, I imagine Man will be more draconian than Piers ever was at stamping down any ghost talk, should any of your coworkers bring it up again. The important thing is, he's keeping Smithy. As long as he remains a bad influence at the gambling table, you all should be fine!

Meanwhile, Eric is mortified. I met with him in Boston over the weekend and we dissected the article. He interacted with the locals more than the rest of us since he did the bulk of our shopping. He admits that Shaun and the guys regularly teased him about living in a haunted house and quizzed him about spooky happenings. Eric admitted he told them about seeing the ghost.

Moreover, he remembers the day we visited Reid for the history lesson about the house. While you and I looked through Reid's photo collection, Eric and Jeff watched TV with Fred. Eric says Fred kept pressing him about whether he'd heard or seen anything strange in the house. At that time, nothing extravagant had happened, but Eric casually mentioned the fires and the way Smithy could defy any lock. He didn't realize Fred would attribute those quirks to the ghost.

Oh, and Trish <u>always</u> waited on him when he ate in the diner and <u>always</u> made small talk. She told Eric she wanted to be a journalist and *was only waitressing until she could finish school. Just for kicks, I went to the library and flipped through some old issues of The Newport Daily News. "Patricia Hartigan" never had a byline before. Want to bet this was her big break?*

Eric is contrite about the whole thing, but I don't blame him. He's a sociable guy, and he always was a sucker for a pretty face. I know he never meant any harm.

This was a purely manipulative piece. It's not even good journalism. Most of it is drawn from hearsay, folklore, and betrayed confidences twisted into a more convenient shape. If you ask me, that crowd was planning something like this all along. Maybe not an exposé, but a book or some such? They all knew each other from way back when. Trish and Fred used to go together, and then she started dating Shaun. This article looks more like evidence of collusion than of a haunting.

I'm tempted to write a letter to the editor to let him know what kind of "reporter" he has working for him. I already wrote Reid a "What the hell?" letter but have yet to send it. Judging by Trish's article, he's graduated already, so I doubt the address he left me is any good. Maybe if I wait a bit, I'll feel less angry and can follow my own advice to watch this mess blow over.

Here's hoping the Dark Lady of Trevor Hall dies another quick and more permanent death soon!

Love and support,
Tammy

LETTERS TO THE EDITOR
OF *THE NEWPORT DAILY NEWS*

October 17, 1976

As a former student of the Bradley Finishing School for Young Ladies, I have a story about the Dark Lady. Back then, I was Alice Snow (Class of 1927). I shared a large room with an adjoining bath[3] with a young lady called Claire Stanley.

One afternoon, I returned to our room, bursting with gossip to share. I called out to Claire and heard her call back to me from the other side of the closed bathroom door. I sat on the edge of my bed and proceeded to tell her about my day, shouting to be heard through the door. Though she didn't respond, I could hear the sound of splashing water as if she were in her bath.

Suddenly, the door to our room opened and Claire stepped in, looking puzzled. She asked why I was shouting and to whom. I leapt up and flung the bathroom door open. The bathtub was empty and dry. Who had called out to me?

Claire and I decided I must have been imagining things. As the years passed, however, and I heard ghostly tales filtered through alumnae, I began to wonder if I had experienced a brush with "the Other Side."

To this day, I still wonder who was in my room.
Alice Vernon
Jamestown, RI

*

3 According to the rooming assignments from the 1926-1927 school year, Alice Vernon's room was on the same corridor where Eric Kaninchen claimed to have seen the ghost.

Your article about the ghost of Trevor Hall brought back so many memories of my own tenure there as a student from 1936-1938. One incident has haunted me for years.

I played violin in the school orchestra and would often stay late in the music room to practice. One night, I returned to find my room in shambles: clothes and papers were tossed all over the floor, though nothing was missing. I was in my first year then and assumed I had been "hazed," so like a good sport, I cleaned up the mess and said nothing. However, the same thing happened the next week, and again a few nights later.

By this point, my good humor was fading. In an attempt to catch the intruder, I sprinkled sooty powder all over the dark floor, hoping the vandals would step in it and leave a trail I could follow back to their rooms. When I crept back to my room later that night, I saw the bed sheets piled on the floor and schoolbooks flung into the corners. I examined the ground but found no footprints. The powder was undisturbed, as if whatever had mussed my room had never touched the floor.

I spent the rest of that night on the floor of the practice room, not getting much sleep. I didn't experience any more vandalism after that, but I always suspected the Dark Lady had had her fun with me.

Raymond Bergeron
Seymour, CT

*

You should be ashamed to print such trash! The Bradleys were splendid people, and their school was an asset to the community. Their reputation ought not to be slandered by this ghost tripe.

Eugene Edgerton
Newport, RI

DIARY OF RUBY DALTON

November 20, 1976

It's been two hours since I hung up the phone, and I can't stop crying. Part of me hopes Tammy will call back to say it was all an awful mistake. The other part of me throbs like an enormous bruise I know will never fade.

I was home by myself when the phone rang. When I picked up, I heard Tammy sniffling on the other end, so I knew it was going to be bad news. I just never imagined this.

Eric is dead. That's what she said after telling me I should sit down. I leaned against the wall, and I was glad for that support.

Tammy had called him earlier today, to wish him happy birthday for next week and to say hello because they hadn't talked in a while. A woman answered. "At first I thought she was a girlfriend," Tammy said, "and I didn't want to give the wrong impression, so I introduced myself as an old coworker of Eric's from Rhode Island and asked if he was around. The woman didn't say anything for a moment or two. Then she asked if I was Ruby or Tammy. She said Eric always talked about living in the big house with us and the chimp. She told me she was Eric's mother. Then she said she had bad news."

Tammy expected her to say Eric was sick or in the hospital recovering from an accident. He was in an accident all right, but he never made it to a hospital. A goddamned drunk driver slammed head-on into Eric's car when he was driving home from school last night. Eric died on impact. The goddamned drunk only got whiplash.

Poor Eric! Why him? He was minding his own business. He had no control over what happened to him. No chance.

Tammy said his mother had gone to his apartment to collect his things and that's why she answered his phone. "She asked me to spread

*the word to his other friends from the project, and I promised I would.
She thanked us for being such good friends to him and said he was happy
during those days in Newport. I didn't know what to say. I never know
what to say to the bereaved. He was her only child, Ruby! That poor
woman!"*

*I don't know what I would have said, either. I've been thinking it
over, thinking I should send a letter or flowers. Or both. There aren't
enough words to explain how friendly and kind Eric was and how much
a part of our family he was.*

*I can't stop thinking about him. I've tried going on with my normal
business: balancing the checkbook, washing the dishes, starting supper.
But nothing distracts me. I keep remembering conversations with Eric,
memorable things he said, or silly ways he had of doing something. It's
like I'm watching a movie loop of Eric's life in my head. So, I'm writing
about it in my journal instead.*

What am I going to say to Jeff? How am I going to break it to him?

LETTER FROM RUBY DALTON
TO TAMMY COHEN

Thank you for your moving description of Eric's service. I cried several times reading your letter, first when I read it to myself and then when I read it to Jeff. We both wanted dearly to come and pay our respects in person.

    It's hard to believe Christmas is just a few short weeks away. I don't feel like celebrating at all. The peppy carols on the radio and the smiling faces on the streets seem to be taunting me. "Smile, Ruby! Get happy, Ruby! 'Tis the season for good cheer, whether you feel it or not." How horrible to be unable to feel pleasure at the one time of year when happiness is practically mandatory. Everywhere I turn, I see reminders of joy to the world. But not to me.

    Not to Eric's family, either.

    I wish I could have been in Medford for Eric. For his mother. I wish I could see you again.

    We'd planned to visit my family for Christmas this year, but with Man still on the warpath, I doubt we can get the time off.

    In other news, we welcomed another scapegoat to CSAM today. Margo Kane looks tougher than her predecessors, with her ripped jeans and shirts and her military-short, dyed brick-red hair. I was afraid to talk to her at first, but she doesn't have an attitude; she just seems really sure of herself. Maybe that confidence will shield her from Man's barbs.

    With my thoughts constantly on Eric, I've remembered something he once said about how the servants at Trevor Hall were disposable. There were always more waiting in the wings to replace them.

    That's how I feel about personnel at CSAM. We come and go so rapidly, we're nothing but shadows. In a few months, I won't remember the names or faces of anyone I worked with, not even someone as striking as Margo. Man never worries about the high turnover because he can always find another fool to work for him. No one is irreplaceable. Any of us can disappear in an instant.

How true that is of life, too.

Please call me when you can. I'd love to chat.

Be well. Be safe.

Ruby

xoxo

CLOSED-CIRCUIT FOOTAGE

Date: December 9, 1976
Location: Corridor D, Research Animal Quarters

The door opens and the overhead lights turn on. Jeff enters, carrying a bowl of fruit. Behind him, Brad shuffles in, hands in his pockets.

"You know," Brad warns, "if Man catches us, we'll both get fired."

Smithy, who was curled up in his cage, hears Brad's voice and crawls toward the door. He hoots in excitement when he recognizes Brad and Jeff, and stretches his hand through the bars.

"Hey buddy!" Brad calls out cheerily.

Jeff hesitates. "Ah, do you mind if I have a few minutes alone with him?"

Brad shakes his head. "I'll stand guard." He retreats into the hall and shuts the door.

Jeff huffs and runs his hand through his hair. Then, he approaches the cage.

"Hey, Smithy! It's good to see you again, pal." He hesitates again, shuffles from foot to foot, and scratches the back of his neck with his free hand. "So, I wanted to ask . . . I know you sometimes see things and know things other people don't. I'm wondering . . . have you seen or heard anything lately . . . from Eric?"

The chimp reaches through the bars for the fruit bowl.

Jeff takes a shaky breath. "Smithy, I need you to tell me: Have you seen Eric?" He signs Eric's name. "I figured if he was still around, he'd come and see you. At least to say goodbye."

Smithy tilts his head and looks back at Jeff, hooting softly.

"Please, tell me, Smithy, have you seen Eric? *Eric*. Come on, it's a yes or no question."

Smithy scratches himself and sits back, apparently losing interest.

"Look, we don't have much time. I know I haven't visited in a while. I want to, but I can't. Don't hold it against me. Please, just tell me. Or if you can't tell me, or you don't want to tell me straight out, show me. If you've seen Eric, eat a banana." He holds up the bowl. "If you have not seen Eric, please eat the apple slices." As he speaks, Jeff signs, "Eric banana; no Eric apple."

"I need to know if he's still around. If he's talked to you, then maybe you can tell him some things."

Smithy watches Jeff for a moment, scratches his nose, then lunges forward and grabs the bowl through the bars. He tips all the fruit into his mouth, stuffing it in until his cheeks bulge. Then, he hands Jeff the empty bowl.

Jeff sighs and his shoulders slump.

"Well, it was worth a try. It is good to see you again. It always is. And I will see you again, I promise. Soon." Jeff signs, "Goodbye," half-heartedly waves, then turns and walks toward the exit.

Smithy lunges forward and spits at him. A piece of banana shoots across the floor, right in front of Jeff. He pauses, stares at it for a few seconds, then slowly turns and looks back at Smithy. The ape leans against the cage door, chewing, watching Jeff.

"You did that on purpose, didn't you?" His voice grows excited, but Smithy doesn't react. "OK, OK..." Jeff looks around the room. A faint smile plays across his face. Then, he picks up the banana and exits.

Smithy watches the door shut, then turns his head and looks to the opposite corner of the room. The overhead lights flicker. The macaques squeal.

DIARY OF RUBY DALTON

January 5, 1977

I need to document what happened at work today. I can't tell Jeff, and I'm not sure about telling Tammy, either. It may be nothing, and I'll feel stupid bothering her with it. I feel like I'm starting to go crazy. Little things suddenly seem portentous. I'd love to write them off as neuroticism. I'd love that more than the alternative.

We ran our eighth gambling trial today. Since the chimps save money so poorly, we allocated tokens in random quantities to the different participants instead of making them earn tokens and then decide how to spend them. We've worked out tables that show how much each chimp is supposed to get each day. I chose a table at random, made up the pay piles, and carried the tokens to the lab . . .

CLOSED-CIRCUIT FOOTAGE

Date: January 5, 1977
Location: Lab A

Taniesha stands behind a large roulette table in
the center of the room, trying to calm six chimps
standing around it. Bashful, Eleanor, Woolly,
Violetta, and Moses are restless, looking around,
hooting, and waving empty drawstring pouches.
Smithy sits apart and stares fixedly at the south
wall of the room; he rocks back and forth in a
seated position. The other chimps ignore him. The
lab door opens, and Ruby enters, carrying a tray
of tokens in small piles.

Taniesha says, "All right, gang, she's here.
Hold still, and we'll get you set up. Who's feeling
lucky today?" Ruby crosses the room to the table.
When she is about four feet from the chimps, she
cries out. The tray flies up and flips over. Ruby
clutches at it, fruitlessly; tokens spray around
the room. Taniesha says, "Aw, shit!"

The chimps hoot loudly and scatter, descending
on the fallen tokens in a free-for-all. Ruby
says slowly, "I'm sorry. I don't know what
happened . . . "

Taniesha turns to Smithy, who is watching the
melee, and signs, "Stay, don't touch."

Smithy continues to rock in place. Bashful
scoops up the tokens nearest him and shoves them
into his pouch. Eleanor launches herself to the
center of the floor and clutches tokens in each of
her hands and feet.

Taniesha says, "No. No! Don't touch. Leave those
be!" She wades among the chimps and struggles to

restrain them from gathering the tokens. Violetta backs away from the crowd. Taniesha says, "Guys! Hey, back up, time out!"

Woolly and Moses reach for the same token and play tug-of-war. Woolly threatens to bite Moses, who releases the token. Woolly then offers the token to Violetta.

Taniesha says, "Well, that's one way to distribute tokens!"

Eleanor screams and all the chimps look up. Eleanor is staring at the south wall. Taniesha and Ruby stare at the wall, then at each other, then at the chimps. Bashful drops his pouch and backs away to the north wall.

Smithy rises and enters the circle of chimps for the first time. Violetta throws the token Woolly awarded her at Smithy's feet and runs to the far wall with Bashful. Eleanor releases all but one handful of tokens, which she hides behind her back, and edges away. Smithy begins scooping tokens into his bag; he also retrieves Bashful's pouch. Ruby stares at him, her face frozen.

Taniesha approaches the south wall, brow creased, hand extended. Ruby turns, sees her, and says, "Taniesha, don't!"

Taniesha says, "There's nothing here. What the heck are they staring at?"

The chimps are quiet now, except for Moses, who growls and postures while watching Smithy gather tokens unopposed. He doesn't approach Smithy or challenge him for tokens, however.

Taniesha asks, "What's up with you? Smithy, stop that!"

He pauses and looks up at her.

Taniesha says, "Leave those be!"

Smithy rises on his hind legs, nostrils flared, and steps toward Taniesha.

He signs, "Black woman."

Taniesha stands taller. Without breaking eye contact, she says, "I have a name," and signs "Taniesha," then, "You, go, please."

Smithy tilts his head, then glances at the chimps, then back at her. He sets his pouch down and retreats to the roulette table, not to the north wall. As he passes Moses, the other chimp scurries to join his fellows against the wall.

Taniesha exhales, looks at Ruby, and asks, "What the hell just happened? Why'd they give up like that?"

Ruby says, "I don't know."

Taniesha says, "One minute, they act like they're at a sale at Filene's, then they all back off by themselves."

Ruby says sharply, "They backed off because you told them to."

Taniesha stares at her.

Ruby shakes her head and says, "Sorry. Let's get these picked up and parceled out the right way before Man comes in here and gives us hell."

Taniesha asks, "You still want to run the trial after this?"

Ruby says, "Why not? It's what we're supposed to do. We give them the tokens, they bet. They're addicted now, just like we wanted."

She and Taniesha scoop up tokens and pouches and put them haphazardly on the tray. Ruby rises with a full tray. Taniesha directs the chimps to stand around the roulette table.

Taniesha says, "Everybody back in place! Let's try this again."

DIARY OF RUBY DALTON

(CONTINUED)

January 5, 1977

. . . *We got the data we needed, in spite of my mishap. Although it was my idea to forge ahead, I felt too shaky to concentrate. When the run was over, I charged out of the lab and was almost sick in the restroom. I made up a lame excuse for Taniesha's sake about sleeping poorly.*

Maybe I am sick. When I walked into that room, I had a firm grip on the tray. I was expecting the apes to charge me and try to grab the tokens off the platter. I never dropped it. <u>I felt something knock the tray out of my hands!</u> I felt an impact, like a little explosion underneath—or an invisible hand punching up. It startled me so badly I didn't try to stop the rush afterward.

It's not as if one of our chimps sneaked up on me and batted the tray away. All the apes were clustered around Taniesha at the roulette table. I could write it off as my imagination or a weird draft in the lab, but the apes were behaving strangely, too: staring at a blank spot on the wall, abandoning the tokens so Smithy could just walk up and collect whatever he wanted. It was as if they saw something we didn't or heard instructions we didn't.

I didn't see anything come near the tray, but I <u>felt</u> it! Now I don't know what to do. For weeks, I've felt something was off at CSAM. First, I blamed it on my body adjusting to a new schedule change. I wish I had time to see a doctor to confirm or deny that.

Even if I did, what if I get a clean bill of health? We're not at Trevor Hall anymore. So, I would have to be nuts.

I don't think I can go through the other kind of craziness again.

UNEDITED INTERVIEW
WITH ISAAC MORGAN
CIRCA 1991

One day, Marianne came to me and asked, "Why are you letting Smithy cheat?" I didn't know what she meant. So, she showed me.

Smithy was winning every round he bet. Every spin, every day. I mean, it wasn't a huge deal because we weren't measuring gambling skill, y'know, but it was *weird*.

We called a technician from the college to see if the wheel was rigged somehow. It was crazy, but all I could think was Ruby, or even Jeff, was somehow fixing the games to make Smithy look better. Well, the tech guy didn't find anything. I had him sit in on my session to see if he could spot Smithy cheating. Of course, he didn't. It was like the chimp was charmed, y'know?

Now, if he'd been a smart gambler, he would've bet red every time. I mean, whatever he picked came up, so why not bet big? All the other chimps, they went red because they understood it was worth more. But Smithy would switch back and forth from red to black. If he'd been human, I would've said he was testing the wheel.

We never found any proof that anybody was behind it, but there's no way he was winning by chance.

Soon Eleanor caught on and started copying Smithy whenever he bet before her. So, we had to get creative to salvage the experiment.

NOTES BY TANIESHA JONES
February 3, 1977

The chimps have effectively transitioned from roulette to a modified form of blackjack. Instead of daring them to reach 21, we draw a series of four cards and ask whether the next draw will be red or black. Red is still double-or-nothing, and a bet on black still results in a consistent but small win.

To further enhance security, I tested each chimp in a one-on-one session so no participant's bet would be influenced by another's. The chimps understood the rules and continued to favor red over black, regardless of whether they were "on a streak."**

**With one exception: In a run of twelve bets, Smithy chose red five times and black seven times. His bet paid off all twelve times.

DIARY OF RUBY DALTON

February 5, 1977

I'm an idiot. My cheeks are still stinging. I don't know whether or what I'll tell Jeff. Is this something we can laugh about?

I went to see a psychic.

The idea popped into my head while I was out shopping. I see signs advertising fortune tellers and psychics all the time, but I never bothered about them before. I think that sort of thing is silly. But today I wondered if maybe one of them could help. Maybe it's not all games and chicanery. Maybe some of them actually do have a smidgen of power. If so, maybe one of them could help me with our problem at the lab.

I'd tried to dismiss the urge, but it was too strong. By the time I made my last purchase, I'd decided to give it a try. I went two blocks past the drugstore, made a left past Madam Yvonne's shop with its beaded curtains and crystals hanging in the window (too over the top), walked past the Friends of the Future Co-Op with the signs of the Zodiac engraved around the window (because that just sounds hokey), and finally, I stopped at "Jean Arless, Psychic" because her shop was a simple storefront with a tastefully painted black-and-gold sign, and a plain, solid wood door, like a CPA or a private investigator.

I didn't have an appointment and wasn't sure if I'd get in, but the young girl at the front desk—about my age, probably a college student—wearing pigtails and an outmoded pink dress with a Peter Pan collar instead of star-spangled robes, assured me I could see Miss Jeannie in an hour because she'd had an unexpected cancellation. I wondered how unexpected it could be if she were psychic. Still, I headed to Coney Island for a very light lunch, considering Miss Jeannie's fee and how much money I had in my wallet. I could ill-afford to spend on entertainment like this. But what if it works? I thought. I __hoped__. What if she really can help?

Before long, I was seated across a table from Miss Jeannie. She looked like an ordinary middle-aged woman with her sensible button-up blouse, slacks, granny glasses, and short curly hair. She sort of looked like the lady who played the Mother Superior in "The Flying Nun." She smiled and greeted me by name, took my hands, and squeezed them. Her own hands were warm and dry, comfortable. "You are most welcome here, and you mustn't be concerned. I'm here to help you. Please don't think you're the only one with questions. Many young people are worried about the future right now, especially about money."

Ah, I thought, she's observant. She had noticed how worn the knees on my jeans were, how the cuffs of my sleeves were frayed, and how I didn't wear jewelry besides my wedding ring.

"Please, tell me what I can do to help you." Miss Jeannie kept smiling, looking into my eyes. Again, I wondered, If she's a psychic, shouldn't she know why I'm here? But maybe the power doesn't work that way. How should I know?

I didn't want to blurt out that I was being haunted. I was curious to see how much she could intuit. I wanted to see how much I could get for my $25 payment without having to give away information. So, I was discreet.

I told Miss Jeannie I was having trouble with another woman who had followed me and my husband from where we used to live on the East Coast, who had caused us some trouble there before, and who I now believed was hanging around our workplace, waiting to cause trouble again. "I haven't seen her myself, but little things make me think she's around. I think a friend of mine knows something about her, but he isn't telling. He might be afraid to. I'm not sure. It isn't the kind of thing I can go to the police about. I was hoping you could give me some advice about how to make her go away for good."

"Ahhh . . . " Miss Jeannie sat back, still holding my hands. Her eyes closed. She hummed in the back of her mouth. I couldn't identify the tune. Maybe it was her version of white noise, clearing her mind so she could feel the vibrations and whatnot. "Yes . . . yes, I see a tall, dark woman . . . "

I flinched at that. I shouldn't have; it's a common enough description. Still, those last words got me: _Dark Woman_. Did Miss Jeannie really sense what was troubling me?

"Oh!" She sounded surprised, then understanding. "Ahhh." She opened her eyes and pressed one of my hands between both of hers. "Honey, you mustn't be concerned." I wondered if that was her mantra. "This interloper will not trouble you, as long as you tell your husband each day how much you love him. Deep down, he knows you care, but he needs to hear it. And when he does, there will be no more reason for this woman to come around."

She said more, but I tuned her out. Did she imagine my troublesome woman was a romantic rival? Hers was probably good advice for most people, but it didn't tell me a thing about Smithy. I smiled and mumbled some kind of thanks and declined to make a second appointment, pleading that I needed to check my ever-changing work schedule. Then, I scuttled home, smarting at having spent so much just to learn I didn't need to worry about my husband cheating on me.

I tried to draw comfort from the fact that Miss Jeannie hadn't said anything about an evil spirit lurking nearby. Wouldn't a psychic have sensed the presence of negative supernatural energy? But she obviously isn't psychic, just a woman full of platitudes with keener observation skills than most, attuned to the typical concerns of young people today. What if I had said outright that I thought we were being haunted? Would she have an answer for me, even something patently false? Or sold me a potion or a magic crystal for an extra $25? Would that have done some good?

If Jeff asks me where the money went, I'll lie. I'll tell him the price of groceries suddenly skyrocketed, or that I overpaid and didn't check if the cashier gave me the right change. I'd rather him think me negligent or unlucky than ridiculous.

CLOSED-CIRCUIT FOOTAGE

Date: February 7, 1977
Location: Lunchroom

Jeff sits at the Formica table sipping a soda and reviewing papers.

Isaac enters behind him, pulls up a chair, and says, "Jeff, man! How's it hanging?"

Jeff says, "Fine, I guess."

Isaac asks, "You having any luck finding a teaching position?"

Jeff says, "No. I've put that off for now. Maybe next year."

Isaac says, "Oh? The market's that bad?"

Jeff says, "I don't know. I've just decided to stay on longer at CSAM."

Isaac snorts and says sarcastically, "You like it here that much?"

Jeff says, "I like keeping an eye on things."

Isaac says, "Well, that's good. Hey, maybe you can help us figure out Smithy. He's a real sneaky number."

Jeff sips his drink, leans forward, and says, "How do you mean?"

Isaac says, "OK, in this session last week? We're getting all the chimps to play roulette. It's like roulette, anyway. All the chimps stand around the wheel—it's like a little casino, y'know? Kinda cute. I wear a visor like a pit boss. And the chimps keep all their tokens in a little drawstring pouch. We found if they held them loose, they'd fight over each other's tokens. Smithy likes doing this mind-control bit where he just stares at the others and makes them give up their tokens."

Jeff motions his finger in a circle for Isaac to get to the point.

Isaac speaks faster and says, "Well, he's figured a way around that now! Somehow, he's getting the tokens out of the sealed pouches! See, everyone was standing around the roulette wheel, and when it came time to bet, the chimps opened their pouches. Moses and Woolly got angry. Moses shook his pouch upside down and kept peeking in it like the chips would reappear, but Woolly threw his empty pouch on the ground and jumped on it and started crying. He should have had six singles and Moses should have had a five-piece and five singles from the last round. So, I had to stop the game and check to see where they went. I looked on the ground first and then I had this feeling, y'know? I started opening the other players' pouches, and sure enough, I found all the tokens in Smithy's bag. It was the damnedest thing! He was standing on the opposite side of the table from the other two. I don't know how he did it. Maybe he bumped them when they were gathering around the table. He's a regular pickpocket. You ever notice that?"

Jeff says, "Hhhmmm . . .Sometimes when we were cooking, stuff would . . . move around. And nobody besides Smithy was in the room."

Isaac says, "Well, we should call him the Amazing Smithy! I never saw him move. And he was so cool about it. He didn't get ruffled when I looked in his bag. He didn't get mad when I took the tokens back and made him sit out a trial. He just looked at me."

Jeff asks, "Did it happen again?"

Isaac says, "Oh, heck yeah! It went on all through the session. A couple trials later, Violetta was reaching into her bag for her tokens, and she started screeching and waving the bag around. I'd swear nothing fell out, but when I checked it out, the bag was empty. She'd just taken a token out on the previous spin. It was like they'd disappeared in mid-air as she was reaching for them. Smithy was standing next to her, and he started edging away while she was freaking out. I caught him and checked his bag and found both of her fivers in there. They were kinda warm. I hate to think about where he was storing them." Isaac shudders.

Jeff rubs a hand over his hair and down the side of his face and says, "Ruby hasn't said anything about this to me."

Isaac shrugs and says, "It's all on tape. Maybe you could look at it later. You're familiar with his tricks, so maybe you can tell how he's doing it. Making coins disappear from sealed pouches . . . I never guessed he was so competitive. When he first came here, he was so intimidated by everything." Jeff grunts. Isaac continues. "But I guess he's found himself now. The other chimps don't bug him anymore. I mean, they're all in separate cages right now for the study, but they always give Smithy his space. I guess he's established himself."

Jeff sets his soda down and stares at the tabletop.

Isaac clears his throat and asks, "Oh, and Jeff, one more thing. What's this mean?" He covers his eyes with both hands, then touches his thumb to his chin and his chest.

Jeff springs to his feet, knocking his soda can to the floor, and yells, "*Where did you see that?!*"

Isaac recoils in surprise and says, "Smithy does it sometimes. They all do. Does it mean he wants to go to sleep?"

Jeff, agitated, says, "Did Ruby tell you that?"

Isaac says, "Yeah . . . a couple months ago."

Jeff, alarmed, asks, "It's been going on that long?"

Isaac says, "Yeah. Why? Where are you going?"

Jeff pushes away from the table and hastens from the room, saying, "Going to see Brad!"

DIARY OF RUBY DALTON

February 13, 1977

Once, I asked Taniesha how she's managed to survive so long in artificial lighting. The doctors have windows in their offices. We have bald concrete. She says she lives in her head. She does her duties, but she's thinking of where she'll be in five years. That's fine; Taniesha will graduate in three months. I have no milestones and no idea what kind of life I'll have in five years. God forbid I'm still at CSAM!

I thought today would pass quickly with two hours allocated to a team meeting, but I had to spend those hours listening to Man blather about his plans for "his" study. (Poor Dr. T.)

Evidently, Man has an offer to partner with a "major marketing firm" to test the appeal of celebrities in advertising (relative to other appealing shills, like semi-nude models or cute kids). How is this going to work with primates?

"We'll offer them the chance to view photos of high-status apes (like Nero or Grandee), or a female in estrus, or an infant. We'll track their preferences, make projections, then get approval to test FYPS[4] based on our pilot."

Man wants to combine that pilot with our gambling study by giving winning chimps the chance to view a photo as an alternative to a food reward. Taniesha thinks there could be intrinsic differences in the types of rewards high-risk and low-risk gamblers choose. She suggested Man use a different subject pool for his marketing study to avoid conflating the effects of gambling addiction with reward preference. Naturally, he ignored her.

4 First-Year Psych Students

I wish I had thought of anything to contribute, even if my input were belittled. My brain has atrophied. I've spent too much time doing mindless office tasks. I can't innovate. All I can think about anymore is how many minutes are left until my next break.

Even this project isn't as exciting as I thought it would be. It's so regimented. There are strict procedures to follow, and every damn thing needs to be documented. Sure, I kept journals for Piers, but a science lab is different. The language is dictated. I can't express myself in my own style; I must adhere to the guidelines. I realize now what we did with Piers wasn't "research." It was something totally new and free and wonderful. And it spoiled me utterly.

I took Piers for granted. He was the first scientist I'd ever met, and I assumed his way of doing things was standard. At least he considered our input, even if he made his own decisions afterward. Piers never talked down to the women on his team. He gave us responsibilities. Man gives us housekeeping.

If this is what research is really like, it's probably best I didn't attend Yale after all. I likely would have been just as unhappy, and that would have made an expensive epiphany.

Now that I know what I don't want, what <u>do</u> I want to do with my life? The years stretch before me like an endless desert: no landmarks to aim for, nothing to look forward to, nothing to sustain me. I'm already having a midlife crisis at twenty-three.

I try to remember how I got into this business. I used to want to change the world. I wanted to be a pioneer and do great things. I'm so far from greatness now, I might as well be in the ninth circle of hell. Cleaning up after chimps and corrupting them with vice won't open vistas for anybody.

My home life isn't great, either. This isn't what I thought marriage would look like. Living like roommates. Having dinner together two or three times a week. Being mired in jobs that make us miserable. Earning only enough to keep us in a tiny apartment. It would help if Jeff could get a teaching job now that he finally has his degree. He hasn't even subbed once yet, and it's three weeks into the new semester. I hope he filled out his application properly—and that he really did submit it.

I don't know how long we can go on like this, but I'm not sure what we're supposed to do instead. Jeff and I never discussed kids when we married. We knew we'd have to find jobs and get established before we could think about a family. We never defined what "established" would look like or when we'd know we'd reached that point.

I hate waking up in the morning. I hate CSAM! I hate this life!

What if this is all there is? What if there's nothing more than waking up each morning in a dingy apartment and dragging myself through one damn day after another into a world of meaningless monotony? No higher purpose, no communication, no understanding, no afterlife.

What if the past few years have been a complete waste, and all the times I told myself I was "contributing to science" and doing something "big" and "worthwhile," were pure delusion?

What if there never was anything like a ghost? What if Smithy is nothing more than a maladjusted animal with no sense of himself or anything beyond the immediacy of being fed? What if we have been fooling ourselves this whole time, seeking significance where nothing exists? Because nothing in this world matters.

Reid was right. People need ghosts. We need meaning. We need to convince ourselves that our rotten routines aren't the sum of our aspirations.

But what if they are? What if that's the true horror?

Life is a trap. It's the ultimate Ponzi scheme. Why doesn't anybody warn you of that?

DIARY OF RUBY DALTON

February 18, 1977

I should have known better than to trust Man. The ad agency deal must have fallen through because now he wants to add a different wrinkle to our gambling study that will, ostensibly, help verify the strength of the test drug.

We're going to compare the efficacy of the drug to the effect of shock treatment in discouraging risk-taking behavior.

Man must be suffering withdrawals from not using his cattle prod often enough, so now he wants to make all our chimp subjects suffer. Of course, he couched his rationale in more scientific terms. "Electric shock is a primary disincentive all organisms respond to. We know a shock can teach an animal not to do something. We don't know if this miracle drug can do a damn thing. So, let's put it to the test!"

The table was silent as we absorbed his words, his glee. That twisted smile wasn't anticipating the joy of scientific discovery. He was thinking of how the chimps would scream and cower. He was thinking of the power their fear would pump into him.

"But Man," Taniesha ventured, "the point of this experiment is to prepare the drug for <u>human</u> trials. We won't be able to give human subjects an electric shock."

His smile twisted further into a sneer. "Do you think I'm a moron, girl? I'm not talking about testing humans! We've got the damn apes for a reason! This is <u>preliminary</u> research! We want to be able to tell those quacks if their snake oil does a damn thing or not. We should give them some real information for their dollars, don't you think? Or don't you think at all? The more detail we can give them, the better. 'Your drug isn't half as good as a plain old noxious stimulus, Mr. Chemist. Don't waste any more of your money in R&D.' Doesn't that sound more sophisticated?"

My brain finally kicked back into gear, impressed by a need to protect my subjects from gratuitous torture. "I see logistical concerns. If we subject the chimps to electroshock in addition to the drug, we won't be able to tell whether any decrease in risk-taking is due to the old treatment—the shock—or the new one—the drug. I think adding too many levels could complicate our study and _weaken_ the results."

Taniesha and I both looked at Isaac, willing him to add his objections. He just stared down at the table. The wimp! But I'm being unkind. Maybe he was creatively drained. Or maybe he decided it was wiser to keep silent.

I continued. "Also, there's no telling exactly what the chimps might associate with the shock. It could be something abstract, like placing a bet, or it could be something as simple as the sight of the roulette wheel or the color red. We wouldn't be able to assert with certainty if the treatment were effective in curbing our target behavior."

The sneering lips pointed downward into a scowl. "This is why girls make lousy scientists." Man spoke as if reading facts instead of insulting half the population and two-thirds of his assistants. "You don't have the stomach for pursuing answers. You're too squeamish about applying a few volts of electricity to a dumb animal. How do you expect our center to advance mankind if we shrink from our calling? Jesus! Sometimes I wonder why I even bother hiring you gals." He squinted from me to Taniesha.

Honestly, I don't know which is worse: being Piers's eye-candy or being Man's verbal punching bag.

"Obviously, we'll vary the treatments! _Some_ apes will get the drug first and some will get the shock, and we'll see if there's any difference between the groups before moving them to a different condition."

Because there are so few chimps in the study, all subjects will have to undergo all conditions in a random order to generate enough responses: ABC, CAB, BCA.

We start the new design tomorrow. I don't know which condition Smithy is in, but I'd put my next paycheck on the red, double or nothing, he'll be getting a few volts thanks to my big mouth.

Jeff hit the ceiling when I told him about our meeting. "He's a sick bastard!" he ranted, pacing up and down. I don't know what I hate more: listening to Jeff shout and complain about things we're helpless to change or seeing him stalk around the room.

"He's a sadist, Ruby! I'll bet this trick was his plan all along. That's why he threw Ed off the study. Man wanted an excuse to hurt the chimps. He doesn't give a tinker's dam about gambling addictions or helping risk-prone people. He wants to be feared. That's why morale sucks. That's why everyone agonizes over writing safe little reports that support whatever Man wants to hear. I'll bet Marianne even fixes the data for him. Advancement of Man! What a sham!"

"Then what are we doing here?" I asked. "We can't change him. We can't change the working conditions. We can't protect Smithy. We're a captive audience to Man's excesses."

Jeff didn't like that, either. He accused me of defeatism. As if I hadn't been criticized enough for one day. As if I loved nothing better than to come back from work, my ears ringing with sarcasm and put-downs, and hear more of the same.

No, that isn't fair. Jeff wasn't belittling me. He's disappointed in me for not sharing his vision and his passion (a passion for butting his head against a wall).

Unless I quit or get fired, I'll have to get with the program to torture Smithy. Maybe that's what Man really wants: to make Smithy develop an aversion to me.

Naturally, I shared the news with the one other person who might be able to help mitigate Smithy's circumstances. Brad was irate, too, but after he finished cussing, he made a valid point.

"Before the university IRB approved this study, Man described exactly what was going to happen to the animals, and electroshock isn't on the list. They're already getting a drug with unknown side effects. Shocks on top of that would be too risky."

Isaac and Taniesha didn't think of that, and they're enrolled in the university.

Then Brad grinned and winked. "Technically, showing them monkey porn or whatever he wants to do now isn't in the contract, either, but that's not gonna do anybody harm. Anyways, I bet you the university stiffs will shit bricks when they get wind of how Man's doing his own thing. They've got to hold him to the original plan."

But how to give the IRB wind of Man's new plan? An anonymous letter? A report from a well-meaning staff member informing them of our progress? Now, finally, my mental wheels are turning. I'll drop by the trailer when I start my shift tomorrow and see what Brad's wheels churn up. Between us, we'll find a way to short-circuit Man's new experiment.

I love how Brad takes the animals' well-being to heart. He's like an adoptive father to Smithy. I wonder if Jeff ever gets jealous.

That gives me a brainstorm. The permafrost encasing my little gray cells is finally starting to thaw and ideas are springing to life.

Brad is invested in Smithy's well-being. Brad has consistent access to the chimps. If I can encourage him to take more action on Smithy's behalf to counteract Man's damage, then Jeff can stop worrying so much about Smithy's future.

Instead of futilely advocating for special programs to enhance Smithy's abilities, Jeff can concentrate on developing his own talents. He can put to proper use the degree he spent the past two years of our shared life earning and get a better job outside of CSAM.

Then we can both leave!

I still can't believe Jeff refused to even look for a teaching position after graduation. Without telling me his intentions. Without asking my feelings on the matter. Without—well, not seeking my approval, but without even soliciting my input on a decision bound to impact both our lives.

If I can make Jeff see that Brad has everything under control and is a fit caretaker for Smithy, then I can convince him it's OK—proper, even—for us to move on. It's going on three years now. ~~I des~~ We deserve it.

It would be nice to have some of my husband's attention for myself. When is the last time he asked me, "What are you reading right now, Ruby?" or "How was that movie you and Taniesha went to see? I wish I had been the one to take you out." No; any time he says something to me other than "Pass the salt" or "Do we have more mac and cheese?" it's about Smithy.

Jeff's completely eaten up about not being included in the gambling study. Instead of being glad at least one of us got picked for the team, he seems to think he should have been the one to work with Smithy.

Personally, I'd be happy to trade roles with Jeff. He's got a better deal working with Dr. Fairbanks and her macaques instead of being put through Man's wringer week after week. It's not as if Jeff never sees Smithy. He spends his breaks with Brad. The two of them take Smithy out for long walks or (more often, now that the weather is rainy) to the trailer where they can sign and talk and drink and (knowing Brad) probably smoke. They're free.

I want to be free. And I know how to make it happen.

LETTER FROM RUBY DALTON
TO TAMMY COHEN

February 23, 1977

Dear Tammy,

I hope this letter finds you well. I hope you're having some fun between prepping for your finals and your dissertation defense. Did Herschel spoil you for Valentine's Day?

I feel like celebrating: I've managed to unite Jeff and Man in serving their separate manias.

How, you ask?

Why, I just mentioned to Man—in passing, you know—how Piers used to have Jeff curate film footage to show potential donors what wonderful progress we were making in our study. And wouldn't it be neat if we could show the school something similar?

He stared at me for a long time but didn't immediately shoot me down. At last, Man told me to get my head out of the clouds and focus on my task at hand "and make sure that data is error-free!" But later in the day, Jeff wandered into the facility looking dazed. What do you know? Man called him to come in with his video equipment so he could capture our sessions for a "special documentary." Isn't Man smart to think of such an opportunity? What a fine idea! I wish I had good ideas like that.

So, for now, Jeff gets to be in the lab, too. He gets to observe everything, including the electroshocks, but he doesn't criticize them because he knows the IRB will do that soon enough. Best of all, he gets to see Smithy more often.

Smithy's happy, too. He keeps signing to Jeff when he's not at the gaming table, mostly asking for food or inviting him to play. Jeff's been surreptitiously filming some of that. You never know what Fresno State might have to say about a signing chimp.

Brad arranged for Jeff to do a walk-through of the chimps' living area for posterity—both indoors and outdoors—to capture where they sleep and what they eat. He does a good job of keeping everybody clean and reasonably nourished within Man's dietary guidelines, but if the good ol' IRB can see a way to make the research animals' living conditions better still, who are we to stand in the way of progress?

Since Man's holding area is an improvement over most medical testing facilities, he supports a filmed tour. He foresees it bringing him more accolades.

I feel reinvigorated about coming to work. I see so many areas where I can make my mark and implement new ideas. For the first time in years, I'm beginning to think I can make a difference after all.

More news to come! Give my best wishes to Herschel and keep plenty for yourself.

Love,

Ruby

ARCHIVAL FILM FOOTAGE

Date: March 8, 1977
Location: Corridor B, Lab D

Man, Taniesha, and Ruby stand around the roulette table. Man holds a cattle prod and faces the camera. He says, "Group C, Electroshock condition, Session four—Begin!"

The lab door opens and Isaac escorts four chimps—Smithy, Eleanor, Woolly, and Moses—into the room. The chimps shuffle in tentatively. Their shoulders are hunched and they look at the ground. Eleanor hangs back and clings to Isaac's hand.

Man calls, "Come on!" He snaps his fingers and points to the table.

Ruby flinches and looks at Taniesha, but she's looking at the ground. As the chimps approach the table, the camera pans over their faces. They're wide-eyed with flared nostrils. Smithy inclines his head toward Ruby. She smiles and signs, "OK. Stay."

Man asks, "Who won the draw?"

Taniesha consults her clipboard and says, "Woolly's first."

Man taps his cattle prod on the floor and Isaac pushes Woolly forward. Man says, "Let's switch things up a bit, keep them on their toes. See just how intelligent these apes are. Make black the big reward condition."

Taniesha grimaces and says, "If we do that, we won't be able to tell if the subjects are betting according to strategy or if they're perseverating under changing conditions."

Man shrugs and says, "I don't see a conflict. We want to know if shocking them will teach them not to risk so much. If they're going to learn that lesson, they'll learn it for black as well as red. Rules change all the time. If they can't figure out how to adapt, they'll go extinct. That's nature's way, doll."

Jeff, off-camera, whispers, "You just want an excuse to shock them, you arbitrary prick."

Man glares at the camera and asks, "Did you say something?

Jeff, off-camera, says, "A note to myself about the new condition." Louder, he says, "Chimps to receive minimal reward and moderate shock for correctly selecting red; maximum reward and mild shock for correctly selecting black, no reward and maximum shock for choosing an incorrect color."

Man says, "Let's go then! Black is double or nothing!"

Ruby asks, "Can we run a practice trial so they can learn the new ru—"

Man snaps, "No! Nature doesn't give practice sessions. Woolly—place your bet."

Ruby holds up two colored rectangles: one black and one red. Woolly indicates the red rectangle and hands over all his tokens. Ruby spins the wheel and the ball bounces from slot to slot, resting in a red square. Woolly chatters in approval. Taniesha returns his tokens and places a small plate with apple slices in front of him. As he reaches for it, Man touches the prod to Woolly's shoulder. The chimp squeals and jumps back, dropping his plate and scattering the fruit. He massages his injured shoulder and stares accusingly at Taniesha. He looks down at his apple slices and then back at her. Taniesha says sternly, "That's all you get now, Woolly. Go back in line."

Woolly, head drooping, steps away without bothering to collect his winnings from the floor. He pouts at Taniesha as if she has betrayed him.

Smithy chatters and steps forward, signing, "More."

Taniesha signs, "No more," and says, "That's all!"

Man calls, "Next!"

Isaac pushes Eleanor forward. She shifts back and forth as if nervous. When Ruby shows her the rectangles, Eleanor chooses red and hands over one of her five tokens. Isaac says, "Subject two is betting red but only using one of her tokens. She appears to have learned from her colleague's example and is hedging her bet."

Man says, "We don't have enough information to make that judgment! Say, 'Subject two is betting one of five tokens on red' and keep your editorializing to yourself!"

Ruby spins the wheel and the ball lands on red. Taniesha hands Eleanor a small tray of apples. Man steps forward to administer the shock and Eleanor screeches and cowers. She tries to evade him, but Man lunges and shocks her in the bottom. He smiles as the chimp cringes away.

Ruby, watching, looks disgusted.

Taniesha clenches her jaw and looks at the ground.

Woolly and Moses watch Eleanor with agitated expressions. Smithy, in contrast, looks at the far wall away from her.

Man calls, "Next!"

Taniesha says, "Smithy," and beckons him forward. He glowers at her and refuses to move.

Man calls, "Come, now!"

Ruby signs, "Please, come, now!"

Smithy stares at Ruby but refuses to budge.

Jeff, off-camera, says, "Go on, buddy. It's your turn!"

Man snaps, "Hush! You don't give instructions; I do. And I'll give someone a shock if he doesn't get his ass in gear!"

He raises the cattle prod just as Smithy approaches the table. He never once looks at Man. Smithy passes Ruby a silver token and signs, "Red."

Man asks, "What's that?"

Ruby says, "He wants red."

Man asks, "How do I know that?"

Ruby says, "It's ASL—"

Man says, "Make him follow the protocol like everyone else! If he can't follow directions, he gets disciplined."

Ruby grits her teeth and crouches in front of Smithy with both colored boards in her left hand; with her right hand, she signs, "Show me."

Smithy bats the red board out of her hand, and she jumps back, startled.

Isaac nervously says, "OK, I understood that!"

Ruby spins the wheel and the ball lands on red. Smithy doesn't take the tray when Taniesha offers it, and when Man stretches out his cattle prod, Smithy turns to stare him in the eye. Man meets his glare and pokes the prod into Smithy's stomach, holding it there a few extra seconds. Smithy squeaks and flinches.

Man's smile widens and he says, "Get back to your place!"

Isaac calls, "Moses." The next chimp approaches with two of four tokens. He chooses red but the ball lands on black. Man sticks his prod against Moses's back. The chimp, cowed, shuffles back into line and Woolly steps forward again. He offers up two tokens this time and chooses the black rectangle.

In line behind him, Smithy shifts and looks around the room. He looks directly into the camera and signs, "Out."

Ruby spins the wheel, and the number comes up black. Woolly is rewarded with a melon, but as he shoves it in his mouth, Man shocks his foot. Woolly yips and jumps up. He back-pedals, staring at Man. Then, he flings the melon rind on the ground and runs to hide behind Isaac.

Isaac says, "The first subject changed his bet. This could suggest he has learned the new pattern."

Isaac pushes Eleanor forward. She looks down when she hands Ruby another single token. Ruby kneels with the colored boards and Eleanor looks up. She hoots loudly and covers her eyes, then scoots back to where Isaac stands.

He asks, "What spooked her?"

Ruby, tense, says, "Nothing. She chose black is all." Ruby spins the wheel abruptly.

Man asks, "How's that?"

Taniesha says, "Covering the face, that's the sign for black. A lot of the chimps know it."

Isaac says, "She's awfully skittish."

Ruby says softly, "She knows what's coming."

While the ball circles the wheel, the chimps shift and look around the room in agitation. Woolly shrieks and covers his eyes. Smithy looks into the camera, then covers his eyes. The ball bounces into the black slot. Taniesha offers Eleanor her melon, but the chimp continues to cower behind Isaac, whimpering.

Man, impatient, says, "Quit your bitching! If you don't want your prize, don't take it, but you won't hide from me."

Man shocks Eleanor, and she rocks back and forth, still covering her eyes. The other chimps chatter and edge away from her.

Man raises his voice. "Knock it off! Get back to your places!" He swings the prod, herding the chimps back together. They shriek and cower from him but still look around the room, apparently frightened of something else.

Man directs Smithy forward with the cattle prod.

Smithy hands one token to Ruby and signs, "Red."

Behind him, the other chimps frantically cover their eyes, making the sign for "black."

Taniesha and Ruby watch them, mouths agape.

Isaac says, "Well, they know better. I guess Smithy hasn't learned . . . "

The ball bounces into the red slot. Ruby, harried, picks up a tray of apples and shoves it at Smithy without looking at him. Smithy steps away without taking it. As he retreats toward the line of frenzied chimps, he looks up at Man, who's raising the cattle prod. As Man brings it down to shock Smithy, the other chimps simultaneously howl and charge across the room.

Man spins around and says, "Where the hell are you going?"

The chimps claw at the lab door, jumping up and down. Occasionally, one turns around and covers its face. The student researchers stare.

Man grits his teeth, face florid, and yells, "Get away from there!" He strides across the room after them.

The camera turns from Man for a moment and rests on Smithy, who remains beside the roulette wheel, watching the disturbance. He turns, as if sensing the camera on him, and looks into the lens. As if cued, he suddenly emits a squeal and covers his eyes, then leaps across the room directly into Man's path.

Man says, "You get the hell away!" Man swats at Smithy with the cattle prod; Smithy manages to roll away before getting shocked.

Jeff, off-camera, says, "Don't!"

Smithy joins the other chimps at the door. When they see him, they retreat from the door, still keening, and launch themselves at Man. Woolly jumps on Man's back and covers Man's eyes. Eleanor wraps herself around his leg. Man falls to one knee under the weight of the apes. He swings his arms blindly, cursing loudly. Moses clambers up Man's back, grabs the light fixture, and dangles from it; in the process, he kicks Man's arm, and Man drops the cattle prod. Eleanor kicks it, and it rolls away, out of the frame.

Man yells, "Goddammit!"

Ruby sidles around the roulette table and approaches Man. He continues cursing and thrashing on the floor while the apes crawl over him. They cling to him, panicked, but do not bite or scratch him.

Ruby calls, "Jeff, stop filming and help us!" She signals Smithy and points to the wall near the table, signing, "Go there now."

Smithy edges away from the door but doesn't go to the roulette table. Instead, he stands in the center of the room, in full view of the video camera.

Man orders, "Shock them! Mother—aggh!"

Isaac runs past the apes and opens the lab door. He yells, "Hey, help! Somebody!"

Taniesha yells, "Close the door!"

As Isaac rushes into the hallway, screaming for help, Woolly springs off Man's back and runs for the door.

Ruby yells, "Stop!"

Jeff, off-camera, calls, "Ruby!"

Ruby attempts to tackle Woolly but the chimp shakes her off. Jeff rushes to her side to examine her for injuries. Ruby shakes her head.

Man pushes himself to his feet, swatting and kicking at Eleanor.

Man yells, "Don't let them escape!"

Eleanor sees the open door and releases Man. She dives between Ruby and Jeff and goes out the door.

Man asks, "Where's my damn prod?"

He searches the floor, but the cattle prod is gone. Moses swings down from the light fixture and makes a break for the exit, but Jeff slams the door before he can get through.

Taniesha approaches Man, who is disheveled, red-faced, and furious.

Taniesha asks, "Are you all right?"

Man asks, "Dammit, what did he do with it?" He whirls and points at Smithy, yelling, "You!"

Jeff says, "He didn't do anything. You can watch the film yourself. Smithy was standing aside the whole time. He didn't go near you; the others started it."

Man snaps, "I don't give a fuck! Every time something goes wrong—every damn time!—he's in the room." He whirls on Ruby, who cringes against her husband, and orders, "You get me my apes back!"

Taniesha says, "Make sure you hold him tight." She points to Moses, whom Jeff blocks; then she slowly opens the door. She steps back as Keith enters, Eleanor in tow.

Keith asks, "What the hell?"

Man advances on Eleanor and slaps her across the face. She cowers. Man orders, "Take them all back to their cages. Find Woolly. And where the fuck is my cattle prod?" He kicks at the ground, looking around in futility. "I don't know how the hell you expect to eat if we can't turn a profit! I don't know how you expect us to accomplish anything with our subjects running wild! How the hell can I depend on any of you? Keith, come with me!"

Taniesha takes Moses by the hand and collects Eleanor from Keith; they fall behind him as they walk to the exit.

Ruby signs to Smithy and he runs to her.

Man walks toward the door, then whirls around, pointing at the camera, and yells, "Turn that goddamn thing off! If you show anybody what's on it, I swear I will break your fucking legs!"

Jeff crosses the room hastily and the camera goes dark.

CLOSED-CIRCUIT FOOTAGE

Date: March 8, 1977
Location: Corridor D, Research Animal Quarters

The door to Corridor D opens and fluorescent lights overhead flicker. Brad enters.

Ruby ducks in behind him and says, "Thanks, Brad."

Brad says, "You won't have much time. Man's cracking down."

Ruby says, "I know. But I needed to see him."

They cross the room, ignoring the animals that cling to the cage doors and call or reach out to them.

Ruby says, "I'm glad he's still here and not in Corridor F. Or worse. I was so afraid of the retribution Man might take against him. Sedating and starving the apes—"

Brad makes air quotes with his hands and says, "'Reducing rations.'"

Ruby continues. "—is bad enough, but I was honestly afraid Man might sell them off or-or even put some of them down."

Brad says, "That'd mean starting the study over with a fresh batch of subjects. Or ending it altogether. And that would mean losing potential profits along with his investment in the research apes so far. Even worse, Man would lose status if he admits he lost control. Downplaying what happened helps keep him looking tough, like nothing's gonna slow him down. It's amazing Man wasn't hurt in that skirmish though. It could have gone really bad. Three apes . . . "

Ruby says, "They weren't trying to attack him. They were frightened. I think they just wanted to get away, but Man was in their way. I think the pressure of being relentlessly shocked without justification got to them. Man changed the rules on them too suddenly and it pushed them over. Made them have a nervous breakdown. Suddenly, they couldn't predict anything, and they got frustrated.

Brad says, "Except Smithy. He looked calm in the film . . . " He stops and glances at Ruby, and says, "Like he knew what he was doing. I noticed he stayed in front of the camera all the time. Like he was making sure he'd be seen. Like he wanted to prove he wasn't causing any trouble."

Ruby stares back at Brad in silence for a moment and says, "Smithy's intelligent, but he's not a mastermind. You sound like Man, blaming him for—"

Brad says, "Uh-uh! I don't think he did anything. That's my point. You can see him just standing around."

Ruby says, "You said he did it on purpose. Like he planned an alibi."

Brad laughs and says, "Nah, I didn't mean that. Only that Smithy's smart enough to stay out of trouble when he sees it. He doesn't cause it. It just happens . . . " Brad falls silent and looks toward Smithy's cage. He asks, "What do you think they were all staring at?"

Ruby says, "I don't know. Maybe a spider crawling up the wall."

Brad says, "A spider wouldn't have scared them! It was like they'd seen a ghost."

Ruby stops and glowers at him. "Don't! Man will skin us alive if he hears that talk."

Brad scratches his head, then laughs. "Oh! I forgot, your ghost! But that was long ago and far away."

Ruby says crossly, "They were probably fleeing the cattle prod."

Brad asks, "Nobody's found it yet?"

Ruby says, "No. It's disappeared."

Brad says, "Too bad he's got more of 'em. Well, here we are." He raps gently on a cage door and calls, "Smithy? Hey, buddy, look who's here to see you!"

Within, a shadow unfolds. Smithy crawls forward to look out at Brad. He sees Ruby and starts to turn away. Brad says, "Aw, don't be like that!"

Ruby says, "Smithy . . . " She pulls a bundled napkin out of her lab coat pocket and unfolds it. Inside are apple and melon slices. Ruby says, "You earned them." Smithy considers the fruit, snorts, and backs away.

Brad says, "Looks good to me." He takes a piece of melon and bites into it, making happy sounds as he chews. The apes in the surrounding cages begin to chatter and reach out their hands.

Smithy crawls forward and signs, "Give."

Ruby places a piece of fruit in his hand, and he chews it.

Ruby says, "Thank you. Can you give us a few minutes? I'd like to talk to him alone."

Brad says, "Ahh . . . I can't really do that. We're in here supposedly so I can change the water." He looks around. "I'll work down at the far end. And I'll whistle so I can't hear you."

Ruby says, "OK."

Brad steps away, whistling loudly. He greets the other chimps by name and stops at the cage nearest the entrance. He clatters the water bottle as he detaches it and crosses to the sink.

Ruby watches him, then turns back to Smithy. He spits some apple seeds at her.

Ruby blocks her face, steps back, and says, "Smithy, there was nothing I could do!" She signs, "Sorry" repeatedly. Ruby says, "Believe me, I didn't want to let him hurt you! I hate it here more than you do. You're just a victim; I have to be complicit . . . and you have no idea what that word means. All you know is, I'm the enemy now."

Ruby stares into the cage for a moment in silence. She signs, "Sorry," again and offers up the remaining fruit. After a pause, Smithy eats another piece. Then he takes the entire cache, napkin and all. Ruby watches him eat, then glances back at Brad studiously refilling water bottles at the sink.

She looks at Smithy and signs, "What happened?"

Smithy doesn't respond.

Ruby says, "Come on, Smithy? What did you see?" She signs, "What did you see in lab today? What happened?"

Smithy doesn't respond.

She signs, "What did you do? Who did you see?"

Smithy grunts and shifts. Ruby closes her eyes and rubs the back of her neck. When she looks up, she signs, "Have you seen Eric? Do you talk to Eric?"

Smithy grows excited, hooting. He signs, "Where's Eric? Long time Eric no see."

Ruby says to herself, "Is *she* the only dead person you get to see?"

Smithy signs, "Smithy misses Eric."

Ruby whispers, "Yeah, I miss Eric, too."

Brad says, "Ruby, Keith's coming on duty. Did you get what you needed?"

Ruby says, "No, but it's all I'm going to get." She steps back from the cage and signs, "Good night. See you tomorrow."

Smithy hoots and signs, "Where's Eric?"

Ruby joins Brad in the doorway and they exit.

CLOSED-CIRCUIT FOOTAGE

Date: March 8, 1977
Location: Lunchroom

Brad and Ruby enter the kitchenette, conversing.

Ruby says, "—they appreciate it so. You relate to them by putting yourself in their position. That's good, Brad."

He shrugs and says, "It's all I know how to do. It comes naturally."

Ruby says, "Not to every researcher. But you really care."

Brad shrugs again and says, "I'm not a researcher." He pulls a soda out of the fridge.

Ruby leans back against the counter, watching him. "You could be. You have a perspective that I think will help you achieve new insights. More importantly, the animals trust you. Trust and respect aren't valued—or practiced—enough. Certainly not here. Man relies on you more and more, especially when Smithy's involved. I bet he'd make you a full researcher. He might not pay you any better, but he'd give you the shot."

Brad fiddles with the pull tab on the can. He asks, "Would you . . . or Jeff . . . teach me how to do research?"

Ruby says brightly, "Of course! I'd love to help get you on a team. Although . . . " She grows serious. "You might have to do some things that aren't a lot of fun. You might have to give a shot or an electric shock as part of an experiment."

Brad shakes his head. He gulps from his soda and says, "No. I won't do that. Man can do it; he likes that part."

Ruby says, "But if you had to do it, you might not stay friends with all the chimps."

Brad turns to her and smiles, says, "Nah. They know I've got their backs. They'd know I had a good reason for anything I did. Did you ever get mad at your mother for making you take cough medicine? Did you hate her because it tasted bad?"

Ruby shakes her head.

Brad continues, "You see? Then they've got no reason to be mad at me. Besides, if anything happened, I'd make it up to them."

He exits and, after a pause, Ruby follows.

DIARY OF RUBY DALTON

March 8, 1977

I behaved foolishly today, and I'm ashamed of myself, both for having been so gullible and for disrespecting Eric's memory.

Was I disrespectful? I was sincere in my wish.

I went to Smithy and asked him if he'd had any news from Eric. Eric always believed Smithy could see and talk to things unknown. Surely, he would turn to Smithy to send us a message.

Smithy didn't answer. I don't know if he even understood my question. Eric always thought Smithy knew more than he let on and was playing dumb whenever we tried to get him to talk about the Dark Woman. Why did I think this time would be different?

No, I didn't really believe I'd get an answer or a message from Smithy. I just <u>hoped</u> for one.

What if it had worked? How would I have reacted if Smithy had signed that yes, Eric was here, Eric had a message for us. I would have been happy and relieved to know he still existed, even if I couldn't see him myself or speak with him directly. I want to think Eric still lives on, and not just in my memory, though I'm not sure what that would look like.

I grew up believing good people went to heaven and bad people went to hell. Surely Eric would be in heaven by now, four months later. Really, he would have no reason to linger and speak with me or Smithy. As far as I know, he wasn't a tortured soul. Perhaps he had "unfinished business" because he went so suddenly and was so young. But wouldn't the lure of heaven be stronger than anything that could tie Eric to Earth?

I never thought of death in such detail before. Why would I? I'm young. Even when we first thought Trevor Hall might be haunted, I was caught up in the "What if?" of ghosts, not in the "How?" If the stories are true that the Dark Woman is the ghost of someone who committed suicide, then I suppose she's earthbound because she committed a grievous sin. That's what my religion taught me, though I always thought that was harsh. Why would a loving God condemn someone who was so obviously tormented that they would go to such extremes, somebody who probably wasn't even in their right mind?

Still, I never questioned that lesson, or anything, aloud. I accepted that suicide was wrong and one must never even think about it, just as I accepted that obeying my parents and going to church was good. It seemed safer that way.

When I was little, I believed in God and guardian angels. I would talk to them all the time, like they were imaginary friends; out loud when I was alone in my room, or in my head. I would confide in them about how I was feeling, what happened at school, or things I wanted. It was comforting to think somebody powerful cared about me and was watching out for me.

As I got older, I grew away from that, but I never completely disbelieved in higher beings. Again, it seemed safer to behave as if there were a God. If I prayed and no one was really listening, then even if I wouldn't be helped, at least I wouldn't be harmed. On the other hand, if God really was there and I didn't show Him the proper respect, then when I finally died, things might go very badly for me.

It was that way at Trevor Hall, too. It was better to behave as if the Dark Woman really did exist so I wouldn't risk offending her. In a weird way, believing in her was also comforting. I could blame our problems on something external instead of thinking Smithy was responsible. At least a ghost was _an_ answer. If she were really watching us, manipulating Smithy, wishing us ill, and causing trouble, then we could stay on her good side and not mock or challenge her or pry too much into her business. That's why it made me nervous whenever Eric wanted to have séances. I didn't want to get her riled up, and I didn't want to risk dragging in anything else that might be worse than her.

"Worse"—that's so beautifully vague. Strangely, I never believed in demons, even when I still believed firmly in angels. Maybe that's because I didn't want to believe in bad things and liked believing in good things. Even now, looking over these pages, I'm tempted to scratch out any reference to the ghost, lest she might somehow know I was writing about her, or I might somehow draw her out. Her—or something worse.

How did I get caught up in thinking about these things anyway? Ah yes, I see it looking back. Eric. Writing about the ghost helped me stop thinking about him. For just a few moments, my throat didn't lock up, my eyes didn't burn, and my insides didn't turn cold. And now I'm experiencing all the sorrow and longing again.

I wish I could tell him how much Jeff and Tammy and I cared about him. I could even tell him how, when I wrote to Gail about his accident, her reply letter was speckled with tearstains. I think he would like that. I suppose he must know that already. When you go to heaven to be with God, don't you get a little bit of God's wisdom and omniscience, too, if not his power? Eric must know how we feel, how we miss him.

Maybe I should go to church and light a candle for him. I haven't been to church in ages or even thought about going until now. I'm not sure how lighting a candle is supposed to help a ghost. Maybe it doesn't. But maybe it would feel better to do <u>something</u>. Maybe it would be a good thing to do, just in case.

LETTER FROM RUBY DALTON
TO TAMMY COHEN

March 14, 1977

Dear Tammy,

I got your graduation announcement in Saturday's mail. Congratulations! I so wish I could be in New York to see you, but I'll be there in spirit. Mazel tov, my dear!

I think we could have afforded the trip, but with everything that's happened at work since Smithy's last gambling session, Jeff and I have decided it's better to stay in Fresno and keep an eye on things. The fall-out is gradually dissipating. After reviewing Jeff's footage multiple times, Man finally admitted Smithy did nothing to instigate the "attack." But that hasn't stopped Man from branding Smithy a troublemaker and booting him from the study.

"Ever since this * * * * has come here, we've had nothing but problems!" he roared during our final team meeting. "He doesn't have to <u>cause</u> trouble. He simply has to <u>exist</u>! He's a f* * *g Jonah!"

After that, I feared Man would sell Smithy to rid CSAM of trouble altogether, but he wants to get the most return for his investment. He'll keep Smithy around but not use him in any group studies for a while.

Man's also steamed about the university's reaction to the way he conducted this study. The IRB was unimpressed with his methodology and ordered him to throw out all data from the shock condition on the grounds that it presents a confounding variable. Actually, they wanted to discontinue the study altogether because cutting data from an already-small sample size would diminish the significance of any results. Complying with that request would mean flushing almost a year's worth of work and a large grant down the toilet. We're trying to compromise by using the sub-group's pre-shock data as a control; the remaining participants will receive the drug. Marianne will have to massage some data, but that's not unethical. It just means a lot of small print in the appendix for the article.

The final compromise was that we can finish the study if Edgar Torrance supervises the remaining trials. Our subjects won't have to deal with Man anymore!

Some good news: Somehow an extra reel of footage showing chimps using sign language was sent to the college along with the marked footage of our plagued experiment. Now, this footage proved so intriguing that they prevailed on Man to institute a language study. If Marianne's big mouth is to be trusted, they implied doing so would be a condition of continuing to work with Man.

Bad news: Neither Jeff nor I will be working with Smithy in this phase of research. I've been assigned to the graveyard shift to tend to the animals' basic needs, and Jeff is working afternoons on some new drug trial. We're separated from each other as well as from Smithy.

Good news: Taniesha and Brad will be assisting Smithy as part of a new study for Dr. Torrance. As I've been demoted to cleaning up after the chimps, Brad has been elevated to a kind of junior-junior researcher, thanks to his rapport with Smithy.

"You know how to keep this bugger in line. Do it!" Man ordered.

One might almost think he was afraid of the little guy (who's no longer so little; he's still below average for his age, but he's about 110 lbs and four feet tall by now).

I'm proud Brad's getting recognition for his talents. I'm confident he can learn to be a research tech without benefit of a degree.

Not-so-good news: Taniesha doesn't want to work with Smithy. She sees this assignment as punishment for back-talking to Man about the electroshocks. She confided in me after the meeting ended: "I don't like telling you this because I know he's your baby, but I get a bad vibe from Smithy. It's been building for a while now; it's not just what happened in the lab."

I pressed her on what she meant. Had Smithy threatened her in any way?

No, but: "To a certain extent, I think Man is right. Weird things happen whenever Smithy's around. He acts like he's in the eye of a storm.

I don't think he's causing any of it, but he knows what's going on. And he knows I know. And he resents me for it."

Brad said something similar, hinting Smithy's too smart for his own good. It hasn't affected their friendship, though, thank goodness.

How can two smart people who know both Smithy and Man blame Smithy for Man's poor judgment? Man's the one who makes everyone edgy and resentful, including yours truly.

I want my own life, separate and untainted by CSAM. But with my weird hours, I can't meet people at civic functions like a normal person. I can't even take night classes now, and the afternoon sessions are already full, so my degree has to take a backseat, too.

All right; enough self-pity.

I'm thrilled about all you have to look forward to, Tammy! Someday soon I hope we'll both have cause to celebrate.

Hugs!

Ruby

xoxo

DIARY OF RUBY DALTON

March 31, 1977

My brilliant scheme continues to unfold. Brad makes an ideal researcher and, despite his griping about school, a great student. He pays attention and asks good questions. I guess he just doesn't like dealing with the BS of grades and papers.

Right now, he's emphasizing practical vocabulary the chimps can use in the lab. Can you imagine them telling Doc Torrance, "I don't want an injection today?"

I explained the apes wouldn't be using precise grammar because their brains don't work that way. Then again, how many of us speak proper Queen's English?

Besides teaching Smithy new signs, we're getting a little relief from our drudgery, courtesy of Dr. Torrance. He recently purchased a new stereo system with a tape deck and record player for his own home, so he's brought his old record player to the office. We can run it in the background when we're crunching numbers or writing reports. Everyone will contribute to the library. I've already made up a small pile of records to take in tomorrow.

Things are changing at CSAM, and for once, it's for the better!

EXCERPT FROM UNCORRECTED PROOF OF
ALL THE RATS WERE WHITE
(AND SOME EVEN WORE LAB COATS):
ON RACISM AND SEXISM
IN THE SCIENCES TODAY
BY TANIESHA JONES

SCHEDULED PUBLICATION MARCH 2001

. . . I had poured six months of my life into that project. For once, it had become more than a job: I was genuinely curious about the work. Ceasing to move through the paces Man set for me, I included my own questions; questions he had neglected to consider. Therefore, I felt some ownership. That was obvious to everyone but him. Or, perhaps he knew full well I had the right to co-authorship and chose to withhold it out of spite.

When I broached the issue, Man became hostile.

"Don't be ridiculous," he'd said. "No review board is going to publish work by 'Taniesha Jones.' It's too ethnic! They'll toss the file in the garbage without even looking at it. You know the stats on hiring: résumés from coloreds and skirts are first to be rejected. Academia is no different. If you think I'm going to let my study get trashed because of your ego, you're f-----g nuts."

Man had spoken crudely to my face on plenty of occasions, but always with the casual dismissiveness that was easy to mistake for humor or ignorance. This was the first time I'd heard him attempt to justify his bigotry with science. I did know the research on hiring qualifications. All of us did. As if personal experience wasn't discouraging enough, now we had exact probability ratios to further subjugate us. For once, Man wasn't completely wrong.

Still, Ruby challenged him. "She could publish as 'T. L. Jones.' That's generic enough that no one can object. And once Taniesha's established, she can always switch to publishing under her full name."

I appreciated that she recognized my need to be fully who I am. "T. L. Jones" would have been an entrée into academia, but it would also have been a disguise, requiring me to suppress my heritage to please faceless gatekeepers. Making the research known was important. Building a reputation was important. But being authentic was important, too. Publishing under colorless, genderless initials would satisfy the first two needs while creating a different quandary. That was a fact of life in 1977. It still is.

Nevertheless, Man finally added my name to the article, albeit, fourth down the list.

For her audacity, Man increased Ruby's hours and transferred her to the graveyard shift so she would be dead on her feet. He assigned her to clean the animals' cages, menial work no scientist had been asked to do in months. Everyone knew the move was a punishment, though Man claimed it was to free up more personnel to assist [Edgar Torrance] with his equilibrium studies.

We didn't see each other at the office for three whole months, but I talked to Ruby by phone whenever I could and managed to have dinner with her and Jeff a couple of times. At one meeting, I brought her a copy of the *Journal of Anthropology* containing *my* article. Jeff photographed us drinking a toast while holding the magazine between us. Ruby then insisted I autograph the article, with my full name, of course . . .

Other women on the research team regarded the status quo as a necessary evil for the right to work in a laboratory, but Ruby and I knew we deserved better. We commiserated with each other, and she would often tell me, "You have it so much worse than I do. He [Man] hits you with twice the arsenal, but you're still standing."

In truth, Man was an equal opportunity misogynist. My skin color didn't make him hate me any more than he hated Eileen [Fenn], Margo [Kane], or Ruby. In some ways, she suffered more than I did.

DIARY OF RUBY DALTON

May 17, 1977

I sincerely hate Man. I've never hated anyone before in my life.

Less than an hour into the day, he stormed through Corridor C, right to my desk. He was waving a stack of papers, and at first, I thought he had another giant assignment for me.

Instead, he found fault with the notes and annotations I painstakingly completed last night, staying a half hour late to do so.

"Why'd you leave this novel on my desk? What the hell am I supposed to do with it?" he shouted.

I reminded him that he instructed me to provide him detailed notes, but he kept talking over me, like a train running over the damsel on the tracks.

"Do you think I have nothing better to do than read all this crap? I'm busting my ass to keep everyone busy! I don't have time to eat a proper dinner (ha!), let alone read. And if I wanted to read something the size of <u>War and Peace</u>, I would read fucking <u>War and Peace</u>, something of quality—not this shit!"

He threw my notes into the trash can and cast one look over all the other papers on my desk that I had yet to read, transcribe, distribute.

"Why is this place always such a mess? Why don't you use some of <u>your</u> time to make your desk look like a professional works here? And what do I have to do to get some damn coffee?"

In a just world, the Dark Lady would attack Man. He's the head honcho. He lords over Smithy and makes his life miserable. He works us all to the breaking point. Whether jealousy or revenge were her motive, he'd still make the perfect target.

Push him in front of a truck, or make his cattle prod explode while he's holding it. Set the chimps on him again, but this time, make them

tear him limb from limb. Frighten him. Show Man even gods can bleed,
and that he doesn't have all the power.

But that doesn't happen. Is it because the ghost can't be compelled?
Because she doesn't care about our plight? Or because she isn't real?

EXCERPT FROM
SMITHY: THE MILLENNIUM COMPENDIUM
BY REID BENNET, PHD

CHAPTER TWELVE: IN THE MAD SCIENTIST'S LAB

This entry, Ruby's last of substance for several months, refuted her earlier optimism. With Taniesha Jones's departure in June, the remaining CSAM staff became so overwhelmed that Ruby was unable to document her own or Smithy's struggles.

As 1977 drew to a close, Manfred Teague drove his team to complete his commercial research for various pharmaceutical companies. However, once those findings were submitted, he unexpectedly shifted tactics.

At long last, he expressed interest in Smithy as something more than merely a body to inject. He even authorized a more formal, albeit unofficial, unsponsored, volunteer investigation of primate language. Researchers gave their own time to the study but submitted regular reports to Teague as if they were on assignment.

This caused the Daltons, Brad Vollmer, and occasionally others to devote *more* time to CSAM, beyond their regular shifts. Despite dissatisfaction with their working conditions, they remained committed to redeeming Smithy's reputation in the scientific community.

The new self-directed study showed promise, until the "Reign of Terror" disrupted all research during the spring and summer of 1978. Yet, warning signs emerged even earlier . . .

CLOSED-CIRCUIT FOOTAGE
VIDEO SESSION #428

Date: November 7, 1977
Location: Lab A

Keith faces the camera. Behind him, Brad connects Smithy to machinery on a table in the center of the room. A vacant chair sits at the opposite side of the table.

Keith says, "It's now two fifteen in the afternoon. I, Keith Branneman, am with Brad Vollmer and the chimp known as 'Smithy.' In a few moments, we'll get this projector behind me going and attach a plethysmograph to Smithy so we can measure his reactions to different imagery."

Brad says, "Dude, you gotta be more specific. We're measuring Smithy's physiological reactions to randomly ordered images of people or chimps. We want to find out if Smithy reacts faster to one species over the other. This will tell us how he identifies himself."

Keith says, "Uh, thanks. I'll be running the video and reporting the output of the readings. Brad is here to assist with Smithy and to translate."

The chimp begins to hoot and sign.

Keith remarks, "Like right now."

Keith steps back, giving the camera a clear view of Smithy.

Smithy signs, "Brad. Dark. Woman. Dark. Woman."

Keith says, "Look, now he's calling you 'dark woman.' What's wrong with this thing?"

Brad looks around the room and asks, "Where is she, Smithy?"

Smithy signs, "Chair."

Brad says, "OK. Out we go." He lifts Smithy and carries him toward the door.

Keith protests, "Hey, where are you going?"

Brad says, "I'm taking Smithy for a little walk."

Keith follows him into the hall and asks, "Wait, what about the study? You can't walk out! Man wants—"

Brad says, "The hell with what Man wants! I'm taking Smithy out. Executive decision."

Keith objects. "Wait! What the hell?"

CLOSED-CIRCUIT FOOTAGE

Date: November 7, 1977
Location: Corridors B and C, Hallway

Brad carries Smithy down the hall toward Corridor D and calls, "Everybody, listen up! Lab A is closed!"

As he passes through Corridor C, the employees turn to stare at him or stand up.

Margo asks, "Where are you taking Smithy?"

Brad calls out, "Everybody stay out of Lab A!"

Dr. Fairbanks steps out of the lunchroom and asks, "Why?"

Brad says, "Smithy farted and it's putrid in there. Everybody keep out!"

Jeff runs out of the lunchroom and walks alongside Brad. He asks, "Brad, what's up?"

Brad says, "Just going for a walk. Be back soon!"

Jeff asks, "Brad, what happened with Smithy? Come on, level with me!"

Brad replies, "He said the dark woman was in the chair next to him."

Jeff curses. "Goddammit!" He spins around and runs back toward Corridor C.

DIARY OF RUBY DALTON

November 8, 1977

It doesn't have to be the same one.

I kept telling Jeff, "Smithy generalizes a lot. Remember how cats and squirrels were all 'dogs' until we taught him new vocabulary? Even if he is signing again about a 'dark woman,' it doesn't mean the same ghost followed us from Newport. We never taught Smithy a concept for 'ghost.' 'Dark woman' is the only sign he knows, so if ever he saw something <u>like</u> that dark woman, he would probably use that sign."

It doesn't thrill me to think Smithy's in contact with legions of spirits, but I'd rather believe he's met some new ghosts than believe the same damn one has tracked him down.

Jeff just looked at me. I saw the worry lines stark on his forehead and the bags under his eyes and realized he's been under the same kind of stress as me. We just don't interact enough to notice.

"Why didn't you tell me he was talking about her again?" he asked.

I didn't understand. "Huh? <u>You</u> just told <u>me</u>. I wasn't there."

"Not the thing with Brad today. This has happened before." Jeff's voice thickened and his forehead lines deepened. "Isaac asked about that sign months ago. He wanted to know what it meant because Smithy kept doing it during that damn gambling study. You must have seen it, too, so why didn't you mention it? We could have done something about it! Why keep this from me? We're supposed to be a team."

What could we have done about it? *I wondered.*

But instead, I said, "If we're a team, why didn't you tell me you didn't actually want to be a teacher? You keep putting it off so you can stay at CSAM. Why even get the degree if you didn't intend to use it? Jeff, I supported you through your classwork because I thought it would benefit us both. <u>I</u> could have enrolled in those classes!"

This time his eyes flashed. "Who says I don't want to teach? And what does that have to do with Smithy? You're changing the subject."

"No, it has everything to do with Smithy! Smithy is why we came here. Smithy is why we're still here two horrid years later. I didn't think it would be this long, Jeff. When will it be enough? What's your plan? Do you mind telling your wife? I am your wife, remember? Not just the other person who pays the rent."

He scowled. "Now you're having a tantrum. We agreed to stay and help Smithy, but we can't help him if he's seeing ghosts and you don't tell me!"

"When did we agree?" I shot back. "We talked about helping him get settled in his new home. We didn't make a pact to stay at CSAM indefinitely. And as for not telling you things, there's nothing to tell. I don't know that he was seeing ghosts. It doesn't make sense. We agreed all of that ended when we left Trevor Hall. That sign could mean anything. Maybe Smithy was pulling Keith's leg or manipulating Brad to take him for a walk. Remember how he used to insist he needed the bathroom when he was just tired of sitting still for his lessons?"

Jeff's teeth clenched. "So, now you agree with Piers? You think Smithy's signing doesn't mean anything?"

"No! Of course he can communicate. But maybe this time, that sign was false. I don't know what to think. I can't tell you what I don't know."

"Just talk to me from now on. Don't keep secrets." Jeff brushed past me on his way to the bedroom, slouching and exhausted. CSAM has made us too tired to even fight.

"When am I supposed to talk to you?" I asked. He was too far away to hear me. "When do we ever see each other long enough to talk?" And when we do talk, it isn't long enough to resolve anything.

Now Jeff and I are mad at each other, there's still no end in sight to our term at CSAM, and we don't know what's going on with Smithy.

I don't think I could bear to go through a repeat of Trevor Hall, not here. I can't imagine feeling so confused and frightened again when I'm already feeling so adrift and isolated. Please let this be a false alarm. Now that Smithy is finally about to get his due, please let everything go smoothly from here on!

DIARY OF RUBY DALTON

Victory today! One month into our investigation and we've already turned in a preliminary report. Brad wrote it himself. I helped him with the formatting and suggested professional jargon in place of his more casual language, but it was Brad who decided what material should be included, interpreted what it meant, and forecasted what we could expect to find next. For a first report, I thought it looked great. Jeff did, too.

 Even Man was satisfied. He didn't praise the report, of course, but he didn't trash it, either. I rushed out to show Brad and found him watering the trees.

 "He gave it back, and it's not all marked up!"

 Brad grinned and said, "Cool."

 I don't think he fully grasped the significance of what he'd achieved. I gave him a big hug and a peck on the cheek. That surprised him.

 "Did I do something really cool?" he asked.

 "You wrote your first research report, without benefit of formal schooling, and Man approved it. That's hugely cool, Brad!"

 "He was probably in too much of a hurry to rip it," he joked.

 "Don't sell yourself short," I cautioned. "This is big. You're moving up. You should be proud of yourself."

 "Hey, I had a good teacher." He slapped me on the back. "It's not like I masterminded this all by myself."

 "But you could," I told him. Brad has more talent for this work than anybody at CSAM has credited him with before. With a little more guidance, he'll be fully capable of running a study and reporting on it without my help or Jeff's.

 Then we can be out of here! I can finally move on with my life. Smithy will be safe, too: a star performer in a new study overseen by a competent and caring researcher.

 This new year is looking better than ever!

DIARY OF RUBY DALTON

April 2, 1978

I'll never be able to listen to my "Ruby Baby" record again.

˜˜˜

I hate to relive it, but I know I need to write this all down. Later, my mind will twist on itself and settle on other explanations. I need to describe what happened while it's fresh.

I had to work last night. Damn Man and damn the night shift! Brad was down with the flu, so I made the rounds and fed the animals by myself. All the exits were properly secured. I checked them myself. I spent fifteen minutes reviewing closed-circuit footage and ensured nobody else was in the building. Phil was patrolling outside, but I was on my own inside.

Or so, I'd thought.

It was a quiet night. Having already completed my major tasks, the rest of my shift unspooled before me as one long penance of silence and dark hallways. It wasn't spooky or uncomfortable. Really. It just didn't feel right that Corridor C should be so quiet, that the typewriters didn't clatter and the hall didn't echo with hushed voices and hasty footsteps. I felt lonely and dislocated. I wanted something in the background to pass the dreary hours until sunrise.

I turned on the little record player so I wouldn't feel so alone. I threw on my little 45 of "Ruby Baby," Jeff's Christmas gift from a few years ago. Its jaunty beat flooded the empty office space. The dingy lighting seemed brighter, and everything grew sharper: the music, my breathing, my high-pitched voice trying to sing the chorus. I tapped my toes along with the music and the sound reverberated from the concrete walls. How funny that I've never noticed that echo during the day!

Even though Man discourages it, I sat down in the break room with a book of my own, hoping to lose myself in another time and place, the world of My Cousin Rachel. It could be counted as sensation fiction, but there's nothing in it to derange the mind. It's a period piece, for heaven's sake! And riveting enough to command my full attention. My imagination didn't wander.

Until the shrieking erupted from the cages down the hall. It startled me, and yet I'd sensed it was coming. It was like a car horn on a foggy road. You know something big is coming, just not <u>when</u> it's coming.

This sound was like a siren. It made the hair on my arms rise. I hesitated, hoping it was a minor squabble. The apes' alarm shrilled again, and my whole body tensed. This was not a normal confrontation.

I closed my book and stopped the record, then hastened down the hall. It sounded like every ape in Corridor D was screaming, and I briefly wondered if a snake had somehow gotten into the room. Then I wondered if Smithy had pulled his old Houdini act and busted out.

I threw open the door to Corridor D, prepared to face anything. I quickly slipped inside and closed the door behind me so nothing could sneak past me into the hall. I scanned the floor for vermin, but it was bare. Then I lifted my eyes to the cages. First, I made sure the cages were locked and the occupants secure within. They were, just as they had been half an hour earlier when I'd first made my rounds. But the chimps were rattled. They shook the doors of their cages, trying to force them open. When Moses saw me, he pounded on his door with little white-knuckled fists. I looked straight into his eyes and saw them dollar-sized and dilated.

"Guys, what is it?" I shouted. I never thought they would answer. I wanted to establish some kind of order and thought the sound of my voice would be enough to do it. But I couldn't even hear myself through the din.

Violetta's cage was nearest me. She rocked back and forth rapidly like she was getting ready to launch herself into a somersault. Instead, she slammed her head roughly against the door. Hard enough to dent it out.

"Stop that!" I told her. I rattled the cage door to make her look up. Chimps' skulls are thick, but I didn't want her to hurt herself. Violetta lifted her head; I sight-checked it for blood but saw none. Her eyes were dark and glassy with fear.

I turned in a circle to see into every corner of the room, trying to find what had everyone so panicked. The room was shadowy but empty. No snakes. No chainsaw-wielding maniacs. Nothing to worry about.

"What is going on?" I shouted again, directly to Violetta this time.

She rocked back, big eyes searching my face. Then she covered her face with both hands.

I looked up at Moses's cage above her. He screamed and covered his eyes. Lowered his hands. Looked at me. Screamed again and covered his face.

My lungs squeezed and crumpled into a ball. The interior of the room felt very hot, almost humid. The air was too thick to breathe. But my skin was cold. My fingertips tingled. My lips parted, nerveless, and my jaw dropped open.

<u>One by one, every chimp began to cover its eyes.</u>

I looked for Smithy. He slumped against the front door of his cage with his head bowed. I heard him snuffling. I couldn't speak, but I rattled his cage to make him look up. He did, slowly. Like he was afraid of what he would see. Or afraid to tell me what he saw. Smithy's eyes weren't enlarged with terror like his neighbors. He looked solemn. Resigned. We stared at each other for a beat. I willed him to tell me what was going on. I wished for him to not tell me what I feared to know.

Smithy pointed behind me.

And the weak fluorescent lighting in Corridor D flickered. Went out.

The shaky moan in my ears almost dropped me to my knees, until I realized it was my own voice.

And then the lights came back on. They illuminated the chimps jumping in their cages. Ajax, Muriel, Eleanor, Moses, Violetta, and Smithy all stared at me—no, past me. All covered their eyes in tandem. All pointed.

"Black, dark," they signed.

It was just dark in the room, I reasoned. Maybe that's what they're signing about. But I looked behind me to be sure. All I saw was the door, and I ran for it, while the apes continued to sign and point.

I burst into the empty, dim hallway, restraining the urge to lock the door behind me. If something unseen was in Corridor D, I didn't want to trap the animals with it. I also forced myself to breathe deeply. I kept telling myself they were spooked about nothing. It was a coincidence. They weren't trying to warn me of anything.

While I stumbled back toward the break room, leaning against the wall to save my balance, a jaunty tune started to play.

"Ruby Baby."

The words I knew so well: "I got a girl and Ruby is her name . . . "

Words I had been singing minutes before. But I had shut off the record player!

I dragged my feet along faster, almost staggering up the hall. I half-thought somebody else might have come in while I was with the chimps, and I hadn't heard them because of the animals' awful squalling.

I teetered into the kitchen, holding my breath. Hoping. But that room was empty and still the record played.

I used to love that song. It was cute and it mentioned my name. But I mustn't have listened to it closely because I never realized before how sinister the lyrics are:

"Like a ghost, I'm gonna haunt you."

Loud and clear, I heard them at last. My stomach turned over because <u>I knew</u>.

"Gonna haunt you . . . Gonna haunt you . . . Gonna haunt you."

Over and over, it skipped.

"Haunt you . . . Haunt you . . . Haunt you . . . "

When it shouldn't even have been playing in the first place!

"Why?" I shouted.

The sour-milk-colored cabinets looked back at me, impassive. The Frigidaire chuckled.

"Why me?" But whatever was in the room didn't answer.

I looked everywhere, not wanting to see it, yet afraid because I couldn't. It could be anywhere. Sitting in the chair I had vacated. Leering from the corner by the trash bin. Right behind me.

The record jumped ahead: "From the sunny day I met ya, I made a bet that I would get ya."

"Get ya . . . Get ya . . . Get ya . . . Get ya . . . "

Tears slimed my face and I clung to the door jamb. I shut my eyes and pressed my face against the peeling paint so I wouldn't have to face my invisible stalker anymore. I wanted to cover my ears but was afraid to let go of the wall.

"Ruby . . . Ruby . . . Ruby . . . Ruby . . . Ruby . . . "

The volume soared louder. My head throbbed. I gagged and my stomach heaved but nothing came up. I thought of Wanda and what Smithy had done to her. There was a whole room full of agitated chimps down the hall. What would they do to me? I felt terrified—but also angry. After four years of wondering and worrying, I felt exhausted and fed up!

"What do you want? Why won't you leave us alone? Tell me or go away!" I yelled.

"Ruby . . . Ruby . . . Ruby . . . "

The chimps howled down the hall. My legs liquified and I began to slide down the wall. And the damn record kept skipping.

"Ruby . . . Ruby . . . Ruby. . . Ruby . . . "

"You don't belong here!" I yelled. Not at CSAM, not in this world. "Go away! Go back where you belong!" To Trevor Hall, to Hell itself; anywhere but here.

"Ruby . . . Ruby . . . "

I tried to crab-walk backward, propelling myself with my arms. Below the waist, I was dead weight. The rest of me trembled. My teeth champed down on my tongue because they chattered uncontrollably. My mouth had become a novelty toy somebody wound up and left to run. Snot touched my upper lip.

"Leave me alone! Leave!"

Clammy hands encircled my upper arms.

I howled. My body jerked and my limbs went limp. I squeezed my eyes shut. Whatever was going to happen to me, I didn't want to see it.

"Ruby! Ruby!"

It wasn't the record. It was a man's voice, distorted. The hands on my arms tightened and pulled, and I felt myself rising up. When I lifted one eyelid to peek, I saw Brad. He looked sweaty and pale, but he wasn't a ghost.

"Are you OK?" Brad asked.

It was the first time I'd seen him in days. He's largely kept to his trailer, recuperating. I sagged against Brad, and he stumbled backward, thrown off-balance by my weight and his illness. I flung my arms around him, dug my fingers into his shoulders. I needed to prove to myself that he was real, solid. Brad rallied and guided me toward the office, but my feet had given up. My body was turning into warm water, and most of it was gushing down my face. Brad leaned me against the wall outside the break room instead.

"I heard the animals screaming and knew something was wrong, so I got dressed and came over. What happened to you?" he asked.

In answer, I pointed to the record player, just in time for it to skip ahead again.

"Gonna get you sometime, Ruby!" it promised.

Brad huffed and yanked the plug out of the wall.

"It started by itself," I whispered. "I shut everything off, and I went to check the animals, and they told me—they all told me—she was there. And then—that!"

Brad pulled over a chair so I could sit down.

"Will you be OK for a moment while I look around?" His voice, hoarsened by illness, was suddenly loud, and I realized that the record wasn't the only thing to have stopped. The screeching from the kennel had ceased, too.

I nodded.

Brad squeezed my shoulder and slipped away. His footsteps receded down the hall, transmuting into voices.

"Hey, man, where'd you come from?"

"I came in the back because I heard the research subjects trying to kill each other."

Keith stuck his head around the corner. His eyebrows knitted when he saw me, then his nostrils flared, and his lips twitched in disgust.

"Jesus, Ruby, you look like shit!"

I turned my head away and wiped my nose on my sleeve. Not that I cared what Keith thought of my looks. So much the better if he was repulsed.

"It's not your night," I said to forestall him asking what had happened.

He crossed the room and took a notebook off one of the desks.

"I forgot this earlier, and I need it to finish my report for tomorrow. It's a good thing I stopped by. I had to break up a riot. Didn't you hear them?"

"I looked in . . . Did you see anything?"

"No!" he scoffed. "They were dicking around as usual. But they shut up quick enough when I showed them the cattle prod." Keith slipped into the kitchen and took a Coke from the fridge. "Did you have a power surge or something? The microwave's blinking."

I shrugged and grunted in reply.

I felt Keith's eyes carving me up, though I looked at the ground.

"Something spooked you, huh?" He stepped closer and dropped his voice. "Want me to protect you?"

So much for my shitty looks discouraging him!

Fortunately, Brad returned to report all clear.

"It's a good thing you showed up," Brad told Keith. "You can cover Ruby's shift. She's not feeling well, so she's going home."

"I've got my own work to do!" Keith protested.

"You can do it here."

Brad stayed remarkably calm through the ordeal. He called Jeff to come pick me up. Poor Jeff was still wearing his pajamas when he arrived. I didn't say a word on the drive, and he didn't ask questions, only held my hand. Once at home, I told him everything. Jeff didn't interrupt or try to rationalize my experiences.

Brad had tried to convince me the power surge reset the turntable—even though I had removed the needle—and made the record keep skipping.

"That thing's always been screwy. That's why Dr. T got rid of it," he rationalized.

Jeff held me when I cried and didn't tell me I was crazy, not even when I told him I didn't want to keep a record player in our place anymore.

"You don't ever have to listen to that record again. In fact, you don't have to listen to any records again. We'll get an eight-track player instead," he promised.

True to his word, Jeff went down to Tower Records today and came back with a used but good player.

He also came back with a 45 of "C'mon, Marianne" for the office.

"Let it mess with <u>her</u> for a change," he said.

MEMO FROM JEFF DALTON
TO MANFRED TEAGUE

April 3, 1978

Ruby is unwell and unable to work. Please apply
her three days of accrued time off. I'll also
donate to her two of my days off. Ruby will be
back to work April 8.

LETTER FROM RUBY DALTON
TO TAMMY COHEN

April 8, 1978

I returned to CSAM today. I don't know what trumped-up illness Jeff told them I had, but I could tell nobody believed him. Oh, folks were polite. Dr. T said he hoped I was feeling better, and Margo welcomed me back, but they all stared when I entered the office. When I passed Isaac in the hall, he greeted me curtly without meeting my eyes. Dr. Fairbanks looked uneasy while giving me instructions, and afterward, she hovered by my desk, watching me.

It's Keith's fault. He told everyone how awful I looked that night—like I'd seen a ghost. Then he claimed I <u>had</u> seen a ghost—the old Dark Lady from the newspaper. He must have made it a hell of a story.

Brad insists Keith is full of shit, and I got spooked by the animals' noise and the power outage. He claims it lasted longer than a little flickering—that I was actually trapped in Corridor D in the dark with shrieking apes for several minutes (though the closed-circuit footage would show otherwise if anyone looked at it). He also says I was sick.

"She must've caught the fever I had. It made me think I was seeing aliens," he said.

His ruse is double-edged. You see, to cover up potential ghostly activity, I have to become crazy.

Man cut me down. "Do you need another week at the spa to recuperate? Did you bring a note from Mommy to prove you're OK now? Are you two years old? No way in hell I'm keeping a frightened little girl who can't even work night shift on the payroll! I need pros!" Nevertheless, he's restored me to day shift, not trusting me to handle nights. I think he wants to keep me under observation.

I apologized profusely—groveled really—for causing him inconvenience and lost productivity. I assured Man I had a clean bill of health.

"_Are you cracking up? You're useless to me if you do. If you can't handle the pressure of working here, a dozen other applicants can._"

I insisted I felt no pressure, argued for the quality of my work, and left his office triumphant but still feeling beaten.

I haven't said anything about that night to anyone else, including Marianne. No one else has been crude enough to ask.

But no sooner had I returned to my seat in Corridor C after meeting with Man than Marianne dragged her chair over.

"Poor Ruby!" She patted my hand. "Five days at home. You must have been scared out of your mind! What did you see? It sounds terrifying. You know, talking about trauma can be therapeutic."

"I don't know what you mean," I dissembled. "I didn't see anything." (True enough). "I have a lot of work to catch up on. Please excuse me."

She did not. Marianne remained at my elbow, patting my shoulder and prompting me.

"Was it very big? Did it have glowing eyes? Was it someone you recognized? Did it speak to you? Did it touch you? Did it try to hurt you?" she persisted.

I refused even to deny, kept my mouth shut, and typed away.

It made me nervous to refuse Marianne. With her penchant for gossip, she might invent her own story about what had happened. If Man suspected a ghost was behind my illness, he would literally throw me out in the street.

Dr. Fairbanks saved me. Passing through on her way to her lab, she scolded Marianne.

"Leave Ruby alone. She's got a lot of work to do. Anyway, don't you have a meta-analysis to finish?"

"I'm trying to help Ruby. I want her to know I'm here for her and she can tell me anything." Marianne winked at me conspiratorially. I stared at the ribbon on my typewriter until she eased away to her own desk at last.

When I came home—alone, of course; Jeff having left for his shift—I lay down and cried. I hate being back at work (though I hated watching daytime TV at home even more), but mostly I cried because of how much I suddenly missed Eric. I kept wishing I could talk to him, not about what he saw, but about how he felt afterward. I remember how we *surrounded him at the gatehouse, joking and questioning him. I wasn't trying to upset him. I was curious. Being on the other side of things now, I feel guilty for my youthful idiocy. I'm impressed that he didn't tell us all to go to hell.*

I don't know what awaits me tomorrow. I have to be prepared for anything. No more freaking out. No more chances after this.

CLOSED-CIRCUIT FOOTAGE

Date: April 26, 1978
Location: Corridor D, Research Animal
Quarters

Marianne enters, whistling and singing under her breath. The chimps rattle their cage doors.

She calls, "All right, gang, it's feeding time."

Mr. Splitfoot hoots as she passes his cage on her way to the fridge.

Marianne says, "I'm not happy to see you, either. It's not my first choice to feed you. Brad's *busy* writing *a proposal* for a new study so he can teach you all how to talk." She laughs under her breath as she takes the food trays from the fridge. "Who knows what you'd say?"

Marianne unwraps the trays and remarks, "At least he made these up first." She sniffs one. "Nut loaf. Oh, boy. And leafy greens and pureed fruit . . . "

Marianne removes a Jell-O cup from the tray and says, "That isn't in the approved diet." She eats the Jell-O with her fingers. The chimps grunt and hiss; some reach through the cage, grasping at Marianne. She ignores them and continues to eat. The lights overhead flicker and the chimps squeal in alarm.

Marianne says, "Oh, hush! It's not the end of the world."

The chimps continue to howl and whimper. Violetta rocks back and forth. Marianne finishes her Jell-O and removes the cups from the remaining trays. She leisurely circulates around the room, distributing trays through the slots in the cages.

Marianne complains, "What babies! I guess that's what comes of Brad coddling you."

A shadow passes across the camera and obscures the image. Mr. Splitfoot howls and throws his loaf at the door of his cage; it breaks apart and spatters over the floor. Marianne whirls to look at him, then looks up at the lights and around the room.

She says, "You're not getting any dessert, so don't fuss."

She pushes a tray into Smithy's cage.

He signs, "Jell-O please. Give Jell-O Smithy."

Marianne puts her hands on her hips and says, "Don't give me any of that gibberish. I don't know what it means. Did Timmy fall in the well? Huh?"

Smithy again requests dessert. Marianne mimics the signs back to him. Smithy hits the bars in frustration.

Marianne says, "Stop that!"

The lights go out for a full five seconds and the chimps screech. When they come up, Smithy has retreated to the back of his cage and is covering his eyes.

Marianne says, "I'm not putting up with this!"

She serves the remaining trays, shoving them through the slots with more force than necessary. She returns to the table, scoops up the Jell-O cups, and puts them back in the fridge.

She says, "Those can be my midnight snack." She turns, hands on hips, to survey the chimps and asks, "Do you all have water? Are we good?"

The lights blink off and on three times rapidly. Marianne tilts her head back to look at them and says, "Then I'm out of here." She crosses to the door. It doesn't open. Marianne jiggles the handle and shoves. Nothing happens. She steps back to examine the door, then pushes her flat palms against it to shove. Her back strains against her blouse but the door doesn't move.

Behind Marianne, the lock on Mr. Splitfoot's cage pops open. The cage door swings out. The chimp leans out. Marianne grips the door handle again and presses down on it with force. She grunts and tugs, griping, "Come on, dammit!" Louder, she asks, "Is someone there? This isn't funny!"

The lock on Violetta's cage pops open, then the one on Woolly's cage, and the one on Eleanor's. Eleanor's cage door swings open with a squeak. Marianne twists around and sees the open cages. She gasps and recoils, pressing herself against the door. As she stares, aghast, the locks on the next three cages pop open, one after the other; each cage door swings out in turn. Bashful crawls to the opening of his cage and sticks his head out.

Marianne pounds rapidly on the door and cries, "Help! Help, somebody! Open this door!"

Mr. Splitfoot climbs out of his cage and stands on his hind legs, sniffing the air. He takes three steps across the floor toward Marianne. She screams loud and long, for forty-five seconds. The latch on Smithy's cage, the final cage, pops off and the door opens. Smithy is still curled up in the rear of his cage. He slowly unfurls and crawls toward the opening. He looks toward the vacant corner of the room, then swings down to the floor.

Marianne shouts, "Help me! Get me ouuuut!"

The other chimps emerge from their cages and tentatively move toward her. Mr. Splitfoot comes closest, within seven feet of her. Eleanor stands behind him. The other chimps sniff the air and look around. The lights go out. Marianne screams again.

When the lights come back on, all the chimps have advanced to within five feet of her. They stand in a semi-circle, hemming her against the door, which she continues to pound and kick. Marianne looks toward the cattle prod mounted on the far wall. Her lips peel back to show her gritted teeth and she stretches toward the prod. Her feet begin to slide in its direction. Mr. Splitfoot steps closer and Marianne freezes. She pulls back, eyeing him. He steps back and Marianne lunges toward the cattle prod. Immediately, Mr. Splitfoot blocks her, growling. Marianne withdraws, raising an arm to block her face. The two remain in a stand-off for several seconds.

Marianne feints to the left, but Mr. Splitfoot isn't fooled.

She looks at all the chimps between herself and the wall and bows her head. Marianne crouches against the door, her shoulder pressed to the wood, but never takes her eyes off the chimps or completely turns her back on them. Marianne rams the door with her shoulder and chops at the handle with her free hand.

She yells, "Let me ouuutt! Brad! Dammit, Brad, answer me!"

The chimps move closer, tightening their circle. Mr. Splitfoot knuckle-walks until he is about three feet from her, then leans back on his haunches. Marianne looks over at the closed-circuit camera, gnashing her teeth. She starts to hyperventilate. The lights flicker.

Marianne exclaims, "No!"

The lights turn bright again. Mr. Splitfoot rocks back and forth, watching Marianne. Woolly draws even with him, sniffing and chuffing.

Marianne gestures to the fridge behind them and says, "Your food's in the fridge. You want your Jell-O? Take it, dammit! It's in there! All the Jell-O you want! Go on!"

The chimps don't move. Gef sniffs the floor.
He looks to the corner, then stretches forward,
still sniffing. He reaches for Marianne's shoe. She
recoils.

Marianne yells, "Stop that! Man will be here
any minute. You hear me? He'll beat you! He'll
sting you with the big stick." She points to the
wall, then points to the row of cages and orders,
"Get back in your cages!" Her voice cracks on the
last word and she wipes her nose. "I mean it! Man
will be angry. He'll hurt you! Go back now!"

Gef looks at Woolly. Woolly grunts and stretches
out as if to lie down for a nap. Gef looks back
at Marianne. None of the chimps respond to her
threats. She starts to moan. Smithy rises on two
legs and walks up to her, passing the boundary of
the circle.

Marianne shrieks, "Not you!"

She takes off her shoe and throws it at him;
the shoe flies over his shoulder and bounces off
Violetta's foot. Wailing, Marianne finally turns
her back to the chimps and punches the door like
a prize-fighter. She screams. Mr. Splitfoot gets
to his feet; he and the remaining chimps rush at
Marianne.

Woolly leaps onto her back. Marianne staggers
away from the door and spins around to throw
him off. The circle of chimps moves with her,
surrounding her. She trips over Eleanor and
stumbles. Marianne gropes to catch the wall and
her chin hits the edge of the serving table.
Blood gushes down her chin and Marianne moans.
Eleanor seizes Marianne's leg and bites into her
calf. Marianne howls in pain.

Mr. Splitfoot leaps onto her shoulder and
grips her hair in both hands. He pulls it first
in one direction, then in another, like a rider
with a horse's bridle, forcing her head to turn.
Marianne thrusts her arm backward to brush him

and Woolly off. Woolly drops but Gef jumps up and hangs on to the end of her arm like he's preparing to do a chin lift. Mr. Splitfoot clambers up to sit on her neck, forcing Marianne's head down.

One by one, all the chimps but Smithy pile on her. They pull Marianne to the ground. Still wailing and howling, Marianne covers her eyes with her free arm. The chimps swarm over her, howling; Marianne wails. Smithy stays back, watching. He jumps up and down, shrieking in shrill, short blasts. It sounds like laughter. Smithy looks at the camera, teeth bared, then leaps into the fray. He grabs the back of Marianne's shirt and rips it down the middle. He tears at her jeans with his teeth.

The door to Corridor D opens and Brad enters the room. He sees Marianne and the chimps and exclaims, "Oh, shit!" He rushes to her, shooing the chimps away. They scatter immediately. Mr. Splitfoot and Smithy jump onto the table. Violetta runs to her cage and climbs into it. The other chimps back away, deeper into Corridor D; none bolt for the door. Brad kneels beside Marianne, who has now gone quiet. His back is to the camera as he examines her.

The image cuts off.

LETTER FROM RUBY DALTON
TO TAMMY STEINMETZ

May 7, 1978

Dear Tammy,
Maybe I should be grateful I wasn't targeted this time, but all I feel is dread. I don't know if you've heard of this yet . . .

"TERROR AT CSAM: HOW I ESCAPED AN ANGRY GHOST AND A ROOMFUL OF POSSESSED APES"

by Gary Wainwright
Fresno Post, May 7, 1978

"I'm lucky to be alive." Marianne Foster's hands tremble as they close around her teacup. She reclines on an overstuffed sofa in her cozy apartment with a view of the Fresno State water tower in the distance. The gloaming of late afternoon casts soft shadows over her face. But the memory of another, more virulent shadow, haunts her still.

Miss Foster is a researcher at the Center for the Scientific Advancement of Man (CSAM). On the night of April 26, as she performed her routine check of the research animals' food and water, she became trapped in a nightmare.

As she prepared to leave, the door connecting the kennel and the corridor slammed shut. "At first, I thought the wind had blown it," she says. "Then, when I couldn't get the door open, I thought maybe a coworker was holding it shut as a prank. The janitor lives on campus and comes and goes all the time."

Though the door failed to budge, the animals' cages—which Miss Foster had verified were secure moments before—inexplicably popped open. "One after the other, I saw the locks give way and the doors swing open by themselves. I was petrified. I couldn't explain what I was seeing, and I feared for my safety. You don't want to be locked in a room where you're vulnerable to chimpanzees. Their strength is inhuman. Some of them went after [Dr. Manfred Teague, head researcher at CSAM] once, and he only managed to save himself because he had a cattle prod. I was utterly defenseless."

As Miss Foster crouched against the stubborn door, screaming for help, the chimpanzees leapt free of their cages and advanced on her, cornering her. Then, she says, she heard a voice shout, "Kill her!"

"I didn't recognize the voice at all. It sounded distorted, almost like it was from a bad drive-in movie speaker."

When she looked around the room, Miss Foster saw she was not alone with the chimpanzees after all. A dark figure stood opposite her, blocking the emergency cattle prod mounted on the wall. Miss Foster estimates the intruder stood at least six feet tall, though it was hard to tell because the figure didn't actually *stand*.

"It hovered above the ground," she reports. "I saw a shadow on the wall, but I didn't see anything below it. Higher up, I saw red eyes. At first, I thought I was seeing smoke and fire. Then the shadow reached out for me. I felt my body turn to ice. The darkness stretched across the room, and I heard it speak again."

The shadow ordered, "Kill her now!" As if on cue, the chimps snarled and clustered about the frightened researcher.

"I thought I was a goner. We had a dozen chimps on Corridor D at the time. One of them had mutilated a caretaker before coming to CSAM." Miss Foster is speaking of Smithy, once renowned as the world's smartest chimp and the subject of Piers Preis-Herald's famous primate language study.

In a 1976 article, *The Newport Daily News* linked Smithy to a legendary local ghost, the Dark Lady of Trevor Hall, whom Preis-Herald's students alleged was communicating with the chimp. Staring across the room at her tormentor, Miss Foster says she realized the Dark Lady had followed the chimp to CSAM.

"I was afraid to look away. I thought if I lowered my eyes, I would seem submissive, and the apes would finish me. But I knew I was close to dead, anyway. In each of their eyes, I saw that same unholy fire. *She* was directing them! I called for help and pounded on the door and prayed for somebody to hear me and let me out before it was too late."

The chimps ringed Miss Foster, pressing close enough to scald her skin with their stinking breath. Then, she says the darkness overtook her.

"I fainted," she admits, lowering her clear hazel eyes in girlish embarrassment.

Fortunately, she was rescued before the deranged chimps could harm her. Seeing the closed-circuit security footage, the janitor realized she was in danger and freed her from her prison. Upon regaining consciousness, Miss Foster went to the hospital for examination, then went home to count her blessings. She escaped her ordeal with various bites, scratches, bruises, and a split lip.

"I wasn't her first victim," she acknowledges. "Two weeks ago, the same thing nearly happened to my colleague, Ruby Dalton."

Dalton was monitoring the chimps during a late-night shift. "The lights went out. Ruby realized something was wrong and managed to escape from the room before the door locked, but she didn't get away. The ghost started calling her name, and when she reached the break room, it was waiting to meet her. A figure in black with skeletal arms reached for her."

Like Miss Foster, Dalton was saved by a coworker's unexpected arrival, and the evil spirit vanished. However, she was so distressed by her encounter that she didn't return to work for a week.

Miss Foster bravely asserts she is ready to face her demon. "I won't let it drive me away from my career. I don't know what it wants, but it won't have the satisfaction of seeing me run." She plans to return to the spiritual battlefield tomorrow.

Foster alluded to other supernatural activity during Smithy's time at the facility. However, no members of the facility have been reached for comment.

LETTER FROM RUBY DALTON
TO TAMMY STEINMETZ

(CONTINUED)

May 7, 1978

. . . I doubt this hack even <u>tried</u> to contact anybody at the facility!

By the time I got to the end of this piece of work, I was completely aghast. Immediately, I feared for Smithy. Then I feared for my job. I decided to be pro-active and go to Man right away. I called the office, but he wasn't in. Instead, I left a message on his answering machine, a rambling self-exonerating screed:

"Man, I want you to know I had nothing to do with this article in the <u>Post</u>! I had no idea Marianne was planning to talk to them. I never collaborated with her, and I certainly never told her any of the things she's claiming. I never saw or spoke to any ghosts. It's preposterous to believe the lab is haunted. I'm so outraged I can barely talk. I think I should sue her for libel. Please give me a call when you get this."

I considered going to CSAM to talk to Man in person but worried that if he didn't get my message (or didn't believe it), seeing me unexpectedly might infuriate him so much that he would fire me on the spot. Instead, I paced the apartment uneasily, stopping to reread the article the way I used to compulsively pick at scabs when I was a kid, knowing it would make things worse but unable to help myself.

The phone finally rang after about two hours. I answered it in a small voice.

"If I find out you're lying to me, I'll kill you."

Hearing that made me feel better. It implied he intended to keep me around long enough to kill me.

I assured Man the story was a nasty shock to me, as I was sure it had been for him.

"Janet says you never said a damn thing about any ghosts and that you asked Keith not to joke about them. I think it's damn strange you brought this ***** chimp into my facility and all these ghost stories came with him, yet you've never said or seen anything. Maybe you're just smart enough to keep your mouth shut.

"As for Marianne, I never thought she would stoop to this. I thought she was loyal! Here, I thought she was contributing to the organization, and then she goes and pulls this shit! After I gave her a shot! Never had a skirt running numbers before. Never thought one could do it. I trusted her. I gave her a position, and she made an ass out of me in bold print! She never could keep her mouth shut. Always wanted attention. Can't get a man to look at her, so she goes crying to a tabloid rag!"

He emitted a string of curses. I kept my mouth shut and let him go on.

"She's out! She's never coming back! I went through every desk until I found all the junk she'd left behind and I burned it in the parking lot. I took her name off every piece this office has going to print. No scandal-monger's going to f* * * up our research. She's a f* * *ing nutcase."

I listened to him abuse Marianne for another fifteen minutes, cooing in approval until Man wound down, threatened me again, ordered me to be in the office by 7:00 a.m., and hung up. I felt relieved to have been spared. For all that I whine about my job, I need it. Besides, CSAM may be a nicer place without Marianne.

For once, I share Man's views. I can't imagine what could have motivated Marianne to throw away her career and her credibility. Did she want her name in the paper that badly? Could she have experienced anything like what this reporter described? I know the things she said about me didn't happen—but part of that story was true. Is Marianne's story exaggerated or completely made-up?

Man says she was careless and left the cage doors ajar. He's blasting everything Marianne ever did. I could accept that maybe she didn't close one or two all the way, but _every_ cage? Feeding the animals wasn't her typical assignment, so it's barely possible she jostled the locks while distributing trays without realizing it. Or maybe Smithy finally figured out how to pick the locks and taught the others to do it the same way he's taught them to sign. The cages opened somehow, and it couldn't have happened by magic.

Brad says Marianne was a mess when he found her. Her clothes were torn off (even her underwear). She couldn't even talk at first, only grunted, and with all the blood running down her chin, "I thought . . . like, one of them had torn her tongue out or something," he confided with a shudder and a whisper.

Hysteria from the shock of the attack? From a haunting?

Whatever! She's gone from my life now and good riddance!

UNEDITED INTERVIEW
WITH ISAAC MORGAN
CIRCA 1991

I remember one specific afternoon. I was reviewing closed-circuit video with Jeff Dalton. We were supposed to pick out footage to put in a reel for donors, something we would send around to different organizations to show the type of work we performed at CSAM.

We were looking at a video of Smithy. I thought it was odd, because in this video, he wasn't participating in an experiment. There was no one in the shot with him. The chimp was by himself in an empty lab. I don't even remember why. Maybe the researcher had stepped out of the room, or maybe we were supposed to investigate Smithy's behavior when no one was watching him.

Anyway, in this surveillance video, Smithy was walking around the room, faster and faster. Jeff said, "He looks worried." Then Smithy picked up a tennis ball and started bouncing it, just playing like he was bored, y'know? Then he threw the ball. It bounced off-screen and bounced back to him. He did this a few times, throwing the ball and chasing it when it came back to him.

I was going to suggest we skip ahead. I didn't see anything of interest to science here, y'know? And then I saw Jeff's face. He was white. You always hear people say that, but this was the first time I'd seen what they meant. You could see all the little veins underneath his skin like ruled lines on white paper. He started muttering to himself: "No, no, no. Oh, shit!"

I said, "Jeff, what is it?" He didn't hear me
at first, just kept muttering and rubbing his
face. He ran his hands up and down, rubbing his
face from brow to chin, stretching out his skin.
The whole time, he kept looking at the video.
Finally, I waved my hand in front of his face and
asked him what was the matter.

"Look at that ball," he said. "The trajectory's
all wrong. See the angle when it comes back to
Smithy? If he was bouncing it off the wall, it
would fall and then bounce up again. It's not.
It's following a high arc. Almost like someone is
throwing it back to him!"

Now, I don't know physics. I couldn't see
anything unusual about the ball in that film. But
I saw the look on Jeff's face. I mean, this guy
finished graduate school, for crying out loud! He
was about six years older than me. He had tons of
experience. And he was terrified!

That did it for me. I gave my notice that same
afternoon, and that Sunday, I went to church for
the first time in eighteen years.

LETTER FROM RUBY DALTON
TO TAMMY STEINMETZ

May 24, 1978

. . . The turnover continues. Margo's quit. I didn't hear that she gave a reason, just took her snacks out of the fridge and left. She didn't say good-bye. Isaac left two days ago under a bigger cloud. Brad says he was acting squirrelly; he thinks Isaac saw something. Before I clocked out today, Brad also confided he's seen brochures on Dr. Torrance's desk for facilities in San Francisco and Sacramento. It looks like he's about to jump ship, too.

Two potential new hires were on site today. May Grier is a transplant from back East and a pleasant, quiet girl. Ross Kalanjian is trying to gain experience before applying to graduate school. He's supposed to be a top-flight mathematician, so I think he's a shoo-in. Neither of them asked about the ghosts, not even informally when they came in to chat with us during our break. Still, I don't see how they could not have heard the recent news about our organization.

Man pulled his classified ads from the local papers because only cranks and "spooky people" were calling.

I forget who said there's no such thing as bad publicity, but I suspect he was referring to Hollywood instead of academia. The shadow of a specter, even in a single report from one disgruntled employee, has darkened our reputation. Man nearly brought down the roof on Monday when he found out we didn't get the memory drug study he's been courting all quarter. He's convinced it's because of Marianne, so now he's preparing a loss-of-revenue/libel suit against her.

I almost feel sorry for her. I'd rather have an angry ghost after me than Man and his lawyers.

"He's losing control," Jeff said when I described the goings-on at the lab. His voice was a blend of awe and disbelief; I couldn't decide whether he was happy about the situation or not.

Maybe <u>this</u> is the worst revenge the ghost could take on Man. My fantasies of causing him to lose a limb pale next to him losing his authority and his ability to direct what happens around him.

WHISPERS IN THE DARK

Broadcast Date: June 3, 1978

Celia: "'She stood in front of my window. The streetlights outside normally shine into my apartment, and I could see the glow bending around her. She was diverting it, like a black hole in space twisting the path of light. And like a black hole, she was sucking all the warmth out of the room. I felt as if an industrial freezer had opened up across the room.' The solid black shadow of a female figure in a flowing gown called her name, but Miss Foster only heard the sound in her head and not in the room. 'It was distorted, like a radio that isn't properly tuned but filled with static. I thought my head would explode.'"

God, that makes my skin crawl, but I'm loving it!

"She felt faint. Coming to, she was shocked to see the specter had crossed the room and was right in front of her.

'I saw her eyes flare up like the pilot light kindling on a stove,' she said. 'I heard my name, Marianne, in that alien static—and then I felt her touch me!' Miss Foster says she felt a searing chill in her arm, 'like a dog with teeth of liquid nitrogen gnawing though my blood and bones.' The pain was so severe it knocked her to her knees."

I feel like I should be sitting in front of a campfire with you all gathered around me roasting marshmallows. Get this: "There is a burn mark around her left bicep. Approximately four-inches long and two-and-a-half-inches wide, it glows a painful pink against the skin on Miss Foster's arm, where she claims the ghost touched her. The injury was diagnosed as a first-degree burn at the infirmary Miss Foster visited."

Can you believe this story? It sounds like a paperback novel but it's in the *Post*. And there's physical evidence! What is up? Yes, you're on.

Caller 1: That girl needs to have her house blessed, fast, before the demon possesses her.

Celia: You think it's a demon, not a ghost?

Caller 1: It's all the same. Demons, spirits—if it doesn't come from God, it's of the Devil.

Celia: I've heard that said, but some might disagree. Caller 2, what's your diagnosis?

Caller 2: That chick needs to get laid! That'll get it out of her system!

Boisterous male laughter rises in the background.

Celia: Did you know, another term for exorcism is 'to lay the ghost'? I know you're talking about laying the *target* of the ghost, but still . . .

More hooting and cheering in the background.

Celia: Anyway, thanks for the tip. Caller 3, what have you got?

Caller 3: It's those damn monkeys' fault. They should all be destroyed.

LETTER FROM RUBY DALTON
TO TAMMY STEINMETZ

June 4, 1978

. . . *Nothing like* that *ever happened to any of us, and thank God for it! As far as I know, the ghost never spoke to Eric or Gail, nor touched them. Why should it start now?*

This account is violent and frightening. I haven't spoken to Marianne about it, and I'm not sure I want to. My dislike of her battles with my impulse to reach out. Anxiety and curiosity have pushed out all normal thoughts since I read the damned article. Even though the accompanying photo is only in B&W, that mark still looks nasty.

Jeff isn't spooked. He's thrilled. When I gave him the story to read, he actually laughed. I was disgusted. "How can you be happy about this, Jeff? I don't like her, either, but I wouldn't wish this torment on anyone."

Jeff took me in his arms and started rubbing my shoulders. He hasn't been that affectionate in, well, months. "Baby, don't you see?" He beamed down at me. "This is the best news ever! If that bitch has fixated on Marianne, then we're *off the hook. All of us! You, me, Smithy." Jeff smooched me enthusiastically.*

I hadn't thought of it that way. The idea opens up many more frightening possibilities.

Given: The ghost is mobile. Therefore, it could return to CSAM whenever it wants. And target one of us.

Given: It can physically direct its malevolence. No more hiding silverware; it's leaving marks and might actually harm, not merely spook, anyone who sees it.

Given: It's stronger than I ever thought possible.

I felt lucky to get away when I did. What if I didn't though? What if it hurts me next?

"ANOTHER ATTACK: 'DARK LADY' NEARLY KILLS MARIANNE FOSTER"

by Gary Wainwright
Fresno Post, June 20, 1978

More mayhem occurred this morning at the seemingly placid residence on Maple Street. Again, Marianne Foster barely escaped with her life.

The ex-statistician from CSAM says a malevolent specter in the shape of a woman, once known as the Dark Lady of Trevor Hall, has materialized to her twice in two weeks and unleashed sinister attacks. Further, Miss Foster is plagued by frightening nightmares.

"In every dream, I'm falling. I can still recall the sensation of my stomach plummeting and my legs kicking desperately in the air as I drop. I remember seeing the sky and trying to touch it, but everything was spinning much too fast. I heard a crunch, and darkness overtook me."

According to Newport legend, a servant once fell to her death from atop Trevor Hall; her ghost is believed to be the 'Dark Lady.'

"I think she was communicating to me about her final moments, wanting me to see in my dreams how terrifying it was to die," Miss Foster says. "Then she decided to show me firsthand."

After one such brutal dream, Miss Foster awoke in a cold sweat.

"I dug my fingers into the sheets to prove to myself I was still alive and in a safe place." Unfortunately, her own bed was not safe enough.

"I couldn't breathe," she recalls with a shudder. "I thought at first I was having an anxiety attack, but there was a literal weight on my chest. I tried to lift my head. I saw only darkness—then those red eyes flaring in the night."

Miss Foster says the ghost put chilly hands around her throat and began to squeeze relentlessly.

"My vision was fading. I felt like my head was going to explode. I started flailing, trying to fend her away."

Through clouds of death filling her head in place of oxygen, an idea came to her.

"Ever since this nightmare started, I've begun to read the Bible, and I keep a rosary by my bed. It makes me feel safer." Miss Foster reached for that rosary and prayed it would indeed save her.

"As soon as I touched it, I felt free! The pain in my throat stopped. I heard a fearful shriek—almost like a car accident with metal screeching against metal—then I felt the weight on top of me dissolve." The darkness dissolved, too, she says, and in the ambient light filtering into her room, Miss Foster's vision of death had departed, fiery eyes and all.

She turned on all the lights, said a prayer of thanks, and then summoned this reporter to hear her story while the details remained fresh. At the culmination of the interview, Miss Foster gently rolled down the high turtleneck collar of her sweater to reveal livid bruises encircling her throat.

"She meant to kill me. I don't know why. Perhaps she feels threatened by me telling my story. But if she would only leave me alone, I would have nothing to tell."

Despite the frightening attack, Miss Foster refuses to leave her home. "She followed Smithy from the Atlantic coast. She followed me from the laboratory. She could follow me to a hotel or any other place I might go." Instead, she will arrange for a priest to bless the apartment, making it inhospitable to the spirit.

Miss Foster takes comfort from the many cards and letters of support she has received since first sharing her ordeal. She admits—with a blush—that some correspondents take an inappropriate interest in her situation.

"I've received a few offers to keep the ghost away by keeping me company at night," she says.

By and large though, her audience has been generous and offers prayers and good wishes to carry her through the dark nights.

With God's help and readers' support, Miss Foster hopes to withstand any more dark surprises.

LETTER FROM RUBY DALTON
TO TAMMY STEINMETZ

June 21, 1978

. . . Now she's trying to kill Marianne, though she's taking her time about it, compared to what she inflicted on Gail and Wanda. Maybe it's harder to pull off her schemes without Smithy's help.

Even Jeff is uneasy now. So much so, I figured something bad had happened.

He didn't want to tell me about it at first, but he saw something on one of the security cameras recently. Isaac saw it, too, and right afterward, he resigned. Jeff's no longer smug because it looks like the Dark Woman may still be around. (Can she be in two places at once? At CSAM by day and Marianne's place by night?)

Ross has already quit. Insert as many four-letter words as you know to get a feel of what Man's reaction was.

Normally, we would dip into the college pool to replenish our ranks, but Man feels that "Marianne's pissed in the pool." Now he's advertising in other markets—Los Angeles, San Francisco, even Portland and Seattle—to bring in "clean minds." It will take longer to find help, but he'll get the kind that won't have seen these news articles.

Hundreds of people <u>have</u> read them, though. I know because Man has punished Jeff and me for our association with Smithy by condemning us to answer the phones. We've received 234 calls by last count! I can hardly keep up with the flood of spiritualists, ufologists, Scientologists, giggly schoolchildren, and perverts. We still occasionally get a request for our literature or an intelligent inquiry about previously published research, but you can tell when somebody is fishing.

I haven't been allowed to see Smithy since Marianne's second article came out. Man removed him from the subject pool, groundlessly. Smithy hasn't caused any mischief. No more than the other thirteen chimps who jumped Marianne. For now, Smithy's housed outside where Brad keeps an eye on him. Yet, if the calls cross a certain threshold or if anything happens on site (God forbid anyone gets hurt!), I fear Smithy's days will be abruptly shortened.

Maybe I should carry a rosary of my own. I know Marianne wasn't Catholic when she worked here because she asked me a lot of insensitive questions about "worshipping idols" when I first started, but if foxholes can convert atheists, the Dark Lady would surely do for her.

I'd appreciate anything you can do for us: light a candle, say a prayer, talk some sense into me. I promise that once things settle down (may it be soon!), I will come out to visit and clear my head. And to meet Herschel at last! Please send me some good news so I can have something else to think about.

Hugs,
Ruby

"DARK LADY CASTS LONG SHADOW"

by Patricia Hartigan-Palmer
The Newport Daily News, July 5, 1978

Recent reports from the *Fresno Post* describe a
series of terrifying encounters between a phantom
woman in black and a young lady employed by the
Center for the Scientific Advancement of Man
(CSAM), the research center where Webster (AKA
"Smithy") was relocated following the dissolution
of the Preis-Herald language study, which ran at
Trevor Hall from 1974-1975.

Marianne Foyster (sic) claims to have been
ambushed in her home, physically assaulted by
animal proxies, and even touched by the icy hand
of death itself. The first attack occurred in
CSAM's chimpanzee enclosure. Later, the spirit
manifested in her home.

Has the Dark Lady of Trevor Hall decided to
become a California girl? Salvatore and Regina
Scolari, who have occupied Trevor Hall since
December, deny having experienced anything ghostly
whatsoever during their tenure and declined
further comment on the story.

Watch these pages for further updates!

LETTER FROM TAMMY STEINMETZ
TO RUBY DALTON

July 8, 1978

Ruby dear,

Never mind waiting for things to settle down—get out of there now! I feel like a moviegoer shouting at the screen when the ingenue goes up the dark stairs to check on 'that noise.' Though I don't think you're in danger (from the ghost, anyway), you could be setting yourself up for a nasty breakdown. Jeff, too.

Take yourselves back to San Jose for a weekend. Or go down to Hollywood at long last. If Man is as hard up for good help as you seem to think, he won't fire you for taking some well-deserved time off.

News of Marianne and the ghost has reached the East Coast. I'm enclosing a tidbit from The Newport Daily News; I subscribe to my own copy now. It doesn't sound alarmist, but I wouldn't be surprised to see more letters trickling in to the editor. I've already told Hersch if any reporters call for my side of the story, he's to tell them I've gone to Tibet to seek the meaning of life and won't be back for decades.

Who gave Gary Wainwright a job? Is he a journalist or a frustrated romance novelist? More disturbing to me than the details of the Dark Lady are his descriptions of Marianne. He makes her sound like a Gothic heroine: "Delicate throat, clear hazel eyes." What does any of that have to do with reporting the facts of a story?

One other thing struck me apart from the indigo prose. Marianne's account of how she fended off the ghost reminds me of one of the anecdotes we heard about a student at the boarding school who was being strangled by the ghost; when she touched the Bible on her nightstand, the spirit vanished. Now, the Dark Lady could be something demonic, in which case holy symbols may repel it, but the story in your paper sounds almost word for word like that other story, even to the fact that the throttling occurred while the victim was asleep. As I read it, I felt déjà vu. I waited for a Bible to appear. A rosary will do in a pinch, I suppose.

I don't mean to sound cynical, but if you had been through a life-threatening encounter with the supernatural, would your first instinct be to phone a reporter? Not a friend, or even a long-distance relative? How unpopular is this girl?

I'm sorry, Ruby. I don't mean to be flippant. It's probably easier for me to see these things because I'm far away from the fuss. And I've never encountered the Dark Lady where I am. All more reason for you to visit us.

I know you don't like when I intellectualize, so I'll stop being a dispassionate observer now and tell you how concerned I am for you. I want to know you're OK, better still that you're happy. If anything happens to you, let me know immediately. Reverse the charges.

Now get some rest and don't let Marianne trouble you anymore.

Love,
Tammy

"THEY WERE ALL OVER ME!" FOSTER MAULED BY DEMON CHIMPS

by Gary Wainwright
Fresno Post, July 17, 1978

"They burn. I can't sleep—the pain is too great—and every time I close my eyes, I worry they'll come back and I won't be able to fight them off." Marianne Foster's normally mellifluous voice is flat, drained of all hope, humor, and even fear as she relates her latest horror story.

The living nightmare that has plagued her since she was attacked in her workplace, the CSAM chimp quarters, has finally overwhelmed her sensibilities. Miss Foster has gone numb. Psychologists say this is one of the first symptoms of the syndrome known as Combat Stress Reaction. Formerly called "shell shock," it is common among soldiers.

Miss Foster has been living in a spiritual and mental war zone for weeks. The latest battle has left scars. As she rolls back her sleeves, red and purple ovals scream against her pale skin like the kiss of a branding iron. Some of the sores still ooze. Day and night, they burn, forcing her to relive the original moments of anguish.

At approximately 4:25 on Sunday afternoon, Miss Foster came home from running errands. No sooner had she entered her apartment and closed the door behind her than she was "ambushed," as she tells it. A powerful force slammed into her from behind, knocking her to the floor on her stomach.

"I thought it was an intruder. Even after everything I've been through, my mind still sought a reasonable explanation." As Miss Foster rolled over to better see who had assaulted her, she was shaken to see nobody in the room.

But she could hear them.

"A roar like a rockslide ricocheted off the walls and then it turned into a barrage of shrieks and howls." From her years at CSAM, Marianne recognized the vocalizations of chimpanzees.

It was then that a phantom army of apes descended on her. Miss Foster cringed under the weight, arms, and teeth of a dozen invisible creatures. She curled into a ball to defend herself, but the blows came from all directions. Invisible mouths locked on to her arms, ankles, and legs. Claws raked her chest and stomach. She watched her own blood flow.

"I couldn't see anything except wounds erupting all over my body, but I knew these were the same chimps that had tried to kill me at the office. They had come to my apartment to finish the job. Their spirits did, anyway."

In Salem Village during the infamous witch trials, victimized girls claimed that witches sent their astral bodies in the form of animals to pinch and bite them. These animal familiars acted as extensions of the witch, carrying out her dastardly vengeance. Miss Foster believes the ghostly chimps that raked her flesh were projections of animals in the thrall of the Dark Lady.

Miss Foster tried to drive the ghosts back by praying aloud, but the holy words had no effect. "They were too strong for me; too vicious!"

The assault lasted nearly ten minutes. "I'd left my rosary in my room. I hadn't thought I would need it at the market. I wish I'd thought to drop it in my purse. It was in a room merely twenty feet away, and I was powerless to get it."

Finally, when she was on the verge of losing consciousness, she sensed a weight lifting, and her tormentors evaporated.

"They must have thought I was dead. *I* did." Miss Foster struggled to her feet and to the bathroom where she evaluated the damage. Bleeding, suppurating gashes covered her limbs, and bruises and cuts peppered her torso. Miss Foster sustained especially severe damage to her arms because she covered her face and so was mercifully spared any facial disfigurement.

The phantom teeth penetrated deep enough that Miss Foster knew she would need medical attention. Unable to drive in her condition, and fearing the attention an ambulance would draw, she called this reporter for help, and I drove her to the nearest practitioner.

There, her wounds were cleaned and scoured with antibacterial solution, then bandaged. Miss Foster was given antibiotics.

"Fortunately," she jokes, "my shots were up to date." Though who knows what protection human medicine can provide against the supernatural?

In addition to performing first aid, the medical specialist photographed the bite marks; the indentations of the teeth are clearly visible in the photos above. Furthermore, samples were collected of the damaged tissue and of the substance oozing therefrom.

LETTER FROM RUBY DALTON
TO TAMMY STEINMETZ

July 20, 1978

. . . *This time, Wainwright held a press conference. He stood in front of Marianne's apartment complex and waved a little vial over his head. He insisted this was ectoplasm, proof that Marianne's attackers came from a world beyond. He spoke as if her story were accepted fact, as if everybody assembled knew ghosts and demons were to blame.*

I know scientists have been studying ESP for years, but do any of them think there are demons in this world or any other? Demons are the stuff of religion. To prove a demon would be to prove that other things in the Bible may be true, too, and I don't think humankind is ready for that. What would the Buddhists say, for instance? These are questions of faith. You can't touch faith.

Despite her pretensions to religious faith, Marianne is not preaching God's love. Her mouthpiece is calling for publicity. I don't know what Wainwright thinks that little vial can prove.

One can believe Marianne's stories or not. She looks pretty bad. Those photos are bites, without question. You can't say she made them up. Where did they come from, though? That's what all of Fresno—and possibly the world—is clamoring to know.

We had so many calls after that broadcast, twice as many as what we've gotten since this nightmare began. People want to know if Smithy is in his cage. Was he in his cage at the time of the attack? Did his astral doppelganger show up on our security cameras? Would we consider putting him in a Faraday cage? Or a lead-lined vault? Or a magic circle of salt? Why don't we just shoot him with a silver bullet?

We've had to hire additional security guards because of questions like that. All chimps have been moved indoors, lest any nut snipe at them. Corridor D is crowded, noisy, and noisome now. If this is what Marianne heard when she was attacked, then she must have been eavesdropping on the forces of hell.

If the stuff in the vial should turn out to be chimp saliva, Smithy's saliva, then I suppose she could have collected the samples beforehand. Although Marianne never had much contact with Smithy. Not close contact anyway, like Brad or I have had.

If the analysis comes back inconclusive, it could be just as bad. People will be free to speculate because the door will still be open a crack. The press will say what they like about Smithy, and the rest of the world will whisper about him. And God knows what Man will do to him.

Already he's preemptively punishing Smithy for crimes yet to be attributed to him. Smithy's back in solitary confinement. Given the crowded conditions in the main housing, it might be sensible to spread the population into "Corridor F," but no! Man would rather keep that dark room empty so Smithy can stew and wonder what he's done to deserve this treatment.

Brad and Jeff are livid. Brad appealed to Man's pragmatism by arguing this will derail any wide-scale language progress. Man told him to try out the other chimps and prove he knows what he's doing.

Then, Brad appealed to Man's sense of self-preservation and argued that, by keeping Smithy locked up, we're implying something is wrong with him. Therefore, we risk attracting more attention and publicity. To which Man replied, "Who cares what the f**k they think? Let 'em think what they want. They do already."

At last, Brad tried to draw on Man's nonexistent sense of fair play, observing that Smithy's behavior within the facility has been normal, unobjectionable. He's done nothing to deserve exile. I drafted a memo following your line of reasoning on the futility of punishment, and Jeff presented it at their meeting. Smithy isn't behaving badly now, "but if he sees he's going to get screwed over either way," Jeff appended, "he may become surly and oppositional."

Demonstrating he doesn't give a shit, Man cut Brad and Jeff's salaries for insubordination. Maybe he was hoping they'd get fed up and quit, though that would be counterproductive considering he's struggling to find good help in the wake of this scandal (I heard someone on the radio call it the 'Reign of Terror'). But nobody ever accused Man of letting logic overrule passion.

Now I'm scared to open my mouth. One of us needs a full paycheck. Jeff curses a blue streak and wishes for Man to get hit by a tanker truck. I still don't talk much to Brad, but when I see him around, he looks stressed. He was always so mellow before. I know he worries more about Smithy than about losing money. I'd like to offer a kind word of support, but I don't want Brad to read too much into it.

Keith is Smithy's primary caretaker now, so there's no chance of stealing a visit or asking him for favors. He's apt to ask them in return.

We all of us wonder when the next crisis will take place and what new, spectacular terrors will unfold. Jeff wishes the ghost would hurry up and kill Marianne. "Then, maybe it can go back to wherever it came from."

Or move to a new target. I thought it, but feared saying so aloud would make it true.

I dreamed last night that I was being chased through the halls of CSAM by something I didn't dare look back to see. As I ran, the corridors turned into the hallways of Trevor Hall. In my dream logic, I knew the only surefire way to escape the monster was to jump off the roof.

Is that an expression of fear or a premonition?

"FOSTER PHANTOM A FRAUD!"

by Gordon Daviot
The Daily Collegian, August 17, 1978

A ghostly reign of terror abruptly ended when the "Dark Lady," which has allegedly been haunting a local woman, Marianne Foster, for three months, was exposed as a fraud and a figment of Foster's imagination.

Spectral evidence has been suspect for over two hundred years. While challenging Foster's subjective experiences would be a non-starter, indirect methods soon undermined her claims. After reviewing the shocking reports of spooky harassment detailed in the *Fresno Post,* this reporter attempted to fact-check certain items and soon learned the following:

*In a report of June 3, Foster claimed the ghost drove her from her home, and she returned under police protection. However, all officers on duty that night deny having seen Foster. No report is on file with Fresno city or campus police to corroborate a complaint by Foster or her claim that police searched for an intruder in her home.

*No hospital or private medical practitioner can be found to have treated Foster for the "demon ape" bites allegedly sustained on July 17. After detailed inquiries, a neighbor in Foster's apartment complex, a nursing student who declined to be named, admitted to having visually inspected the bites and determining they were infected. However, she denied making any claims as to the origin of the bites.

*Analysis of the specimen sent to the Fresno State chemistry lab revealed the "ectoplasm" taken from the bite is a combination of cleaning solvent and human saliva.

Why would anyone perpetrating such a blatant fraud dare to submit their fake evidence for scientific review? In fact, reporter Gary Wainwright never intended to have the sample analyzed. But the road to hell is paved with good intentions, and a gesture of goodwill brought the fraud to light.

After showing the vial at a press conference, Wainwright displayed it on a shelf in his office, alongside mementos from college and souvenirs from celebrity encounters. The following day, his assistant brought editorial corrections to his office for approval, found her boss out for lunch, and spotted the "evidence" labeled and apparently forgotten on the shelf. The unsuspecting secretary packaged the vial and shipped it to the university as a courtesy.

Wainwright's sudden and inexplicable resignation later that afternoon suggests his active participation in the deception. However, Wainwright himself has not been found for comment.

"SO LONG, MARIANNE!"

by F.C. Howe

The Fresno Bee, August 18, 1978

Angry crowds gathered outside the home of disgraced hauntee Marianne Foster. Just days ago, Fresno quivered with awe and terror at the stories and photographs of abuse Foster claimed to have endured at the spectral hands of a "Dark Lady." Foster's claims have been featured in the *Fresno Post* since May. Ardent readers even met with Foster to comfort her, pray with her, and hear of the haunting from her own lips.

Now, in light of *The Collegian's* exposé of Foster's lies, her public feels betrayed.

"She took us for fools," fumed Daniel Lister. "We cared about her, and she lied right to our faces. But now she won't even show her face!"

Indeed, Foster appears to have vacated the building; she has not been seen there since the press conference. Phone calls to her last known number have gone unanswered.

A woman fitting Foster's description was seen checking into the Econolodge under the name Teresa Neele. Ms. Neele has not responded to inquiries.

VIDEO FOOTAGE: "20/20" INTERVIEW
WITH TANIESHA JONES

Broadcast Date: April 6, 1989

Do you have any comments about your former colleague, Marianne Foster?

Taniesha smiles and shakes her head.

Who would've thought she'd turn out to be so weird? It's one thing to lie, but she actually attacked herself! She choked herself—or got Wainwright to do it—and bit herself. That's what I struggle with. Marianne would've had to chew directly into her arms or contort herself into a pretzel to reach her—other places. On top of that, she rubbed bleach into the lacerations. I can't imagine how painful that must've been! Despite what people say, I don't think she was crazy, though. She showed far too much determination and attention to detail.

How would you diagnose her?

Oh, I'm not qualified to make a clinical diagnosis. But I believe she was desperate to be the center of attention. Maybe she was lonely in her life outside CSAM. She definitely loved to gossip. Loved the sense of power, I imagine. Marianne always was nosy and an instigator. I don't know if she planned all along to go public with concoctions about the ghost or if she got the idea after she got locked in Corridor D. That part happened; I saw the video.

Taniesha hesitates and frowns.

It came out later that she'd contacted the reporter
in Newport who had written about Smithy and asked
her for other clippings about the haunting. That
was about two years before Marianne went public.
After she was exposed, the reporter suddenly
produced the original letter containing Marianne's
request. So maybe she *was* planning something that
far back. What really inspired her was that case
in Long Island where the family said the ghosts
followed them from house to house. That turned
out to be a spectacular fraud, too, but it got
plenty of attention at the time. It still does,
as a matter of fact.

Was Marianne's story fully discredited?

Oh, absolutely. Wainwright, her accomplice, fessed
up, even though Marianne never did. And after she
worked so hard to get into the spotlight, she
vanished. Jeff suspected she would pop up and fake
a fugue state next, pretend she couldn't remember
any of the stunts she'd pulled, but I figured
she'd done enough.

**What about the ghost stories? Were those done,
too?**

Not entirely. . . Though of course, later, people
cited Marianne as proof that everything was made
up. She hurt the cause.

CLOSED-CIRCUIT FOOTAGE

Date: November 7, 1978
Location: Corridor F, Isolation Ward

Smithy sits alone in a five-by-six-foot cage, eating lettuce and staring out of the cage. He drops his lettuce and knuckle-walks to the corner, peers through the bars, then returns to his original position.

The camera cycles to two different angles: the main door, closed and locked; the supply cabinet at the opposite end of the room, closed and locked.

The camera returns to Smithy, staring out the cage in the same place as before. He leans forward, placing his weight on one hand.

A shadow crosses in front of the camera, darkening the frame for about ten seconds. When the shadow lifts, Smithy can no longer be seen.

The camera cuts to the two other angles in the isolation ward: it shows the main door, still closed and locked, and the sealed supply cabinet at the opposite end of the room.

DIARY OF RUBY DALTON

November 7, 1978

Now I finally know. I thought the haunting would end with Marianne's exposure, but now it's happened to me. I should feel frightened. Yet, I feel clearheaded. Maybe that's a sign of shock. Maybe the fear will set in later. For now, I'll use the calm to write my account.

My encounter happened in the middle of the day, around 2:20 p.m. as near as I can tell. I was alone (I thought) in the ladies' room. It was my tenth visit since 7:00 a.m., and if I were anxious about anything, it was the prospect of having a UTI.

I was considering how much trouble a doctor's appointment would be since I don't have weekdays off. My mind was on the cost and how Man would scream at me if I asked for sick time. As I washed my hands, I wondered how much CSAM has sickened me over the years. I wasn't thinking about ghosts at all. I haven't since Marianne's fiction fell apart.

Gradually, I noticed it had become dark in the bathroom, as if a cloud had come over the sun, yet no bulbs were out or even flickering in the light fixture. I could still see clearly, but my surroundings were growing dull.

Then I turned my head and looked right at Her.

She hovered between me and the door. She was solid but flat, just as Eric said. I couldn't see through Her, yet She had no substance. No dimension. No contour. She was like a shadow. She was taller than I expected, though maybe that was because She wasn't standing on the ground. Her head was above mine, but She had no face. Instead, I gazed up at a shifting curtain of ink. I distinguished an hourglass outline below; shoulders, a skirt.

I knew I should be afraid. I always thought I would be terrified if I ever saw the ghost. Look how I reacted when I heard Her taunting me.

I'm going to scream, I thought. I'm going to open my mouth now and scream. Thinking it through, envisioning the process of drawing breath and expelling it, I knew I would scream as in a nightmare; my voice would pop out like a squeak and nobody would hear me.

My mind played the scenario, and yet I did not scream. I opened my mouth, then closed it, realizing I wasn't frightened. Instead, I felt extremely *awake*. My every fiber was alert. I could feel the air from the ventilation tickling the back of my neck and the drops of water from the sink settling into the whorls in my fingers. The muscles in my legs quivered from the force of holding so still. The rim of the sink protruded into my belly and my stomach squeezed into a ball. Still, I didn't cry or collapse. I didn't want to. Now that we were together, I most wanted to see what would happen.

The ghost, Marianne's fabled tormentor and Smithy's plague, hung in place. She didn't reach for me. She didn't threaten at all. I couldn't even tell if She was looking at me or if She was locked in her own vortex. Maybe She floated over me because She was standing on the floor of yesteryear. Maybe She didn't even know I existed.

Wouldn't that be something? What if we've been living in terror of Her all this time, worrying about what She might do to us, and She was never even aware of us?

Or what if *we* were ghosts and She saw us as shadows in Her time? If She is a poor, benighted little maid, what must She have made of the strange dark people thundering up Her staircases day and night? What must She have thought of the little dark dwarf that climbed the walls and swung from the trees? What would a Victorian maid know about chimpanzees? Dear God, that might have been enough to frighten Her into jumping off the roof!

I can think of these things now, but I didn't then. At that moment, I held my breath and stood perfectly still. I turned my head to face the mirror over the sink so I wouldn't appear to confront Her, but I kept my eyes angled on Her shadow. Naturally, I didn't glimpse any sign of Her in the mirror. She didn't move.

What do you want? I thought to myself, but then I thought it again more consciously. I directed my thoughts to Her, thinking I could communicate with Her. *What do you want? What are you doing here? Are you the same lady from Trevor Hall?* She didn't budge. And I didn't hear any voices echoing in my head. I tried to say it out loud.

"Who are you?" I mouthed the words. I saw my mouth blurring in the mirror, but I didn't hear any noise. For an instant, I had the weird thought that the ghost was absorbing all the sound in the room. But in fact, I hadn't been able to raise my voice to speak. I tried again.

"Who are you?" Now my voice, though soft, echoed off the walls. The plumbing chuffed in response. The fluorescent lights hummed. The ghost didn't move.

I couldn't remain in a stand-off with her all day long. "Please go," I whispered. "Nobody wants to hurt you. Please leave us alone."

I forced myself to close my eyes. They were burning from holding them open so long. How long had we been frozen like that? I felt tears wash over my gritty pupils and stream down my cheeks, but I didn't wipe them away.

When I opened my eyes again, She was still there. She was no closer or farther than before. She hadn't changed Her pose or indicated any wish to communicate with me. But She couldn't be in my imagination or She would have disappeared.

I closed my eyes again, and this time when I opened them, the path to the door was clear. The bathroom felt slightly warmer, though the lighting still felt off. It was as if the sun were visible again but now it was setting. I wondered where She went. Thought She might be behind me. Decided I didn't want to check. I ran to the door and burst into the hallway, half-expecting Her to be waiting for me outside the bathroom or down the turn in Corridor C. I kept walking, toward the front office and the atrium, past the fountain and out the front gates. I was supposed to feed the chimps, but I didn't think about that. I wanted to get out.

I walked all the way to the convenience store down the street and dialed Brad's number from the pay phone. He didn't answer, but to my surprise, he had an answering machine. I told it, "Brad, I can't work anymore today. Please take care of Corridor E for me. It's—" Here, I had to look at my watch. My watch had stopped half-way between 2:20 and 2:25. That's how I can guess when the manifestation took place. Feeding was supposed to be at 2:30. How long had our encounter lasted?

"—after 2:30. I'm going home." I felt relieved not to have to explain myself directly to him.

I walked some more, going up and down the street, marveling at how normal everything looked. The sun reflected off the mirrors and windows of cars in the parking lot. A pair of little kids fought over who got to ride the mechanical horse in front of the supermarket. People crossed the street. Traffic filled the streets.

I reflected, "It shouldn't be this normal. How can these people go about their business? What would they think if they knew I'd seen a ghost? What would they think if they had seen Her?" I admired and envied their ignorance.

I walked all the way home. My feet hurt and I had to pee again, but I wasn't tired, nor did I feel scared. Even now I'm not scared. I felt charged up, like I'd stuck my finger in a light socket. When I caught sight of my reflection in a shop window, I was surprised I wasn't glowing.

Jeff was surprised, too. "What are you doing back so early?" he asked. "I saw Her." I said "Her," not "it."

Jeff freaked when he heard my story, even though I told him nothing happened and I felt fine. He hugged me, then he got up and paced around the room, then he came back and squeezed me tightly, and then went back to pacing. "You can't go back!" he insisted. "This is the second time she's targeted you. You're lucky—_we're_ so lucky—she didn't do anything to you." He stopped pacing and held me and stroked my hair. "I'm sorry, Ruby. I'm so sorry I brought you there." He kissed the back of my neck and rubbed my back. "No more. I promise!"

I put up a token argument with Jeff, pointing out that if I'm not safe at work, neither is he. I told him not to act macho with me. Jeff countered that he's never been approached or addressed by the ghost, so he faces less risk.

After I finish this entry, I'll write my resignation letter to Manfred Teague. I'm not sorry to leave, but I'm surprised to be going out this way. Obviously, I can't tell him I'm resigning because his lab is haunted, only that I'm unable to continue and I thank him for giving me the opportunity to work with him.

I am glad not to have to go back tomorrow, but part of me is bitter. I tell myself Man didn't beat me. CSAM didn't beat me. Instead, _She's_ driving me away again. Because that's why She appeared to me, obviously. She couldn't tell me to clear out because she hasn't got a voice or there's some barrier that prevents Her from communicating with me, but by materializing to me, She knew I would want to avoid Her and avoid CSAM. She wanted me to leave CSAM. And that's good. It's good She wants me to go as opposed to wanting me dead or mutilated. Still, it's hard not to think She's really haunting me and not Smithy.

Poor Smithy. I hope you'll get by OK with only Jeff and Brad looking out for you. I hope I'll see you again someday.

UNCUT INTERVIEW WITH KEITH BRANNEMAN

In Search of . . .
Broadcast Date: January 17, 1982

Hell, yea—ah . . .boy howdy, I remember that day!

*Keith looks off-camera, nods, then faces the lens
again.*

A reporter for KMJ was interviewing Man about
upcoming experiments, his reaction to the Marianne
fiasco, and so forth. Then, they went to tour the
grounds. Man took him up the hill to view the
beautiful, landscaped grounds right as Smithy
came bounding over the grass.

Ruby was supposed to be on duty then, but she'd
gone home early. The cameras show her walking out
the front before Smithy disappeared, so she didn't
have anything to do with it, either. Something
spooked her. Again! She gave notice the next day,
before Man could fire her. Oh, he was pissed! Just
when we need her, she's gone.

Yeah, I was on duty, and I monitored the cage
but I didn't see anything. I saw a shadow or a
glitch on the screen. Nothing more. That happened
sometimes. It was an early closed-circuit model;
it was fritzy. Smithy stepped out of the frame
and the image changed. I saw three different views
of the room flashing in succession. None of the
angles showed anything wrong. I never saw him
leave and all the exits stayed closed. I swear!

Keith holds up a hand as if taking an oath.

The cage and the entry door were locked every time they appeared. If one had been ajar, I would've raised an alarm, but as far as I knew, everything was fine, and Smithy was hiding. I never figured out how he did it. The camera never showed anybody else. Man thought Brad was involved at first, but he was in the kitchen when it happened. I could hear him running water and opening cupboards and even singing from down the hall.

Well, after a few minutes, I didn't see Smithy in the cage anymore. I got worried about why he wasn't showing up, and I called Brad in. I asked him, "Can you see him? Is he hiding somewhere I don't know about? Am I blind?" Brad looked real hard and shook his head. He acted puzzled. Then Man called in on the walkie-talkie to report the breakout.

Smithy took off across the complex. Man worried he'd get over our fence and escape into the world. Maybe run wild on CSUF's campus. Can you imagine him jumping on cars or climbing into some girl's dorm room? Yeah, he could've done a lot of damage if he'd made it out. Frightened people. Caused a panic. Brought more bad publicity. We couldn't have that.

Brad and I rushed outside. Man was screaming and his face was all red. The reporter was holding his notepad in front of his face like he wanted to block the shouting. Or maybe he was using it as a shield because Man was waving his gun around while he screamed. "Catch him, damn you! This is your fault! Why weren't you watching him? Where's Ruby? What kind of effing morons work here? Hustle! Now!" Brad scrambled out to the garage to get the Jeep . . .

Keith laughs.

I always read things like that in books: "scrambled." I never could picture it until that moment. Brad was nearly tripping over his own feet.

We kept vehicles onsite, but we hardly ever used them except for tours. Ordinarily, Man would've taken the Jeep to show off the place to the reporter. But when Brad pulled up, Man turned up his nose. "I can't use that clunker! See what *you* can find with it." Then he told the reporter, "Come with me" and hurried away. The reporter ran after him—but didn't scramble.

I told Brad to hurry up because if Man caught us dawdling, he'd probably shoot us both. Brad kept shaking his head and saying, "Man, oh, man!" but he wasn't talking about our boss. Then he said, "Wait a minute," and ran back into his trailer. I was getting fed up and about drive out myself, but he came back carrying a box of those Oreo knock-offs from the grocery store: Hydroxy-whatsits.

Brad started the car and away we went. He was weaving from side to side, trying to follow the trees and yelling, "Smiitheee! Here, buddy, buddyy!" at the top of his lungs. Like the thing was going to answer him!

But damned if I—oh, sorry. But, what do you know? All of a sudden, there's Smithy flying through the trees. He looked like Spiderman swinging from his thread in the superhero comics I used to read as a kid. Or Superman leaping from tall building to tall building.

Keith falls silent. A muscle in his cheek stretches.

I guess that's because apes really are superhuman. They're stronger and faster than we are. They've got excellent balance and proprioception. They can brachiate as naturally as we can put one foot in front of the other. That's what Smithy was doing: swinging arm to arm from tree branch to tree branch. He'd vault up into the leaves and then swoop down onto the next branch. And he was fast! Brad wasn't driving at top speed because we didn't want to crack up, but we had to go fast to gain on Smithy.

Brad stuck the box of cookies out the window and yelled, "Come on down, buddy! Let's have a bite and chat!" He kept waving and trying to get the ape's attention. He tried signing to it, too! While driving! I had to grab the wheel a few times because I thought we were gonna go into a tree while he did his hand-jive nonsense.

It didn't stop Smithy, but he *was* paying attention because he signed back. He waved his hand—the one that he wasn't swinging from—and covered his eyes. I asked Brad later what he was saying, and Brad said it meant, "Go out." Brad thought Smithy was telling us to go away so he could escape to freedom.

Keith pauses and inclines his head to listen to the interviewer.

Oh, covering his eyes? Yeah, that usually meant "dark." I think he was telling us to look the other way so he could jump the fence.

You know, thinking about it now, it's kind of funny, but at the time, I was pissed. The ape was out, we didn't know how. Our jobs were on the line, and instead of trying to force it down, Brad was trying to bargain with it. And *the chimp* was telling him how things were gonna be!

Then we heard this revving sound coming from behind the trees and suddenly there's Man on his little ATV motorbike with the reporter clinging to his waist coming up ahead of us. He took that thing on safari with him and shipped it back and forth as needed. I had to grab the wheel and swerve so we didn't crash into them. Man kept looping around the trees and around us. He sounded like the Atomic Wasp. *Rrrrrrrrrrr!*

Smithy went nuts and started flying deeper into the trees. Man went after him, but our car was too clunky to pass between the trees, so we had to stay behind.

That motorbike shot ahead into the overgrowth, and after a few seconds, we heard a shot. Brad fell apart. He started crying, propped his hands up on the steering wheel and buried his face.

Then the ATV came back. Man had the chimp across his lap along with the gun. He pulled up alongside and scowled at us both. He said, "Stop crying, you sap"— only he really said something else you won't be able to broadcast. "It was a tranquilizer, moron. Keith, take the car back and don't smash it up."

I switched places with Brad and drove back to the Center. Man put Smithy in isolation to recover from the drugs. The reporter kept gushing over how daring Man was and how he took on the ferocious ape and brought him down with one shot. They recorded a radio spot that aired that night. I was mad because I hoped he would also interview me about how I was a hero for helping chase down the escaped ape.

Keith sighs, then smiles.

But *you're* interviewing me now!

UNDATED (PARTIAL) MEMO FROM MANFRED TEAGUE TO CSAM STAFF

Directive: To examine how higher cognition, operationally defined as language-based interactions, persists in the presence of traumatic brain injury, using chimpanzee analogs.

Goals: The findings of this investigation will enable us to make predictions about the likelihood of higher cognition in humans continuing after catastrophic events (e.g., stroke, blunt-force head trauma, extended oxygen deprivation). By measuring the chimp's performance, we can determine the limitations of spontaneous rewiring and recovery and establish a baseline for reparative treatments.

Subject: Webster presents the highest ratings on measures of both verbal comprehension and fluency (i.e., ASL); ergo, his characteristics are most congruent to human performance.

Design: Over the course of six months, portions of the subject's cortex will be sequentially destroyed (TBD: through a combination of electrical cauterization, physical impact, and hemispherectomy). The subject's performance on language-based tasks will be measured following each intervention to test at which point advanced cognitive functioning ceases. Following onset of incapacitation, we shall investigate therapies for restoring basic functioning . . .

DIARY OF RUBY DALTON

November 8, 1978

It's unbelievable how fast things are happening. I'm trying to keep track of the sequence of events for future reference.

I fell into a deep sleep last night shortly after eight, only to be awakened just before midnight by a raucous banging on the front door. I thought it was a police raid, until I heard Brad's voice shouting, "Jeff, man! Hey, Jeff, Ruby, open the door!"

At first, I thought he might be drunk, but as Brad's entreaties grew louder, and his pounding made the pots and pans in the kitchen shake, I realized something awful must have happened.

"I better let him in before the neighbors complain." I couldn't see Jeff's face in the half-light as we got dressed, but I could picture it from his tone: grim. We stumbled along, flipping switches and blinking against the brightness. When Jeff pulled open the door, Brad staggered inside. The sight of his mismatched clothes, blotched face, and teary eyes increased my dread.

"I'm gonna kill him!" Brad sobbed. "You'd better keep me here for the night, 'cause if I go back out, I'm gonna kill the son of a bitch!"

Jeff pulled out a kitchen chair and asked Brad to explain.

"The bastard has it in for Smithy! Did you get the memo? Or a phone call? I was already in bed when this little paper came under my door. When I first heard the mail slot scrape, I thought someone was trying to break in. I could've shot a burglar and called it self-defense, but this—"

"Spit it out, Brad!" Jeff demanded.

His face twisted and he punched our table. "I mean murder! Butchery! Lobotomy!" He glanced at our shocked faces. "Man plans to cut up Smithy's brain to see what effect it will have on his language abilities!

He's singled out Smithy specifically because he's got the most developed signing skills. That's what our language study has done for him!"

Brad reached into his pocket for a crumpled paper and slapped it onto the table. I stared at it as if it would bite me if I touched it. But part of me still hoped Brad was drunk or high, so I tentatively smoothed out the creases and began to read as Brad continued raging.

"That fucker's gonna bash in one side of his head just to see what happens! Then he'll smash in the other side to see if Smithy can still perform. Then he'll try removing a chunk of his cortex and another and another and—" Brad's voice choked off, but I saw it all in print, as black as an executioner's mask, against the page.

Jeff ripped the memo out of my hands, read it to himself, then started tearing it to shreds. "Christ, that asshole wants to turn him into a vegetable!" His voice sounded like a frightened child's. The muscles in Jeff's face pulled in different directions, twisting it into an expression I couldn't recognize.

I pulled out a chair for myself and listened to the men beside me sniffle and curse while I stared at the scraps on the floor, the death decree, that infested our carpet. They taunted me: "You can't get rid of me now! I've multiplied!" My stomach heaved and I just reached the kitchen sink before I became ill. I stared down the void of the drain and tried to think beyond the rage and helplessness wracking my body.

"He can't do this," I rasped once the bile settled back into my throat. "Smithy is crucial to the language study. CSUF wants this study. They won't let Man get away with this! They'll stop him."

"Unless Man spins it as part of the study," Jeff countered. "Man's thinking, 'We taught him language once. Now we'll mess him up and see if we can teach him again. Smithy's the best we've got, so if he can't recover, nobody will.' Something like that. It's not the first time Man's added his own twist to a university study."

We all remembered how electroshocks found their way into a drug trial.

"I can talk to some of the students I know," Brad suggested, "maybe get them to stage a protest. Make up some fliers. Get the word out about what's going on at CSAM. That'll make bad publicity. Man doesn't want more of that."

Jeff was skeptical. "Protestors have been trying to oust the university president since before we got to town. It hasn't worked yet. We can't rely on protestors to help." He kicked the wall. "We've been telling Man about our progress for weeks! He's never hinted anything this diabolical! Why is he doing this?"

"Maybe Smithy busting out pushed him over the edge." Brad then regaled us with details of how Smithy mysteriously escaped his cage without disturbing the lock, leaving a mark, or showing up on camera all while Man had a visiting reporter on hand.

That all must have gone down around the time I was in the bathroom. She must have been trying to distract me.

Jeff and I looked at each other wordlessly throughout Brad's story. I could see he wanted to tell Brad what had happened, but I shook my head. I didn't want to add Her to this mess, but I wondered: did She set Smithy up to face Man's ire, or was She trying to help him escape before Man could sharpen his scalpels?

"Why didn't anybody from CSAM contact us?" Jeff kicked the paper fragments. "Why didn't we get one of these?"

"Maybe Man was waiting for us to come back to work to tell us the deed had already been done," I suggested. "Maybe he's planning to make you work with Smithy throughout this new 'study.' It would be like him to twist the knife."

"He was probably dealing with so much shit, he didn't think about you," Brad pointed out. "I live out back. It was easy to tell me. Or maybe he's planning to fire you." He looked at me when he said that, but the chill that crept up my back with all claws extended made me look at Jeff. Yes, Man would punish me for dereliction of duty, but if he retaliated against Jeff by firing him, how would we stay afloat?

Jeff gritted his teeth. "To hell with that! Ruby's quitting anyway, and I sure as hell won't work for him if he's planning to butcher Smithy!"

"Brad, talk to your friends at the university," I urged. "I'll go, too. You work on the students; I'll go to the IRB."

"Better yet, we should go to the ASPCA," Jeff interjected. "This is animal cruelty. Pure sadism."

"We can bring in the press: The Collegian and The Bee. Turn public opinion against him." Brad sighed and covered his face. "But public

opinion has no authority. CSUF doesn't own Smithy. Man can do whatever the hell he wants to him. Sure, maybe the IRB will get its dander up, and maybe in a year or two, the school will sever its partnership with CSAM. The gambling study was two years ago and look where we are. We need to help Smithy _now_!"

Urgency was our goal. Brad was talking like he wanted an injunction against Man. How could we get one? _Could_ we get one?

I said quietly, "Maybe we could ask the university to file an injunction to delay the surgery because Smithy is such an important subject. He really is unique, and if Man tinkers with him, once-in-a-lifetime opportunities could be lost. Besides, the IRB will want to review this proposal for cruelty. CSUF requested the language study. We have to prove they've a voice in what happens to Smithy."

"What if CSUF doesn't want to play?" Brad objected. "We should get a whaddyacallit anyway because Man is wrong!"

Jeff asked, "Can _we_ get an injunction? Us three? As concerned parties for Smithy's welfare?"

I had no idea who had the right to request an injunction or not. "Maybe . . . Tammy might know. Her husband's a lawyer. I can call her tomorrow and ask her."

"No," Brad insisted, "call her now! We don't know when Man is planning to start cutting. Tomorrow could be too late." I protested it was three in the morning in New York, but Jeff backed him up.

Thank God Tammy answered the phone herself and accepted the charges! I'd have been mortified if my first conversation with Herschel involved me waking him before daybreak to ask a favor. Once she heard our story, she shared our shock and outrage. I asked about an injunction. Tammy got quiet. Then, I heard her whispering to Herschel.

"What you need to do is file an ex parte motion," she said at last. "Request a guardian ad litem. That's a lawyer who represents the interests of people who can't represent themselves—children, the senile—when they get into a jam. Now, it's never been done for an animal before. Hersch says this would be highly experimental, but he's intrigued from an academic perspective."

"We're not lawyers. We don't know how to do all that. Would Hersch represent Smithy?" Brad asked. I squeezed the phone and held my breath while I awaited Tammy's answer.

"First of all, Herschel is a contract lawyer. He's never acted as a guardian ad litem. Second, he's not licensed in California. But once the sun comes up and it becomes socially acceptable to start calling people, he will reach out to his buddies from law school to see if anybody knows somebody who can help. Keep in mind, Brad, what you're proposing is revolutionary. You'll need a brilliant attorney to be able to pull it off, and the best doesn't come cheap."

My stomach dropped, sinking my hopes with it.

"But a brilliant attorney might possibly take on the work pro bono for the challenge or the publicity. Don't give up. We'll do all we can for you and Smithy. But nobody thinks clearly in the middle of the night."

She chided Jeff for destroying what should have been Exhibit A in our complaint. I taped the memo back together as best I could. I think it's legible enough to get the point across, if anyone will take the matter up for us. For now, we're waiting. ~~Tomorr~~ In a few hours, we'll hear more about our fate and Smithy's.

~ ~ ~

Herschel came through for us! A cousin of one of his friends went to law school with a guy who's now partner of a firm in San Jose that handles torts, personal injury, and civil rights violations. Tammy referred to him as "an iconoclast" (i.e, he has an open mind). We're leaving shortly to meet with an attorney at Rhymer & Prest's branch office in Clovis.

~ ~ ~

Conrad Hegge is hardly the tenacious bulldog Brad envisioned. He's an elderly man with a kindly smile and a distracted stare when he talks, almost as though he's reviewing an invisible law-book hovering before his eyes. He was patient with us, explaining logistical points over and over again. He's sympathetic, the right person to take an interest in Smithy—and exactly the wrong person to charge into unknown legal territory on our behalf. The same compassion that makes him open to taking this case will make him vulnerable to Man's vitriol. Man'll claw Hegge to shreds.

At least Hegge seems well-prepared. When we arrived, he already had a stack of papers in hand: notes about the case, including information provided by Herschel and Tammy. Rhymer & Prest has a telecopier machine, and Hegge was able to have their summaries transmitted all the way from New York! It's faster than a letter and more detailed than a telegram. We were all impressed.

After considering the printouts and reading Man's tattered memo, he said, "It sounds to me like your Mr. Teague is trying to have it both ways. On one hand, he claims Smithy is the only appropriate candidate for this surgical experiment because of his supremely developed language skills. But if his skills are so sophisticated, then it would be criminal to subject him to this kind of destruction."

I remembered Tammy once arguing something similar about how Piers was upholding Smithy's language abilities but simultaneously denying he was making true statements; I wondered if she'd put that in her notes to Hegge.

"That's exactly what's happening!" Brad agreed. "We need to show people how smart Smithy is. I can talk with him. I've been practicing sign language ever since he came to CSAM. But he'll talk to other people, too. If you get somebody who signs to interview him, they can vouch for him."

"I can provide film footage," Jeff offered. "Some of it's in Man's possession, but we can still access it, and I can make copies before he knows we're suing him. We can show it to the judge, the jury, whomever, and convince them Smithy's the real deal."

"No," Hegge said. "We don't need to <u>convince</u> anybody. We just need them to keep an open mind. Just like fostering reasonable doubt in a criminal trial, we need to use a preponderance of evidence to persuade a judge that Smithy <u>could</u> possesses higher intelligence than the average primate. Call it 'reasonable belief.' Your evidence could help, but let's not rely on evidence from CSAM. For one thing, if Manfred Teague owns the rights to your films or your data, he can try to suppress it. Besides, I think outside verification will be more persuasive."

Brad's forehead furrowed. "You mean like an expert opinion?"

I felt my stomach clench. Looking in Jeff's eyes, I saw the same resignation.

The corners of his mouth tightened. "Only one person's expert enough to testify that Smithy is genuine." Hegge took out a pen to write the name, but Jeff's lips twisted shut.

I said it. "Robert La Fontaine."

Brad let out a long whistle.

"He has an excellent reputation," Hegge said. "He'll make a powerful witness."

"*If* we can get him to testify. He may tell us to go stuff ourselves," Jeff grumbled.

I tried to be hopeful. "Not necessarily. This could be his chance to get back at Piers. By validating Smithy's ability, La Fontaine would be calling Piers's judgment into question. It could be a coup for Osage, too."

Jeff continued to shake his head. "Robert La Fontaine . . . I never thought my work would be used in support of his or vice versa."

We made a list of all the people we thought might testify. Jeff promised to give Hegge a copy of the rebuttal to Piers we tried to publish a few years back. I've already talked to Taniesha; she'll help. I'm certain the Meyer schoolteachers will, too. I'm not sure about Gail though, and I'd like to avoid involving Wanda.

Brad promised to get his contacts at the university involved. He spent most of our drive home rehearsing his manifesto aloud. Hegge further suggested we incorporate into a 501(c)(3) organization. This will give us a higher profile and greater legitimacy. I'm to start filling out the paperwork once I finish with my diary.

Finally, Hegge determined he had enough material to get to work. "I'll start drafting the order now and have a runner take it to the courthouse. My assistant, Sam, will contact you to take your statements. We'll file them later."

The boys were getting up to shake his hand when I asked about payment. Abruptly, they sat down again, grave-faced.

"This will be handled on a pro bono basis." Hegge winked at us.

When we left, Jeff was radiating confidence. He and Brad alternately plotted their strategy for countering Man and sang Hegge's praises.

"We lucked out with him," Brad insisted. "He gets it. I wasn't sure a lawyer would. I always figured they were in it for the money and their clients were always guilty. I used to be down on lawyers, but from now on, Conrad Hegge is my main man."

I'm glad they're upbeat. They'll need optimism. I have no illusions that this will be anything but an ugly slog.

EXCERPT FROM "CALL TO ACTION"
by Brad Vollmer

Distributed on California State University Fresno Campus, November 9, 1978

Brothers and sisters—Children of Mother Earth—All freedom-loving, violence-shirking, decent human beings—Unite!

Terrible crimes against nature are unfolding around us!

Manfred AKA "THE MAN" Teague, director of CSAM, wants to torture the innocent animals in his care in the name of science!

He wants to cut up the brain of Smithy AKA Webster, a cookie-loving, playful, mellow, innocent, boss chimpanzee while he's still alive, and he calls that progress!

It's time to take a stand against this monstrosity! Tell CSUF enough is enough! Break your alliance with the mad scientist and his torture chamber!

Rise up together and Free Smithy!

PETITION IN FRIENDS OF SMITHY V. CENTER FOR THE SCIENTIFIC ADVANCEMENT OF MAN AND MANFRED TEAGUE

FILED NOVEMBER 9, 1978

Ex Parte Petition to Nominate Guardian ad Litem and Motion to Compel Habeus Corpus for "SMITHY," a Chimpanzee," Filed in FRIENDS OF SMITHY V. CENTER FOR THE SCIENTIFIC ADVANCEMENT OF MAN AND MANFRED TEAGUE.

Comes now the Plaintiff, the FRIENDS OF SMITHY, a charitable organization devoted to improving the welfare of primates in captivity and providing public education about primate species, to demand Respondents MANFRED TEAGUE and the CENTER FOR THE SCIENTIFIC ADVANCEMENT OF MAN ("CSAM") produce the animal "SMITHY" AKA "WEBSTER" a chimpanzee aged seven years, for examination.

The Plaintiff enters the following facts into evidence:

1) That Respondent has expressed intent to injure SMITHY under the guise of medical experimentation (see Exhibit A);

That such experimentation as described would create irreversible impairments to SMITHY's functioning and quality of life;

That SMITHY is a being of higher intelligence and remarkable capabilities whose impairment would represent untold loss to the interests of science by jeopardizing its understanding of the relationships between human and animal cognition and communication, and;

That the aforementioned medical experimentation (see Exhibit A) would constitute cruel and unusual abuse against a being of higher intelligence and complex emotion, as prohibited by the State of California and the Geneva Accords.

The Plaintiff makes the following prayers:

That the Court immediately impose an injunction prohibiting MANFRED TEAGUE and/or any representative or agent of CSAM from performing any operation upon SMITHY or otherwise interfering with the physical and/or mental functioning of the animal;

That the Court appoint a *Guardian ad Litem* to oversee SMITHY's interests;

That the Court remand SMITHY to such *Guardian ad Litem* for protection for the duration of proceedings, and;

That the Court assign SMITHY's residence and care to a neutral third party until the *ex parte* hearing obtains resolution.

Submitted on this 9th of November, 1978 at Clovis, California.

RHYMER & PREST, LLP

By: Conrad Hegge, Esq.
Attorney of Record for Plaintiff

ASSORTED NEWS HEADLINES
NOVEMBER 12, 1978

FRESNO COURT TO HEAR ONE-OF-A-KIND CUSTODY
DISPUTE; CHIMP'S FREEDOM AT STAKE

"FRIENDS OF SMITHY" FILE
CHIMP EMANCIPATION SUIT

"DR. FRANKENSTEIN?" ALLEGATIONS OF
ANIMAL ABUSE AT CSAM SPARK LAWSUIT

CSUF TO END PARTNERSHIP WITH CSAM:
QUESTIONS SURROUND TREATMENT OF RESEARCH
SUBJECTS; "FREE SMITHY" PROTESTS ON CAMPUS

LETTER FROM RUBY DALTON
TO TAMMY STEINMETZ

November 15, 1978

. . . As promised, Hegge immediately filed his petition to prevent Man and CSAM from further experimenting on Smithy. We'll have our first hearing on December 18 before the Honorable Nathaniel M. Borley.

Jeff just applied to incorporate the "Friends of Smithy" to educate the public about the dignity of primates everywhere (and to generate tax-free money and publicity to aid Smithy's cause). The Friends are named Plaintiff in our complaint.

At present, Smithy is housed at a local zoo, though not on display, to prevent either Man or us from having any advantage. The lawyers can visit him to check on his welfare, but Brad, Jeff, and me (and anyone from CSAM) are excluded.

We've been working the streets, too. Brad's convinced Isaac to help gather signatures on our petition to the CSUF chancellor to "fire" CSAM. We already have several hundred! Brad's been barnstorming on campus and even had a rally at Ratcliffe Stadium where he and Isaac shared first-hand eye-witness accounts of life in CSAM's trenches. Brad said he read aloud from a photostat of Man's memo "and the stands vibrated when the crowd booed!" He's led one march on campus already this week, and more "Friends of Smithy" are sitting in at the cafeteria and science labs or picketing in front of CSAM.

Of course, the press has noticed. I had a good laugh today watching Channel 30's coverage. The newscaster referred to Man's institute as "SCAM!" He read the full name correctly but then he went on to mispronounce the acronym five times: "Representatives of SCAM . . ." "Director of SCAM . . ." SCAM, SCAM, SCAM! I bet Man sues him for libel.

The media doesn't seem to know what to make of the story. I've seen our case described as a custody dispute and an attempt to win emancipation for Smithy. One wag even referred to us as the "Simianese Liberation Army." I guess that shows how avant garde this trial is going to be; I hope such misrepresentation doesn't hurt our standing.

I asked Hegge if he thought Man might settle amicably before our court date. He responded by describing what happened to the process server who delivered our petition. When Man saw the summons, he started cursing lustily—and when he saw what it was for, he chased the server out the front door with a gun! He even fired it into the air a few times, shouting that he was going to kill us expletives deleted. So much for thinking Man might negotiate reasonably.

Hegge emphasized the importance of painting Smithy as distinct and special. "Animals are routinely treated as property. The law sees them as interchangeable. In divorce cases where the parties argue over who gets to keep the dog or cat, or in civil cases where a beloved pet has been killed through negligence, the animal owners typically don't get much of a hearing. Unless you've lost a prized racehorse or a purebred show dog and you can support a claim for monetary reimbursement, one animal is just like another.

"We need to show the judge—and the world—Smithy is unlike any other animal, and if he is irreparably damaged at Teague's hands, the whole world will suffer damages from his loss," Hegge explained.

The whole world is going to be watching us, Tammy. This case is the first of its kind, and no matter how it ends, it will go into the record books. Judging by the way the press has already responded to our filing, our every move is set to become News with a capital 'N.'

"Some of the interest will be serious, from academics who study cognition and supporters of animal rights. Some will be prurient, from people who think we're fools and want to be entertained at our expense. Embrace it all. We want all the attention we can get because we want to stimulate conversations," Hegge said.

It's finally dawning on me that our lives are about to be upended. Jeff and I have arranged to change our phone number because of how many reporters and cranks have been calling. Some of them said truly disgusting things. It wouldn't surprise me to learn Man has hired goons to harass us. I'll let you know our new contact information once it's been established.

At least the super is chasing away unauthorized visitors from the apartment complex. I hope he doesn't evict us on account of the trouble we've attracted.

Yesterday, Jeff and I gave our statements to Hegge's paralegal. It turns out "Sam" Stone is a woman. Her full name is Samantha and she's been with the firm two years. She's a petite, polished brunette with a voice made for radio. Sam says this case is the most fascinating she's ever been part of and she's excited and grateful for the opportunity.

I thought about that while she interviewed us, and when she was packing to leave, I asked her what I've been afraid to ask Hegge: Why take this case? Why work for free and incur hours of effort and untold expenses on something guaranteed to be a massive headache?

Sam studied me beneath drawn brows as if deciding whether I could manage the truth. "The short answer? For the fame. This case gives Rhymer & Prest the opportunity to blaze trails and potentially create a new branch of law. There have always been agitators wanting to close circuses or zoos, but they're on the fringes. This might actually be the start of a mainstream animal rights movement.

"But not all of us are in it for the glory. Some of us want the challenge of crafting arguments and shepherding an unusual case. And some of us think it would be a damn shame if a chimp who can do all the things Smithy does spent the rest of his life as a vegetable in some creep's science experiment."

That was all Jeff needed to hear to decide Sam Stone is our new best friend. I think she's sincere and I'm glad she's on this team. I'm sure everyone at R&P will work hard to achieve success for their clients—but they'll work harder if they have a personal stake in the outcome.

Though Jeff and I will be involved in the case, I've discussed with him the importance of finding real work, too. Needless to say, Jeff and Brad are now unemployed—and Brad is homeless. Brad says he doesn't care; he's got friends who will let him crash on their couches for now. For that matter, we'd take him in, if need be—provided we can keep our own roof over our heads. To that end, I suggested to Jeff we each at least get a part-time job. Working nights, we could still attend court proceedings by day.

His folks have mostly been understanding about what's happened, though Mama Martha confided to me her worries that Jeff is putting his future on hold and making the wrong name for himself with this court case. However, she respects his devotion to Smithy. She doesn't like the idea of Man cutting up chimp brains for fun, either. She agreed to wire us some money to help us stay afloat. I got so choked-up, I couldn't thank her properly.

I haven't yet told my folks what's happening. They live far enough away that the story may not have reached Scranton. I always told Dad I'd make my mark someday but never imagined this.

For now, I'm pursuing as many job interviews as I can and crossing my fingers that my name won't be in the headlines prominently enough for any potential employers to notice. I'd appreciate your good wishes. I appreciate more than words can express all the help you've given us so far. I couldn't be happier with how things are unfolding.

Love,
Ruby

DIARY OF RUBY CARDINI

November 15, 1978

I'm not at all happy with the direction of the trial strategy.

I told Tammy part of Hegge's plan but held back the rest because I'm still hoping to talk him out of it. Also, I didn't want her to regret steering us to someone who would pull such a bone-headed stunt.

We began our meeting by reviewing our accomplishments so far; then Hegge introduced his plans. "We've got to use all the arguments available to us. Our goal is to create reasonable belief, as I said. We also need to win public opinion. We won't have a jury trial, but the public can still be our friend. It will demonstrate on our behalf, as we've seen. Some individuals may write letters to local newspapers or otherwise make known their opinions. The law will decide the case, but where the law is vague or silent, the judge has leeway, and often, for better or worse, public opinion plays a guiding role. Therefore, we must find an angle that appeals to our public."

"We'll humanize him," Brad asserted. "Maybe we can bring Smithy into the courtroom for demonstrations! Hell, maybe we can even get him to testify! Let the people, let the <u>judge</u>, see him interact with us and answer questions. They can watch him ask for his freedom. Then let's see if the judge tells Smithy he's got to go back to Man's prison and die."

Hegge nodded and made a note. "That's a compelling idea, and well worth a try. But I want to introduce another element into our strategy." His eyes skimmed over us.

"I'm concerned it won't be enough to persuade the judge that Smithy's language abilities make him unique. Other apes use language." He raised a hand to forestall Brad. "Maybe not as efficiently as Smithy does, but one could argue 'talking' apes are common enough. However, there is one claim about Smithy no one can rival: that Smithy can talk to the dead."

I was sure he was joking. The surprise on Brad's face seemed to confirm that. But Hegge wasn't laughing, and when I saw dawning resignation spreading over Jeff's face, I got scared.

"That's—" I almost said 'insane,' then I switched to, "untenable! You can't be serious. You can't prove the supernatural! Scientists have tried for ages. They've gotten nowhere. It's a matter of faith. If you go down that route, you'll trap us. You'll throw away any goodwill we can earn." I stopped for breath—and realized the words coming out of my mouth weren't my own; I could hear them echoing across the years in Wanda's voice. "Our premise is going to be hard enough to prove because it's so novel. We've got to be careful, please!"

"There are three reasons your chimp is famous," Hegge stated. "One is his language skills—which have been in doubt ever since Preis-Herald denounced him. Two is Wanda Karlewicz's face. Three is the ghost. These stories are well known to the public and have been for years. A forest of rumors has had time to grow around this ape. People will want to know more about them. Let's own them. Let's bring them into the open and make people question what they signify. Let's make them our back-up plan."

I pleaded—first with Hegge not to do this to us and our case—then with Jeff and Brad to make him see reason. But they want to go along with it! They even suggested I testify!

I felt nauseated just thinking about talking to a judge—and a room full of strangers and reporters and maybe even video cameras—about what I saw and sensed. Man's attorneys would make me out to be as mad as Marianne.

And suppose She doesn't like being talked about? She let me off with a scare and a warning to leave Smithy to Her. I didn't need more than a gentle push; I was ready to walk out of CSAM anyway. If I get involved again and drag Her into the spotlight, She might hurt me like She did Gail or Wanda.

"Please, let's stick to the facts! We'll lose credibility from the scientific community if we start talking about spooks. The experts will think we're credulous and begin to doubt Smithy's real talents."

"Science isn't as snooty as it used to be, Ruby," Hegge said. "Highly respected institutions are exploring the paranormal. Duke and Princeton

have been conducting ESP experiments and publishing their findings for peer review. Even the military has an ESP program. Ghosts aren't so laughable. Consider this tactic one more arrow in our quiver.

"Besides," he added, "I guarantee you the opposition won't be expecting it."

Damn right, I wanted to shout. I wasn't expecting it!

The thought of tainting our case with ghost stories left me retching (seriously, I've been hovering near the toilet all day). After we closed our planning session with serious conversation about witness lists and community outreach, I called Sam at the Clovis office and urged her to talk down her boss. But she backed him!

"Remember, Ruby, we don't have to prove ghosts are real. We just have to persuade the judge to consider the <u>possibility</u>. If he thinks Smithy's the missing link to the Other Side, then how could he rule in Man's favor? It's worthwhile." I'm reconsidering my opinion of her as an asset.

For now, Hegge is adding names of "parapsychologists" (and for all I know, faith healers and snake handlers) to our witness list. I can't imagine Robert La Fontaine taking the stand after Uri Gellar. I'm hoping—no, <u>praying</u>—that Hegge (or someone! Can the partners, Rhymer and Prest, be in favor of this?) comes to his senses before then.

ASSORTED NEWS HEADLINES
NOVEMBER 21, 1978

MASS SUICIDES IN GUYANA

CULT LEADER AMONG 400 DEAD

WOMEN AND CHILDREN POISONED

LETTER FROM RUBY DALTON
TO TAMMY STEINMETZ

November 21, 1978

. . . It's unbelievable! Did you know those people had a church right here in Fresno? They had temples all over California, it seems. To think Jim Jones or some of his people might have driven past our apartment, or that I might have sat next to one of them on a bus or passed them in the street without ever guessing who they were or what they were about. And now they're all dead. It gives me the creeps.

They killed their children, too. Little babies who never had the chance to think or make any choices for themselves. I cried when I read that. How can such things be? The paper said Jones isolated his followers from their families and friends so he became the most important person in their lives, the only one they would listen to, but didn't these people have consciences to listen to? Didn't they know wrong from right in their hearts?

Jeff's upset, too, but for a different reason: Jonestown has pushed Smithy off the front page.

"There'll be a massive investigation, Ruby. A congressman is dead. Nobody will want to read about our lawsuit anymore. In a couple of days, Smithy will be pushed out of the A-section and then forgotten altogether. All the momentum we've built will be lost! All because some nut thought he was God!"

Jeff's attitude staggered me. I wanted to ask, "How can you think about your own needs at a time like this? Babies are dead and hundreds of relatives are grieving." Then it occurred to me: Jeff doesn't know anybody from People's Temple. The blurry corpses in the photos don't mean anything to him personally. Smithy is and always has been his primary concern. Of course, he's going to worry about him even during a tragedy like this.

As it turns out, Jeff needn't have worried. Those bastards had a chimpanzee.

The press, in its zeal to investigate every aspect of the story, mentioned that fact. And because both Smithy and the People's Temple are 'local' interest stories, they've been tied together. One of our local radio stations interviewed a zookeeper from San Francisco who complained of how untrained individuals have been given the chance to own valuable exotic animals. "These precious and delicate creatures are at their mercy. At the least, they risk neglect from caretakers who don't understand their needs. At the worst, they face abuse and exploitation." Poor Mr. Muggs in Jonestown faced execution along with the rest of the cult.

Even though that zookeeper was speaking about Jonestown, I sensed he was also condemning any non-professional who would dare to own an exotic animal. That would include us and Piers—but not Man, who can hide behind the legitimacy of his scientific organization. I'm not sure how I feel about that insult or if I have a mind to feel anything about it at all. It's hard to feel offended when hundreds of innocent—if misguided—people are rotting in a jungle tonight because they trusted the wrong person.

We've another meeting with Sam and Hegge to discuss how we might spin the Jonestown massacre to our favor for publicity. Hegge was serious about exploiting every possible argument. I feel ill thinking about it . . .

LETTER FROM RUBY DALTON
TO TAMMY STEINMETZ

December 11, 1978

Tammy,

Now I understand why I've been feeling sick these past few weeks.

I understand, too, why She appeared to me. She wasn't warning me away; She was offering a deal. She was telling me, "Leave Smithy to me. Get out of here now, and nothing more will happen to you. He'll be mine, and you'll have yours."

I'm pregnant.

Can you believe it? Right now, of all times? It's a miracle when you think of how little Jeff and I have been together. Mom and Dad will be thrilled. I haven't told them yet. I haven't even told Jeff! Isn't it strange I should tell you first? Yet, by the time you get this letter, everyone else will have known about it for days. You're my rehearsal, Tammy.

It helps to see the words on paper. It's still hard to accept. When the doctor gave me my test results, I almost asked him, "Are you sure it's not a tapeworm? Or cancer?"

Not that a pregnancy is impossible, but after four years together, when we weren't even trying, when we've only got my earnings from Gottschalks on which to live and the Trial of the Century looming over us, I wanted to scream, "Wait!" I want to hit pause, like on a tape deck, and play this part of my life later, when I can afford to pay more attention to it. And when Jeff is around to share it.

Right now, he's downtown with Brad and Isaac, leading a demonstration against CSAM as a prelude to opening statements. Hegge wants us to remain in the public eye even though nothing is happening in court yet. I doubt anyone has forgotten this case, but reminders like this are a part of our strategy.

To my surprise, Jeff had qualms about the rally. The public has been receptive to our anti-CSAM talk. Even people who believe mankind has dominion over animals don't necessarily want them to suffer. Hence, Man is very unpopular these days. That means his facility is suffering, too. No university funding and no research partners means no money to feed and care for the research animals still on-site. It means we're rescuing Smithy at the expense of Rosalie, Woolly, and the others.

"I didn't want to hurt any of them." He sounded like a little boy explaining he didn't mean to hit the baseball through the window. "It isn't their fault their owner is a sadistic bastard. I wish Judge Borley would send them all to foster facilities. Knowing what Man is like, the judge shouldn't let that prick near any animal."

Jeff called during a break to see how things went at my appointment. I didn't want to give him the biggest news of our lives when he was on a pay phone in a parking lot, so I told him I was healthy and I'd have more details when he got home. He seemed satisfied. He didn't even notice my voice sounded funny; I had been crying, you see.

Will he be so sanguine when he knows? We've talked about children from time to time. We'll say, "Let's send our kids to a Montessori school." Or "Remind me never to yell at our kids like that," when we see a frazzled parent and her squalling offspring in a store. But we've never sat down to plan a budget or where we'll put the crib. We haven't talked about which church our kids should attend. Responsible parents-to-be do things like that.

But always something else has been more important than attending to our future. Smithy has always been more important.

Jeff will have to accept our priorities have changed. I need him here. I need him to get some kind of job because in a few months, I may not be able to stand anymore, let alone work a register or take inventory. And I want Jeff with me for all the highlights: the weigh-ins and the check-ups and the first kick. I deserve to have my husband back for all those things.

"Get out of here. Go live your life and do all that you wanted. Move on." How I want to!

LETTER FROM RUBY DALTON
TO TAMMY STEINMETZ

December 16, 1978

. . . We've finally met our first expert witness. Robert La Fontaine has consented to testify for us about primate language. He's in town already to meet with Smithy and to convene with us.

When he walked into the office, and I finally set eyes on him, I abandoned any idea of him as an arrogant celebrity. He looks so normal. He was even dressed in jeans and a turtleneck, not a sport coat or cravat. I was also surprised by how much younger (and shorter—and nicer) he is than I expected.

I believe I can tell when someone is being socially polite, and when La Fontaine shook hands with me and Jeff, he seemed genuinely interested. He repeated my name like it belonged to an old friend. He called us pioneers and said it was an honor to join our team. After all the years we've spent griping about him and painting him as our rival, I wasn't prepared for that.

He did express some skepticism about our mission, though. "As I'm sure you know, primate language research has always been viewed with suspicion. I don't know how many Planet of the Apes jokes you've had to tolerate, but I've heard hundreds, and received twice as many letters from anti-evolutionists. I believe these noble and intelligent beings deserve to be treated with dignity, but I can't wholly endorse ape emancipation. They can't take care of themselves, you know. Most likely, Smithy will simply be transferred to another facility. Have you thought about that?"

"He could stay with me," Brad said. "I can look out for him. We get along fine. We're buddies."

"I'm sure you are, but try to see things as the court will," La Fontaine urged. "The fad for apes living in people's homes has passed. The risks and liabilities, you know."

I always thought the way we'd raised Smithy was unique. I was shocked when La Fontaine told us how many private citizens over the past decade have somehow gotten their hands on chimps to keep as pets or sideshow attractions to bring in extra cash. Many of these apes end up at a facility in Georgia where La Fontaine works to re-socialize them and help them acclimate to the loss of their human families. ("And to wean them from junk food.")

He went on, "I can hear the slippery-slope arguments now: 'You want apes to live like people? You want to give them rights? You mean you want them to vote?! Next thing you know, you'll have people wanting to marry their dogs or their horses. It's the end of the world as we know it!' I'm anticipating the worst of the backlash, you know. Playing devil's advocate. You're going before the firing squad."

I could see a vein pulsing Jeff's forehead, so I cut in to preserve harmony. "Emancipating apes isn't our goal, either. All we want is to get Smithy clear of CSAM and into a place where he'll be respected and comfortable. Making that happen means getting a judge to recognize that apes' higher intellect entitles them to better treatment. It's a package process."

Jeff put an arm around my shoulder. "Even if the judge doesn't declare apes a special class of person but grants <u>Smithy</u> special immunity, we still win. If he does recognize ape rights, we win big time. If we lose . . . we might as well put everything we've got into the fight. Now, are you going to fight with us, or undermine us?"

To my relief, La Fontaine smiled. "I'm with you, certainly. Especially now that I see you do understand what's at stake."

La Fontaine hasn't met Smithy yet, but he has several (supervised) appointments scheduled so he can observe him and provide his own insights into Smithy's abilities. He didn't want to hear from us about Smithy's vocabulary or special characteristics. "I've read some of your research, but I prefer to form my own, untainted opinions."

I couldn't refrain from asking about his research. We've always wondered about the overlap, after all. La Fontaine surprised me again. He said he honestly had no idea Piers was preparing a primate language study at the same time he released his preliminary studies about Osage. "I follow others' research through the academic journals, but your professor announced his study through popular media."

La Fontaine said he reached out to Piers after his first publication to compare notes "and to mend fences; I didn't intend to upstage him," but Piers snubbed him. "He seemed to think I was insincere. And he's held it against me ever since."

That sounds about right. Piers probably couldn't believe anyone wouldn't have heard of him and his Webster study.

La Fontaine intends to be in court as much as he can, even if he's not testifying himself. Like Sam, he believes this case may signify a new trend for animal rights. "In which case, I should learn as much as I can to prepare for any future situations in which I may be called to testify."

Is this the man we accused of breaking into our house and scrawling Wanda's name in filth on the walls? Did we really think <u>that</u> was a more likely explanation than a ghost?

What other crazy things have we convinced ourselves are true? Are we deluding ourselves that we can obtain a favorable verdict on such unconventional grounds?

LETTER FROM RUBY DALTON
TO VINCENT CARDINI

December 18, 1978

Dear Vince,

The judge has set the first hearing for March 13. Because our matter is so unusual and the Court has so many more important cases pending (though he didn't phrase it that way), Judge Borley is going to fit Smithy in where he can (probably on Friday afternoons when things are slow), but we may be postponed for long stretches "if matters of urgency intercede."

Borley said he wasn't even sure whether we belonged in civil or probate court, and it's unclear how long this matter could stretch. Hegge said we're lucky the judge didn't simply dismiss our petition.

The three-month gap will give us time to conduct "discovery," a fancy legal term for gathering evidence we want to present. We'll need to show lots of documentary evidence, which we don't own, so we have to issue requests for CSAM to "produce" it; that is, give us access to view and copy the films, logbooks—and the thousands of hours of closed-circuit video and audio recordings we've just learned exist.

It turns out Man was taping us in secret the entire time we worked for him! I knew he had cameras on the animals for security reasons; we wanted that footage to prove Smithy spontaneously signed with the other chimps. But Man also taped in public areas: the break room, the office, the labs—though thank God not the bathrooms. He probably heard everything we ever said behind his back. No wonder he hated us so much.

Meanwhile, Smithy sits in a cage at the zoo. Brad wanted to request an Order allowing visitation. Hegge cautioned, "One thing at a time. This will be a big fight. Let's be sparing in what we demand." He knows Man will oppose us at every step.

Jeff, Brad, and Hegge's paralegal are responding to Man's latest allegations now. He's filed a civil suit against us for defamation of character and lost earnings. Man claims all the bad publicity has affected his ability to conduct business, find researchers/investors, and perform routine daily tasks because his employees have to push through a picket line of angry folks in gorilla masks every day.

I nearly flipped out when I heard about that. I never dreamed we'd be counter-sued (though I should have guessed from the constant threats Man always made against Piers).

"How can we fight two lawsuits?" I asked Hegge. Rhymer and Prest only agreed to help us with our habeas corpus matter, you see. But there's hope! People for Primates has joined Friends of Smithy in raising donations for Smithy's welfare. We'll have enough money to hire a second lawyer. Hegge also suggested filing a breach-of-privacy suit against Man for not informing us about the surveillance cameras. He thinks Man might crack if he's juggling three lawsuits. If only!

Jeff wants to help draft interrogatories for trial. He's never spent five minutes in a law school, but he thinks his intimate knowledge of Smithy's life qualifies him to participate in the process. Sam told him he's welcome to help. I hope she's humoring him.

This is all more than I bargained for: files and loose papers piled on our kitchen table, Jeff poring over documents at all hours, questionnaires the size of novellas demanding to be filled out. I wish there really were a Friends of Smithy organization with a mature Jane Goodall type at the helm and a staff of volunteers to run everything.

I tried to share my skepticism with Jeff and Brad. I thought it was important they stay grounded and prepare for potential failure. Jeff especially is flying high, determined to make Smithy a hero to the world.

Brad needled me about being a "team player." "Someone has to fight, Ruby. Didn't you want to make history? Here's your chance! We need you with us. Smithy needs you. Even though he can speak for himself, he's got no authority to speak. He's not much different than women were one hundred years ago. You couldn't vote. You couldn't be on a jury or run for office. You couldn't even keep your own money if you had a job or an inheritance. You were property. Well, that's Smithy's life now, only he's worse off. At least a woman's husband couldn't force her into a crazy experiment that would kill her." I was tempted to educate Brad about the risks of childbirth in an age before birth control, but I didn't have the energy for a debate.

"Someone stood up for you, Ruby, even though it was hard and women's rights sounded like a dumb idea. Someone fought so you could have a good life. Can't you give Smithy the same opportunity?"

Hearing Brad's lecture angered me, but some of my ire was at myself for not being a better fighter or a true believer. I do think Smithy deserves better, and Brad's right that nobody will <u>give</u> him a better life; we have to fight for it.

"Smithy didn't ask to be here.," Brad argued. "He never wanted to be a research subject or be taught to act human."

True. But I never asked to be here, either. What about my wasted years at CSAM, slaving under Man's tyranny? I don't want to while away another four years of my life on this trial...

EXCERPT FROM PRIVATE INTERVIEW
BETWEEN REID BENNET AND SAMANTHA
STONE, ESQ., CIRCA 2000

Samantha Stone: No, Smithy's wasn't the first case where I assisted, but it gave me the foundation and confidence to manage the cases I would take in the future. More importantly, it gave me a new outlook on life. That may sound trite, but it's true. That was the first time I thought beyond winning a case and considered my profession a tool to change lives for the better.

I saw the first glimmer of hope the day we won permission for Smithy to have visitors. We were surprised opposing counsel acquiesced; it seems his client wanted to have a look at Smithy, too. We insisted on supervised visits. So did they.

I escorted Jeff Dalton and Brad Vollmer to the zoo and, in the presence of a guard and opposing counsel, I met my client for the first time.

He was demurer than I'd expected. I'd been to zoos before. All the primates I ever saw were raucous creatures with more energy than a preschool class. I was expecting a howler monkey. Smithy did make noise when he saw his visitors. It was like someone had popped batteries into him. He went from lying in a heap in the corner to flying. Smithy was living in a six-by-eight cage, and he ran back and forth in the tiny area, bouncing off the bars at one end and ricocheting back to the other side, hooting. I was afraid he'd break an arm or hit his head, but the guys just laughed. Opposing counsel looked disgusted. He didn't get it.

Brad started signing, and Smithy gradually wound down—meaning he bounced in place instead of soaring around his cage—and began signing back. They chatted a bit—*I missed you. How are you?* Brad translated the conversation so I could follow along. Smithy wanted them to take him out for a walk and play with him. It was amazing to watch. They were really communicating! It wasn't orchestrated. Then Smithy remembered his manners and asked who I was. Jeff named me: S with the sign for "strong," so Smithy would know I was fighting for him.

That first visit lasted less than an hour, but the memory of it and the meetings thereafter in which I was privileged to sit have lasted forever. I'd never connected with another creature that way before. I saw intelligence in Smithy's eyes and love in his face when he signed to Brad. I knew then I was doing the right thing. No matter where the fight took us, I'd be in it with all flags flying.

Ever since, I've been proud to stand and fight for those who need a voice, for women and children who have been abused, ignored, or oppressed. It gets nasty, but it's necessary.

Smithy was an incredible *person*. I know that isn't fashionable to say but I can't say otherwise. He changed my life for the better, and thanks to him, I've been able to do the same for others. I feel blessed to have known him.

SIGNS CARRIED BY PROTESTERS
OUTSIDE THE COURTHOUSE
MARCH 13, 1979

MAN IS A MONSTER

SAVE OUR SMITHY

DEATH TO DR. FRANKENSTEIN!

DOWN WITH THE MAN!

FREE SMITHY!

(Drawing of hands signing, "Freedom")

"SMITHY TRIAL BEGINS"
BY ELIZABETH MACKINTOSH

The Fresno Bee, March 13, 1979

This morning began the second great "Monkey Trial" of the 20th Century. Not since John Scopes was arrested over fifty years ago has the world been so riveted by testimony involving apes.

The Honorable Nathaniel Borley heard opening statements in "Friends of Smithy v. the Center for the Scientific Advancement of Man," a case that aspires to set at least one ape on legal parity with humans.

COURT TRANSCRIPT, *FRIENDS OF SMITHY V. CENTER FOR THE SCIENTIFIC ADVANCEMENT OF MAN*[5]

Opening Statement of Conrad Hegge (Plaintiff)
March 13, 1979

Your Honor, I thank you for hearing this motion on behalf of Webster, a chimpanzee also known affectionately as Smithy. Be assured that by any name, he is an extraordinary being. We are here today because a series of extraordinary circumstances have jeopardized Smithy's life and welfare. Now, you might say animals face peril every day, such as when dogs serve the police department. What makes this situation unusual?

To begin with, Smithy faces an appalling danger to his person. For the past four years, Smithy has been an inmate of the Center for the Scientific Advancement of Man, a private research facility operated by Dr. Manfred Teague. Although this organization has undertaken a number of worthy projects over the years, Dr. Teague's latest venture is a proposal torn from the script of a horror movie.

The Friends of Smithy, led by three former CSAM researchers, came to me for help when they learned Dr. Teague planned to mutilate Smithy's brain. I submit as Exhibit A this original memo, in which Dr. Teague states his objective will be to surgically remove pieces of the animal's brain, one at a time, to see how his overall behavior

5 Hereafter "Court Transcript"

changes. Allegedly, this will shed light on the experiences of humans suffering brain injuries.

Is harming another sentient creature the best way to assist humans in need? Indeed not! There are many other ways to gain the knowledge Dr. Teague claims to seek. One way is to interview and test humans who have already experienced brain injuries. Another is to dissect the brains of cadavers who suffered impairments in life. However, this proposed experiment fits an ongoing pattern of sadism and disregard for the creatures in Dr. Teague's care. You will hear about other experiments he's conducted, many of them gratuitous, all involving the infliction of mental and/or physical suffering, some of which have resulted in the deaths of his animal subjects. This is a deplorable situation! It is intolerable that Smithy should remain in the power of Dr. Teague or CSAM!

Although it would be a tragedy to condemn any creature to the fate Dr. Teague plans for Smithy, it would be particularly shameful for *this* animal to be subjected to such treatment. Smithy is distinct from Dr. Teague's other subjects. He was raised in the image of man with the goal of helping him communicate with mankind. Smithy grew up among humans and learned to act like a human. In fact, he was taught to do something it was once believed only humans could do: communicate. Smithy is educated in American Sign Language. He understands over four hundred signs and can converse with people and even with other chimpanzees he has helped to train.

Animal language is a controversial subject, and you will hear points of view on both sides. I believe you will agree, however, that the evidence supports Smithy's talents. As a sentient animal with advanced cognitive capabilities, he can offer much more value to science alive and intact than lobotomized. By continuing to investigate Smithy as a linguist, we can learn more about how to build connections with the animal kingdom. We can learn more about ourselves, our origins, our abilities, our destinies.

Not only can Smithy talk; he can talk to the dead! He is a conduit to the Other Side, a missing link between life and the afterlife. As you will hear, Smithy spent his formative years at Trevor Hall, a house shrouded in ghostly lore. While some people have claimed to see Trevor Hall's resident specter, the Dark Lady, this chimpanzee has actually interacted with her. In candid film footage, you will see him signing with and about an entity whose presence can be supported by Trevor Hall's other occupants, all trained scientific researchers.

You will hear some challenging testimony. I urge you to maintain an open mind. Scientific investigation of the powers of the human mind is yet in its infancy. Mankind has long desired to know more about what comes after death, and science has made nascent attempts to find these answers. Smithy offers the opportunity to discover more about the true final frontier. It would be a tremendous loss to the human race to harm this chimpanzee and thereby interfere with his ability to tell us what we so dearly want to know.

Given Smithy's special characteristics and the unusually harsh consequences facing him and all mankind if Dr. Teague is successful in his countermotion to keep Smithy, I pray that this Court grants a *habeus corpus* order to release Smithy from CSAM and from the threat of any further harm.

Smithy possesses enough cognitive sophistication to be nearly human. Like any human living in these United States of America, he deserves the right to life, liberty, and the pursuit of happiness.

Never before have you heard arguments to this effect. But never before have you encountered anyone like Smithy. Again, I pray you keep an open mind and consider all the evidence with an aim to administering a just ruling.

COURT TRANSCRIPT

Opening Statement of Lance Latimer
(Respondent)
March 13, 1979

Your Honor, I don't know how to proceed after an opening like that.

I thought we were convening today to address a simple issue of purported animal abuse. The plaintiffs, the Friends of Smithy, through their attorney, have alleged undue cruelty and malicious intent on the part of my client, Dr. Manfred Teague, director of the Center for the Scientific Advancement of Man.

It's easy to develop affection for an animal. Most people have had at least one cherished pet. Animals are cute and they appeal to our sensitivity. The plaintiffs have developed an intense affection for the chimpanzee, Webster, whom they call Smithy.

But their affection has become pathological. They have developed an inappropriate level of possessiveness toward him. They believe they know what is in his best interests and are prepared to label any action with which they disagree as a "barbaric and criminal affront." That phrase comes directly from the Fresno State *Collegian* student newspaper. The plaintiffs have been actively mustering support on the campus that was formerly associated with CSAM. That relationship has since terminated.

The plaintiffs forget that the name of the facility—and its purpose—is the scientific advancement of *man*. The species as a whole. The needs of the many outweigh the needs of the few. Rather than see their fellow men prosper thanks to scientific investigation, they are prepared to enlist the Court's resources to obtain special treatment for an animal. This is unheard of. This is unbecoming. Frankly, this is unbelievable.

Your Honor, Dr. Teague is engaged in legitimate, promising research that requires the use of primates. As the saying goes, you have to break an egg to make an omelet. No one *wants* to see an animal injured, but it is a regrettable necessity, just as it is necessary to cause a child suffering by administering a vaccination so the child doesn't develop a life-threatening illness. If the animal's sacrifice will lead to benefits for humankind, the ends justify the means.

Furthermore, I will show you that contrary to rumor, Dr. Teague's methods are not inhumane, barbaric, or motivated by anything other than a desire to do good for humanity. By attempting to deprive him of his subject, a chimp Dr. Teague legally purchased in 1975 under the terms outlined in this agreement, Respondent's Exhibit A, and by further attempting to shut down his laboratory, the plaintiffs are inflicting immeasurable harm on the world.

They will try to tell you this is a special chimp, so he deserves special treatment. He can talk. He's intelligent. But the research they cite was discredited by its own designer years ago. The entire body of research on primate language is at best inconclusive. Yet, the dubious promises such research offers continue to captivate the public and tempt people who ought to know better into creating a self-fulfilling prophecy. The people who surround this creature are merely seeing what they wish to see in his actions. In effect, he's the Chance Gardener of the animal kingdom; high-minded humans project their desires onto the animal and read great import into his every gesture and random word. There is no definitive evidence verifying the ape's so-called abilities. Their arguments in favor of his personhood are specious.

As for their other allegations—which I just heard for the first time as you did—these are patently absurd!

Indeed, there is no foundation for the motion for *habeas corpus*. Such action is motivated by personal prejudice, ego, and spite against my client, as well as childish wishful thinking.

I move for dismissal of the action.

I further request punitive damages in the amount of one million dollars in lost revenue, pain and suffering, and legal fees.

We beg the attention and the impartiality of the Court as we present our evidence.

DIARY OF RUBY DALTON

March 13, 1979

I'll never forgive Hegge for his opening statement.

After he declared Smithy could speak to the dead, you couldn't hear a breath in the courtroom. By the time he announced Smithy was the 'missing link' between worlds, snickering and whispers filled the void. I wanted to hide my face. I wanted to walk out of the room to escape the questioning and criticism I knew would result.

I stayed to put up a united front. And because I knew if I left then, I would forever be singled out as "one of those nutty plaintiffs" rather than someone who happened to be sitting on the plaintiffs' side.

Jeff didn't mind. Neither did Brad. My husband looked defiant, and our friend looked eager to see how everyone in court would react to the announcement. The most frequent reaction has been ridicule, but some people are intrigued. I pray the judge will be unbiased.

I don't know how Latimer went on with his opening argument. I was too anxious to attend to his words, though I have the vague idea he was scolding us for bringing the motion. I watched as his lips kept twitching, sure he would burst into laughter at any minute. I half-hoped he would because I thought it would make him look petty and improve sympathy for our side. He didn't. Instead, he entered a motion to countersue us for one million dollars!

Dear God, that's worse than the libel suit. Hegge says not to worry. There's no way the judge will grant it; Latimer's doing it to scare us. I don't know if I can trust him, though.

Although, apart from his absurd statements about ghosts, Hegge did well in introducing our first witness and initial evidence.

"SMITHY TRIAL BEGINS"

BY ELIZABETH MACKINTOSH

The Fresno Bee, March 13, 1979

. . . The chimp's attorney called renowned primatologist Robert La Fontaine as the first witness. La Fontaine, who has taught at McGill University and Georgia State University and has authored several books about his own primate language research, offered his expert opinion on Smithy's ability to understand and produce language.

Having performed multiple interviews with the chimp, La Fontaine testified that Smithy possesses intermediate language skills. "He addressed me without prompting, asking me to tell my name and to take him out of his cage for a walk. He responded appropriately to my questions and discussed objects and people both present and out of sight." Understanding *object permanence*—the continued existence of a thing even when it is out of sight—is a hallmark of advanced thought in children.

Under cross-examination, La Fontaine conceded that Smithy's vocabulary was "non-standard." He explained the chimp has invented his own signs for certain objects and actions instead of adopting the approved sign from Ameslan vocabulary. However, La Fontaine viewed this as a strength rather than an object of criticism.

"When we attempt to understand the world by developing new vocabulary based on our existing knowledge, we exercise our language faculty. Portmanteau words (*e.g. seahorse*) and metonymy (*e.g.* using a brand name such as Kleenex or Jacuzzi to describe a product) are examples of how we do this. Smithy has independently displayed both." In support, La Fontaine detailed Smithy describing a wristwatch as a "hand clock" and a refrigerator as a "cold box."

Further, La Fontaine cited Smithy's use of proper names. "The zookeeper's name is Erwin McDonald. The name sign Smithy created for him translates to 'hamburger man.' Thus, Smithy carried over his association of the name McDonald with the famous restaurant chain's food."

While the primatologist spoke earnestly in support of Smithy's language skills, attorney Latimer still managed to use his testimony to cast doubt on the chimp's credibility . . .

COURT TRANSCRIPT

Testimony of Robert La Fontaine
March 13, 1979

Latimer: You've written in *Osage's World* that your own chimpanzee subject, Osage, "displays the most sophisticated language faculties of any ape alive today." Do you stand by this statement?

La Fontaine: I do.

Latimer: Even though Osage has demonstrated a stable vocabulary of two hundred and fifty signs—according to your book—and Webster has allegedly mastered twice as many words?

La Fontaine: Osage has consistently been subjected to double-blind trials and third-party observations over the past six years. Over time, witnesses and researchers have developed consensus on two hundred and fifty signs. The other apes I've observed—namely Kiki and Chanticleer, who use sign language, and Kenji, who uses a patented computerized pictograph language—show persuasive, albeit less sophisticated, mastery. For almost five years, Smithy has been locked away in a research facility where his language skills have not been systematically studied, so I cannot vouch for his four hundred reported signs. However, I observed approximately seventy-five signs during my own interactions with him, not including the signs he has developed himself, and I believe that Smithy's mastery is at least on par with Osage.

Latimer: I see. So, this ape is intelligent?

La Fontaine: Certainly!

Latimer: At least as intelligent as Osage?

La Fontaine: Absolutely!

Latimer: Doctor, I'd like to summarize an anecdote from Chapter five of your book. In "Growing Pains," which describes Osage's penchant for mischief, you recount an incident when she stared out the office window and repeatedly signed "Jane here." Jane was the name of one of your assistants at the time. You opened the door expecting to see your assistant arriving, but Jane was not there. Instead, Osage took that opportunity to run past you out the open door and to an ice cream truck on the next block. You believed Osage had heard the music of the ice cream truck and created a ruse to convince you to open the door so she could escape.

La Fontaine: Yes, I remember that.

Latimer: You write about this incident with pride. It would have aggravated me.

La Fontaine: At the time, I was furious—Rather, I was embarrassed with myself for falling for the prank and for not at least looking out the window first. However, I respected Osage's creativity and determination. That escapade illustrates both the chimpanzee's ability to engage in advance planning, a trait typical of humans, and in deception, something also been thought to be specific to humans. That story illustrates how advanced Osage's cognition truly is and how similar to the human brain is the chimpanzee's.

Latimer: Hypothetically, if Osage is capable of using language to tell an untruth to manipulate her keeper, and if Webster's abilities are similar to Osage's, then would Webster also have the ability to deceive humans by telling them something untrue? For instance, could he claim that a person was present in the room when such a person was not in the room, just as Osage falsely claimed Jane was at your door? More specifically, could Webster claim the presence of a non-existent woman to manipulate the people around him? Are his skills *that* advanced, doctor?

La Fontaine: I cannot make a judgment about that. I didn't personally witness him engaging in deception.

Latimer: But is it possible?

La Fontaine: My observations so far are insufficient for making any claim about such abilities. I would have to observe Smithy in more detail, over time and perhaps in a controlled situation.

Latimer: Are you withdrawing your testament in support of the chimp's language skills?

La Fontaine: No. I believe Smithy uses language. However, I don't know if he can deceive.

EXCERPT FROM
"SMITHY TRIAL BEGINS"
by Elizabeth Mackintosh

The Fresno Bee, **March 13, 1979**

Greater public interest centered on the second witness, Lorna McKenzie, described in the witness list as Smithy's foster mother. The McKenzies were originally selected to raise the chimp within a family structure because their son already communicated using ASL. Preis-Herald hoped organic exposure to the language would enhance Smithy's skills. McKenzie's testimony shed light on the first year of research and the chimp's personality in infancy.

She claimed that although Smithy (then called Webster) could only produce a half-dozen signs when he was removed to Newport in anticipation of McKenzie's expecting a child, he evinced comprehension of a broader array of signs. Under cross-examination, McKenzie also admitted that Webster had bitten several family members during his residency, but that she and her husband had treated the problem as a matter requiring greater discipline. She denied the family experienced any ghostly activity and resisted suggestions that the chimp ought to be euthanized for his own good or the safety of others.

McKenzie issued an impassioned defense of her erstwhile foster child:

"We must pity him. He deserves our protection! We shaped him according to our mores and made him dependent on us. He'll never be able to function in the wild. He's too humanized. He couldn't even get along with the other apes [at CSAM]. He's more human than ape now; that was the intent of everyone involved in the project. We alienated Webster from his own species to make him more like ours, and now we're punishing him for following our lead. I regret my part in all of this. As much as I loved Webster, I wish I had told Piers I wouldn't foster him. Then maybe the experiment could have been nipped in the bud. I hate to read about what's happening to Webster these days. I cry when he comes on the news. We've betrayed him."

POLITICAL CARTOON

Fresno Gazette, March 14, 1979

A sad-faced chimpanzee sits on a stool, facing
the reader. Behind him stands a solid-black,
feminine silhouette, holding a paintbrush. In the
background, large, dripping letters on the wall
spell, "SOME CHIMP."

DIARY OF RUBY DALTON

It's cute; I'll give them that. It's also completely misleading. Nothing She's done has helped Smithy; rather, she's made him a pariah, a laughingstock, and a lightning rod.

Perhaps the cartoon is predicting the ghost will help save Smithy, now that Hegge has made Her a crucial part of his defense. I'm sure that's Hegge's hope.

Plenty of credulous observers are hoping for an interspecies/interdimensional collaboration, but I never expected Jeff to be one of them. He was so pleased when he waved the paper in front of me. "This is the reaction we're trying to get, Ruby! Imagine if the ghost really did appear in the courtroom and everybody saw her. What would that do for us? What could it do for Smithy?"

What would it do for mankind's concept of life and death?

I sensed Jeff wasn't just idly speculating but was building up to something I wouldn't like. I tried to dissuade him. First, I pointed out that ghosts don't materialize in full view of witnesses on demand, no matter how much you might want them to. Ghosts showing up at a crucial moment to solve a problem or make a scene only happens in the movies. In real life, they're much more subtle. Tammy read a book about ghosts and hauntings while we were at Trevor Hall and told me some of what she learned. Real spirits tend to materialize to one person at a time and only for an instant. Most of the time, spooks just make weird noises and move objects around—basically the kind of stuff we experienced. That isn't dramatic or persuasive enough. Jeff wants to go big.

I also warned him that trying to force the ghost to appear is a terrible idea because we have no idea what She might do. Most likely, She'd be angry with us for disturbing Her and drawing Her into the open. We wouldn't be able to control Her response. But it would suit Jeff just fine if She did something unpredictable, something nobody would be able to ignore, something for the headlines. The bigger the better!

"We both want the same thing," he insisted. "We want Smithy to be healthy and intact. The ghost can help us. It would be in her best interest to help us. She should want to cooperate."

"She _should_ nothing," I protested. "How do you plan to secure Her 'cooperation,' anyway? Will Hegge summon Her to materialize in the courtroom and take the stand? Are you going to ask Her to speak through Smithy? Make a table levitate in front of the judge and opposing counsel and all the reporters? Tap once for yes and twice for no?"

Jeff looked disappointed, like I was slow or being stubborn. "All those things would be good. They could only help us. If we could encourage her—ask her politely, if you prefer—to be more communicative and maybe give us information we could use, like who she actually is and where we can find supporting evidence, or if she could produce some kind of news that you and I and nobody else has, _that_ would be proof."

I didn't like where the conversation was going and flat out asked him if he was planning to hold a séance. Jeff laughed, but that's his way of dodging. I pressed him again. "Are you going to ask the ghost directly for Her help? How would you ask Smithy to ask Her, since we're not in communication with him, either?"

"We'll politely put our request out to the universe. You seem to think she can see and hear anything we do, anywhere we go, like Santa Claus. If that's true, then she'll be aware of our needs and can act on them accordingly."

He doesn't grasp the risks of that approach. I don't want to call Her attention to us. I want Her to leave us alone. She existed in relative obscurity for years. If She had wanted to put Herself on the front page of the national newspapers, She could have done so. She wants to be left alone, and in turn, She'll do the same for us. That was the truce. She wants us to back off and leave Smithy to her. If we meddle or try to bend Her to our will, She'll make us pay.

I tried to explain, but Jeff was too stubborn to listen. Now that Smithy requires a savior, Jeff's forgotten how worried he was on the day I saw Her. "'Truce' is what you call it. She didn't actually speak to you *about what she wanted. If she'd been explicit, we could be sure of not doing anything to offend her. Instead, everything's open-ended."*

"All the more reason to be careful," I argued. "We don't know what will make Her mad, so why take a risk?"

"Because we've been tiptoeing around this ghost for years. We've always been afraid—of getting fired for talking about it, of what it might do to hurt someone. Now, for once, the ghost can finally help us! We can leverage the haunting for Smithy's benefit, even use it to save him."

I pointed out everything that could go wrong with his strategy, how silly we could look and how we would hurt our cause if we acted like spiritualists instead of scientists. "What if you summon Her, but only a few people in court can see Her? Or what if only Smithy can do so? It would look like mass hysteria. It would be a fiasco."

"But what if it wasn't? What if it worked even better than we expected?" Jeff countered.

"Or what if it works and you regret it? What if She hurts you? Or me? Or the baby." I cradled my belly and let my eyes tear up. I was willing to play any card to divert him. I had no shame.

My gambit worked. As Jeff consoled me, I pleaded with him. "Promise me you won't hold any séances to contact Her. Promise me you won't try to communicate with Her at all. I'd rather abandon the supernatural angle altogether, but if you must use it, just discuss the existing evidence. Don't try to create anything new." Jeff grimaced and looked downright constipated, but he gave his promise. I hope he means it. If not, by the time he realizes his mistake, it may be too late for us all.

COURT TRANSCRIPT

Testimony of Piers Preis-Herald
March 14, 1979

Hegge: Who designed the program for teaching Webster?

Preis-Herald: It was a collaborative process between me and my assistants. I set certain guidelines, such as requiring the research team to use sign language in their day-to-day communications, but my lieutenants, Ms. Karlewicz and Ms. Ehrlich, established the logistics of which words would be taught and what benchmarks would be set. They oversaw the study in my absence and made regular reports via letter or the occasional phone call or telegram.

Hegge: What percentage of the time were you actually working hands-on with Webster?

Preis-Herald: It varied. In the beginning, I lived on-site at Trevor Hall, but once the new school term began, I returned to New Haven and only visited Newport on my days off. Ergo . . . one hundred percent of the time until September and thereafter about forty to sixty percent of the time.

Hegge: If you weren't on-site, how could you investigate Webster's language displays?

Preis-Herald: Mr. Dalton filmed many of Webster's interactions with his teachers and I reviewed that footage, which was as good as seeing it first-hand.

Hegge: Based on what you reviewed and what you experienced, what did you determine about Webster's language skills?

Preis-Herald: My evaluation was lengthy and difficult. Initially, I believed, based on glowing reviews from my assistants, that the chimp was making impressive progress. However, when I investigated more thoroughly, I found many concerning factors they had overlooked.

Hegge: When did you form these conclusions?

Preis-Herald: This happened after the project had ceased, and I had more leisure to consider all the research we compiled.

Hegge: Did you work alone in your evaluation or in concert with your assistants who had gathered the data?

Preis-Herald: I was on my own. My assistants, sadly, had scattered to the winds by that time.

Hegge: Please tell us a little bit about this team. Who were they and how were they selected for the project?

Preis-Herald: I was proud of the team I assembled. There were six students, drawn for convenience's sake from schools along the Eastern Seaboard. However, the students themselves were remarkably diverse. We had a mixture of men *and* women from different parts of the country—California, Missouri, Wisconsin, Pennsylvania, Massachusetts, and New York. They possessed different ethnic and religious backgrounds. They even had different specialties, ranging from general cognition to education to language dynamics. The youngest was a nineteen-year-old freshman, Gail Ehrlich. Ruby Cardini was also an undergraduate, an incoming transfer student from a junior college. Jeff Dalton and Wanda Karlewicz, my own graduate assistants, were the eldest at twenty-four.

Hegge: You must have received a tremendous number of applicants for this project.

Preis-Herald: We had about two hundred legitimate inquiries.

Hegge: Did you winnow these down on the basis of academic merit?

Preis-Herald: I looked for qualities each person possessed that could be of greatest use: technical expertise with audio-visual equipment, experience with childcare, or characteristics like ambition and enthusiasm. I met personally with all the volunteers I eventually selected, and my final decision was somewhat subjective, based on my gut feeling about whether they would work well on the project and with one another.

Hegge: Do you believe the team you assembled was intelligent? Capable? Trustworthy?

Preis-Herald: Yes, I placed great faith in them. I left them to their own devices for long stretches and trusted that they would conduct themselves and the research responsibly.

Hegge: So, you had a team of experienced, ambitious, accomplished students whom you trusted with your *magnum opus* of research, yet when the time came for you to release your formal conclusions, you completely discounted their input. I refer here to Exhibit H, a letter to the journal *Science* written in response to Dr. Preis-Herald's October 1975 article penned by four of the primary researchers: Tammy Cohen, Jeff and Ruby Dalton, and Eric Kaninchen. The letter details their objections to their former supervisor's alleged findings and their own observations to the contrary. Have you reviewed this letter, Doctor?

Preis-Herald: Yes.

Hegge: Do you believe it has merit?

Preis-Herald: No. It's an elegant rebuttal, but it's founded on illusory evidence. The authors wrote from the heart, not from the brain. Their letter is based on personal anecdotes, not on descriptive statistics, probability, or content analysis. Understand, these students were highly impressionable. They were excited about the project and wanted it to succeed, both to secure their own futures and because they had developed an emotional attachment to the chimp. I had not foreseen that their fondness for Webster would shape their view of the data. They were well-intentioned, but they simply weren't hardened enough, or experienced enough, to understand what they were seeing. They looked at the data and saw confirmation of what they already believed, whereas I looked at the data for things a critic or skeptic might question and asked myself if I could refute those doubts.

Hegge: Are you saying your team was good enough to perform your study but not good enough to judge its outcome?

Preis-Herald: You're confusing data collection with data analysis. Research professors commonly employ assistants to gather data that better-trained scientists will then interpret. I was confident my team could teach a chimp and record his responses, but interpreting what those responses meant was a matter for someone with greater expertise. My experience in the field exceeded my team's, so I performed the analysis. I had been conducting scientific research for more than twenty years, whereas my most seasoned graduate student had only four years under her belt.

Hegge: Describe your experience.

Preis-Herald: Prior to the Webster study, I specialized in the study of persuasion and language. I had authored or co-authored eight published papers and several popular books, including *The Language of Yes: Using Cognitive Research to Persuade Customers to Buy Your Message,* and *The Language of No: How to Dissuade Others and Plant Second Thoughts.*

Hegge: So, you worked in advertising. Did that qualify you to analyze a chimpanzee's behavior?

Preis-Herald: I've worked for thirty-five years in both academia and the private sector. I was a tenured professor for over ten years at one of the country's most prestigious universities. I also hosted a syndicated radio program covering a broad array of psychological topics. Please don't try to dismiss me as a mere ad-man.

Hegge: All right. You were a seasoned psychologist, and your assistants were neophytes. On the other hand, the teachers at the Meyer School for the Deaf were not naïve and self-deluded kids. Why not involve their input in your analysis?

Preis-Herald: The teachers were not trained scientists.

Hegge: But teachers habitually evaluate their pupils and determine whether they have achieved mastery. I have here Exhibit J, copies of Webster's report cards from September 1974 through February 1975. They all show ratings of satisfactory performance.

Preis-Herald: Bear in mind, the teachers were used to judging human students' progress. They didn't know about animal conditioning. Also, I'm afraid that in my efforts to engage the Meyer faculty in my project, I emphasized the groundbreaking nature of their role to such an extent that they may have tricked themselves into believing in progress that didn't actually exist. Ultimately, I determined from objective, scientific analysis that Webster could not communicate, and the project had failed.

Hegge: What tipped you off?

Preis-Herald: Various things. First, Webster didn't accumulate words like a human child. He appeared to learn the signs and could reproduce them in an appropriate context, but once the lesson plans changed and he was given new vocabulary to master, he would seldom use the prior set again unless deliberately prompted.[6] He's a crammer. He would memorize signs, reflect them back during the evaluation period, then forget about them, like a student prepping for an exam.

Hegge: That doesn't sound so bad. I myself have forgotten most of what I learned in high school;

---

6 The affidavit of Sarah McMann-Lukovic of the Meyer School later countered this claim.

in my daily life, I never use Boyle's Law or the quadratic equation. Sherlock Homes, in "A Study in Scarlet," tells Dr. Watson that he doesn't bother to learn facts that are irrelevant to crime-solving because they will push more important knowledge out of his head. Why shouldn't Webster follow Mr. Holmes's example?

Preis-Herald: Sherlock Holmes's creator believed in fairies and ghosts. Considering your position, I'm not surprised you would defer to him.

Hegge: *Touché!* Well, did any other evidence lead you to discredit Webster's skills?

Preis-Herald: Yes. He was also a lazy communicator. Even when he had acquired a sign, he wouldn't always use it. For instance, he was taught the signs for "spoon," "fork," and various food items. Yet, when at table, he would sign, "Give me that," and reach for what he wanted. I recall one occasion when Ruby was eating strawberries at a picnic. Webster simply signed "Give me" and held out his hand.

Hegge: Did Ruby request clarification?

Preis-Herald: She asked that he sign "please," but she didn't insist on "strawberries."

Hegge: Was what he wanted clear enough from the context of the situation?

Preis-Herald: In that case, it was.

Hegge: That still sounds like communication.

Preis-Herald: It's ambiguous and doesn't show a true mastery of language.

Hegge: But such shorthand is typical in regular communication. Instead of "Please, pass the potatoes," people say, "Give me some of those." Webster could have witnessed such language patterns.

Preis-Herald: Oh, no. My team was scrupulous in explicitly signing all their vocabulary words. Their lessons simply failed to take root. Furthermore, he never acquired a grasp of grammar. He strung words together at random in a word salad. Instead of "Give me strawberries," he might say, "Eat me Webster you give." His displays were often redundant: "You Gail me Webster give now." No direct object, but a repetition of the subject and indirect object. That's a semblance of communication, but not communication itself. B.F. Skinner trained pigeons to dance using operant conditioning, but a dancing pigeon isn't Fred Astaire.

Hegge: In your exploration of language, have you encountered any research about a subject called Eugenie?

Preis-Herald: I have.

Hegge: Can you please summarize the details for us?

Preis-Herald: Hers was a tragic case of child abuse. From a young age, Eugenie was locked in a closet and given food and drink but no human interaction. When social workers liberated her at the age of eight, she had no language skills at all. Diligent care and painstaking attention helped her to finally learn a few basic words, but researchers concluded Eugenie had no framework for real language, no understanding of grammar or syntax and no ability to form words. Essentially, she was incapable of communication because she had missed her critical period for learning language. Because she was not exposed to language early in life when her brain was best capable of acquiring it, she never could use it. Sadly, she died at the age of sixteen of an infection, all without speaking as even a toddler is capable of doing.

Hegge: In your estimation, was Eugenie's language ability worse than, on par with, or better than Webster's?

Preis-Herald: I cannot render that judgment. I never examined Eugenie.

Hegge: But you read the reports about her? The journal articles?

Preis-Herald: Yes.

Hegge: Very well. Judging by the information in those reports and the information in the reports about Webster, which subject would you estimate had the more sophisticated language skills?

Silence.

Hegge: Doctor?

Preis-Herald: It's a specious comparison.

Hegge: After reading the reports on both subjects, do you believe Webster and Eugenie were comparable?

Preis-Herald: No. Webster expressed a broader vocabulary, but—

Hegge: Interesting. By your admission as a psycholinguist, Webster demonstrates language skills while Eugenie did not, yet Webster is slated to have his brain carved up by Dr. Teague.

Latimer: Objection! Argumentative!

Hon. N. Borley: Sustained.

Preis-Herald: You're trying to establish a false equivalency! Webster was cued.

Hegge: I am trying to establish how Webster compares to other humans since the issue at hand is whether he possesses human cognitive characteristics. For instance, how does he compare to a human child with special needs? No child would be subjected to such a study as Manfred Teague has designed.

Preis-Herald: Human beings are fundamentally different from animals—

Hegge: To date, that's been accepted as true. This hearing will determine whether some animals, particularly animals demonstrating humanlike characteristics in fact, deserve the same basic protections as humans. Now, one last point: What did you think when certain members of your team, namely Mr. Kaninchen and Ms. Ehrlich, reported they had seen the ghost that you derided?

Preis-Herald: I thought they were deluded.

Hegge: Had you found them to be reliable and trustworthy up to that point?

Preis-Herald: Yes, both were good researchers, but that doesn't preclude the fact that they were wrong. They may have honestly believed they had seen a ghost, but they were mistaken.

Hegge: Did you give credence to their other observations pertaining to the study?

Preis-Herald: To a point. Remember, these researchers also convinced themselves Webster could communicate. They saw what they wanted to see.

Hegge: According to you, your assistants deluded themselves because they wanted to believe in Webster's language skills. Do you think that they also wanted to believe in ghosts? Were Mr. Kaninchen and Ms. Ehrlich happy about their purported encounters?

Preis-Herald: No, both were quite shaken. Mr. Kaninchen even insisted on new rooming arrangements, which caused some upheaval. But he wasn't the only assistant unhappy with the accommodations. Perhaps the whole thing was a ploy to secure a more desirable room. To address your original question, I don't believe either Eric or Gail wanted to see a ghost specifically, but both were suggestible. They wanted to believe in extraordinary things, including talking chimps and visitations from beyond the grave.

Hegge: I see. Your Honor, I've no more questions at this time, but I reserve the right to recall this witness.

Latimer: I've no questions for Dr. Preis-Herald at this time, but I also reserve the right to call the witness in the future.

Hon. N. Borley: Very well. Doctor, you are dismissed for the present.

WHISPERS IN THE DARK

Broadcast Date: March 14, 1977

Celia: All these researchers and lawyers are so
hung up on the sign language, asking "Can the
ape talk?" I want to hear more about the *ghost*.
I want to know more about life after death. I
think there should be more questions about that
issue . . .

DIARY OF RUBY DALTON

March 20, 1979

Another sleepless night. If the baby doesn't keep my body from getting comfortable, my thoughts keep my brain from powering down.

In two more days, Jeff testifies. Hegge and Sam have coached him, and Hegge promises to keep his own questions brief and concentrated on Smithy's tenure at Trevor Hall; he'll re-call Jeff when it's time to address the doings at CSAM.

"We're going to establish what Smithy's routines were and what sort of communication he engaged in. It will all be very straightforward." That's how Hegge plans it anyhow. No telling how Jeff will behave once he has a platform.

And what about when Latimer starts questioning Jeff? He's condescending and confrontational. Even though it's imperative that we take the high road, I know if Jeff is provoked, he'll erupt. Then he'll look like the nut instead of Man.

Sam has been role-playing Latimer to prepare Jeff for hostile questioning. They've practiced scenarios that insult his intelligence, his motives, Smithy's intelligence, and the quality of Jeff's recordings. "And I didn't punch her in the face once. I've got this," he insists.

It's easy to hold yourself together when it's all pretend. What about when Jeff's in the courtroom with eyes and cameras on him and he feels pressured to defend himself? Or Smithy? Those thoughts stab my mind day and night and make my stomach ache.

As much as I'm dreading Thursday for Jeff's sake, I'm eager for it because of Tammy. She testifies that day, too, and she'll stay in Fresno through the weekend. It's been half a decade since we were face-to-face! I wonder what my "big sis" will think of me after all this time.

At least I know she'll be collected and mature, whatever Latimer throws at her.

Thank goodness Hegge isn't making me testify at this point. I begged him not to, and he finally concurred I could add little that Jeff wouldn't know. Eventually, I'll have to speak about CSAM though. Even if Hegge doesn't call me, Latimer will.

That doesn't bear thinking about yet. If I start considering how I'll respond under pressure, I won't sleep for a week.

COURT TRANSCRIPT

Testimony of Jeffrey Adam Dalton
March 22, 1979

Hegge: How long have you known the chimpanzee?

Dalton: About seven years, since shortly after he was born.

Hegge: In what capacity did you meet?

Dalton: I was a psychology student at Yale. Piers Preis-Herald was my graduate advisor and he invited me to assist in his new study. I thought it sounded exciting, so I agreed.

Hegge: What was your role?

Dalton: At first, I provided basic caregiving: I bathed Smithy—I nicknamed him Smithy and I've always thought of him that way. I fed him with bottles and later mashed up his solid food. I tried to play with him sometimes, keep him happy.

Hegge: Did you work with him on his language development?

Dalton: Not to the same extent as Wanda and Piers. I didn't know sign language at the time, and I had to take lessons with Wanda before she would approve me to teach Smithy. She and Piers insisted that I master signing before I worked with him. They didn't want Smithy adopting bad habits if my signing was sloppy.

Hegge: Did you have any other tasks?

Dalton: Yes, I managed various recording devices: film and still cameras and, occasionally, audiotapes of notes describing Smithy's behavior.

Hegge: What sort of behavior did you film?

Dalton: All the visits we made when Smithy lived with Lorna McKenzie, his formal training sessions at Trevor Hall, him playing, hanging out with us, cooking. Smithy loved being in the kitchen. He'd hand Wanda things she asked for and help mix ingredients.

Hegge: Approximately how much of Smithy's life at Trevor Hall did you film?

Dalton: Oh . . . maybe forty percent of his waking hours.

Hegge: What did you do with the footage?

Dalton: Piers showed some of the films in his classes or to donors. Our research team reviewed footage from time to time to see if Smithy was struggling with any tasks or if he had any activities he especially liked to do. We looked for signs he used more often than others, and counted how often he used each sign.

Hegge: Did he sign certain words more often than others?

Dalton: You, me, give, eat, good, dirty, play, woman, dark.

Hegge: Your Honor, we have sample reels of such footage from the study that we'd like to show; they are Exhibits C, D, and E.

Hon. N. Borley: Proceed, counselor.

Entered:
Exhibit C: "Smithy's first training session" –
Running time 20 minutes
Exhibit D: "Color training session" – Running
time 15 minutes
Exhibit E: "Imaginary friend" – Running time 6
minutes

Hegge: Mr. Dalton, have you altered this footage
in any way?

Dalton: I trimmed it down from its original
length. That first session, Exhibit C, was about
two hours long.

Hegge: Apart from shortening the run time, have
you made any alterations?

Dalton: No.

Hegge: Thank you, Mr. Dalton. Nothing further at
this time. Your witness, counselor.

Latimer: We reserve the right to call this witness
again.

Hon. N. Borley: Noted, counselor.

COURT TRANSCRIPT

Testimony of Tammy Steinmetz
March 22, 1979

Hegge: Drawing from your professional background in education and your personal experience in Dr. Preis-Herald's study, do you believe Smithy understands language?

Steinmetz: Yes, I do. He doesn't process language the same way you and I do, but he comprehends it well enough to respond to it. Smithy has passed through the basic stages of language acquisition and developed original signs to represent new ideas. I understand he's also been able to teach signs to other chimps.

Latimer: Objection! Hearsay!

Hon. N. Borley: Sustained.

Hegge: I'm informed your grandmother passed away during your first year at Trevor Hall and you took a few days' absence to attend the funeral. Afterward, you dressed in black for two weeks to show mourning, didn't you?

Steinmetz: I did.

Hegge: Did you notice any change in Smithy's behavior between your departure and your return?

Steinmetz: Yes. He was more reluctant to interact with me after my return.

Hegge: How did you interpret that behavior?

Steinmetz: At the time, I thought he resented my absence.

Hegge: Did you later revise your interpretation?

Steinmetz: Yes; over time, Smithy developed an aversion to the color black, and I later realized he must have been alienated by my mourning wardrobe.

Hegge: Do you know what fomented this dislike?

Steinmetz: He often signed about a "dark woman" when he was upset, so I imagined a woman in dark clothing had frightened him at some time and he then generalized his dislike. When I stopped wearing black, Smithy treated me warmly again.

Hegge: Where did he see this woman? On TV? In a picture book?

Steinmetz: I don't know. Often, his signs suggested he saw the figure in the house.

Latimer: Objection! Your Honor, this line of questioning calls for speculation. And what is the relevance?

Hon. N. Borley: Sustained. Please restrict your questions to verifiable details, Mr. Hegge.

Hegge: Did you ever experience anything unusual in the house that you could not explain?

Steinmetz: I heard strange noises—scraping and pounding—coming from the third floor. When I investigated, I saw no one there. Smithy was asleep, so he wasn't responsible. Wanda was awake at the time, but she denied hearing any noises.

Hegge: What do you think caused them?

Steinmetz: I don't know.

Hegge: Did you consider natural causes?

Steinmetz: The foundation settling? Underground streams? I think those noises would have been more consistent and less dramatic.

Hegge: Did you consider you might be hallucinating or ill?

Steinmetz: Oh, yes. About a week after the nighttime incident, I saw a local doctor. He assured me I was healthy.

Hegge: What about gases? Something chemical in the house causing everyone to imagine things?

Steinmetz: I'm sure Dr. Preis-Herald or Mr. Pierson, the owner, had Trevor Hall inspected before we moved in. Also, if noxious gases had built up in the house, the plumber would surely have noticed them on one of his many visits.

Hegge: Did you explore the notion of a ghost?

Steinmetz: Ruby and I researched the history of the house but didn't find enough documentation to support or refute a haunting. Eric and I . . . attempted communication.

Hegge: Please, explain.

Steinmetz: We held a séance the night Gail claimed to have encountered the spirit. After everyone else had retired, we went to the pantry. Wanda and I had gotten stuck in there once, and she sensed a presence. Eric laid out cards illustrating the ASL alphabet as our makeshift spirit board, set a wine glass in the center, and placed candles at the cardinal points. We each put a finger on the glass and tried to clear our minds to be receptive.

We concentrated on the questions, "Who are you?" and "What do you want?" but the glass didn't even wobble. That in itself was odd. Usually, so I've read, the unconscious mind spurs the body to move the planchette involuntarily. Eric grew frustrated. He had previously tried to communicate with the spirit and asked Smithy to tell him more about it. I want to emphasize we never specifically asked about a ghost or even a 'dark woman,' only general questions about who or what Smithy saw in the room, and he never acknowledged anything unusual. Eric believed he was holding out on us. This was our first attempt to make contact without Smithy, and it was still going nowhere. Then I thought . . .

Pause

Hegge: Go on, Ms. Steinmetz.

Steinmetz: I thought I could provoke the spirit by pretending to be her. I thought if a spirit were watching but choosing not to interact with us, and it saw me impersonating it, it would react: become angry, intervene in the séance, materialize and confront me. I wanted something to happen, even if it wasn't something good. I was tired of sitting in the dark talking to myself.

Hegge: What did you do?

Steinmetz: When Eric next asked, "Is there a presence in the room," I pushed the planchette to "Yes." He whooped so loudly, I thought the others would hear and come running. I tried to hush him, but he was too excited.

Eric spat out a stream of questions: "Are you the Dark Lady? Do you talk to Smithy? Did you appear to me?" I had to keep swirling the planchette to keep up with him. Then he asked more specific questions about the ghost's identity: "Were you a teacher at the Bradley School? Were you a servant in the Trevor household? Did you die in this house? Who are you?"

I wasn't sure what to do then. I hadn't thought through what my identity should be, and while I pondered, I didn't move the planchette at all. Eric became agitated, thinking the spirit had abandoned us.

He called out, "Don't leave us. Come back." I suppose I could have answered yes or no at random, but I developed second thoughts. I felt guilty about misleading Eric. I worried I had gone too far and my ruse could backfire, so I abandoned the deception. The planchette never moved of its own accord. If a spirit were watching us, my gambit to get its attention failed. I finally convinced Eric we weren't going to learn anything and persuaded him to say nothing of our activities. He was eager to tell the others we had contacted the ghost, but I pointed out we hadn't learned anything useful, and it wasn't worth angering Piers. Eric kept quiet, and I've never spoken about the incident until now. I never told Eric I was his ghost. I was too ashamed.

Hegge: Were you disappointed you couldn't make contact with the spirit?

Steinmetz: I was relieved. I'd been worried about stirring it up even more.

Hegge: If there was a spirit, what do you suspect was its intent?

Steinmetz: I can't imagine what it wanted. Its appearances didn't seem to accomplish anything. Maybe it enjoyed playing tricks on us? Or scaring us?

Hegge: Why did it only appear to one of you at a time?

Steinmetz: I've considered that. Maybe to manifest, the spirit needed to adjust its electromagnetic frequencies to match our individual brainwaves and could only produce one frequency at a time, the way a tuning fork can only trigger one certain register. Over the years, I've read several books about the occult. They hold that only certain people have the ability to see or communicate with ghosts. Some researchers believe in an underlying physical cause, akin to the genes that make certain people color-blind. Others cite psychological factors, like belief in an afterlife and openness to new experiences. I couldn't say which factors might have been at play for Eric or Gail. Or myself.

Hegge: Would you describe Smithy as . . . *open*?

Steinmetz: He was receptive and eager to learn.

Hegge: Thank you, Ms. Steinmetz. Your witness, Mr. Latimer.

Latimer: Mrs. Steinmetz, I couldn't help noticing how uncertain your testimony sounded. You answered "maybe" to the ghost questions several times. Are you also ambivalent about Webster's signing ability?

Steinmetz: No; enough evidence has amassed across time, situations, and people to validate Smithy's abilities. Incidentally, I prefer to be addressed as *Ms.* Steinmetz.

Latimer: How can one validate the chimp's abilities? If the issue had been settled, we wouldn't be here.

Steinmetz: Multiple witnesses possessing various levels of expertise have been able to sustain logical conversations with Smithy. When he expresses a request or a question, others correctly interpret his intent. When they ask him a question in turn, he provides a response that fits the context. That fulfills the Turing test. That's communication.

Latimer: What is "the Turing test."

Steinmetz: Alan Turing was one of this century's foremost cognitive psychologists. He worked with early computer models and developed theories about artificial intelligence. Turing believed that in the future, computers would be able to simulate human interaction so well that a real human wouldn't be able to tell the difference. He proposed a thought experiment wherein a person would communicate with an unseen partner by typing messages on a computer screen. The subject would have to guess, solely from the responses, whether their partner was another person or a machine. An incorrect guess meant the imitation was successful. If you transcribe Smithy's interactions, they resemble human speech closely enough that he could pass for a person.

Latimer: Have you performed this Turing test and found that independent judges mistook the ape for a human, Mrs. Steinmetz?

Steinmetz: No, *Lance*, I have not, but I think it should be done. I'm confident in the outcome.

Latimer: Perhaps Mr. Hegge will perform the test in his arguments. He's fond of spectacle.

Hon. N. Borley: Mr. Latimer . . .

Latimer: I apologize, Your Honor. Let's shift gears. You've talked about the animal's cognitive abilities. What about its behavior? Was the chimp sweet-tempered or violent?

Steinmetz: It's disingenuous to characterize Smithy's personality as either/or. He wasn't exclusively one thing or the other. Most of the time, he was compliant, but he had occasional outbursts.

Latimer: "Outbursts" sounds mild, Mrs. Steinmetz? Didn't you see him attack the household pets?

Steinmetz: No, Lance, I did not.

Latimer: No? Mrs. Steinmetz, do you deny Smithy assaulted one of the cats and it had to be removed from the house for its own safety?

Steinmetz: I don't deny that, but I didn't see it happen.

Latimer: Were you present on the night of November 14, 1974, when Webster attacked Eric Kaninchen and two cats in Ms. Karlewicz's room?

Steinmetz: I was present, but I didn't see Smithy attack the cats. I saw him attempt to capture the cats by climbing up the bookcase where they had retreated, but he didn't lay hands on them. I don't know what his intention was. He did drag Eric around the room, but it was a reaction, not an act of spontaneous aggression. Eric was keeping Smithy from reaching the cats.

Latimer: Didn't Webster also set the dog on fire that same night?

Steinmetz: I don't know. The dog was shut up in a room that caught fire, but I don't know if Smithy locked her there, if he set the fire, or how any of that happened.

Latimer: Do you believe the various fires in the house—over twenty before the end of 1974—were due to spirit influence?

Steinmetz: Possibly. Possibly poor wiring was responsible.

Latimer: During your stay at Trevor Hall, the plumbing broke down six times. Do you believe that was also due to spirit influence?

Steinmetz: Possibly, but unlikely.

Latimer: Why blame the fires on ghosts but not the backed-up toilets?

Steinmetz: The electricians didn't find anything amiss with the wiring, whereas the plumbers made temporary repairs to the pipes, substantiating that pipes caused the problems.

Latimer: But *ghosts*, Mrs. Steinmetz? Why not arson? Smithy frequently left his room and roamed the house at odd hours. Did it ever occur to you he might have been playing with matches?

Steinmetz: We considered that. Wanda started counting the kitchen matches each night and morning and even locked them in a drawer. Jeff hid a camera in the kitchen to record Smithy in case he was taking the matches. We never caught him doing that.

Latimer: But why not natural causes? Nerves? Imagination?

Steinmetz: Six different people sharing hallucinations for fourteen months? I think a ghost is a much simpler explanation than trying to cite multiple different causes for each experience. Besides, it's not incumbent on me to explain what happened. I'm just telling you what I experienced.

Latimer: Did you fabricate other hauntings the way you fabricated your séance with Mr. Kaninchen?

Steinmetz: Never.

Latimer: No further questions.

DIARY OF RUBY DALTON

March 22, 1979

After all my worrying about Jeff, I never expected Tammy would be the one to talk back.

"Latimer is such a monumental ass, I couldn't control myself," she explained. I can't disagree.

But her outburst wasn't the most surprising part of her testimony. I never knew she and Eric held their own séances. I was always too scared when he'd suggest them, lest we open a door we couldn't close and make things worse. Maybe that's why they left me out of their plans.

I worried Jeff might ask her for more details about their sessions, but he left us to ourselves to catch up while he and Brad compared notes on the case. I started filling Tammy in about the next stage in the hearing, but she cut me off. "I can read about the trial in the newspapers, Ruby. How are you?"

I can't remember the last time anyone asked me that when it wasn't just a social pleasantry or a veiled attempt to get an update on Smithy. For a moment, I wasn't sure where to begin. I made a joke about being pregnant, and she made a joke about changing diapers, and then we were talking, really talking again. Our words flowed more freely than they ever did over the phone because we could see each other's reactions.

I fretted about how to make ends meet with only one part-time paycheck (soon to be discontinued) and about Jeff's single-mindedness. Tammy listened with a patient smile.

"You're doing a hell of a job," she finally said, "more than I ever could, did, or wanted to. Remember, I left the project. You're still here, and carrying the fight further than anyone else has." So often, I feel frustrated about all that I haven't been able to accomplish in my life, and how different everything is from what I imagined it would be. Tammy's

support mitigated that sense of failure immensely. It felt so good to have someone care about me for a change.

We're going out tomorrow after my shift to see the sights of Fresno, such as they are. Tammy is taking me shopping as a belated Christmas/early birthday gift. For a few hours, at least, I can put my worries behind me and enjoy time with my best friend. And for a whole week, I don't have to go back to court!

COURT TRANSCRIPT

Testimony of Gail Beveridge
March 28, 1979

Hegge: How did you determine when Smithy had mastered a word?

Beveridge: The sign had to be crisp and clear. He had to use it at least three times in the proper context, and at least one time he had to use it without any prompting.

Hegge: What does "crisp and clear" mean?

Beveridge: Oh, that the sign was formed according to standard Ameslan. He couldn't be sloppy and droop a finger or only motion halfway.

Hegge: Did Smithy ever make up his own sign instead of using a standard sign?

Beveridge: Yes, but it still had to be repeated consistently three times and he had to use his own sign in conversation in a way that made sense.

Hegge: Could more than one sign have made an acceptable response? For instance, if you held up a banana to demonstrate the concept "yellow" and Smithy signed "fruit" instead, would that count as an appropriate response?

Beveridge: Yes, and he did exactly what you said. We once had a list of fruit words. I showed him an apple and he signed "red" and "food," but I was trying to teach him the sign for "fruit." I had to show him the new sign in combination with lots of different fruits—apples, pears, bananas, oranges—until he understood they were all part of a group called "fruit."

Hegge: Now if he signed, "Give Smithy apple," did that carry the same validity as, "Give Smithy fruit" or "Give Smithy food?"

Beveridge: Yes, technically. Because it was a true sentence. An apple is fruit, and fruit is food. But we'd try to encourage him to use one word or another depending on what the vocabulary assignment was. Wanda was a big proponent of making Smithy be as specific as possible. She wasn't satisfied if he signed "clothes"; she wanted him to sign "sweater." You see?

Hegge: Instead of "Gimme that thingamajig," she wanted the specific noun?

Beveridge: Yes.

Hegge: But did you all still understand his request?

Beveridge: Yes.

Hegge: Did you believe Smithy's substitution of one word for another represented a true transitive understanding? I mean, did you believe he used synonyms because he grasped—

Beveridge: Yes, I thought any time he used a sign, he understood what it meant.

Hegge: So, as long as *you* understood Smithy, you believed *Smithy* understood his own signs?

Beveridge: That's right.

Hegge: So far, Mrs. Beveridge, I've asked about your experiences with Smithy. Now, I'm going to ask about your experiences with the house.

Beveridge: OK . . .

Hegge: What happened on April 8, 1975?

Beveridge: We had a big dinner party.

Hegge: Did you attend that party?

Beveridge: No.

Hegge: Why not?

Beveridge: I wasn't feeling well.

Hegge: Were you physically ill or were you upset about something that had happened earlier in the day?

Beveridge: Something happened.

Hegge: Mrs. Beveridge, please tell the court what happened that day.

Beveridge: I was coming downstairs from my room. I used the servants' stairs instead of the main stairs because they were closer to the kitchen, and I was going there to see if Wanda needed help. I was going downstairs and—I can't remember now if I first heard my name or if I felt a chill like another door had opened—but I knew I wasn't alone anymore. I looked up, thinking one of my housemates had come looking for me. And I saw a figure. But I couldn't make out who it was because it was all black.

Hegge: What did the figure look like?

Beveridge: It was a woman. I'm not sure how I knew that because she didn't have any features. I couldn't see her face. It was covered by something. But . . . she wore a dress, I think. She . . . didn't have any legs. Just terminated in shadow. But I could see a long black gown billowing around her, like—

Pause.

Hegge: Mrs. Beveridge? Mrs. Beveridge, can you please continue? Mrs. Beveridge, what is it?

Witness screams.

DIARY OF RUBY DALTON

March 28, 1979

Gail's mouth opened and closed like a fish's, and her eyes strained from her head. I thought she was having a seizure until I followed her frightened stare.

And I saw Her again.

The figure of a woman, her skirt billowing above the ground, her face a solid sheet of black. Pointing up at Gail on the witness stand.

I squeezed my eyes shut, but when I opened them again, She was still there in the very back of the room, still pointing. And Gail still looked like she was about to pass out.

Gail sees it, too, *I thought.* It's not in my imagination. This is really happening! She's returned! *Then my stomach squeezed, and it took all my strength to hold my teeth together and keep my breakfast down.*

I pinched and shook Jeff's arm. He'd been gaping at Gail, but he swung around to me. I couldn't speak, but I twitched my head in Her direction so he would turn around. I wanted him to see Her, too. But Jeff just kept asking, "What? What is it?"

Then Gail's scream blew through the packed courtroom and brought the spectators to their feet, and I lost Jeff's attention altogether. He and Brad—and half the front row—rushed forward to help Gail, who had slumped over the podium.

And that black figure continued to point.

FROM "SPECTER IN THE COURTROOM; WITNESS FAINTS" BY GORDON DAVIOT

The Daily Collegian, March 28, 1979

Proceedings in Smithy v. CSAM *came to a screaming halt this afternoon while Gail Beveridge was on the stand. A former Preis-Herald researcher, Mrs. Beveridge now resides in Jefferson City, MO, with her husband and two children.*

Mrs. Beveridge had testified in detail about Smithy's lesson plans and his helpfulness with household chores when attorney Conrad Hegge turned his questioning toward the supernatural. As Mrs. Beveridge described her alleged encounter with the infamous Dark Lady of Trevor Hall, the witness pointed and shrieked, then collapsed. A bailiff revived her with smelling salts.

Mrs. Beveridge's anxiety was provoked by a woman cloaked in black who had appeared at the rear of the courtroom during her testimony. Other attendees at the hearing also saw this dark lady and reported that she pointed accusingly at Mrs. Beveridge.

Proof of the paranormal? Hardly.

Bailiffs apprehended the dark lady, who failed to disappear before being brought up on charges of contempt of court and disruption of the peace. Amy Paulson, 21, a Fresno State student, admitted she had followed the case and planned the hoax to coincide with "really spooky [stories]" about incidents at the Newport, RI mansion. Ms. Paulson wore a long black skirt and reversible jacket to court; she also smuggled a black veil under her blouse. When Mr. Hegge introduced the alleged haunting, she turned her coat, put on the veil, and took a position where Mrs. Beveridge would be able to see her.

The witness remained so distraught, even after learning the ghost sighting was bogus, that court recessed.

CSAM defense attorney Lance Latimer told the _Collegian_, "Regardless of how juvenile this prank was, Mrs. Beveridge certainly seemed to believe in it. I hope she recovers from her shock. However, I can't help but question the lady's reliability. If she could be so easily fooled by this "ghost," then about what else is she mistaken?

Was this hoaxer a plant intended to cast doubt and disdain on the plaintiff's witness? Time will tell.

For now, the jury remains out on the existence of ghosts.

COURT TRANSCRIPT

Testimony of Gail Beveridge
March 29, 1979

Latimer: How are you today, Mrs. Beveridge?

Beveridge: Better, thank you.

Latimer: Thank you for being here today.

Beveridge: I didn't think I had any choice. *(Witness laughs).* Um, you're welcome?

Latimer: I'll try to make this brief, so as not to tire you. To review yesterday's testimony, you and Webster got along well together, and he was receptive to your teachings and eager to please. Is that accurate?

Beveridge: It is.

Latimer: You said before that during your sign language lessons, you would "try to encourage him to use one word or another depending on what the vocabulary assignment was," and he was receptive to that.

Beveridge: Yes. I mean no, no! It wasn't like . . . I mean, we didn't lead him. He knew how to make the signs and what they meant. We just needed to make him understand when we wanted him to show a certain sign. Like I said before, "fruit" still describes an apple, but we wanted him to ask for the apple by name.

Latimer: I see. And when you gave him these cues, he understood how you wanted him to respond and was perfectly willing to do what you asked.

Beveridge: It wasn't like you're making it sound. Smithy *learned*! He's very smart. He was a good student.

Latimer: Did you never know him to misbehave?

Beveridge: Well, he was a prankster. One time, he hid these brownies—

Latimer: Did Webster ever misbehave, above and beyond simple childish naughtiness?

Beveridge: Yes . . .

Latimer: Do you recall the events of November 14, 1974?

Beveridge: Yes. Smithy got loose. We searched everywhere, including the closed-off part of the house. He was there, and he was very angry. He broke a skylight and nearly cut me and my friends very badly. Then he went back to Wanda's room and threatened her cats. And when Eric—our now-deceased friend Eric—tried to calm him down, Smithy pulled him off his feet and towed him around the room.

Latimer: What did you think of that?

Beveridge: I was terrified! I'd never seen Smithy act that way. Sometimes he'd squeeze the cats too hard when he hugged them or pull the dog's tail when he wanted to play, but this time he was *trying* to hurt somebody. I didn't know he was capable of that, and I didn't know what he might do next. I was afraid he might really hurt Eric. Like, throw him across the room or-or break his legs. Eric couldn't stop him. Or maybe he was too afraid to try.

Latimer: What happened to Eric?

Beveridge: We finally knocked over the bookcase as a distraction so Eric could get away. He had a sprained ankle and bruises but nothing as bad as it could have been. I think Smithy purposely held back. That, in his own way, he was still playing. Or he just wanted to scare Eric but not actually hurt him.

Latimer: Did you invite your younger sister Vanessa to Newport three months after this incident?

Beveridge: Yes.

Latimer: Why?

Beveridge: She'd wanted to visit since Christmas. I'd told her when I started working there that she could visit, and I owed it to her to keep my promise.

Latimer: Did you intend to keep your promise even if it meant compromising your sister's safety? You allowed her to interact with Webster, didn't you?

Beveridge: I did. She wanted to meet him, and we thought it would be good for him to see new faces. Vanessa learned some signs and helped teach him.

Latimer: Mrs. Beveridge, do you love your sister?

Beveridge: Of course!

Latimer: Then why, after witnessing the chimp's capacity for violence, would you knowingly bring her into a situation where she might be harmed? Webster had already attacked Ruby and Eric, two beloved caregivers. Vanessa was a stranger to him; he had no loyalty to her.

Beveridge: Nothing happened! Smithy liked her, and Vanessa adored him. She was crushed when she had to leave.

Latimer: But something *could* have happened, could it not? Webster could have dragged Vanessa the way he dragged Eric. He could have broken her legs. He could have *bitten* her.

Beveridge: Smithy didn't have any reason to hurt Vanessa. He just had a bad day those other times. It happens. Everybody has bad days. It wasn't his fault he was so much stronger than everybody else. He didn't know his own strength. And we didn't know what was wrong. He could have been sick and didn't know how to tell us.

Latimer: You mean Webster, the Great Communicator, couldn't properly convey his message?

Beveridge: As many words as we taught Smithy, there were always more he didn't know. It's harder to describe how you're feeling or what you're thinking than it is to ask for second helpings at dinner.

Latimer: Mrs. Beveridge, did you not consider the risks to your sister before you brought her to Newport? You're an intelligent young woman. You had been observing this animal for more than a year. Did you not foresee the possibility that her visit might end tragically?

Beveridge: Smithy had been so good for three months. I didn't believe he would hurt her.

Latimer: But you *did* consider the possibility Webster might hurt your sister, so you didn't invite her to visit in December but waited until March when his behavior appeared to stabilize. Isn't that right, Mrs. Beveridge?

Witness begins to cry.

Latimer: Please answer the question, Mrs. Beveridge.

Beveridge: Ye-es . . . I thought . . . I knew he *could* but I didn't believe he *would*. He was so young and innocent, like a child. And he was so cute . . . I didn't want to believe he was dangerous.

Latimer: Did you ever suspect he would hurt you?

Witness sobs.

Hon. N. Borley: Would you like a recess for your witness, Mr. Latimer?

Latimer: Do you need a break, Mrs. Beveridge? Some water? No? We'll continue, Your Honor. Now, what happened the night of July 4, 1975.

Beveridge: We . . . were watching fireworks. On the roof.

Latimer: And?

Inaudible.

Latimer: Did you say Webster tried to hurt you? Please speak up, Mrs. Beveridge.

Beveridge: Yes.

Latimer: Tell the court what happened.

Beveridge: We were watching fireworks, and I wanted a closer look, so I stepped toward the little wall that separated us from the edge. I said, "Come see, Smithy." I'd been looking at the harbor, and when I turned around, I saw him—all bristly. His eyes were big, and he looked like he was going to attack. I put my arms in front of my face to protect myself. And he launched himself at me. I felt him hit me. In the chest and shoulders. And I went backward. I barely managed to grab on to the little wall as I was falling.

For an instant, I wasn't sure what had happened. But I could feel the air all around and below me, and when I kicked my legs, there was nothing to stand on. I started screaming. Then I felt Smithy's hands on mine. I couldn't see him, but I knew they were his from all the times I'd held them or molded them into words. They were pulling at my hands. First, I thought he was trying to help me up. Then I felt him strike the back of my hand . . .

Witness cries.

And I knew he was trying to *loosen* my hands! I don't remember much else. I know I kept screaming because I stupidly thought my voice would carry to some of the other houses nearby. And people would come help. Stretch out a blanket below me or something. So I could finally let go and land safely. I seemed to hang like that forever. Then I felt more hands. And Eric pulled me up. I don't remember anything else until a neighbor was helping me into an ambulance. I've been told I was in shock.

Latimer: I'm sorry to put you through this, Mrs. Beveridge, but it's important the court know what kind of animal Webster is. You said you were watching fireworks when he pushed you off the building. You did nothing to provoke him?

Beveridge: No.

Latimer: He jumped at you. Without warning. Without provocation. He *intended* to push you off the roof.

Witness cries.

Latimer: Did you see anyone provoke him? Touch him or tease him?

Beveridge: No.

Latimer: Did any of the firework sparks touch the house or spook him?

Beveridge: No.

Latimer: Mrs. Beveridge, what do you think happened? You must have some opinion after all this time.

Beveridge: I figured I did something. I don't know what. Maybe I raised my voice to be heard over the noise, and he thought I was shouting at him. Or maybe I'd done something earlier in the day that Smithy didn't like and still remembered. I've never understood it. We were such good friends! We spent so much time together. I thought I understood him. I was never scared of him. But after hearing the other witnesses, I think maybe they're right. Smithy depended on us to take care of him because he didn't know how to take care of himself. And somehow, I let him down.

Latimer: Mrs. Beveridge, it's common for victims of violence to blame themselves or consider things they might have done differently. But you must realize your actions could not have affected Webster so dramatically. The chimp acted of its own volition. It *chose* to injure.

Beveridge: I *do* think it was me! Smithy wouldn't have come at me like he did unless he felt threatened. You don't know. You weren't there. You didn't see what went on.

Latimer: What went on, Mrs. Beveridge?

Beveridge: Things happened in the house. He tried to tell us, and we didn't understand. We let him down. He must have been frightened. Maybe he resented us.

Latimer: Are you implying a supernatural intervention?

Beveridge: It could have been. I didn't see anything that night, but maybe Smithy did. He wasn't violent by nature. I can't believe . . . I don't *want* to think he did those things on purpose. I never will.

Latimer: No further questions.

DIARY OF RUBY DALTON

March 29, 1979

Poor Gail. I didn't realize how hard on her this whole process would be. I spoke to her before court this morning and told her she was a trooper for getting back on the stand. She seemed embarrassed by the ghost hoax (I didn't tell her I fell for it, too) and by Latimer twisting her testimony to make it seem like we fed Smithy words we wanted him to use. She seems to believe she hurt our case, but Hegge says she's done us a good turn by refusing to blame Smithy outright for attacking her.

It may be mean of me to say so, but I'm glad that stupid prank happened when Gail was testifying. Her hysterical reaction isn't such a black eye for our case because, for some reason, Gail seems to have the least credibility of any of us. Had Tammy or Jeff responded in kind, it would have been more bruising. Maybe it's because she's the youngest of our group, or because she's no longer involved in academia. I was surprised to hear she went into cosmetology instead of finishing her degree. (We have fallen out of touch; at least I remembered she got married). I suspect some people may see her as flaky or dumb for doing that, though her decision sounds pretty clever to me. As Gail explained, being a hairdresser allows her to be her own boss and choose her own working hours, so she has flexibility to be with her children when she wants. Maybe I should do the same. "Entrepreneurial manicurist" sounds more impressive than "waitress" or "store clerk."

Tomorrow, the Meyer teachers, represented by Simon, Hope, and Sarah, will testify. I hope they give Smithy another glowing report. . .

EXCERPT FROM
"THE LATEST WORD ON 'SMITHY'?"

Time Magazine, October 9, 1978

. . . While Dr. Preis-Herald's fortunes have dipped, the Meyer School still draws accolades. Graduation rates remain at 90 percent, and on average, 60 percent of pupils go on to college.

Senior instructor Hope Wellborn and Principal Simon Gagnon are the only remaining faculty who taught Smithy (April Heath married and left teaching in the summer of 1977 and Sarah McMann joined the Peace Corps in 1976). They recall him as a bright and mischievous pupil who loved attention—good or bad.

According to Wellborn, "He had a sweet disposition. When you interacted, he'd watch you and anticipate your next move."

"Try to figure out how to outsmart you, you mean," Gagnon jokes. "You could almost see little wheels turning behind his eyes."

"Smithy could persuade you to give him snacks or play another round of chase when you both knew he was supposed to be drilling. Sometimes he grew frustrated. He'd sulk in his corner and refuse to sign with you. But if you gave him a hug, he would give one back. He always responded to kindness." A nostalgic smile crosses Wellborn's lips but doesn't reach her eyes. "Even though they pulled him out of school because they said he was becoming violent, he never bit or scratched or hit me."

"He knew your limitations," Gagnon adds. "He knew what he could get away with and how far he could push you, but he also sensed how you could be hurt. With April [Heath], he would threaten her property; during a tantrum, he'd tear up the artwork other students had made for her walls or throw books. She was a little thing, so he never got physical with her. Nor with Hope. She's a soft, motherly type. He didn't mind pushing *me* now and then, but he didn't do it hard enough to cause any damage. And he could have."

Wellborn claims, "At times, you could almost forget Smithy was an ape. He became a funny-looking little child. I signed with him as casually as I would with any kindergartner. It didn't matter to me that he didn't know all the words I was using. The important thing Preis-Herald impressed on us was to normalize signing for him."

Gagnon agrees. "Smithy was fascinated whenever I showed him a new sign, but he didn't always adopt the new word right away. I remember teaching him the sign for 'coffee' one day. He immediately lost interest, but about a month later, he watched me drinking from a mug—something I'd often done in the intervening weeks—and he abruptly signed, 'Give Smithy coffee.' I almost dropped my mug."

DIARY OF RUBY DALTON

March 30, 1979

. . . *Simon was wonderful. Latimer tried to make Simon say he had to partner with April and Hope when they taught Smithy because they were afraid he might attack them. Simon acted shocked. "None of us ever worried about that. Smithy never made a move against any of us. April was petite, and Hope has a bad back, so they couldn't lift him. I was muscle, not protection."*

Tammy always used to complain that Smithy behaved so well for his teachers and saved his bad moods for us, but I'm glad now that he was selective. It really helped to have credible educators give him glowing reviews.

Hegge also read a declaration from April in court. She described how Smithy would sometimes sign to himself the words for pictures in books he was looking at, showing that he didn't only sign when in conversation. She also described how Smithy used language to manipulate the staff by signing "dirty" to indicate he needed to use the toilet. In fact, he was only pretending so he could interrupt the lesson, knowing the staff would respond quickly to this sign. "By these actions," she wrote, "I always perceived that Smithy possessed strong intelligence, a will of his own, and a satisfactory grasp of language."

Pretty soon, Hegge will have to get a declaration from me. I won't be able to come to court much longer. As it is, I have to get up every twenty minutes or so to use the bathroom. The bailiff keeps giving me dirty looks.

Of course, after the instructors finished testifying, Hegge brought the parapsychologist to the stand, and my sense of triumph withered . . .

COURT TRANSCRIPT

Testimony of Lyle Ohrbach, PhD
March 30, 1979

Hegge: Please state your name and occupation for the court.

Ohrbach: My name is Lyle Owen Ohrbach. I've been a professor and researcher in the psychology department at Stanford University for three years. I've held my PhD since 1969.

Hegge: What is your research specialty?

Ohrbach: I focus on the field known as parapsychology. I'm currently engaged in a joint project with members of the physics department.

Hegge: Is that unusual?

Ohrbach: Hardly. Parapsychology is a plastic rather than a rigid discipline. There are no degrees in the field, no basic curriculum. Rather, various practitioners apply their own specialties toward understanding the more mysterious aspects of the human experience from various angles.

Hegge: Is parapsychology a science?

Ohrbach: Oh, yes. It has been recognized by the American Association for the Advancement of Science.

Hegge: How interesting. Perhaps we can now put an end to rash accusations of "voodoo" and "chicanery" in the courtroom. How long have you been a parapsychologist, Doctor?

Ohrbach: I suppose since 1971 when I met a student, a Vietnam vet, who related to me an unusual experience he'd had in the service. He'd enrolled in the psychology program to better understand what had happened. In brief, he had what we call an out-of-body experience or OBE that helped him avoid an ambush. I'd never heard of anything like it, but as I read the available literature, I became intrigued, and I've been on a quest to learn more ever since.

Hegge: After eight years of study, you must be a real expert.

Ohrbach: There are no experts. It's a wide, wild area of study, but I'm doing my best to chart one piece of it at a time.

Hegge: What does your piece cover? OBEs? Ghosts? ESP?

Ohrbach: The last. I've performed experiments in telepathy, remote viewing, clairvoyance, and precognition. Soon I'll begin an investigation of telekinesis, the power to move objects using the energy of the mind.[7]

---

7 In a subsequent paper, Dr. Ohrbach reported that target objects were warm to the touch after having been (allegedly) psychically manipulated. He claimed this resulted from the build-up of kinetic energy, which psychics then manipulated. Dr. Ohrbach further suggested so-called poltergeist phenomena are not due to ghosts but to living psychics subconsciously using telekinesis.

Hegge: Those topics sound pretty far out, Dr. Ohrbach. I'm surprised the university sees fit to fund them.

Ohrbach: The university encourages inquiry and open minds, but much of my funding comes from outside sources. We've even had inquiries from government agencies, though I'm not at liberty to elaborate. Suffice it to say our exploratory research is encouraging enough for us to continue.

Hegge: Encouraged by the CIA?

Ohrbach: No comment.

Hegge: Fair enough. Now, I asked you a minute ago about whether you studied ghosts. Do you?

Ohrbach: I do not. In fact, I don't even believe in traditional ghosts. I believe that when we think we're seeing or communicating with a ghost, we're actually experiencing a kind of telepathy, a communion with a bygone energy trace that's left an imprint on the environment. Some of my experiments have required psychics to describe the history of an unknown, unseen, wrapped-up object by reading its energy. I study precognition, which is psychic knowledge of the future. There's also retrocognition, psychic knowledge of the past, the ability to peek through a window in time and see and hear the dead. It's one-way perception. The dead don't interact with us. But sensitives can still read the thoughts and actions of the deceased. If you consider those living memories to be ghosts, well then, I suppose that is part of what I study.

Hegge: Is that a standard, accepted explanation about ghosts?

Ohrbach: Oh, no. There are as many different ideas about what makes a ghost as you can imagine. Just as I believe a ghost is the lingering trace of energy from the past, some parapsychologists believe ghosts are actually visions of the future that we glimpse at odd moments. Many others uphold the traditional notion that a ghost is a conscious, earthbound spirit. Some believe ghosts are the souls of people who died with unfinished business—because they passed away suddenly or in extreme circumstances. Some believe ghosts simply cling to the places that were most familiar to them in this life without necessarily suffering a tragedy, as if they continue their routines unaware they're dead.

Hegge: Based on your research findings, how would you account for the stories about Smithy and the dark woman he and the students at Trevor Hall claim to have seen?

Ohrbach: I suspect these witnesses psychically tapped into the history of the place and glimpsed an image of a woman who really did occupy the house at some point. They were no doubt confused and alarmed by what they experienced. The humans called it a ghost. The ape, lacking the concept of a ghost, simply thought he was seeing another person and attempted to communicate with it as if it were another member of the household.

Hegge: How could an ape see such a thing, regardless of whether it was a true entity or lingering energy?

Ohrbach: Animals possess a broader range of senses than the average human. Dogs can hear high-frequency sounds that don't register on human ears. Certain predators, like snakes and sharks, can see infrared light. We don't know exactly how a ghost manifests. It often appears through a combination of visual and auditory, and sometimes tangible stimuli. Therefore, an animal would be more likely to perceive a ghost than a human. Many reports from so-called haunted houses describe agitated pets reacting to something no one else can see. In fact, I understand that the other animals at Trevor Hall also reacted to an unseen presence in the house; that the dog would bark at thin air and the cats would react defensively, absent any visible threat.

Hegge: Now, humans also encountered the presence. Ms. Beveridge testified that she saw a dark figure, and Ms. Steinmetz claimed to have heard noises. How could that be?

Ohrbach: Theirs were not consistent, continuous experiences. The women didn't always see what Smithy and the house pets saw. I speculate that they may have been only temporarily attuned to the phenomena, just as humans can hear certain high-pitched tones as teenagers but not when they reach adulthood. Or possibly the witnesses are themselves sensitive to extrasensory phenomena. Just as a minority of the population is color-blind while most people can perceive a full color spectrum, certain people can perceive unusual phenomena that most others cannot.

What separates people from apes is that humans are very good at rationalizing. The women may have been able to tune the ghost out or talk themselves out of what they were experiencing because it didn't fit within their preconceived notions of the world. A chimp would have no such reference framework, and so Smithy continued to respond to the ghost, even after the humans did not.

Hegge: Given the opportunity, would you test Smithy in your lab?

Ohrbach: I'm definitely intrigued by all I've heard about him, but I wouldn't know where to begin. I don't specialize in ghostly communication. I think Smithy would be better off in the hands of my colleague in England, Wilbur Roland; he's conducted numerous investigations of poltergeist phenomena, which many of the peculiar activities reported at Trevor Hall, especially the spontaneous fires, seem to match.[8]

There's also Klaus Kleiner of Austria. He frequently works with mediums. I've heard some tantalizing stories filtering through the Iron Curtain about work being performed by our counterparts in the Soviet Union. It wouldn't surprise me if Moscow made an offer on the chimp once this trial is concluded.

Hegge: Can you account in any other way for the experiences you've heard described?

Ohrbach: I've repeatedly heard that Smithy has the same intellectual capacities as a human being. Well, keep in mind human beings don't always tell the truth. They may deliberately lie or make mistakes. They may hallucinate or become self-deluded through denial or repression.

Hegge: Are you suggesting Smithy could be psychotic?

Ohrbach: Oh, no. I'm not a trained psychoanalyst. I'm not qualified to make pronouncements on the

8 The fires, allegedly, also resulted from the build-up of kinetic energy and the residual heat produced.

human mind, and I certainly don't claim to be able to diagnose the mind of a chimpanzee. I'm merely suggesting reasonable alternative explanations for Smithy's behavior could exist that wouldn't necessarily undercut the validity of his basic communication skills. However, I will defer to the primate ethologist who, I understand, will be testifying later.

Hegge: Very good, Mr. Ohrbach. That concludes my questions for you. Mr. Latimer, your witness.

Latimer: No questions.

DIARY OF RUBY DALTON

. . . *Ohrbach wasn't on the stand for long. After the big build-up Hegge gave him in our pre-trial planning, I was afraid he would ramble for days. He was actually quite restrained. I'd had nightmares of a swami in a turban describing solstice rituals conducted at Stonehenge with Shirley MacLaine, but Ohrbach stayed within the loose bounds of scientific possibility. He didn't make any official pronouncements or confirm Smithy as a channeler. I listened to his different interpretations and wondered what I saw in the bathroom: An echo? A premonition? A true spirit? I can't believe what haunted us was anything other than an intelligent force. But what could she want? Ohrbach never attempted to guess.*

After he stepped down, I thought, "That's it?" I was surprised at myself for wanting more when I hadn't wanted Ohrbach to testify at all, and I wondered whether the spectators might feel the same way. Nevertheless, I recall Hegge's initial advice: we just need to introduce reasonable belief. Ohrbach has kept alive the idea that Smithy represents something far greater than a simple research subject, and that's all we need.

WHISPERS IN THE DARK

Broadcast Date: March 30, 1979

Celia: Hey, night owls! Were you watching the trial today? If you're like me, then you were eagerly anticipating the testimony of Parapsychologist Lyle Ohrbach, supernatural expert from Stanford. And maybe, like me, you feel a little bit . . . let down. His testimony was *so* dry. *I* wanted to hear about the ghost. I thought that's why they brought him in. All this ESP business just didn't cut it for me. I thought maybe Dr. Ohrbach was holding back, trying to keep things professional while he was in the courtroom, so I invited him to talk with us a little bit further about the Other Side.

Before you get excited, he begged off. He said he *really* doesn't know anything about ghosts, and he *really* wants to focus on the powers of the mind because that offers the best chance of obtaining verifiable evidence and professional respect.

But rather than leave you all hanging tonight listening to little ol' me mouth off, I give you Dr. Armand Stokes, a psychology professor at UCLA who researches the occult in his spare time and who was in Fresno today observing the trial. Dr. Stokes is more than happy to answer our questions about ghosts, poltergeists, and what the heck went on in that house. Thank you so much for coming, Doctor.

Stokes: It's my pleasure, Miss Armendariz. I'll do what I can to enlighten you and our listeners as to what is known about the spirit world. I hope I shan't bore you.

Celia: I'm hoping you can answer some of our burning questions. First of all, I thought the whole earthbound spirit thing meant a ghost was stuck wherever it died. If a ghost is haunting a house, it can't leave the house, right?

Stokes: That's what's commonly believed. However, Dr. Ohrbach discussed different theories about ghosts in his testimony. If you believe a ghost is nothing more than a memory that has imprinted itself on the environment, then you're correct that a ghost cannot leave the location where the memory is fixed. It would be like trying to play a 45 record in an eight-track player. The medium and the machine are designed to go together; if you mix them up, you won't achieve the same effect. But if a ghost is more than a mere recording, the possibilities are—well, maybe not limitless, but much more elastic.

It would be helpful to know if we were dealing with the spirit of a dead person or some other type of entity. For instance, Dr. Ohrbach referred to poltergeists. Unlike a traditional ghost, a poltergeist is not tied to a place, but to a person. Where the individual goes, the phenomena follow. The students' reports of objects missing or moving by themselves definitely resemble poltergeist activities, so it would seem Trevor Hall isn't haunted, but *the chimpanzee* is haunted.

Celia: I'm shivering.

Stokes: However, a poltergeist may not even be a ghost—

Celia: Whaaat? I'm getting confused . . .

Stokes: Imagine how we feel. We're supposed to be the experts.

They laugh.

Stokes: In some instances, poltergeist phenomena seem to be tied to ESP. Objects are moved unconsciously through a form of telekinesis exercised by the focus person, the figure who seems always to be present whenever mysterious events occur and who may even be a target of the violence or pranks.

Celia: Are you saying the chimp could be doing all this himself?

Stokes: Possibly. Chimps are fundamentally physically like humans. ESP is a human ability. I don't see why chimps couldn't share it. However, that doesn't explain what this shadowy figure, this Dark Woman, could be. Now, another possibility is this Dark Woman could be a completely different type of force. Not a spirit of the dead, not a form of ESP, but some other type of intelligence—

Celia: A demon?

Stokes: Well, that's one popular bugaboo among certain occult investigators. If anything unusual or frightening is going on, why, a demon must be causing it. So, yes, I suppose we must consider that possibility.

Celia: I can recommend a *curandero* . . .

Stokes: Maybe not so fast. This being could be an elemental. Many cultures believe in spirits that aren't necessarily spirits of the dead. They believe inanimate objects like rocks, trees, or rivers possess awareness. Even weather phenomena exercise intelligence and intention. Certain places are supposed to be inhabited by nature spirits—

Celia: But wouldn't an earth spirit or a river spirit be tied to one place?

Stokes: I mention those only as examples. If these traditions are correct, many, many spirits or deities could exist around us in the unseen world. People throughout history have written of beings neither human nor ghostly that possess great power and can take on humanlike form to interact with us.

Celia: The Dark Lady could be an evil fairy, and she's cursed Smithy because she wasn't invited to his big birthday party!

Stokes: That's . . . something to consider. My point is, a nonhuman entity needn't be tied to a specific place. One of my colleagues at the university has been working with a young woman who claims she is being stalked and assaulted by an invisible entity—

Celia: Assaulted how?

Stokes: Pushed, slapped, thrown . . .

He mumbles.

Celia: *Violated! Are you kidding?*

Stokes: We think she's credible.

Celia whistles.

Celia: How am I supposed to sleep tonight?

Stokes: The young lab technician from CSAM discredited in your school paper claimed something similar. Her story was so frightening because such things do happen—though they evidently didn't actually happen to her. We don't understand what these entities are. There's so much we don't know about the world!

Celia: More things in heaven and earth . . .

Stokes: Indeed. We do ourselves a disservice by clinging to stereotypes and make-believe rules about what a ghost can and can't do or can and can't be. We simply don't know. This is why it behooves us to study such questions and maintain an open mind, lest we cut ourselves off from an answer just because it doesn't fit what we think we know. I don't believe a ghost need necessarily be tied to one location. I think it's perfectly plausible that this Dark Woman, whatever it may be, has indeed followed the chimpanzee across the country. We can only hope Smithy will see fit to tell us more about it. If he's all his keepers claim, he's a priceless treasure that must be protected.

Celia: And if he's not?

Stokes: Then he still deserves some dignity.

Celia: Thank you, Dr. Stokes. I'm going to put away my other questions and instead take some questions from our listeners who are lighting up the switchboard.

Stokes: Oh. Is that necessary? I'm sure whatever you plan to ask is comprehensive—

Caller: Hey, it's Isaac Morgan, from CSAM . . .

Celia: Hey, the chimps' keeper!

Isaac: I'm all for Smithy, y'know.

Celia: Right on!

Isaac: Anyway, you were talking about other things the ghost might be, and I thought, "What if it's aliens?" I mean, you hear about them kidnapping people to study, like the interracial couple on TV, and that lumberjack last year. Well, if aliens are interested in humans, it stands to reason they'd also want to study chimpanzees, chimps being humans' closest relatives, y'know?

Stokes: That's, ah, a very innovative suggestion, Mr. Morgan. However, the phenomena described at CSAM and in Newport don't align with a typical UFO abduction narrative. No one, to my knowledge, has reported seeing any lights in the sky, or missing time, or losing memory.

Isaac: Oh, sure, right. I didn't mean it could be a little green dude in a spaceship, y'know, but that *this entity* could be extraterrestrial. Like, from another dimension. A thing like that, we wouldn't understand it with our puny brains and weak senses. To us, an alien entity could seem like a ghost. Except it could do things a ghost wouldn't, like move from place to place.

Celia: And it would focus on Smithy because he can communicate.

Isaac: Exactly! Maybe these beings have given up on people because of how warlike we've ended up being. Chimps are the next best hope.

Celia: You could be on to something, Isaac. Thank you for sharing your thoughts.

Isaac: Wait, I'm not d—

Celia: Hi, what's your name?

Caller: Never mind. Hey, Doc, just what exactly did that ghost do to that lady you're studying?

VIDEO FOOTAGE: "20/20"
INTERVIEW WITH TANIESHA JONES

Broadcast Date: April 6, 1989

Taniesha shakes her head and smiles.

No, I don't believe the Dark Lady was an alien. I never saw anything I couldn't explain, but if the Dark Lady existed, I have no idea what it was or what it wanted with Smithy. He was much less attractive than either Brad or the Daltons liked to think. You never knew what you were going to get with that chimp. Some days, he was fun to be around, but others, you worried about getting too close to him. He'd look at you like he couldn't stand you, but he knew he couldn't get along without you, and he resented you even more for it. Maybe a ghost would've fared better. It wouldn't have had to worry about being bitten or scratched, and if the chimp got too obstreperous, I suppose it could just disappear.

I suspect it latched on to him because it wanted to communicate. If it had wanted to learn how chimps functioned, it had the whole laboratory to work with, but Smithy seemed to be the point of focus. That's probably because Smithy acknowledged it. Just being noticed, having someone look at you and *see* you, maybe for the first time ever, is priceless. Having someone say, "Yes, I know you're there. I think you're worthy of attention," is alluring. If I were a spirit wandering in the wilderness and someone finally started paying me a little attention, I'd be happy to follow wherever he went.

LETTER FROM TAMMY STEINMETZ
TO RUBY DALTON

April 2, 1979

. . . I thought you might crack a smile at the enclosed. Of course, it was in yesterday's paper, so caveat emptor . . .

EXCERPT FROM
"TALKING NONSENSE WITH CHIMPANZEES"
BY RANDALL JAMES

Buffalo News, April 1, 1979

Lily Dale, NY, has been a haven for mediums and other otherworldly minded souls for the past century. It's seen its share of colorful characters, but one channeler with the pungent name of Sylvia Shallot outshone them all with her performance yesterday.

Shallot, a self-proclaimed "animal conduit," advertises the power to communicate telepathically with pets and wildlife alike. In an invitation-only séance in her home last night, she applied her gift toward connecting with the mind of the world's most famous plaintiff: Smithy.

During a half-hour session, Shallot "evoked" a stream of consciousness from the controversial chimpanzee, including the following:

Who are you? Where go? Who are you woman?

Help. Woman help Smithy. Why no help? Bad woman. Smithy afraid.

Go away. Go away woman. I no like. Ugly! Away! No play with you. My cat! My dog!

No dark woman! Bad. Go away. Why you here? Get out. Out out. Go away. Stop.

Dark ugly. Cats mad. Dark make Smithy ugly. Smithy mad. No like. Bad cat. Dark make bad.

Smithy no see dark woman. Stop. No look. Dark go away. You hurt. Smithy hurt you hurt Smithy hurt you break you.

No more! Go away! Smithy make you let go. Let go woman.

Bad place. Smithy afraid. Where friends? Where cats? Where dog? Smithy sad. Want go home. Go out. Out. You. dark again. No. No, go. Want go. Go out dark.

Grunt. Grunt. Hoot hoot scream. Hoot scream. Grunt. Grunt.[9]

Such valuable testimony surely belongs in the court record.

---

9 The Shallot séance was recorded to audiotape for posterity. Multiple primatologists who have heard the tape note the animalistic noises the medium performs match the vocalizations chimpanzees use to signal a predator sighting in the wild.

WHISPERS IN THE DARK

Broadcast Date: April 3, 1979

Celia: Our guest tonight is Madame Zelda, a psychic who's experienced numerous hauntings, specifically involving poltergeists. Madam Zelda, please share with us your insights about the Smithy case.

Mme. Zelda: Thank you, dear. This case has all the hallmarks of a poltergeist haunting, considering that the spirit can manipulate objects, make them disappear, and so forth. Above all, poltergeists haunt people, not places, though in this case, the poltergeist is haunting an ape. In my experience, poltergeists usually target people who are powerless or oppressed, often young women or children, particularly those who have experienced something traumatic.

Celia: Powerless? But apes are so much stronger than people. The prosecution is even arguing that Smithy is dangerous and needs to be put down.

Mme. Zelda: This chimpanzee, though it is physically strong, has no status and lacks self-determination. It is subject to terrible treatment, to pain and suffering. It is a thing that is owned, an object. It is abject. If anyone ever needed a poltergeist for protection, it would be Smithy.

Celia: How is this thing *protecting* Smithy? It sounds like it's frightened him and put everyone around him in danger.

Mme. Zelda: Paradoxically, the poltergeist, although it appears to attack the target, is actually offering protection. It shows others the target is a figure to be reckoned with, someone with heretofore unsuspected strength and powers.

Celia: Now, I've heard different takes on this subject: Do you believe the poltergeist is actually a separate entity, or is it an extension of Smithy, kind of like a psychic alter-ego?

Mme. Zelda: That I cannot yet be sure, but a poltergeist is involved. The pattern of activity is unmistakable.

Celia: Fascinating! Callers are already ringing in. Maybe you could answer some questions for them about how poltergeists operate . . .

DIARY OF RUBY DALTON

April 4, 1979

Whatever the outcome of this trial, I don't think I'll ever forgive Hegge for playing the ghost card simply because of the headaches it's caused. The snide remarks on the news. The laughter in the courtroom. The believers are just as bad, treating us like we're messengers of the New Age: whatever we do is going to reflect on the entire paranormal community, so we'd better not screw up.

And, as usual, we've got weirdos coming out of the woodwork. Tammy sent me an example. Closer to home, the university radio station has been hosting psychic crackpots. Jeff's tickled, but I half-wonder if this Ceelee person staged the stunt in the courtroom to generate material for her program.

Hegge thinks it was sabotage, and Sam said a PI is seeking ties between Latimer and the student who played the ghost. Personally, I don't believe Man's side has to stoop to such tricks; our ghost story sounds so far-fetched anyway.

Next up, the long-term CSAM employees will testify about Smithy's linguistic abilities. Taniesha will also testify generally about her experiences working for Man. Though that won't pertain to our claims about Smithy, it depicts Man's character. "If he would treat a young woman in his employ so cruelly, how would he treat a helpless animal in his power?" Hegge pointed out. "It will be good for us."

I'm fearful it will open us (or Taniesha) to another libel suit, though that case apparently is going well. Hegge seldom discusses it, and the papers don't comment on it at all. Hurray for small favors.

I won't be able to watch Taniesha's testimony because I'll be at my second trimester check-up. I'd hoped Jeff would come with me and learn something about the child he's going to be parenting in a few short months.

Ha! Sometimes I wonder if he's got fatherhood jitters and throws himself into the trial to hide from his responsibilities. Then I think maybe he just doesn't care.

I couldn't help noticing how professional—and pretty—Sam looked in court last week. She wore a little suit dress because women are required to look feminine. She told me the judge almost sent her home the first time she wore slacks to court. Ever since, she makes sure to wear stockings and a knee-length skirt with her blazer and blouse. I haven't worn a skirt in ages, and I couldn't even zip up my slacks if I had a mind to wear them. Not that Jeff would notice. He barely looks at me, let alone that way. Am I stupid for worrying about the time he spends with Sam? Or stupid for not worrying more?

Jeff says tomorrow is just a check-up, and he'll be with me for the birth. Ninety-nine more days until delivery.

God knows how many more days until a verdict.

WHISPERS IN THE DARK

Broadcast Date: April 4, 1979

Celia: Thank you for tuning in. Tonight, my guest is Zachariah E. Lane, a medium who has been cultivating his talents since age nine. He oughtta have plenty to say about this case. Welcome, Mr. Lane.

Lane: Thank you, child. I hope your welcome also extends to my spirit guide, Athuravasta.

Celia: Oh, certainly. Please tell us more about him.

Lane: *Her*. She was a priestess-shaman of her society, a tribe long lost to time that once ruled the kingdom of Galt.

Celia: Galt? Where's that? Do you mean Gaul? Like, France?

Lane: That's not important. All you need know is that Athuravasta possesses great wisdom and insight. She instructs me and protects me in my dealings with the spirit world.

Celia: What can she tell us about the spirit in this case? Can she identify it?

Lane: We cannot give you a name. We cannot be that specific. There is no telephone book in the spirit world that one simply consults, but there's information in the ether and the Akashic records, you see?

Celia: OK.

Lane: Such sources Athuravasta has inspected and relayed to me. From my conversations with Athuravasta and from my own observations, I can tell you that the spirit is a woman who has lost a child. Either the child passed at a very young age or was stillborn in the womb. The specifics are unclear, but she is a bereaved mother seeking a replacement for her child. She cannot move on to the next life because her grief keeps her on this plane looking for her loved one. She believes she has found it in the form of this ape.

When it was brought to the house of the earthbound spirit, it was very young and treated by its teachers as a child. This confused the spirit and led her to believe the ape was her child. That's why she's fixated on it and why she has followed it. She has imprinted on the ape and is determined to protect it. She watches over it and defends it from harm. She nurtures it as a mother does her baby and awaits the opportunity to claim it for herself.

Celia: Wait, are you saying this ghost wants to *kill* Smithy?

Lane: I make no specific predictions. I can only tell you what she wants. A woman is not complete until she has a child. She needs something to love and care for. It is her reason for being. This spirit has been in agony without her baby. She must have this chimp for her baby to find peace.

Celia: That's what your guide told you?

Lane: This is what I know from my own experience. I was a woman in a past life.

Celia: Really?

Lane: Yes. I was Athuravasta, a priestess and shaman of Galt.

Celia: But . . . I thought Athuravasta was your spirit guide. How can she be a separate spirit if you were her in the past?

Lane: My feminine energy has become dissociated and stands apart. The yin in the yang, you see.

Celia: Uh, sure . . .

Lane: In my past life, I was mother to three children who were slain before my eyes by barbarian invaders, so I can verily remember the agony, loss, and longing this spirit is feeling now.

Celia: How terrible. What else do you remember about your past life?

DIARY OF RUBY DALTON

April 5, 1979

All's well. My weight and blood pressure are normal. The baby is the right size. We can't tell what it is yet, old wives' diagnoses about cravings and carrying to the contrary.

I told Jeff all this—after he first finished giving me the low-down on all that had happened in court.

Isaac went first, was nervous and stammered a little, but looked clean-cut. Jeff thinks he still made a decent impression. "He said Man liked that he could get away with tormenting the animals. The apes couldn't quit or threaten to report him. Isaac felt sorry for them."

He admitted he knew Brad would slip extra food to the animals or sneak them out of their cages to play, "but he looked the other way because he thought it was good for them to be treated decently."

Latimer jumped on that, suggesting Isaac deserved Man's criticism by being lax in his work. When he testified about Smithy's signing, Isaac had tried to build Smithy up by saying he knew more words than Isaac himself was able to learn. Latimer questioned whether Isaac was qualified to judge Smithy's signing at all.

"He said, 'For all you know, he could have been making random gestures and you, in your ignorance, merely believed they had meaning, isn't that right, Mr. Morgan?' And Isaac said, 'If it were just me, maybe, but someone else was usually around, like Jeff or Brad, and they knew the words when I didn't.' Then Latimer asked, 'Couldn't they have been lying?' and Isaac said, 'Maybe. Why don't you have your own expert look at the films and find out?'

"He kept trying to make it look like Isaac had a chip on his shoulder and was out to ruin Man and that's why he's been organizing on campus. So, Isaac reminded Latimer he wasn't fired, he quit CSAM because of the ghosts. Then Latimer said, 'No further questions!'

Next, Dr. Torrance described the gambling/vaccine trial and how Man railroaded him off the project he'd initiated before converting it into a shock-aversion trial. "Latimer tried to paint him as a vengeful rival wanting to get back at Man for stealing his study. Ed described how the school reprimanded Man. He said that censure would have been payback enough. He admitted seeing Smithy sign on his own plenty of times during tests, and over time, he saw the other apes pick up signs, too."

Jeff said Torrance was a good witness because of his academic credentials, because he kept his cool under questioning—and above all, because wasn't invested in language studies, so his observations were impartial.

Dr. Fairbanks's were less so. "Right away, she started defending Man even when the questions didn't pertain to him: 'Dr. Teague is a fine researcher. He protected the animals in his care as well as he could, but sometimes sacrifices have to be made for the good of humanity.'"

Jeff's voice pitched higher in a parody. "'Dr. Teague is _such_ a humanitarian. If he saw one of his fellow men burning to death on the side of the road, he would absolutely piss on him to put it out.' Well, what can you expect? She still works there. She always was a suck-up."

Besides singing Man's praises, Fairbanks denied Smithy had any special skills beyond recognizing people by name. "But Conrad shut her up by presenting her own reports in her own handwriting about how many words Smithy used and how he even 'chatted' with his cage-mates. These all dated from the time the university asked us to start paying attention to things like that, when it was desirable to show Smithy in a good light.

"So, Conrad goes, "Were you lying then or are you lying now?' Then she says Smithy wasn't consistent, that he called Taniesha a dark woman instead of using her name sign. So, Conrad reminds the court 'dark woman' is what Smithy calls the ghost, and even if he wasn't talking about a ghost, Taniesha _is_ dark and a woman so it's still a true statement." Ultimately, Fairbanks tied herself in so many knots that Latimer didn't even want to question her much when it was his turn.

Instead, Hegge called Taniesha, who gave the court an earful.

She discussed a former colleague, Dr. Paul Pankhurst, a kind man who loved opera and ballet. Man thought he was weak. He mocked him in front of the staff, calling him "Pauly" or "Paulyanna" until the junior researchers picked it up, too. Pankhurst eventually quit and Taniesha hasn't heard from him or seen his name in print since.

I'm amazed Man hasn't driven more people out of the discipline. Jeff repeated a story Taniesha never even told me about a project he once assigned her and then deliberately sabotaged. Man was throwing a big holiday party and told Taniesha to personally invite the donors and other important people he'd selected as guests. He gave her a handwritten list of their names and telephone numbers, but every number she dialed was either disconnected or wrong. "Eventually, Taniesha checked the list against the phone book and discovered every number had one digit transposed. No way Man made a mistake like that. He wanted her to look incompetent.

"She said Man never really wanted her there. He wanted it to look like he'd made an effort to bring in some diverse workers, but they were unfit. Then Man wouldn't have to bother with minorities anymore. She called herself his 'Potemkin hire'—said it looked progressive to have a black woman on staff, but in reality, all the work he gave her was menial."

That's Man all right: butchering his smartest ape, squandering his most talented assistant, destroying everything good. I'm so glad Taniesha got away from him and didn't let him crush her spirit. She'll be outstanding in her PhD program and wherever she goes next.

COURT TRANSCRIPT

Testimony of Taniesha Jones
April 5, 1979

Hegge: Would you characterize Dr. Teague as a violent man?

Jones: He was mean and needlessly cruel. He would shock the animals to punish them, and he'd also do it arbitrarily to keep them on their toes, but the cattle prod was just one of his tools. Man did other things to make their lives harder. The first study I assisted tested a prospective drug treatment. Before giving the antidote, we had to expose our subjects to the disease. The symptoms were debilitating. Some animals developed motor and coordination problems, even partial paralysis. We had to keep them in that state before we could try to cure them with the vaccine. Some animals were assigned to a placebo study and received no curative measures at all. At one point, Man observed the apes' condition and decided to complicate it. He said, "Let's cut back on their daily rations. We should see how this drug acts on a starving body, not a healthy body. Then we'll know how it'll work in the real world." So, we starved our animal subjects to extrapolate how their recovery might progress under conditions of natural deprivation. Man did that because he could, not because the protocol required it.

Hegge: Did the animal subjects recover?

Jones: Five chimps died, and many survivors suffered neurological or mobility detriments. Man later sold them to another facility for high-impact testing. Their bodies were already so ravaged, they weren't worth using for anything else.

Hegge: How many animals died in CSAM's medical trials?

Jones: That's hard to say. I remember how many animals died during my tenure at CSAM, but I can't judge if they died because of the drug manipulations or because of their abusive treatment.

Latimer: Objection! Witness is admonished to stick to facts and not speculation.

Jones: It's a fact that if you abuse an animal or don't feed it properly or keep it in a state of stress, you'll exhaust its body and it will die faster. Our animal subjects were under continuous stress. I believe that made them more vulnerable to the risks of the medical studies.

Hon. N. Borley: Objection overruled.

Hegge: Did Dr. Teague mistreat Smithy?

Jones: He treated Smithy more harshly than the other animals. He frequently placed Smithy in solitary confinement. This was a punishment reserved for the most recalcitrant, dangerous animals, or to contain highly infectious diseases.

Hegge: Was Smithy contagious or violent when he went to solitary?

Jones: No, he wasn't contagious, and he hadn't been openly violent, but . . . bad things happened when he was around. Smithy may not have caused them. In fact, I was watching him on several occasions when something weird happened, and I know he didn't cause it. Still, Man blamed him and chose to punish him. He was against Smithy from the beginning. He thought Smithy was a prima donna because he had received special treatment at his previous home and because he was a celebrity. I think Man was jealous.

Hegge: Did Dr. Teague mistreat Smithy in other ways?

Jones: He handicapped him. Smithy had participated in a major language study and was supposed to have linguistic gifts, but in all my time at CSAM, Man never bothered to pursue that line of study. Smithy was left to stagnate intellectually. Man never acknowledged Smithy's abilities except to mock them. His only motive for investigating Smithy's language deficits now seems to me to be cruelty.

Hegge: If Dr. Teague's behavior upset you so, why didn't you quit?

Jones: I didn't want to give Man the satisfaction of running me out. I wanted to prove I was tough enough to withstand anything he could throw at me, personally or professionally. People in my position—a woman, a black person—have to be strong. If one of us falls short, our entire sex or race is held accountable. I didn't want Man to use any perceived weakness of mine as an excuse to write off an entire group. I also wanted to prove to myself I had the stomach to be a real scientist. I know the results aren't always pretty. Mostly,

I wanted to be sure I was the one caring for the animals. Not all the assistants were sympathetic. Some believed they had the right to treat animals as the means to an end. Even though I had to hurt the animals sometimes, I wanted to do what I could to mitigate their pain. Finally, I'd hoped we'd eventually move on to a study of cognition and behavior. That's the type of research that attracted me.

COURT TRANSCRIPT

Testimony of Taniesha Jones
April 6, 1979

Latimer: Ms. Jones, you've made a number of incendiary remarks about your former employer. You've accused Dr. Teague of bigotry and oppression. Yet, you've stated you were the sole black woman on his research team. By hiring you, he gave you the experience you coveted and helped you complete your research program. He was your benefactor. Don't you owe him a bit of loyalty?

Jones: We didn't have a mentor/protégé relationship, and he was hardly my benefactor. I was hired based on my qualifications, not as a favor. My achievements at CSAM were in spite of Manfred Teague, not because of him.

Latimer: Ms. Jones, the disparaging remarks you've made against your employer of five years could damage Dr. Teague's reputation and future prospects. Have you no remorse about this?

Jones: If your client experiences any fallout as a result of *his* choices and *his* actions, I fail to see how that could be my fault. I didn't swear a loyalty oath to Manfred Teague. I owed him the hours I was scheduled to work and my best work during those hours. I gave him that. I owe him nothing more.

[Cut]

Latimer: Did you ever express your concerns to Dr. Teague about using the cattle prod to discipline his subjects?

Jones: I kept my head down during the first year, but finally I couldn't swallow my distaste any longer. He'd just shocked a young ape who had been playing with a cage-mate and wouldn't settle down when it was time for lights out. You see, Man expected the animals to go to bed at a set time like a camp counselor with a cabin full of children. The chimp wasn't behaving in a threatening manner; he simply didn't do what Man wanted when he wanted it to happen. Rocky was lying on his back, twitching, with drool pouring from a corner of his mouth. I asked Man why he had to shock Rocky.

Latimer: How did Dr. Teague respond?

Jones: He said, "These are wild animals. I need to teach them they're not in charge: I am! They're stronger than we are, but they'll never use that strength if they think I'll use *this*." And he caressed his cattle prod like it was the hood of a classic convertible. He said, "One of these days, you'll be damned happy I have this. It's for your safety! Would you rather—"

Pause.

Latimer: Ms. Jones? What did Dr. Teague say?

Jones: "—end up like that broad whose face got torn off?"

Latimer: Did he mean Wanda Karlewicz?

Jones: I believe so.

Latimer: Then you both were aware of the hazards Webster posed and the damage he had already done to other people before Dr. Teague acquired him?

Jones: I didn't know Smithy was the same ape at first. When I made the connection, I thought Man was crazy for buying him and bringing him around us. But I talked to Ruby and worked with Smithy and saw he wasn't a foaming-at-the-mouth monster. Still, I always kept my guard up and worked to stay on Smithy's good side.

Latimer: Did you understand Dr. Teague's precautions better?

Jones: I didn't believe he would need such precautions if he didn't keep apes with that kind of reputation. In fact, after Teague opted not to pursue any language experiments with Smithy, I decided he'd only bought the chimp so he could use his cattle prod on him.

Latimer: Your Honor, I ask that the witness's last remarks be stricken from the record.

DIARY OF RUBY DALTON

April 7, 1979

... *Even though Latimer tricked her into acknowledging Smithy's history of violence, Taniesha's time on the stand has done more benefit than damage for our side. Yet after her provocative testimony, Hegge has opted to rest our case instead of riding the tide of outrage! He's not going to call Man to the stand, which I think is insane. Our supporters will also think we're nuts to pass up this opportunity.*

Jeff assures me he'll still question Man eventually. "Latimer's bound to call him to speak in his own defense. We'll cross-examine him then and expose Man as a lying, vicious, racist, sexist, sadistic son of a bitch."

Likewise, Hegge will delay questioning Jeff or Brad until after Latimer has had a go at them, the better to counteract Latimer's strategy. Latimer won't be lobbing any bombs just yet, though. He's asked Judge Borley for a continuance to gather witnesses, and since the Easter holiday is next week, followed by spring break at the private school Judge Borley's kids attend, the judge has given Latimer until the beginning of next month to prepare.

Now Man's team has three whole weeks to build a case when I had expected them to follow us within a few days. What will they do with that much time? How much new, damaging evidence can they uncover? How many new, persuasive witnesses? Not to mention, by the time Man takes the stand, the roiling ire Taniesha has generated against him will have lapsed, and we'll lose one of the best weapons in our arsenal.

But the others don't see it that way. "Don't you understand, Ruby? Man's scared!" Brad declared. "If his lawyer needs all this extra time to come up with a decent defense, it's because he's desperate and trying to pull a parachute out of a hat!"

That's how Hegge and Sam see the situation, too. Everyone is in such good spirits now, they figure they can relax for a little while. I think it sounds too good to be true, but I'm going to push the issue out of my mind for a fortnight. Instead, I will enjoy having my husband back with me. Next weekend, we'll drive up to San Jose to spend Easter with my in-laws. When we get back, maybe I'll get Jeff to help me plan how to fit a nursery into a one-room apartment. I hope this interlude will wake him up to how little time we have to prepare for the real trial of our lives.

I hope he's right that victory is near so we can return to our real lives full time.

WHISPERS IN THE DARK

Broadcast Date: April 10, 1979

Celia: Welcome, eavesdroppers! Give a hand to our guest, Elise O'Shea, a former member of the International Association of Psychic Investigators. She's an amateur investigator who has spent more than twenty years researching paranormal occurrences. Sometimes she's worked alone, sometimes in the company of other investigators, scientists, or mediums. O'Shea has a robust store of experiences from which to draw in analyzing this case. Elise, thank you for joining us.

O'Shea: It's my pleasure. Thank you for giving me the chance to share what I've learned about the spirit world. First of all, it's important to understand that a spirit is a liminal figure. That is, it exists in a place where boundaries cross. A spirit belongs to the realm of the dead, yet it moves through the world of the living. It observes and can learn from us, but it may not always be seen, except by those with special faculties to do so. It cannot affect our world without drawing upon the energies of a medium. Even then, it can only perform small acts—levitating or breaking an object, for example. It is caught between.

Celia: You mean it's earthbound?

O'Shea: Many spirits do not understand that they are dead. They don't know why they can no longer do things they used to do. They feel trapped and confused.

Celia: Why do you think this spirit is trapped?

O'Shea: I cannot guess at that without further information, but I believe I understand why it has fixated on this chimpanzee. Smithy is also a liminal creature. He is caught between the world of animals and the world of humans, neither fully one nor the other, yet both. He is an animal raised as a human. He lived in a house, wore clothes, and was treated as a child, and then suddenly, he was returned to an animal state, stripped, put in a cage, and subjected to abuse. Naturally, he is confused, frightened, and probably angry about his condition. Like calls to like. In this case, Smithy's tumultuous emotions would have called to the spirit. It would understand and empathize with the chimp and so would be attracted to it.

Celia: How amazing! Could the ghost leave the house and follow the chimpanzee?

O'Shea: Why not, if the chimpanzee is more compelling than the location where the spirit died? I should love to investigate further. I even contacted Manfred Teague, but he refused to take my calls.

Celia: That's not surprising, but it is too bad. Just think of all we could learn if you were able to test your theory . . .

DIARY OF RUBY DALTON

April 11, 1979

*People say "Whispers in the Dark" is good for our case, but I'm not so sure.
I heard the latest in Celia's parade of paranormal experts last night. At
least this one was a bona fide investigator and not some quack channeler.*

*I just don't see how programming like this can help us. Celia's creat-
ing the circus I so desperately wanted to avoid in the courtroom. Why do I
stay up to listen to her program? I tell myself it's important to know what
adversity we might face, not just from Latimer but potentially from her.
I wonder how many of her listeners are tuning in out of morbid curiosity
and how many of them actually believe this stuff.*

*And yet, even though I think these experts are full of it, there's a seed
of sense in what each of them says. Even the guy with the reincarnated
spirit guide, whom I don't believe for a moment, made one good point.*

*He said the ghost is Smithy's protector, and that's true. I saw the way
She shielded him from the other apes when he first came to CSAM. I
didn't see Her materialize in the cage, but who else could it have been?
Even Eric pointed out how She had saved Smithy from choking and cited
that as an indication She wasn't malevolent.*

*However, I don't get the sense that She's maternal at all. I'm starting
to experience those feelings myself, and the attitude She's taken toward
Smithy is not nurturing and loving. It's interest and curiosity. She's more
like a big sister looking out for a little brother than a mother shielding
her young. Vince and I were like that. He teased me all the time when we
were little, but he didn't like when anybody else did it. If he saw somebody on the playground bossing me around, he'd go over and push them.
It was like he had a monopoly on me. Over time, we mellowed out and
learned to depend on each other. When you're in a family, you're stuck
together. She and Smithy are bound that way, too.*

Although, I do remember the tour guide at the Breakers telling me Mrs. Trevor lost a baby. That story doesn't circulate nearly as often as the one about the dead housemaid, but it happened. It would be a matter of historical record. Could the medium have known about that? Maybe he did research before the show to sound credible. Or maybe he does have some genuine intuition.

The poltergeist lady also talked about the spirit being a protector because Smithy is downtrodden and oppressed. That was certainly true at CSAM, but not at Trevor Hall. Smithy was happy in the beginning, before She started to appear. Later, he learned to fear Her. If Smithy's fears and anxieties summoned Her, why was She present so early in the study? If She's caused his anxieties, then Her presence is counterproductive.

Celia's guest last night, Dr. O'Shea [sic10] made the most sense of all. Smithy and the ghost are drawn to each other because they're both caught between two worlds. I still remember a dream I had once at Trevor Hall: I was walking through the house, and I could see everyone, but they couldn't see or react to me. It gives me the creeps when I think about it. I felt frightened and angry in the dream; I believe that's how She must feel. I'm sure it's how Smithy feels, too.

Even if Celia's guests made some good points, their speculation doesn't benefit us. If she were to bring in more experts like Dr. O'Shea, people who actually have a CV, that might give substance to a supernatural defense. Right now, her show's a distraction at best, and at worst, a pillory.

Oh, god, I just had a thought: What if Latimer puts these "experts" of hers on the witness stand to discredit us? He could enter their silliness into the record to show the world the caliber of person we're depending on for our defense. I can just hear him: "If none of these experts can agree on what's going on, then what value do supernatural arguments have?"

Stop thinking about it, Ruby! Don't give him any ideas!

---

10 As stated in the broadcast, Elise O'Shea is an amateur investigator and has no academic credentials.

LETTER FROM RUBY DALTON
TO VINCENT CARDINI

April 14, 1979

. . . [W]e're on break right now while Man's lawyer is building his argument. Hegge heard a rumor that Latimer is tracking down a witness he badly wants. I'm afraid to think who that might be. But then, lots about this case frightens me.

Good news: we won the libel suit! The judge determined that Jeff's and Brad's characterizations of how Man treated his research animals and what he meant to do to Smithy were factual. The "mad butcher" bits all came from the general public's interpretation of those statements. The damages Man's claiming aren't our fault but John Q. Public's, and good luck suing <u>him</u>! I hope this outcome bodes well for the remaining action.

Ever since the trial began, Brad's been pushing to bring Smithy into court and have him testify. "At the very least, he should be able to hear the charges against him, like a human defendant."

Hegge agreed with him!

He's petitioned to have Smithy present during the trial; there'll be a separate little hearing about that issue before we resume. Since Smithy's in the zoo's custody, we'll need his custodian's input and approval as well as the judge's.

I'm surprised anyone is contemplating this proposal, but to my utter shock, Latimer has already consented to it. He's made no secret he thinks the trial is a farce. He complained when Ohrbach testified. I'd imagined he would think bringing in a chimpanzee would cheapen proceedings even more. At the least, given the stink Latimer has made about how dangerous Smithy can potentially be, I'd expected more uproar about him posing a threat to the court.

I said, sarcastically, "Maybe Latimer's hoping Smithy will go crazy and bite off a few more people's faces. Then he can claim Man was right all along."

Hegge showed no concern. "Undoubtedly he hopes this will backfire on us. Maybe he hopes to make his own client look better by depicting us as delusional and foolish." I fear that's exactly how we look.

"Or," I said, "maybe Latimer knows Judge Borley would never agree to it, so he's willing to appear magnanimous."

Hegge winked at me. "Don't write Borley off so quickly. Haven't you seen how he courts the press? Our judge loves the attention this case is bringing him. There's no such thing as bad publicity, you know. The added drama of Smithy's presence may appeal to him."

I can't envision him coping with an unpredictable animal in his courtroom; Judge Borley always seems focused on keeping order. Even though Smithy would be restrained (i.e., caged) and not exactly swinging from the rafters, I still can't imagine Borley would find anything appealing about having an ape observing (or participating in) the proceedings.

DIARY OF RUBY DALTON

April 17, 1979

Some women are "football widows" or "baseball widows." I'm the world's only chimp/trial/ghost widow.

Jeff's just announced he and Brad are going up to the Bay Area this weekend as reconnaissance for the trial. There, where the occult is big business, they hope to find experts who can help us get insight into how to substantiate the haunting.

I can't believe he plans to leave me on my own in my condition! When I confronted him, Jeff suggested I could invite a friend to stay over (What friends? Taniesha's busy getting her PhD, and it's not like I've had the opportunity to make friends anywhere else.), or come along. I turned him down; I don't want any part in this trip, and I know I'd slow them down by needing to stop for a bathroom every twenty minutes.

I'm doubtful this excursion will have any value. They're not likely to find more scientists of the caliber we need. Talking to fortune tellers won't give us sound evidence. When I said as much, Jeff reiterated with some exasperation: "We've got to follow every possible angle to save Smithy. If we don't, we'll regret it forever. Now is the time to act, before testimony resumes. It's only for a couple of days, Ruby. I'll check in with you from the road, if I can."

I asked whether he really believes this junk or whether he's just talking it up for the case. Jeff was never much interested in the supernatural before, even when we lived at Trevor Hall. He didn't try to contact the ghost then. "Do you really think ghosts exist? Can the dead go back and forth between this world and wherever they end up? What about reincarnation? If we cycle from birth to death to rebirth, then where do ghosts come from?"

Jeff was quiet for a long moment. "This isn't really about my philosophy on life after death. You want to know what I think about Smithy. Well, I'm not sure I believe in ghosts, but I definitely believe in Smithy.

"When Eric realized what "dark woman" signified, it made sense to me that some other force was at work in the house. I knew Smithy wouldn't hurt anybody unless he was provoked. I knew he wasn't making up lies or messing around with language. Why would he? Besides, he couldn't fake his emotions. He was terrified because he saw something he didn't understand.

"I don't know if this thing is really a ghost, or a visitor from another dimension, or a being from the future, or some memory of the past that was caught in the house and keeps skipping like a record. And I don't care. What I do know is it's real. What matters is how it's affecting Smithy. Is it scaring him? Is it hurting him? Is it helping him? How does he feel about it?"

I interrupted him then. "Really? You don't ever wonder where She comes from or how She can exist in this world without form and without being visible all the time?"

Jeff frowned. "No. Look, I don't understand how electrons or mitochondria work, either, and that's never bothered me. It's someone else's job to know about that stuff. As long as the world keeps turning, and I get a clean bill of health, that's what matters."

"But we don't have a clean bill of health anymore, Jeff. We have to deal with a ghost."

"That's why I'm taking this trip. To figure out how to deal with it! I don't need to know its whole etiology. Ohrbach and people like him get paid to know that. We may never find out who she really was or where she came from, but maybe we'll find out how to control her, how to drive her away, or how to communicate with her ourselves. If she's a dead human, I can reason with her. If she's not, I'll try something else. She's got to follow rules, like everything else in the universe.

"Science is constantly making progress with quantum mechanics and other discoveries. You heard Ohrbach talking about how the military's getting into psychic research. The rules controlling the Dark Woman and the answers about her origin might be just out of our reach now, but maybe one day soon, next year or in the next decade, some psychologist or physicist will figure all that out. Someday, we'll understand everything.

"And then people won't be afraid of ghosts anymore."

POSTCARD FROM JEFF DALTON
TO RUBY DALTON

April 20, 1979

Hey, babe,
We stopped in Sta Cruz to fill up and get food. We passed the board-
walk & of course I thought about walking there with you on our first day
as man & wife. Thinking of you & missing you.
Love,
Jeff

DIARY OF RUBY DALTON

April 21, 1979

I dreamed again like I did at Trevor Hall years ago. It's funny how that dream remains almost as sharp as a real experience and how it intrudes in my thoughts from time to time. Will this dream do the same?

Instead of Trevor Hall, I was in a plain, empty room with no windows and no visible door. The color of the walls was solid but indistinct. It could have been white or gray or cream. At first, I thought I was in a laboratory at CSAM, except the labs usually contained furniture or equipment. Smithy was there, too, hunched over in a corner, his back to me, moving his hands over the ground. I thought he was fingerprinting or drawing and wanted a better look.

Seeing Smithy cheered me. I was eager for him to notice me. He finally did look up, but he didn't run to give me a hug. He didn't sign my name or even 'hello,' but I knew he knew I was there and recognized me, and I felt elated. He wouldn't pretend I didn't exist or look through me like others. I wouldn't have to struggle for his attention. I had only to show myself, and he would respond. After all this time, we were finally connected.

I stretched out a hand and he came toward me. I didn't have to tell him I wanted him near; we were in accord. How good that felt! It was like enjoying a filling meal or slipping into a soothing bath. I wanted to say, "Show me what you're doing," but I had no voice. No <u>mouth</u>. It was like being under anesthesia at the dentist. I could think but not act.

Before I could sign my question with my hands, Smithy scampered back to his corner and retrieved his drawing. He <u>knew</u> my thoughts; I need only concentrate on what I wanted, and he would obey me. I had that power over him. I, who had always simpered and tried to be good and obedient. I, who worried about pleasing others, could now do as

I pleased. I, who had no power before, was now stronger than I'd ever imagined.

Smithy's little drawing consisted of swirls of indigos and blues slashed with faded greens: shadows of night and trees, the outdoors he craved. I knew what he intended, though anyone else would see only random blotches and lines.

"I'll take you to the trees," I thought. "I'll take you out of this dull, stifling room. Only heed me."

Smithy panted and bounced on his knuckles like a dog about to go bounding after his leash.

"We can go wherever you like," I promised. "We can do anything together."

Or, more accurately, I could do anything because of Smithy. Before, I was alone, but now that we were together, I knew my own power. He knew it, too. That's why he obeyed. No one else could do what I could. And there was no one else like Smithy who could do what he could, either. We belonged together.

When I woke, I tried to make sense of my vision. It's not that I don't dream about Smithy. I do, especially since the trial began. But I usually dream we're in court and he goes crazy, overturning benches and biting the heads off people in the audience, or that Judge Borley rules against him and he's dragged away in manacles to a torture chamber, unable even to sign to us for help. Less often, I dream about being at Trevor Hall and doing routine things, like trying to prepare Smithy's breakfast and discovering we don't have any food in the house, or giving Smithy a bath only to have him run away and force me to chase him through the labyrinthine halls.

This was different. I wasn't myself, but I'm not sure who I was or how I knew the things I knew. My sensations and thoughts were all based on things that didn't actually happen in the dream, but I knew about them anyhow, just as I can dream about being in a strange place and nevertheless know my way around. I felt so <u>confident</u>. That certainty was a new experience, and even the memory felt intoxicating.

When I tried to sleep again, I saw blue and green swirls against my eyelids. Before finally drifting off, I wondered how She'd get him to the jungle. In the instant before succumbing, I knew <u>that's</u> who I had been.

Somehow I had merged with the consciousness of the Dark Woman. It was Her power and influence that held Smithy.

Was that a real encounter? Was it taking place simultaneously across town? I doubt the zoo has any white rooms like I saw.

Or was the room symbolic? Her isolation reified? She's cut off from the world because she's a Spirit.

But Smithy is aware of Her, either because he has some innate power or because he's more open to things people tend to choose not to see or believe. Because of that, She's imprinted on him. And he's imprinted on Her. They've some sort of bond. He gives Her acknowledgment and . . . validation? Yes, that feels right.

But what does She give *him*? Promises of a better life? Of freedom? Are those real promises or opiates to keep him compliant?

Smithy's been isolated, too, from his human family and from other chimps. He must be desperate for companionship.

Yes, the dream symbolism emphasizes they're alone together. They're "unique in their clique, so to speak," in the words of an old song I heard on the radio one Halloween. She's probably telling him these things to keep him calm and under control.

That's what She wants: control. She likes being in charge. That would make sense whether She'd originally been a servant under a domineering master, or a teacher accustomed to managing a room full of students. Or perhaps all spirits become possessive in the afterlife.

Was She possessing Smithy? Not exactly, but She was directing him. She was using Her influence, telling him what to do and where to go. Smithy went along with her wishes because . . . why? Because he wanted the promised reward? Because he actually felt some affection for Her?

How could that be? That spirit tormented him for months when we were at Trevor Hall.

Or did She? My earlier dream of the fury and frustration I felt at not being acknowledged or understood keeps seeping into my thoughts. What if all She wanted was to catch Smithy's attention?

They understand each other better now. They're on the same side.

But what do they both want? If I had stayed in the dream longer, would I know? Why am I receiving these glimpses or messages in the first place? Is She intentionally transmitting them? Is it an accidental slip? Do I share an underlying rapport with the spirit? Or have the others dreamed of Her, too, and just don't talk about it? Should I ask Jeff and Tammy? No, Jeff might try to use me as a conduit to talk to Her.

Of course, these dreams and speculations could be coming from my imagination. My subconscious could be stringing together random ideas to solve the mystery. Wasn't there a fictional detective who solved mysteries by dreaming about them? Only I don't feel like I've solved anything. I'm more confused than ever.

No, I'm only confused as to the ultimate end game. I know better now why things happened as they have.

These two are kindred spirits.

LETTER FROM JEFF DALTON
TO RUBY DALTON

April 22, 1979

Ruby,

    Even though I'll get home before this letter does, I'm writing it now to tell you about our trip and to organize my thoughts because I don't remember everything the way you do.

    I feel like most of this trip's been a waste of time. We've visited head shops and places that sell crystals and incense. The people who work these shops know astrology or tarot cards. They're not ghost experts. Still, they got excited when they found out who we are. One woman demanded I tell her Smithy's birthday and where he was born so she could make his horoscope and tell us how the trial will turn out for "only" fifty bucks. I had to pass.

    Outside Berkeley, we attended a gathering where a channeler was talking. I'm not sure what the difference is between channeling spirits and being a medium who communicates with the dead. I guess some of these spirit guides were never technically alive. More likely they're just hooey. This second-rate Ramtha mostly babbled repetitious, Age of Aquarius wishful thinking: She predicted Russia will set off the bomb and the survivors of the massive war will have one thousand years of peace and live in underground cities until the air is clean enough to go back up. Yet we'll still be exposed to enough radiation that we'll develop superpowers to read minds and levitate and crap like that. Honestly, you can find better stuff in comic books. Why do people waste their time sitting around listening to this BS? Why did we? Curiosity and hope that she would spill something worthwhile.

    We did meet up with some students who are amateur parapsychologists, but they're more interested in ESP like Dr. Ohrbach. They do tests with cards and dice and practice telepathy and remote viewing. One guy suggested our Dark Woman might be somebody who's astrally projecting herself—not the ghost of a dead person, but the spirit form of a living person. Maybe a Russian spy trying to eavesdrop on us. Why a Russian spy would hang out with a bunch of chimps instead of at the Pentagon he couldn't really say, just that Smithy might have evolved psychic powers and this hypothetical Soviet agent could be trying to cultivate them. It was something different, anyway.

Finally, outside Millbrae, we met a shop owner and self-taught student of the occult who's read books by all the people in the secret society of the Golden Dawn and by scientists like William McDougall and J.B. Rhine. She calls herself Claire de la Lune. She changed her legal name from "Louise Friedlander" because she wanted to honor the power of the moon goddess or something. I didn't tell her "Claire de la Lune" is the theme song of the sociopathic child in <u>The Bad Seed</u>. I figured she wouldn't appreciate it.

Miss Lune actually wasn't that loony. She talked about an experiment a ghost-hunting group in Toronto tried. They attempted to contact a ghost, only their ghost was imaginary, and they all knew it. They'd made up a fake back story and a name for him, and then started holding séances to talk to him. Get this: the ghost talked back.

It wasn't really a spirit but something they conjured up through their combined willpower. Miss Lune said the people in the experiment created and maintained the "ghost" because they needed it for some reason. She suggested that Smithy could have conjured the Dark Woman in a similar fashion. If so, that'd explain why the ghost is still with him. But why did he do it? And how?

Do you think he somehow understood what we were talking about when we joked about Trevor Hall being haunted? Wanda worried we might somehow influence him. Could she have been right? I've no idea how we would go about investigating or proving that idea. Maybe Dr. Ohrbach could help us understand more? It's a fresh idea and I think we should consider it.

I'm taking a nap after I post this. We'll start driving back tonight. I'm glad; I miss you lots.

Love,

Jeff

KHJ-TV NEWS BROADCAST

April 30, 1979
In the Newsroom

A well-coiffed female newscaster sits behind a desk, rifling papers and reading from the teleprompter.

"A stunning twist in the Smithy trial was announced today. Attorneys for the plaintiff have requested that the famous signing chimp be allowed to sit in the courtroom during testimony and even give testimony himself. Like everything else in this case, the motion was unprecedented. Equally surprising, Judge Borley is said to be seriously considering it. We go now to Esther Cox and Erwin McDonald at the Fresno Family Zoo, where Smithy has been staying since his removal from CSAM six months ago."

The scene cuts to a daytime view of a gray-haired man with a seamed face who wears a plaid shirt, overalls, and a baseball cap standing in front of an outdoor enclosure, approximately twenty-by-fifteen feet, with vertical, prison-like bars. Within, a few skinny trees are scattered throughout, a wading pool is at one end, parallel bars are at the other, and a blanket lies on the ground. The man speaks to a brunette reporter in a tan dress suit with a microphone.

Cox asks, "Do you think Smithy is ready to testify?"

McDonald says, "He looks to me like he is. He's been talking to himself since he got here. I guess he's lonely; nobody around here can sign to him, but he keeps trying. He's always moving his hands and looking around."

The camera cuts to Smithy, crouched in a corner of his cage with his back to the viewer. The camera zooms in over his shoulder and focuses on Smithy's hands. He signs, "When go out? Open door. Smithy hungry. Give me cookie melon soda. Where you go? Go out open again." As he signs, he gazes into space.

Cox asks, "Would you bring him to court, if asked?"

McDonald says, "Sure, if I got the summons. I won't answer for what he does though. The judge'll have to keep order himself."

Over a montage of different angles of Smithy sitting in his cage, the newscaster's voice-over says, "No summons is forthcoming yet, but it may only be a matter of time before Smithy gets his day in court. Testimony resumes next Monday."

WHISPERS IN THE DARK

Broadcast Date: April 30, 1979

Celia: Haven't I always said I support freedom
for Smithy? All right, I suppose I've mostly been
talking about his ghostly predilections. Let me
say it loud and clear now: Smithy deserves to be
free of CSAM and any other organization or person
that would try to control him.

As a woman, I feel personally invested in seeing
that Smithy doesn't continue to be manipulated,
physically or psychologically, by others with
more power. Women have always had to struggle
to secure simple freedoms that most men take
for granted: freedom to own property, freedom to
participate in civic life, and freedom to control
our own bodies. We've only recently achieved that
last part. Unless you're in a position where
someone else can completely take over your life
and wipe out your dreams on a whim, you won't
understand. If you don't own yourself, if you
can't count on yourself at the bare minimum, you
are *screwed*. You've got no hope. *Nothing*.

Any modicum of freedom is precious. I want
this chimp to have whatever it takes to achieve a
peaceful, healthy, and happy life. He ain't gonna
get that with Manfred Teague. We need to see that
he's protected. Whether you believe he's got the
power or not, you've got to show him some basic
human decency. Do no harm. Do unto others as you
would have them do unto you. That's our mission.
We owe that to Smithy. He's earned it after all
he's been through.

TRANSCRIPT OF KMJ RADIO BROADCAST

May 2, 1979

The facetiously named Simanese Liberation Army, or "new SLA," departed from its tongue-in-cheek humor and amiable activism last night when it led nearly one hundred people in an attack on the zoo, where the chimpanzee known as Smithy or Webster is being kept.

Five individuals attempted to destroy the generator for the facility while the remaining protesters gathered at the entrance and demanded to see owner Erwin McDonald. When he emerged, the group seized him and attempted to take him hostage but were prevented by zoo security guards. One guard fired his pistol into the air to disperse the crowd. Nobody was shot, but while retreating, over a dozen people sustained minor injuries such as sprains and bruises.

Police arrested the vandals of the generator storehouse. Additionally, fifty-seven protesters were taken into custody; twenty-nine are members of the new SLA, and twenty-eight are unaffiliated attendees who learned of the demonstration through flyers circulating on the college campus or by listening to the AM radio program *Whispers in the Dark* hosted by CSUF student Celia Armendariz.

Peter Jones, head of the new SLA, contends the gathering was a peaceful demonstration to petition for the release of Smithy into their custody. He would not confirm or deny allegations that the chimp would then be removed to a sanctuary outside the state and possibly the country. "The New SLA does not condone violence. Vandals and thugs learned of our plans and used our gathering as a cover for their mischief. We intended no harm, and we did not engage in destruction of property."

Jones further disputes that Mr. McDonald was injured during the conflict. "We were merely gathering to speak with him when a security guard fired his weapon. As our group fled what we believed was an incipient massacre, Mr. McDonald was pushed and shoved, but at no time was he taken captive. Our group should not be judged by the actions of a few hooligans, and Smithy should not be penalized at all."

WHISPERS IN THE DARK

Broadcast Date May 2, 1979

Celia: All right, everybody, it goes without saying, but I'll say it anyway: We need to be peaceful in our actions. No violence, ever. I understand you all want to see Smithy freed. I do, too. But we have to go through the proper channels, the courts, and not use vigilante actions. So, if you must go to the zoo to make your point, remember, hands off and be polite.

But if you *can* grab him without making any fuss or making anybody the wiser, go for it!

DIARY OF RUBY DALTON

May 2, 1979

I wish Celia Armendariz would raise more funds for Smithy's defense and raise less hell.

I understand she means well; I understand she's sincere; and yes, I acknowledge that her show has brought more attention and sympathy to Smithy, but she's made a ton of trouble for us by bringing a mob down on the zoo, intentionally or not.

Police will be patrolling more frequently to deter any other breakout attempts. Hegge says they may also order people to stop amassing outside the court if they don't have a permit. That would be very bad. The crowds of protesters with their colorful signs are a visible indication of support for Smithy in the community. If they're not there for whatever reason, it will look like apathy has set in.

The bigger harm is that now, Smithy's supporters are being perceived as rabble-rousers and troublemakers. A letter to the editor this morning said, "If they can't control who turns up at their gatherings and can't vouch for the quality of people they're bringing in, they shouldn't be allowed to operate." Who has time to do background checks on everyone who might show up to a protest?

I pray this is a singular snafu. If it signifies a new direction for the movement, it could be the end of all we're trying to accomplish . . .

FRESNO TODAY WITH JOHN BELL,
COURTESY OF KJEO

Broadcast Date: May 4, 1979

A male voiceover says, "The Smithy trial has
stimulated plenty of curiosity regarding the star
chimpanzee." As he speaks, the picture cuts among
various caged animals: monkeys, birds, foxes.
"The biggest question everyone has right now is,
How is Smithy doing? We're at the Fresno Family
Zoo today to find out."

The camera zooms in for a close-up on Smithy
swinging from a set of parallel bars. "Here we
see the ape in his temporary home, oblivious to
the strife beyond the safety of his cage."

Smithy looks toward the camera, drops, and runs
up to it. The camera zooms out, showing a dark-
haired mustachioed man in a brown corduroy suit
standing outside the enclosure. Smithy pauses
before the reporter. His lips pull back, showing
a toothy grin, and he starts signing.

John Bell laughs. "He's glad to have visitors.
Look at that smile! I only wish we knew what he
was saying. Mr. McDonald, can you help us out?"

The older man, wearing a flannel shirt and dark
jeans, enters the frame. "I wish I could, but I
don't know sign language. I see him gesturing
like that all the time. It sure would be nice to
know what he's saying."

Smithy looks backward at the pool, then back
to the reporter. He tilts his head, then runs to
the corner and stops beside the pool, keeping his
back to the camera and visitors. He leans over

the rim of the pool and tilts his head again, as if listening.

"I understand this is a larger enclosure than he had when he first arrived. He seems well here," Bell remarks.

"Yes," McDonald agrees. "Smithy's always running around, playing, doing something. Tuesday's excitement didn't rile him, thank goodness. I don't suppose he even knows about it. He's holding up well in general. Some apes don't like to be alone. They sulk and turn listless, and their health declines."

"How's his appetite?" Bell asks.

"He eats everything we give him and maintains a healthy weight," McDonald responds.

"Well, he certainly looks like he's in good hands," Bell says. "I'm pleased to see it, and I'm sure our viewers are happy to check in with our favorite chimp." The camera zooms in on Smithy at the pool. The chimp looks backward and signs something. Bell chuckles and says to the camera, "Back to you in the studio."

DIARY OF RUBY DALTON

May 5, 1979

Turn around.

Literally, he signed, "Turn behind," but he could've meant, "Look behind you."

"He was telling the reporter something was behind him," Jeff insisted. "If he'd turned around just then, he might've seen the ghost. He might've even caught it on camera."

For an instant, I flashed back to the night in the laboratory, when all the chimps were screaming and covering their eyes and Smithy was pointing just over my shoulder. If I had turned around faster, if I had looked over my left shoulder instead of my right, what might I have seen?

"Did you ever catch the ghost on camera?" Hegge asked.

"No, but there's a first time for everything. Look, it's even possible they filmed something important unawares and it wasn't used as part of this broadcast. We should ask for that footage before they record over it. It could have a clue. Even if there's no actual ghost in the image, we might see footage of Smithy signing to her, or some other indication that she's still around, that she's visiting him at the zoo. That would cement the case, wouldn't it?"

"It would definitely be thought-provoking. It would keep the question open," Hegge agreed.

Brad had a totally different take. "He could've meant to tell the reporter, 'Turn your back,' or 'Look away.' It looked to me like he didn't want any visitors, at least not strange ones. Did you see his teeth? That reporter thought he was smiling, but when chimps show their teeth, they're showing aggression. They're saying, 'Go away before I hurt you,' not 'Hi, it's nice to meet you.' It's the opposite of humans. I always get creeped out when I see chimps smiling in movies because I think, 'What do their trainers have to do to get that reaction?'"

"Normally Smithy likes visitors," Sam observed. "I wonder why this crew put him off."

"Maybe he didn't like the camera. Maybe he's tired of being a spectacle," I suggested. "Maybe McDonald was wrong, and he does know a bunch of strangers broke into the zoo looking for him. That would make him wary."

Brad shook his head. "He wants to see his people. He wants to see _us_, not strangers. We need to get him back before he sours on people altogether."

"Now, that's a good point." Hegge looked serious. "If the circumstances of his captivity are making Smithy uncivilized, things could go badly for him."

Sam translated. "If he's not cute and approachable anymore, the public won't care and won't be invested in him."

There's our real problem: Smithy deteriorating, losing his mind anyway, even without Man's scalpel. Smithy losing himself, losing his personality, becoming something vengeful and vicious that might attack another woman.

"That's why we need this footage," Jeff continued. "It will help our case and help get him his freedom that much sooner."

"Jeff, I hear a lot of silent 'ifs' in that statement," Hegge noted. "If their footage contained anything significant that could help us, it would have been broadcasted. Smithy didn't even cover his eyes and sign 'black;' he signed 'turn around.' That's vague. It could mean anything. We would need footage of him signing something clear and unambiguous: 'The Dark Woman is here.' 'Look, the Dark Woman is behind you.'"

"How about a yes or no in response to someone asking him if a ghost is present?" Jeff asked.

"I would love to see that footage."

Jeff leaned forward, eyes narrowed in concentration. "Do we have access to all of CSAM's footage?"

Hegge raised his eyebrows. "From the last six years, since you, Ruby, and Smithy were there? Technically we could subpoena it, but I don't want to sit through thousands of hours."

"You won't have to," Jeff said. "I want a specific piece of footage from Corridor D. Give me a day or two to get back to you about the date.

Maybe we'll have to check a couple of dates, but I'll do it myself, so you won't have to."

"What are you looking for?" Hegge asked.

"I asked Smithy once if a certain ghost was present, and he gave me an answer."

That was news to me. As far as I knew, Jeff had never tried to perform a séance. He didn't even suspect the Dark Woman might be back until after the gambling study started.

"If Man was recording in Corridor D—and he seems to have been recording everything—then he would have that exchange on tape. We can use it for evidence."

Hegge still frowned. "I would have thought you would have mentioned sooner if such persuasive evidence existed."

"I didn't think of it before. I could kick myself for being such an idiot." Jeff didn't look like somebody who wanted to kick himself, though. He was beaming. I couldn't fathom what he was up to and what he hadn't told me.

Jeff must have sensed my thoughts because he turned and smiled at me. "Don't worry, Ruby. I'll explain it all. Once we get that footage, you'll see for yourself. Everybody will."

EXCERPT FROM
SMITHY: THE MILLENNIUM COMPENDIUM
BY REID BENNET

Most of what we know about the trial and the plaintiffs' strategy comes from the transcripts or Ruby's diary. The following ephemera—notes evidently scribbled between Samantha Stone and Jeff Dalton while in the courtroom listening to testimony—fascinate, both because they survived and because of what they precipitated:

> *We checked CSAM film of you & fruit. H says no good, too vague, looks random. You = rube. Best: Wishful thinking/Worst: S toying w/ you. Need better proof.*

Can you get us into zoo? We can talk to him and you'll see

With trial ongoing???

We deserve another visit. Even supervised. It's been months. Let OC watch us. Better if he sees something go down. Could convince him (or scare him to death, ha ha)

Big ask.

Cmon. Please try. If no we try something else. If yes we could win now

EXCERPT FROM "'DR. FRANKENSTEIN' IN THE FLESH: MANFRED TEAGUE TESTIFIES" BY ELIZABETH MACKINTOSH

The Fresno Bee, May 8, 1979

Crowds flocked to the Fresno County Courthouse yesterday for the most highly anticipated appearance in *Friends of Smithy v. CSAM*. Some spectators even camped overnight in the hopes of snaring a seat and hearing Dr. Manfred Teague, alleged persecutor of the chimp known as Smithy, testify in his own defense . . .

COURT TRANSCRIPT

COURT TRANSCRIPT

Testimony of Manfred Teague
May 7, 1979

Latimer: Please tell the court your name and credentials.

Teague: I am Manfred Teague. I hold PhDs in psychology and biology. Seventeen years ago, I used a family inheritance to start my own foundation, the Center for the Scientific Advancement of Man, to privately explore questions concerning human behavior and cognition and to find ways to improve the lives of people all over the world.

Latimer: What's the focus of your research?

Teague: Our vision is broad. We explore any question relating to mankind. We've investigated medical questions and questions concerning humans' hereditary relationship to primates. Until recently, much of our research was carried out in conjunction with the local university. We had more sophisticated facilities than the campus and were equipped to address more research questions. Furthermore, that partnership allowed us to provide students the opportunity to conduct research in a professional environment under the supervision of trained scientists. Regrettably, that partnership has been dissolved in the wake of outlandish accusations and smears against my reputation and that of—

Hegge: Objection. Relevance. Your Honor, the matter at hand is not libel against Dr. Teague. That case has already been settled.

Hon. N. Borley: Sustained. Mr. Latimer, please redirect your client.

Latimer: Dr. Teague, I understand negative publicity surrounding this case has disrupted CSAM's research. What projects were you undertaking at the time this case was filed?

Teague: We were about to launch a longitudinal study on motivation and achievement and a medical trial for a new drug to treat diabetes. I was also in discussions with a private medical foundation to investigate the effects of brain damage on cognition.

Latimer: Was that the study that triggered the allegations about Webster's peril?

Teague: I believe so. Unfortunately, Mr. Latimer, medicine is not a tidy field. When science makes breakthroughs, its triumphs are celebrated. However, the road to those triumphs is often littered with the bodies of test subjects—and human beings who didn't receive treatment in time. It's difficult to hear the testimony of former employees and their mischaracterizations of me and my work. I'm not thin-skinned, but I'm galled by their lack of understanding about scientific research.

Latimer: Please elaborate.

Teague: CSAM has investigated serious issues affecting—*threatening*—humanity. The cognition study I mentioned is one example. Thousands of people—

parents, children, spouses—are incapacitated by head injuries, strokes, and other brain damaging events. It behooves us as a species to find ways to alleviate their suffering, preserve what faculties remain, and if possible, rehabilitate them to a higher standard of well-being. The ultimate goal of my research is to save and improve human lives. Because most of our research is exploratory, we cannot use human subjects in our trials. We are first obliged to test treatments on animal subjects. Cosmetics companies use rabbits and mice, but my lab uses primates because they resemble humans physiologically and neurologically. During our investigations, out primate subjects sometimes experience discomfort. Some are irreversibly injured, and some even die. That's a regrettable but unavoidable fact of this line of work. I don't set out to torture monkeys. That's what the press and the plaintiffs want people to think, but it's untrue. My goal is to benefit mankind! If I could test these drugs without killing a single animal, I would do it. But if I had to kill every animal in my inventory to find a drug that works, I would do that, too. The benefits to the human race far outweigh any harm that a sampling of animals might suffer. We wouldn't have Salk's vaccine if we hadn't been able to test it on animals first. Think of the millions of people who might be paralyzed by polio today. Should the world revert to that state?

Latimer: Is it true you planned to enroll the chimp Webster in a study that had the potential to harm him but also had the potential to ease human suffering?

Teague: Yes.

Latimer: Was Webster your only subject in that trial?

Teague: Of course not! A study wouldn't be scientific with only one subject. You have to test your treatment on enough subjects to achieve statistical significance. With a pilot study, where your goal is to see if your manipulation has the desired effect, you can use a smaller sampling. Once you've validated your procedure, you move on to a larger subject pool. My pilot test would have involved six chimpanzees; Webster was just one of them.

Latimer: Did you choose Webster because he allegedly possessed language skills?

Teague: Yes. I chose my other subjects for the same reason. They'd all had some exposure to language. I thought it worthwhile to see if they retained these abilities and to what degree following neurological trauma.

Latimer: Incidentally, which apes were you planning to test?

Teague: Their common names were Woolly, Bashful, Nero, Wendy, and Violetta.

Latimer: Would it be incorrect to claim you designed this study specifically to punish Webster?

Teague: Quite incorrect.

Latimer: Were you confident the outcome of your study would be beneficial?

Teague: I had hopes.

Latimer: Have your previous studies involving animal subjects yielded positive returns?

Teague: Yes! In the past fifteen years, we've tested seven drugs that have since either been approved or are pending approval from the FDA.

[Cut]

Latimer: What about the allegations of animal cruelty over and above what was required to test the medical treatments?

Teague: Absurd! Any force I used was a preemptive measure to ensure my security and the security of my staff. If anyone had ended up like that poor, unfortunate Karlewicz girl, I'd have been sued for negligence. People would have said, *Man let those poor kids get torn to shreds by his mad apes!* I thought it was better to shock them upfront so they were docile and cooperative later, rather than let them run wild over the lab. As it is, the damned thi—brutes mobbed *me* once before I could use the prod. Fortunately, I wasn't harmed. And look what happened to Marianne Foster! What *really* happened to her. Those chimps bruised her, frightened her, and might have done a lot worse if Vollmer hadn't dragged her out. That never should have happened, but it might have happened more often if I hadn't disciplined the animals the way I did.

Latimer: Were those actions entirely necessary?

Teague: Yes.

Latimer: What about the accusations of racial stereotyping and insults?

Teague: Look, I have more to worry about than being politically correct. I've got to worry about the logistics of the studies I'm running, keeping our facility in the black, safety procedures. Could I have made some jokes that rubbed people the wrong way? Sure. You never know how somebody's going to react to a thing like that. But nobody ever told me I'd said anything offensive.

Latimer: Then your remarks were not intended to harass or humiliate?

Teague: If I said or did anything that made one of my employees feel targeted, it was completely unintentional.

Latimer: You didn't single out or sabotage Taniesha Jones?

Teague: That's ridiculous!

Latimer: Did you persecute Paul Pankhurst?

Teague: I ribbed him a little, the way I do all my colleagues. The man simply didn't have what it takes to survive in this field. I criticized his methodology and instead of shaping up, he resigned.

Latimer: Did you demean the women you employed?

Teague: I've got as many women working for me as men. Or I used to when I could afford to hire lab assistants. I didn't bring them on board so they could all make coffee. A man can only drink one cup at a time. I hired people I thought would work hard and do good science. If they weren't awarded plum assignments as fast as they wanted them, maybe their expectations weren't realistic. So,

no, I did not bully my female employees. If their
feelings got hurt, maybe they're in the wrong
field. Maybe they should be teaching kindergarten
instead. I've got high standards. Not everybody
can meet them.

EXCERPT FROM "'DR. FRANKENSTEIN' IN THE FLESH: MANFRED TEAGUE TESTIFIES"
by Elizabeth Mackintosh

The Fresno Bee, May 8, 1979

. . . Dr. Teague repeatedly made excuses for his behavior, often blaming others for being easily offended, downplaying his actions, or attempting to justify them as serving a greater good. Much of his testimony emphasized the accolades he received for work he conducted or facilitated.

Teague cited the polio vaccine as an example of a scientific breakthrough made possible by animal testing, implying that those who support animals' welfare jeopardize humans' well-being. However, Jonas Salk himself denounced using monkeys in polio vaccine trials because the disease is communicated differently in that species. Reliance on the monkey model of contagion and treatment actually harmed humans who should have benefited from the vaccine. The moral value of medical testing on animals to benefit humans remains an ethical conundrum, but Teague's example undermines his self-proclaimed credentials as a top scientist.

Occasionally, his disregard for the feelings of his employees and the suffering of the animals appeared callous. When cross-examined by plaintiff attorney Conrad Hegge, Teague claimed not to know the number of animals that had died at his facility. Hegge introduced records subpoenaed from CSAM that revealed thirty-two animals have died in the past ten years; seventy-two have died since the facility opened. Compared to other medical testing facilities, CSAM's fatality rate is 0.7 times higher than the next highest fatality rate.

Testimony is expected to conclude next month when Brad Vollmer and Jeffrey Dalton, who initiated the lawsuit, will take the stand.

COURT TRANSCRIPT

Testimony of Keith Branneman
May 7, 1979

Latimer: Mr. Branneman, would you agree that Webster differed significantly from the other animal subjects in attitude and behavior?

Branneman: Yes, sir.

Latimer: Did you attribute these differences to anything particular?

Branneman: I thought he was a spoiled brat.

Latimer: Did you consider any other explanations for his behavior?

Branneman: *I* didn't, but then this news article came out that said the house where Smithy used to live was haunted, so some of my coworkers wondered if that's why he was so weird. Like, maybe the ghosts were still haunting him. I thought that was bul—bogus, a pack of nonsense. Man was annoyed when he heard the rumors, but people still talked. Smithy participated in a study where the chimps played roulette, and any time one of them picked black, rumor had it they were communicating with the "black woman," the ghost.

Latimer: Did Mr. Vollmer or the Daltons share this view?

Branneman: Oh, yes! One time, I was working with Brad on a project. It was just him, me, and Smithy in the room. I was setting up the camera and Smithy started making signs that Brad translated as "dark woman." He got real upset and asked Smithy, "Where is she, boy?" And Smithy signed, "the chair," so Brad unilaterally canceled the experiment right there and then and took Smithy out of the lab. He acted like Smithy was in danger. Man was pi—pretty upset. Brad's action set back our progress on that study. Even when we resumed trials, he wouldn't go back into that lab.

Latimer: What did the chimp sign, exactly?

Branneman: He signed "chair."

Latimer: Is that all?

Branneman: I saw him sign, "Brad, dark, chair." Then Brad freaked out and took Smithy outside.

Latimer: The chimp didn't sign "dark *woman*"?

Branneman: No, just "dark."

Latimer: What meaning did you take from this message?

Branneman: Nothing! It didn't mean anything; it's a random word. But people kept freaking out over stuff like that. All the time! And then loonies and reporters would get underfoot, interfere with our business. Like now.

Latimer: What impact has this court action had on your work at CSAM?

Branneman: We haven't been able to do *any* work! No new research, anyway. Just reanalyzing old data. I could barely even get into the building for the first month after this case was filed. Man had to hire security guards to clear a path for employees to walk through the protesters. I had to start taking the bus in to work, or park a mile away and walk, because if I left my car in the lot, one of those PETA freaks would trash it. There's not much point going to the office anymore, anyway. We've lost all our research contracts. Man has had to sell off half of the animals because he can't afford to provide for them. ASHRAAM just bought Woolly, Rosalie, Kidd, Camille, and her baby. Did you know that, Brad? Jeff? If you thought they had it bad at CSAM, you've really fixed things for them now. They'll never walk again. They'll never see daylight again!

Hon. N. Borley: Order! Mr. Branneman, confine your responses to Mr. Latimer and do not address the courtroom!

Branneman: Sorry, Your Honor. Sorry, Mr. Latimer. It's just so unfair! Man's been a good employer to me. Even if he's made some mistakes, lots of innocent people work at CSAM, too. People like me and Dr. Fairbanks can't make a living or do the work we love anymore. It's a mess!

DIARY OF RUBY DALTON

May 7, 1979

Keith was a terrible toady, putting the ghost stories into a contemptuous light. However, he lost his cool, Judge Borley yelled at him, and he didn't stand up too well under Hegge's questioning. Jeff acted out the scene for me with gusto.

First, Hegge ripped into Keith about his assumptions that Smithy was a troublemaker: "Did you have any proof Smithy bit any chimps? Did you see any fighting on the monitors? Oh, you saw the other chimps attacking Smithy but not the other way around?"

More importantly, he zeroed in on a slip Keith made: "Mr. Branneman, you testified the other chimps in the roulette experiment would, quote "sign black" unquote. Is that true?"

"Uh, yeah . . . "

"These animals signed a word that you recognized! How did they come to learn this word?"

"Ummmmmm . . . "

"Did they acquire it from Smithy?"

"I guess. . . "

But the best part was when Hegge got Keith to admit he was assigned to track the video monitors on the day Smithy escaped. "Is it fair to say if you had done your job properly, the escape wouldn't have happened?" Jeff told me Keith's face looked like a giant beet and all he could do was mumble.

Hegge showed me the roster of witnesses for next week, including the one Latimer has been able to keep secret until now. Even though I'm sure the press will be staking out the courthouse now that Smithy's allowed to attend, I've decided to squeeze into my nicest maternity gown and watch the testimony in person one last time.

SURVEILLANCE FOOTAGE
COURTESY OF FRESNO FAMILY ZOO

Date: May 11, 1979
Location: Smithy's Enclosure

Smithy sits in the far corner, his back to the camera. He appears to be tracing something in the dirt or smearing dirt around the ground. A bewhiskered man wearing overalls opens the gate to the enclosure and Sam, Jeff, and Brad enter. Brad wears a bright red baseball cap turned sideways. The attendant enters behind them and locks the gate. He says, "I gotta stay with you at all times and make sure there's no funny business."

"That's fine, as long as we get to talk to him. Fifteen minutes, that's the deal." Jeff speaks quickly, as if in a hurry. His tone changes as he calls out, "Hey, Smithy, how've you been, old pal?"

The chimp freezes. He sits up straighter and inclines his head but doesn't turn around. A moment later, he resumes tracing in the dirt.

Jeff approaches him. "Hey, Smithy, look who's here!" The ape doesn't react.

Sam adds, "It's nice to see you again, Smithy. We've all missed you." Smithy turns when he hears her voice, considers Sam, then turns his back and continues ignoring his guests. She mutters to the others, "What is this, the silent treatment?"

"Smithy . . . " Jeff sounds pained. "Please don't be mad at us. I guess you're upset because we've left you here by yourself for so long, but that wasn't our choice. We *want* to see you, but

Man won't let us." He signs, 'Bad man.' Smithy doesn't look or respond.

Brad walks around the enclosure, whistling. Smithy's ears twitch when the music starts. Brad says, "Let's see what you've got here. This doesn't look so bad." He flops onto a hammock strung between two trees. The hammock sags precipitously and the trees creak. Smithy turns his head again in time to see Brad roll—or fall—out of the hammock and onto the ground. "Whoa! Guess it's not my size."

Smithy makes a chuffing sound, almost like chuckling, and runs over to Brad on all fours. As Brad starts to rise, Smithy pushes down on his shoulders, pinning him. The attendant cries out, "Look out! No!" He reaches for a tranquilizer gun on his belt.

"It's all right," Jeff insists.

"Oof! What are they feeding you in this place? Pretty soon, you won't be able to fit in that thing, either." Brad's voice is calm. "Hey, Smithy, check this out. What do you think?" He turns his head from side to side to emphasize his hat. "I'll give it to you if you get off me."

Smithy lowers his face toward Brad's and looks at him a long moment but doesn't budge.

"Please, buddy? This is starting to hurt."

Slowly, Smithy backs away and Brad hands him the cap. Smithy turns it around in his hands as if unsure of what it is, then plops it on his head, brim backward. He hoots in excitement. The attendant objects. "Hey, you can't leave anything in the cage from outside!"

"We didn't sew a hacksaw under the brim, if that's what you're worried about," Jeff says sourly.

The attendant frowns and says, "The other guy doesn't bring him presents. I'm pretty sure you're not allowed to bribe him."

Smithy runs a lap around the enclosure. Sam smiles and says, "That's more like it." To Jeff, she says, "Now we can get down to business." She raises her hand and indicates her watch.

Smithy stops running when he reaches a couple of blankets in the corner. He reaches under them, pulls out an apple, and bites into it. The attendant exclaims, "Hey! Outside food is definitely not allowed in here." He turns on Brad. "Did you give that to him?"

"No, man," Brad responds. "It was already there. He's had apples before. It's not a big deal."

"It is if he chokes on it, or if those seeds poison him. We never give them whole apples, just mushed. One of you had to have brought it." The attendant glowers at each of them in turn. "It wasn't there this morning when I cleaned his cage, and I'm the only one who's been in here all day. It's my job to watch over him."

Jeff says, "If you're that worried, you can check who brought it; you've got those security cameras now." Jeff points up toward the camera.

The attendant says, "I can try. We don't keep the film very long. We're not like your boss, keeping stuff in a closet for years."

"Ex-boss," Jeff grumbles. The attendant walks away and speaks into a walkie talkie, but the conversation is garbled.

Sam, watchful, approaches Smithy and remarks, "An apple, huh? Not a banana?"

Smithy, still crunching away at the apple, stops, cocks his head, and then slowly closes and opens one eye, as if winking.

Sam flinches and says softly, "Seriously? Smithy, we're trying to help you. Don't hold a grudge."

"Yeah, where did that apple really come from?" Jeff adds, signing his question. Smithy rotates the apple so the uneaten side is facing out and extends it toward them, as if offering it.

The attendant snaps, "What are you up to? You better not be giving him any instructions."

"We're just asking him how he likes his snack," Brad calls back. In a lower voice, he asks, "Can't we just *visit* with Smithy instead of interrogating him? Our time's almost up as it is."

"We came here to gather more proof," Jeff insists.

Sam shakes her head. "Go ahead, Brad. I don't think he's going to tell us anything, anyway." She looks back up at the camera. "Maybe he doesn't have to. If contraband food *is* teleporting into the cage, wouldn't that be something to see?"

TELEVISION BROADCAST
COURTESY OF KFSN

May 13, 1979

The camera tracks a middle-aged man with salt-and-pepper hair and mustache wearing a suit as he walks in front of a neutral background, speaking.

"Good evening. I'm Rob Mannheim, and I welcome you to the first episode of our four-part investigation into animal research labs.

"In recent days, an employee at CSAM testified that the facility's apes had been sold to an organization called ASHRAAM. I suspect most of us had never heard of ASHRAAM before, nor understood why the very mention of it so distressed the plaintiff's team and the witness himself. To satisfy our curiosity, this network will go behind closed doors to see how CSAM's top competitor in the research industry conducts itself and to get a better idea of what lies in store for CSAM's chimps now that that organization is swiftly unravelling."

The picture spins and the voiceover explains, "Because ASHRAAM is not open to the public, I will be visiting incognito as Mr. Alistair Smith, a wealthy foreign investor."

The picture stabilizes. Mannheim now wears a high-quality tweed suit and leans heavily over a cane with a large rectangular handle shaped like the barrel of a gun. He's been aged by makeup and wears an almost bald pate with strands of grayish hair and thick, coke-bottle glasses. Wrinkles spread across his forehead and a thick beard covers his mouth. His voice drops into a Scottish brogue as he says, "I've adopted the name 'Smith' partly as a tribute to the young chimpanzee that launched my investigation. Tomorrow, I'll meet Jim Sema of ASHRAAM to tour the facility. I'll be depending on my trusty cane to help me get around. Inside the handle is a micro-sized spy camera. It will be your eyes as we explore this venue."

The image of a jet taking off fills the screen. Then, the picture suddenly becomes grainier, and the perspective shifts lower than eye level as the camera pans over a spacious, neon-lit examination room. A four-legged animal is stretched out on a table. A surgeon flays open one leg while three younger doctors stand by taking notes. Across the room, a woman weighs rabbits of various sizes.

A dark-haired man in a lab coat with a receding widow's peak and a pinched mouth steps into the frame. "You said you were primarily interested in how monkeys and apes are used. Down this way is our head trauma unit." Sema gestures down a side corridor from which emits shrill shrieks.

The camera pauses. "You mean for testing crash helmets and the like?" Mannheim asks in his adopted accent.

"Partly. After we break the animal, we see how well we can put it back together. The damaged material provides the young surgeons at the medical college an excellent chance to practice their techniques. If they make a mistake, well, it's better it's on a chimp than on a child, don't you agree? Come, I'll show you." Sema beckons Mannheim down the hall.

They come to a large window, behind which sits a primate restrained in a chair. A weight shaped like a battering ram retracts over its head. The ape looks up at it. Its teeth are pulled back in a grimace of fear. It strains at its bonds, screeching. The chimp has already soiled itself.

"Do you get useful results from these impact studies? These apes have much thicker skulls than any human. I expect you have to extrapolate quite a bit to be able to use the—"

The weight falls. The camera jumps as Mannheim clutches it more tightly. The chimp slumps forward, immobile. Blood streams from its nostrils.

"—data," Mannheim finishes quietly.

"Very valuable results," Sema says calmly. "Just now, though, our principal line of research is communicable diseases. This way, please." Sema returns to the main corridor.

As they walk, Sema explains, "We've been working on a longitudinal study of hepatitis, infecting the animals, observing the progress of their disease, and then attempting various treatments. We've followed the same process before with syphilis. Just now, the industry is most interested in hepatitis as a template for diseases that might evolve in the near future. Now that we're so close to putting smallpox to rest, at long last, it's time to see what else we can eradicate." He indicates a row of refrigerators. "Here we are."

"Ah, is that where you store the drugs?" Mannheim asks.

"No. This is where we store our specimens." Sema pulls open one of the middle doors, revealing not a refrigerator but a chimpanzee crammed into a small cage. The unit is coffin-like. It's entirely dark inside, and the animal hasn't space to turn around. Steel mesh covers the front. The ape's legs are folded under him, and his arms are pinned at his sides. The chimp quivers, grunting faintly, but doesn't react to the two men. Instead, it stares vacantly into space.

"Is it comatose?" Mannheim moves closer, aiming the camera on the glassy, dark eyes.

"They get like that sometimes when they've been shut up for a while. Others try to stimulate themselves. Here." Sema opens another door. A smaller, younger chimp sits behind it. This one rocks back and forth, its arms around itself in a tight hug. It whimpers when the door opens but also stares forward blindly.

Sema shuts the door. "They go a bit gaga after being isolated for protracted periods. Some of them fail to thrive and die, true, but it's entirely necessary to separate them for their own safety and ours. We can't risk allowing these animals to infect any other specimens or any lab workers."

"But why not allow the ones that have already been infected stay in one cage together?" Mannheim's voice wavers slightly as he struggles for a neutral tone. "Isn't that how CSAM does it?"

Sema's lips curl. "Cutting corners may save CSAM a few bucks, but it weakens the results. When you isolate the specimens, you have better control over them. We obtain better data this way."

"How can you determine if their conditions result from the disease, the test drugs, or their indefinite isolation?" Mannheim's voice takes on a harsher edge.

Sema doesn't rise to the bait. "We manage. If you're concerned about the isolated specimens, I can show you where we keep some of our others."

The picture cuts away to a darkened theater. Mannheim's voiceover says, "I've omitted the remainder of the tour for the sensibilities of our audience. The segment you've just reviewed is an accurate depiction of how ASHRAAM treats its quote unquote specimens. I screened this footage for primatologist Robert La Fontaine, who's spent the past decade working closely with chimpanzees. I wanted his opinion of the conditions at ASHRAAM."

La Fontaine enters the theater, shakes hands with Mannheim, who is no longer in costume, then sits to watch the film. The camera shows a montage of La Fontaine's reactions to various sequences. His mouth twists in disgust. He covers one eye and turns his face away. Finally, he walks out of the theater. Mannheim pursues him into the hallway.

La Fontaine is visibly upset, gesticulating. "That's all typical of these institutions. It's disgusting! Some of these labs are funded by government research dollars. Your and my tax dollars are paying to help torture animals. ASHRAAM makes me ill. An ashram is meant to be a peaceful retreat, a place for meditation and enlightenment. Instead, that facility has perverted the term to connote a chamber of horrors for our closest living relatives."

The image returns to Mannheim addressing the camera before a neutral background. "ASHRAAM is currently the leading facility for independent animal research in the nation, conducting experiments that leave it with an inexhaustible need for new material.

"If Judge Borley should rule against Manfred Teague, it is all but certain he will sell his remaining specimens to ASHRAAM to recoup some of his losses. Even if Dr. Teague should prevail and maintain control of Smithy, he will likely sell that chimp to ASHRAAM, too. Is this the future that awaits this beguiling and beloved chimp? How do other, less prestigious research facilities compare to ASHRAAM? Join me next week for the second part of this investigative report."

DIARY OF RUBY DALTON

May 16, 1979

Everybody's still in the kitchen talking about Smithy. They're not even trying to keep their voices down so I can sleep.

They're worried about how Smithy will handle himself tomorrow. They fear he may have developed a bad attitude and maybe resents us. Truth be told, I sort of resent <u>Smithy</u>. Smithy's the reason Jeff is never around. He's the reason we stayed so long at CSAM in the first place.

What would my life be like if we didn't have to cater to Smithy? Where would we be living now? What jobs would we have? Would we have started a family years ago? I'll never know because we're stuck in Smithy's orbit, and consequently, stuck in Man's orbit. It's like Earthbound.

<u>It's like I'm earthbound</u>. Trapped like a doomed spirit.

My God, is this what it's like for Her? No wonder spirits become vengeful and destructive. If I had to spend eternity stuck somewhere I hated, if I had to endure unending tedium and bitterness, if I didn't think I could ever escape, I would go mad. I'd want to hurt everyone within reach.

If I were to be struck down now in an accident, would my restless spirit be marooned at CSAM? Perish the thought!

Is She lashing out like I would? Is She as frustrated and full of despair? She's tied to Smithy, just like I am. I'm tired of it. Did She have a choice? Did She want to follow him, or was She drawn into his wake despite Her wishes, like a swimmer in the riptide? Did he free Her from Trevor Hall, or simply trap Her elsewhere?

Is this why I've been granted a glimpse into Her psyche? Because I'm trapped against my will, too?

I begin to understand. I can pity Her now instead of fearing Her. Maybe Smithy feels sympathetic toward Her, too. After all, he's also bound against his will.

If he were to die now, would he also become a terror?

EXCERPT FROM
SMITHY: THE MILLENNIUM COMPENDIUM
BY REID BENNET, PHD

CHAPTER THIRTEEN: THE MONKEY TRIAL

For the first time, though only for two days of testimony, video cameras from CBS, ABC, NBC, and BBC were admitted into the courtroom to film the unprecedented appearance of the ape. Other news agencies still had to rely on courtroom illustrations and photographs, like Ben Martin's now-iconic pair of images: Smithy at his third birthday party, behatted and stretching out his hand to accept a slice of cake from Wanda Karlewicz, juxtaposed with Smithy, four years later, his hand reaching through the bars of his cage as if grasping for freedom.

CBS cameras captured the high feelings pervading the courtroom . . .

ARCHIVAL FOOTAGE

COURTESY OF THE COLUMBIA BROADCASTING SYSTEM
MAY 17, 1979

The courtroom feed alternates between two cameras: Camera A is focused on the front of the courtroom, foregrounding the judge's bench, where the Honorable Nathaniel Borley sits, the vacant witness stand, and a portable seven-by-ten-foot metal cage in which Smithy is held positioned between the two; Camera B is positioned at the left of the courtroom and focused on the plaintiff's table up-close and the unoccupied respondent's table to the right. A buzz of conversation permeates the background, punctuated by the voices of audio technicians setting up the network's feed. A large chimpanzee paces inside the cage. The court bailiff paces at the left of the cage, watching the chimp intently. At the plaintiff's table, Samantha Stone, Brad Vollmer, Jeff Dalton, and Conrad Hegge engage in whispered conversation.

Smithy grabs the bars of his cage and scans the seated audience. He spots Sam and signs her name; she waves to him. Smithy makes another gesture, which she doesn't recognize. Sam elbows Brad, who is twisted around in his seat talking to a reporter in the audience.

Sam asks, "What's he saying?"

Brad faces forward and cringes. "'Help.'"

Smithy sees Brad and becomes excited. He signs, "Brad help." Brad starts to respond, but the approaching bailiff interrupts him. "You aren't permitted to talk to that thing."

Brad says, "Why not? I'm part of his defense."

The bailiff moves to block Brad's view of Smithy. He says, "How do I know you aren't coaching him to cause trouble?"

Brad says loudly, "For real? If you're gonna accuse me of conspiring with Smithy, then you must believe he can understand me. If you agree he can communicate, maybe we can end this right now and go home."

The bailiff says, "Keep your hands still unless the judge instructs you to talk to the ape." He steps away.

Smithy rocks back and forth and signs with greater agitation. Brad signs, "No," and gestures to the bailiff. When the bailiff passes his cage, Smithy squirts a stream of urine at him. The bailiff exclaims, "What the—"

The courtroom audience roars in surprise and laughter. Judge Borley bangs his gavel and calls, "Order in the courtroom!"

The bailiff says, "Your Honor, that thing just peed on me!"

Judge Borley says, "It's a wild animal, Hank. We have to expect such things. Honestly, I expected it sooner. Please have the janitor clean up the mess and then go clean yourself up."

The bailiff points to Brad and says, "Your Honor, he told it to do that!"

Brad protests, "I did not! This Nazi is trying to prejudice the court against us."

Hegge puts a hand on Brad's arm to restrain him. Judge Borley says, "Please be quiet, Mr. Vollmer. I'll trust my own eyes and ears in making my decisions. Mr. Hegge, if any of your clients disrupts my court with another outburst, I will have them removed."

Hegge says, "I apologize, Your Honor. It won't happen again."

Brad says, "Your Honor, this is a brand-new situation for Smithy. He's anxious, and sometimes when he's stressed out, he acts up. If I could talk to him, I could calm him down, tell him to behave in your courtroom. I won't coach him to do anything bad, I swear."

Judge Borley says, "I'm trusting the court's impartial ASL interpreter to monitor your communications for possible malfeasance. You may have limited interaction with the chimp, but only to reinforce that he must behave. Court will come to order in five minutes. I expect him to be in order by then, too."

Brad says, "Thank you, Judge! I mean, Your Honor!" He rushes up to the cage as flashbulbs go off. Smithy clings to the bars and stretches out his hand. Brad squeezes it briefly, then signs, "Sit down."

Smithy rapidly signs, "Brad, out. Out. Out."

Brad replies, "No out. Smithy sit. Be good. Be quiet." Brad points to the judge's bench and signs, "Nice man help Smithy. Smithy sit still." Smithy slides down the bars to the floor, watching Brad with a sorrowful expression. Brad wipes at his eyes and signs, "Good Smithy."

Smithy signs, "Drink."

Brad asks, "Your Honor, can Smithy have some water? Please?"

Judge Borley says, "He may, if he doesn't spray it anywhere."

Brad says, "You got it, Your Honor! I'll tell him to go in his bucket." Brad fetches his own water glass from the plaintiff's table and passes it to Smithy through the bars.

Smithy drinks it empty and signs, "Thank you."

Brad signs, "You're welcome. Be good," and returns to his seat.

The bailiff returns, wearing a fresh uniform shirt and announces, "All rise! Court is now in session!"

COURT TRANSCRIPT

Testimony of Piers Preis-Herald
May 17, 1979

Latimer: Doctor, I have a few follow-up questions concerning your research and your observations of Webster. First, in your estimation, is Webster intelligent in the way a human being might be considered intelligent?

Preis-Herald: Considering that the ape's favorite telly program was "Hee Haw," I'm inclined to say no.

Latimer: Setting aside taste, do you believe the animal is capable of understanding and responding to human language?

Preis-Herald: For a long time, I chose to believe so. However, as I've already testified, with time, distance, and a clear-eyed analysis, I eventually determined the evidence wasn't strong enough to support primate language skills.

Latimer: Do you believe primates generally are unable to communicate using human language or that Webster himself is deficient in that regard?

Preis-Herald: It's tempting to hope primates may someday show evidence of language. I've followed Dr. La Fontaine's research closely, and I have in mind things I would do differently if I performed a similar study again. I never have attempted another study, however, because I doubt further study would yield meaningful findings, and I've no wish to waste funds. Dr. La Fontaine's claims are based more on wishful thinking than on evidence of complex, spontaneous chimpanzee communication. As for Webster, he simply doesn't possess the capacities we were seeking.

Latimer: Will you address Webster for us now? Ask him a question.

Preis-Herald: All right, but I don't believe it will do much good.

Preis-Herald signs, "Who am I?"
Smithy snorts, tosses his head, and turns away.
He signs to Brad.

Preis-Herald: He didn't answer me. He's asking those gentlemen to play and to let him out. Those requests have won him prompt attention in the past.

Latimer: Is he giving you the silent treatment?

Preis-Herald: It's tempting to project an anthropomorphic motivation on his actions, but I wouldn't dare make that assumption. It's possible he's ignoring me. It's also possible he didn't understand me, or he thinks he'll get a more desirable response from the crowd at that table.

Now he's signing "dirty." That's the sign he gave when he wanted to use the toilet. Oftentimes, he used it as a ruse to escape his lessons.

Latimer: What does that sign mean? Making a circle of his fingers and touching them to his lips?

Preis-Herald: I've never seen it before. It could be a sign he invented or a random motion that won him reinforcement in the past, so he's decided to repeat it.

Latimer: All right, thank you for that demonstration, Doctor. What did you do after you concluded your study?

Preis-Herald: I terminated our lease of Trevor Hall and discharged the students under my supervision. I also spread the word within the ethological and comparative cognition communities that Webster was available for purchase and possible use in a future study. I recognized that he still possessed great value because of his unusual background and the degree of cunning he had demonstrated. Yet, Yale had no other chimpanzee studies in the works and no place to house him. Because Webster was officially university property and had been purchased with a grant, I was authorized to re-sell him by the president of Yale.

Smithy screeches and makes a sign.

Latimer: Dr. Preis-Herald, do you know what that gesture means?

Preis-Herald: Yes, it was a vulgarity. It means, "Fuck Nixon." One of my students taught him that. It used to get a good laugh from everyone. This is exactly what I mean. Webster is not truly communicating. He's merely performing in the manner prior experience has taught him will draw attention.

Latimer: Since disassociating yourself from Webster and dissolving the research program, have you benefited financially in any way from the project?

Preis-Herald: Yes. I wrote a book about my investigation, *The Webster Project*, and articles for various magazines. I also sometimes receive honorariums for lecturing about the case. However, when I believe it expedient to share my knowledge, I will speak without charging any fees.

Latimer: Do you speak about the ghost?

Preis-Herald: No, I discuss the language study and the pitfalls in interpreting its findings.

Latimer: Why not write about the haunting of Trevor Hall? Surely that would be more profitable than primate language.

Preis-Herald: It might be more lucrative, but it would be a betrayal of logic and reason since ghosts don't exist. Nothing justifies that cost.

Latimer: Very well; you've made money from your writings and appearances; did your colleagues who performed the research receive any residuals?

Preis-Herald: No. They performed their work within the context of a school assignment. Their reimbursement was in the form of school credit, room, and board. If any of them should write a book about the study, I suppose they might profit that way.

Latimer: You've been criticized for not acknowledging the contributions of Wanda Karlewicz, who designed most of Webster's program of study, in your books or articles. Why not share the recognition or the remuneration?

Preis-Herald: This is painful to discuss. After her accident, Wanda didn't want her name associated with the study. She asked me to omit it from any articles I might write about Webster. She claimed it would be pointless to put her name forward when the rest of her couldn't follow, and she joked that nobody could pronounce her name, anyway. I think, at that point, she wanted to hide. She didn't want to be contacted about Webster or associated in any way with our language project. She wanted to concentrate on putting her life back together.

Latimer: At Trevor Hall, did you also have a research assistant named Eric Kaninchen?

Preis-Herald: Yes, I did.

Latimer: Did Mr. Kaninchen tell you he had seen a specter on the estate?

Preis-Herald: He believed he had seen one. He was quite distressed about it.

Latimer: Did he believe Webster could also see this specter?

Preis-Herald: Yes.

Latimer: But you don't believe this to be the case. Why not, Doctor?

Preis-Herald: In part, I struggle to accept the idea because of Eric himself. You see, he died tragically in an automobile accident a few years ago. Such a waste of talent! Eric was fond of Webster, and as you say, he firmly believed Webster could see and speak with the dead. Yet, Eric has not come back from the dead to communicate with him. If he believed Webster could take messages from spirits, why not come back to say, "The

afterlife is real. Believe in Smithy."? It would
seem an obvious thing to attempt, if such a thing
could be done. But he cannot because ghosts don't
exist. Since time immemorial, all so-called
proof of ghosts has been anecdotal. Most high-
profile cases have been exposed as fraudulent. The
phenomena have never been studied or predicted
with regularity, as they must be for science to
recognize them.

Latimer: Some people, scientists included, claim
that animals, with their heightened senses, can
perceive ghosts better than humans. What do you
think about that?

Preis-Herald: Bats communicate with sonar. We
have machines that measure sonar. Dogs can see
infra-red. Machines perceive infra-red. Anything
an animal might be able to perceive can also
be perceived with technology. If our technology
hasn't captured a ghost, it's because ghosts
don't exist.

Latimer: Do you believe the unusual incidents at
Trevor Hall resulted from Webster interacting
with a ghost?

Preis-Herald: Certainly not. There are abundant
natural alternative explanations. My students
placed great significance on the fact that Webster
frequently got out of his locked room. He was a
skilled escape artist. That trait seems endemic
to the breed. Chanticleer, the ape living on
the University of Oklahoma's campus, routinely
escaped his cage by unwinding the wire of the
fence enclosing him and tying it back up again
when he returned. I misspoke earlier when I
implied Webster was unintelligent. Despite his
lack of language fluency, he was extremely cunning

and capable of evaluating and manipulating his environment. I believe he caused most of the mischief, including setting fires and hiding objects in unsuspected places. Everything else, such as the noises, can be attributed to basic characteristics of an old house. The association of these events with ghosts is solely the product of impressionable minds.

Latimer: Thank you, Doctor. That concludes my line of questioning. Your Honor, I respectfully ask that the chimpanzee be removed from the courtroom before I introduce my next witness. This is a matter of the greatest delicacy. Securing this next witness has cost me considerable time and trouble, and I don't want the animal's presence to disrupt these proceedings. If you will review the witness list we provided, I'm sure you will understand my motivations.

Hon. N. Borley: Yes, Counselor. Bailiff, please remove the chimpanzee and its cage for the remainder of the day. Court will adjourn until 1:00 p.m.

LETTER FROM RUBY DALTON
TO TAMMY STEINMETZ

May 17, 1979

. . . Wanda took the stand today!

Specifically, she was brought to court on a bench warrant. It seems she ignored or dodged three summonses from Latimer. He finally sent a sheriff's deputy to bring her to the courthouse. Hearing how she was inconvenienced, I thought of how she must hate Smithy and this business.

When she came in, she was all bundled up like a coy movie star with a big floppy hat tied down around her face by a scarf. All the reporters flurried about her, but the judge was unimpressed . . .

COURT TRANSCRIPT

Testimony of Wanda Karlewicz
May 17, 1979

Latimer: I call Wanda Karlewicz to the stand. Your Honor, I would like to state for the record that this next witness is a hostile party. She has disregarded prior attempts by my office to contact her and testifies today under penalty of contempt.

Witness is sworn in.

Hon. N. Borley: I don't allow disguises in my courtroom, Ms. Karlewicz. Remove your coverings, please.

Karlewicz: Please, Your Honor, may I keep them on?

Hon. N. Borley: I won't ask again, Ms. Karlewicz. Your behavior is already pushing the limits of contempt. Remove them now, or I'll ask the bailiff to do so for you.

Karlewicz: Your Honor, please! My face is disfigured. I know from experience that the sight of it distresses others, and their reactions are painful to me. For the sake of those in the courtroom and for my own peace of mind, please may I be allowed to wear them?

Hon. N. Borley: This disfigurement was caused by the chimpanzee's attack in 1975?

Karlewicz: Yes.

Hon. N. Borley: What was the nature of the injury?

Karlewicz: He bit through my cheek. He tore away a six-by-four-inch patch of skin, muscle, and nerves.

Hon. N. Borley: You required reparative surgery, did you not?

Karlewicz: Five surgeries in total, Your Honor, with two skin grafts, and physical therapy. I had to practice eating, speaking, and smiling again.

Hon. N. Borley: I'm sorry for your suffering, Ms. Karlewicz. I mean no offense, but it's my duty to render a judgment on the fate of this chimpanzee. To do so, I must be fully informed. I ask you now to please remove your hat and scarf. You may turn your back to the court and face me only.

Witness rises and faces the judge's bench. Witness removes hat and scarf.

Hon. N. Borley: Thank you for your cooperation, Ms. Karlewicz. I appreciate your help and apologize again for these measures. It's not my intention to upset you by reminding you of past events. However, I must have a full and clear picture of the animal Webster's capacities in order to render a decision.

Now, we may proceed with the examination. Counselor?

Latimer: Ms. Karlewicz, I wish to echo Judge Borley in saying I don't wish to cause you further distress during this line of questioning.

I recognize that the attack you suffered must have been enormously painful. You and Webster were very close, were you not?

Karlewicz: Yes. I was one of his primary caregivers. I'd worked with him since he was an infant living in the McKenzie household. Because I had the most experience with American Sign Language, I was Webster's main instructor. I have a younger brother who was born deaf, and my family uses ASL for his sake. At Trevor Hall, I fed Webster, cooked for and with him, and dressed him. Either Jeff Dalton or I would give him his nightly bath and tuck him into bed. Some nights, I even slept in the room with Webster. He was affectionate with me. He constantly gave me hugs and kisses or tried to groom my hair.

Latimer: But he wasn't always so affectionate, was he?

Karlewicz: No.

Latimer: Can you describe what those times were like?

Karlewicz: It was like he had the devil in him. I don't know how else to put it. He would turn on a dime and suddenly fuss or scream and resist instructions. Maybe we shouldn't have been so cavalier in joking about evil spirits while we were in that house. Maybe we brought bad luck on ourselves.

Latimer: Did you believe a ghost was haunting the premises?

Karlewicz: Not really, but many strange things happened during our stay at Trevor Hall. I personally experienced things I couldn't easily explain. Kitchen utensils seemed to vanish as soon as I set them down and reappeared once I looked away. At first, I thought Webster was playing pranks, but over time, I came close to wondering if that really were so.

Latimer: Do you attribute your and your colleagues' experiences to the supernatural?

Karlewicz: No. I believe it was all Webster. I don't know how he did it, but I know he's intelligent. And willful. Webster successfully manipulated the people around him to get what he wanted time and again. Somehow, he tuned into the group's paranoia about ghosts and played it up. I can't imagine why he did that, but I also can't believe the alternative.

Latimer: What do you believe prompted his attack on you?

Karlewicz: I don't know. I prefer not to speculate, frankly. Animals are unpredictable—even the best of pets. I can't bear to be around animals anymore—not just chimps, but also dogs or cats. I don't trust them.

Latimer: Ms. Karlewicz, what do you think should be done with Webster?

Karlewicz: He shouldn't be around people. I certainly don't want him to stay at that research center. People work there, don't they?

Latimer: What would you recommend?

Karlewicz: Send him to Africa and turn him loose in a jungle, or put him in a sanctuary or a zoo, but don't put him into anybody's home or give him the chance to interact with people who aren't specifically trained to handle primates. He's too volatile, too tricky. If given free rein, he will take advantage of it.

Latimer: By "take advantage," do you mean he might turn violent again?

Karlewicz: Yes.

Latimer: Do you think Webster's violent tendencies merit more intensive measures?

Karlewicz: I don't want him to be put down, if that's what you mean. I don't want revenge. I'm opposed to capital punishment. I wouldn't wish death on a murderer, and I certainly don't wish it on Webster.

Latimer: Even after everything you've been through—the disfigurement, the pain, the surgeries, the public humiliation, the total alteration of your lifestyle—you don't resent the chimp for doing that to you?

Karlewicz: Webster hurt me badly and changed my life, yes. I'll never understand why. I always thought we were good friends. But I don't bear him ill will. I don't believe he's really responsible for what happened. The fault was ours. We failed to understand his true nature. We didn't understand how erratic a wild animal could be. Within the context of the study, we were instructed to treat Webster as a human child in every way. In doing that, I think we forgot that he wasn't human. I slipped up, and this happened.

Witness touches her cheek.

But I consider it an accident, not an act of malice. When I think of Webster, I don't think first of my injury. I remember the good times we shared. Truly! I'll remember how his eyes would light up when we signed with him. I'll think of him dancing, or of his excitement the first time we pushed him on a sled. Webster could be mischievous and exasperating and even frightening, but much of the time, he was like a little child.

Latimer: Ms. Karlewicz, can you please summarize for the court what impact Webster has had on your life?

Karlewicz: Webster caused me heartache, but he gave me a gift, too. It was awe-inspiring to see how quickly he developed. Over a few months, his vocabulary tripled. I was amazed by how much he could remember and do. He *learned*! I never saw an animal perform that way. I'd like to enter into the record that I disagree with Dr. Preis-Herald. He doesn't fully understand how signing functions since he's not a native user. It's a performative language. ASL doesn't have a one-to-one correspondence with spoken English. Meaning comes from the rate or direction of movement and how signs are combined. I tried to explain that during the study. The emphasis Dr. Preis-Herald placed on Webster's word order always struck me as excessive. It's somewhat true that Webster's signing was modular, largely because he was taught with individual words instead of holistic phrases, but he *did* sign. Webster signed to us without prompting. He knew us and wanted to communicate with us. You can't imagine what it felt like to look in his eyes and see real understanding there. I got to make a connection with a fabulous being who was something so *other* than myself. I was able to reach across the gulf

of evolution and connect with a member of another
species. I felt like an astronaut on Mars. It
was incredible, and I wouldn't give back that
opportunity for anything, not even a normal life.
So, to answer your previous question, no, I don't
resent Webster. I feel incredibly privileged to
have been a part of the study and to have worked
with him and all the other people associated with
the project.

Latimer: Thank you, Ms. Karlewicz. No further
questions at this time, Your Honor.

Hon. N. Borley: Mr. Hegge, your witness.

Hegge: No questions, Your Honor.

Hon. N. Borley: In that case, Ms. Karlewicz, you
are dismissed.

LETTER FROM RUBY DALTON
TO TAMMY STEINMETZ

May 17, 1979

. . . Wanda's testimony blew everybody away. I teared up. Seeing her for the first time in years and hearing how she really felt made me ache. I feel guilty for not trying harder to keep in touch with her after the study dissolved. I assumed she had such terrible associations with the project and anyone involved with it that she wouldn't welcome hearing from me. I didn't want to make her feel worse.

Brad passed us a note during recess. Apparently, Wanda's coming to court was Hegge's doing! It seems she's remained involved with chimpanzees from afar. She regularly makes donations to People for Primates. The treasurer of the organization recognized her name and wrote to Hegge with Wanda's address and phone number, advising him to contact her about speaking in Smithy's defense.

"It probably wasn't ethical of her to share that information, but it sure worked in our favor," Brad wrote. Is that ever true!

Hegge knew Latimer's side was trying to bring Wanda in but that she had so far resisted his summonses just as she had ours. Instead of ordering a bench warrant himself, Hegge wrote her a friendly letter encouraging her to testify. He told her that "by sharing her unique perspective" she might be able to save Smithy's life. That probably wasn't very ethical to do, either. If Borley found out, he'd probably cite Hegge for witness tampering or some such.

Brad approves. "It was brilliant of him not to cross-examine her. He just let her answer Latimer's questions and speak her piece. We got our point across without anyone knowing Hegge was involved, and he came out looking like the sympathetic attorney because he didn't grill Wanda about her accident."

I looked for Wanda during the recess. I didn't see anyone leave the courtroom from the time she testified to the time the judge adjourned, but I couldn't spot her, even with the big hat. Maybe the bailiff sneaked her out through the judge's chamber so she could avoid the cameras and curiosity-seekers. I hope she got away unmolested, but I'm sorry I didn't get to talk to her. To tell her I'm sorry and wish her well. To say thank you.

I'm grateful Wanda testified. I hope she made a good impression on Judge Borley. Jeff will testify next month; I have my deposition in two weeks! I'm so nervous my guts clench up when I think about it. But if Wanda could come forward, in spite of everything, so can I. Wish me luck!

> *Love,*
> *Ruby*

LETTER FROM GAIL BEVERIDGE
TO VANESSA RALSTON

May 17, 1979

. . . Over and over, I see people I used to know and can't believe how much they've changed in five years. Ruby looked so tired today. I've been waiting for her to testify, now that the other side is calling witnesses, but they say she won't because of the baby. It's her first, and I guess it's taking a real toll on her. I'm happy for her and Jeff. I think he'll be a good daddy. He was always so good with Smithy.

I still haven't been able to talk to him except for those few minutes after I finished testifying. He acted like he didn't have much time for me then. Maybe he was mad about what I said. He looks like a new man without his beard. A lot younger. Ruby said the lawyers made him shave. The other guy, Brad, wouldn't do it though.

I finally saw Piers! He's gotten heavier and his expression looks like he smells something sour. Maybe he thinks the trial stinks. I almost went over to say hi to him, but I was afraid he'd look down on me because I testified about seeing the ghost. I know he never believed me about that.

And then there's Wanda. Nobody has seen her since her accident. I couldn't really recognize her voice when she was on the stand. She sounded like she had a bad cold or was getting over tonsillitis. But the things she said sounded like her. I was impressed with her for getting on the stand. She stayed calm and didn't cry like I did. She made a good argument for Smithy.

Wanda left the courtroom as soon as she was dismissed. I guess she didn't want to deal with the cameras. It was probably rude to chase her, but I went after her anyway. I didn't want to let her disappear from my life again without at least saying hello and letting her know I was thinking of her. I was sort of hoping, too, we could talk about Smithy and compare notes since we're the two he turned on. She didn't say in her testimony why she thought he did it. I always wondered what we could come up with if we put our heads together.

Lots of other people had the same idea to catch Wanda as she left, and a group of photographers got between us as I was trying to leave. By the time I reached the hallway, Wanda was gone. I looked for her and even went outside, but I couldn't spot her. I figured she must have jumped into a waiting taxi and run away. I saw the photographers standing around looking put-out, and I figured they couldn't catch her, either. That made me glad.

I went back inside and to the ladies' room to freshen up. I stepped inside and almost bumped into a nightmare. It looked just like the thing that scared me when I was testifying and the thing I saw long ago on the stairs. It was tall and all black with no face and a long scarf that wrapped around its head and fluttered around its shoulders like a hanging rope cut free from the gallows. It didn't move or come after me. It stood there and I froze, wondering, What is this now? What does it want?

Finally, the thing said, "Hello, Gail," and I realized it was Wanda! I was shocked. I felt relieved—first that it wasn't a ghost and then because I hadn't missed her—but I was shook up, too. She looked just like the ghost, all black, billowy, and faceless. I never thought of that while I watched her on the stand. But seeing her in the bathroom where I didn't expect her gave me the willies.

And then I felt ashamed! Wanda must have seen me staring at her in fright (I was on the verge of screaming. Why am I so jumpy?) and thought I was scared of her because of how she looked. Well, she was partly right, but not for that reason. Oh, Vanessa, I felt like dirt.

To make up for it, I threw my arms around Wanda and gave her a big hug. She stiffened but she didn't pull away, and I think (I hope) she got that I was sorry.

I said, "Wanda, I didn't recognize you! And then I thought you were a ghost or another jerk trying to spook me."

She said, "I heard about that. I'm sorry. I was just waiting for the press to get bored and go away so I could leave."

I told her she had the right idea, and maybe it wasn't such a bad thing that they don't let too many women be courthouse reporters because nobody could follow her. I told her how glad I was to talk to her again because I'd always looked up to her and I missed the old days and I was so sorry about what happened. I said a lot of things I don't even remember. I babbled a lot. There was a lot on my mind, but I couldn't get it to come out smoothly.

The whole time I talked to her, I looked past her, over her shoulder at the back of her reflection in the mirror. It's stupid but I didn't want to look her in the face. I figured she must hate people staring at her and wondering what's underneath that scarf and veil. But also, it was creepy the way she reminded me of the ghost.

Wanda didn't say much back to me, and I noticed her shuffling from side to side. I figured she was tired and wanted to leave. I offered to see if the coast was clear, and it was. Before she left, I asked her what she thought would happen.

She said, "I don't know, but it's not my concern anymore. It's not yours, either, Gail. We've done our part. Smithy's fate is in others' hands now. You don't have to stay and watch over him. Go back to your own life and enjoy it."

I told her good luck, but I stayed in the bathroom after she left. I didn't want to look like I was following her, and I didn't want to go back in the courtroom, either.

But Wanda made a good point. Instead of staying for the end of the trial, I'll call my travel agent about going home. I've spent long enough chasing ghosts. Maybe I shouldn't be surprised I keep seeing them.

HOME VIDEO FOOTAGE

Date: May 18, 1979
Location: Dalton Residence, Living Room

Jeff and Brad sit at opposite ends of a sofa.

Jeff looks into the camera and says, "Good evening. I'm Jeff Dalton. This is Brad Vollmer. It's about 8:00 p.m. on May 18. Not exactly the witching hour, but it's dark enough outside, so it will do. Now, we've got to get through this before Ruby gets home from work—or else she'll divorce me. Tonight, we'll do our best to communicate with spirits on the other side. We've set up this camera in anticipation of our success, so if anything happens, it will be on film for all the world to see. So, here goes."

Jeff clears his throat, lowers his head, and lifts his palms to the ceiling. "Hello, out there! To anyone who might be listening, we come in peace, and we ask that you kindly consider our plea. We mean you no harm and apologize in advance for disturbing you, but we need help."

Jeff licks his lips and clears his throat. "Eric? Eric Kaninchen, are you out there? If you can hear me, give us a sign, please. Any little thing. Knock the glass off the table or make the doorbell ring. Or make a knocking sound. Anything!"

Jeff pauses. Brad looks around the room, but nothing happens.

He continues. "Eric, it's been a long time, man. I miss you. I'm sorry we didn't talk more after we left Newport. I know Ruby and Tammy wrote you letters, and I should have done that, too, but how many guys write letters, right?" He chuckles weakly. "But I regret now that I didn't talk to you more when you were here and I had the chance. I'd love to talk to you now—I really would. I'd love to hear your voice again."

He sniffles and wipes his nose on the back of his sleeve.

Brad slides farther back to the end of the sofa, watching Jeff. "Hey, man, if you want me to give you space, I can go in the kitchen."

Jeff waves to him to stay seated. He's quiet for a moment while he regains his composure. "You were a great friend. It was a pleasure and an honor to work with you. I'm hoping you'll do a solid for your friends now and work with me again. You might have guessed this isn't just a social call. We need help. Actually, Smithy needs your help. If you've been watching, then you know he's in big trouble. People want to hurt him bad. But we have a shot to save him and give him everything he deserves. But we can't do it alone.

"We've told everyone about the Dark Woman, the one you saw, the one Smithy sees and talks to. I don't know her name, so I can't summon her, and I'm really not supposed to. But I'm hoping that wherever you are, maybe you know something about her, or you can find her and spread the word. Ask her nicely to please put in an appearance or give Smithy a message, something he wouldn't otherwise know on his own, something he can tell the judge and the world so they'll believe in him and give him his freedom. Or better yet, come forward yourself. I know how much you cared—care—about Smithy. I know you would help him if you could. I'm hoping you will. Piers asked why you don't appear and talk to Smithy. I've been wondering that, too. You know he's a conduit; you know you could get through to us anytime. I thought, 'Well, maybe Eric's already crossed over and he's at peace now. He's not thinking about us anymore and doesn't need to say anything.' Or maybe the ghost is interfering, keeping you from us, keeping Smithy for herself so only she can talk to him. I don't know. But if you can hear me, Eric, please do something to help us. Anything! Any little thing at all!"

Jeff looks at the ceiling, then around the room. His nose is red and his eyes are still watery.

"Please, man, help us. Help Smithy, won't you, please? I don't know who else to ask. Please say you can hear me. Please give us a sign. Anythi—"

The image winks out.

FIRE INSPECTOR SAYS
CSAM FIRE WAS VANDALISM
BY GORDON DAVIOT

The Fresno Bee, May 19, 1979

Last night, at approximately 8:15 p.m., fire broke out in the east wing of CSAM, destroying two laboratory rooms and a quarantine facility for sick animals. All were empty at the time, and no employees or animals were injured. The fire originated in the facility's electrical system. Representatives from the Department of Water and Power are investigating whether the fire at CSAM could have triggered the widespread blackout that struck most of Fresno at approximately the same time and lasted for two hours.

Investigators discovered a cattle prod identical to the type used by CSAM staff to train and discipline research animals among the debris, suggesting the fire was deliberately set. It is believed that the arsonist jammed the cattle prod into the electrical box, causing it to explode. Use of the prod in this way is doubtless a symbolic protest of the techniques used by CSAM director Manfred Teague. Recent testimony in the matter of *Friends of Smithy v. CSAM* has emphasized the authoritarian techniques Teague has fostered in his other researchers. Public disapproval of his behavior has spawned violent outcry, including protests in front of CSAM and the courthouse.

Dr. Teague expressed his own outrage and frustration. "These rascals[11] are trying to destroy me. They've attacked my reputation and now they're attacking my business. They're imperiling the animals they claim to want to help and threatening the lives of human beings. Nobody who sincerely values the health and well-being of a living creature could do that. These are monsters, and they must be stopped before they do worse."

He specifically cited Jeffrey Dalton, Ruby Dalton, and Bradley Volmer, the former CSAM employees now battling for custody of the chimpanzee Smithy, as enemies with the means and motivation to commit this crime. However, all three accounted for their whereabouts at the time of the incident.

Police are currently investigating whether the same persons who attempted to disable the generator of the Fresno Family Zoo earlier this month also committed this attack against CSAM. Authorities are exploring all possibilities, including that the arsonist is a current employee of CSAM. CSAM operations have temporarily halted, and the animals will be transferred to other facilities, zoos, and parks across the southwest.

Anyone with information about this attack is encouraged to contact Fresno police.

11 The word was changed for print media.

"FRIENDS OF SMITHY BECOME DISCIPLES: INSIDE FRESNO'S NEWEST RELIGIOUS MOVEMENT"

BY DAN ROSS

Fresno Gazette, May 22, 1979

Remarkable claims have emerged from the Fresno courthouse over the past six months about the seven-year-old chimp called Smithy. Now an audience smitten by Smithy is acting out its ardor in equally dramatic fashion.

They have read about the trial in periodicals, watched news broadcasts, and listened to the late-night radio show, "Whispers in the Dark," hosted by Celia Armendariz, who regularly champions Smithy's cause. Stimulated by Miss Armendariz's call to arms, inspired by personal visions, and espousing an unlikely faith in a unique animal, these adherents have united to form the Disciples of Smithy.

They are not Smithy's first or only supporters. The Friends of Smithy—animal rights activists—initiated the lawsuit against CSAM, but as the Disciples point out, the Friends view Smithy's talents as earthly, whereas the latter see Smithy as a spiritual guru, one who has seen a world unknown to most men, spoken to spirits, and touched lives on this plane and others.

Desiring to learn more about the movement, I visited one of the Disciples' meetings, held in an erstwhile nightclub space in the Tower District, now a coffee house that hosts nighttime poetry readings. Below is what I experienced.

As approximately thirty-five people assemble over coffee, they testify about Smithy's impact on their lives. The first to speak is Larry Sharp, an employee of the Fresno Family Zoo, where Smithy is housed. Sharp has often observed Smithy alone in his cage.

Or maybe not so alone.

"Smithy's always running around like he's playing tag with someone, but no one is there. The first time it happened, I thought he was chasing a bee or butterfly. But I watched Smithy closely and I didn't see anything else around."

Then there are the mysterious appearances.

"We manage the animals' diets very carefully. We don't let them have outside food because it could make them sick." Yet, somehow Smithy manages to come up with whole apples and pears, not pureed like the zoo serves. "Once he had a whole melon slice, another time a candy bar. He watched me as he unwrapped it and kind of smiled at me. Then he winked. I swear! He knew I was thinking, *Where did that come from? How did you get it? Something* must have brought it to him."

Sharp acknowledges recent unrest at the zoo. "A camera's there for Smithy's security, but it also shows that no one comes in or out with these gifts." The Disciples are fascinated by these stories from someone in such close contact with their hero.

Twenty-two-year-old Tina Rausch, whose pink baby doll dress and bow-tied ponytail belie her age and her compelling presence, is a self-proclaimed sensitive. She operates The Magic Eye, located off Van Ness and Tulare, where she reads palms and tarot cards. Now she claims to read Smithy's mind.

"He came to me in a dream. He asked me to bring a message to all of you: a message from the ghost." Rausch explains Smithy is the Dark Lady's messenger, chosen because he can hear and see her while ordinary people cannot. "But most people can't understand Smithy, either, or they just don't want to pay attention, so he needs a human to carry the message the rest of the way."

According to Smithy, via Rausch, the ghosts (plural) want to be left in peace. "That woman's not the only one who died at Trevor Hall. So did people in the family, people who worked there, that teacher who killed herself when her fiancé jilted her. They're all still there, wandering, frustrated and angry. They missed their chance to move on. The door is only open a short time, you see, and they didn't leave when they had the chance. Some didn't know any better. They were confused and didn't realize they were dead until it was too late. Others just wanted to stay on. They had their reasons. But now they can't find peace. They keep trying to drive people away, but every time they do, more people come in.

"The Dark Lady speaks for them all because she's been there the longest. She said everyone needs to leave Trevor Hall for good. Move out now and don't come back, and don't let anyone else in. Nobody may live at Trevor Hall again. The house must become a refuge for the dead."

How did Smithy communicate this, since Rausch knows no sign language: in words or in pictures?

"Both," Tina says. "I experienced a rush of impressions. I saw images of the woman in black, but I also sensed words. They just flared up in my mind. Smithy made a circuit between me and the Dark Woman, and I could feel her emotions. I felt this blast of cold coming from her, like from an industrial freezer. She's frustrated and angry. And she's tired of being ignored. After everything she's done, nobody pays attention. Not really. They make a big show, but they don't honor what she's really saying.

"If we don't obey soon and empty Trevor Hall for the spirits to have the run of the place, she'll come back with a vengeance. If you thought all the other stuff was bad—a few fires, some noises in the night, a girl falling off a building—then you'll be knocked off your feet by what she's got planned next."

Not to be outdone, Joanna Edwards, a young single mother, says she was watching the trial when Smithy spoke to her.

Through the TV.

Some people might think he was looking at the camera, but Edwards insists Smithy was looking directly at her. "He knew I was there, and he told me he needed my help. He said, 'Set me free, and I'll help you in return.'"

What help could she expect from a young chimpanzee? "He promised to help me win the lottery. He would tell me what numbers to play so I could move out of my dumpy apartment and send my little boy to college."

How does Smithy expect Edwards to free him, and why ask her for help instead of approaching somebody with more authority? "I don't know. Why was Joan of Arc chosen, or Saint Bernadette? Alls I know is he picked me, and now I'm telling you about it so we can free him like he wants."

The Disciples ask what Smithy's voice sounded like, and Edwards clarifies that it didn't sound like a *voice*, exactly. She didn't *hear* it. Like Rausch, she *sensed* it. The words were clear in her mind.

After testimony comes fellowship, when the Disciples of Smithy mingle and speak to one another or address the group more informally. I speak to a young man called Barry who worked security at the nightclub in its heyday and declines to give his last name. His own vision inadvertently mirrors the design at Delphi thousands of years ago. "We're going to build a big church, and people will come from all over the world to talk with Smithy, and he'll help them with their problems." Why would Smithy do that? "He likes people. He's been around people all his life. Why wouldn't he want to help them?"

Barry elaborates. "We'll build [Smithy] a big temple and call it the Monkey Palace. Why 'Monkey Palace' when Smithy is a chimpanzee? "Because it sounds cool." Barry further explains, "Monkey Palace" was the name of an Indian restaurant near his home, which has since closed. "We can use the same building and the signs and the decorations."

I also take the opportunity to ask whether anybody in the church is raising money to help with court expenses, or perhaps to buy Smithy. If the imperative is to free him, that seems the best way—and the most legitimate—to do it. The Disciples hem, haw, and hedge. Rausch says they have chosen to assist in other ways; I gather nobody has any money to spare for the cause.

I ask why they hope to install Smithy as a prophet in a temple. If his goal is to be free, shouldn't they release him into the wild? Wouldn't the Monkey Palace become a different kind of cage for him?

A young woman called Bethany chastises me. "You just don't get it. 'Free' means free to do what he wants. Smithy wants to spread the word about his gift. We need to help him use his talent for the betterment of mankind."

I inquire if any of the Disciples know sign language or are prepared to learn it to better communicate with their god, since it appears his telepathy only works in one direction. "If Smithy wants us to learn it, we will," Rausch vows.

My questions inspire some more practical discussion among the Disciples. They debate the best way to raise awareness of their mission and hit upon the idea of a letter writing campaign to reach important people: the mayor, city council persons, Judge Borley, the attorneys for CSAM. Edwards declares she will write to former Governor Reagan because he worked with chimps in Hollywood and is sure to be interested in Smithy. "Maybe he can get some of his movie star friends to donate to our cause."

Someone else proposes a public demonstration to raise awareness of their church. They agree to wear all black when they march, "because that's Smithy's favorite color," Rausch declares. (While I understand Smithy allegedly uses the word "black" frequently, I don't recall anyone mentioning his preference for it). Discussion focuses on where the march should take place: In front of the courthouse for symbolic reasons? In front of CSAM in protest? Or in front of the zoo to be closer to Smithy? Sharp quickly discourages this last suggestion. "There's been too much drama at the zoo already.[12]" Finally, consensus determines it's best to march through downtown Fresno to attract the most attention.

The meeting closes with all attendees holding hands and bowing their heads while forming a circle around a stuffed ape. As an effigy in a voodoo ceremony represents a specific person, this toy is a stand-in for Smithy and intended to better focus our thoughts and energies on him. We are to contemplate our good fortune at being born during the same time Smithy walks the Earth and to mentally send him good vibes, imagining him free, whatever that might mean to the circle.

---

12 Sharp was briefly a suspect in the zoo vandalism and was believed to be in league with the Simianese Liberation Army. However, no supporting evidence ever emerged.

The group seemed enthusiastic and well-meaning, though that never prevented idealists from turning into extremists before. While they all sent good vibes for Smithy, each person seemed to have a slightly varied understanding of what the best outcome for him would be. The lack of a consensual goal suggests the organization might flounder. Time will tell, particularly when the verdict is issued, which is expected within the next month.

LETTER FROM TAMMY STEINMETZ
TO RUBY DALTON

May 25, 1979

. . . The fire was unexpected, though it wasn't exactly news; I'd already heard about it on the radio by the time I got your letter. However, from the way you underlined the bit about the cattle prod, I take it the fact of the fire isn't what you meant to convey.

You once mentioned that a cattle prod vanished from a lab study practically before your eyes. Are you implying that that prod was the one used in this incident? Do the prods have serial numbers like guns? Is there any way to track them? Could you definitively determine if this is the same one?

If you're thinking the ghost magically hid the prod until she could use it to enact this mischief, I'd say that's a long shot. Our Dark Lady has always been low-key. I don't see her trying to grab headlines like this. Besides, as eye-catching as this fire was, it seems somehow petty. Beneath her. She's also always been drawn to Smithy; why attack CSAM when he's no longer there?

It's fortunate your neighbors could provide an alibi for Jeff and Brad, though I suppose the police will still investigate whether they might have colluded with somebody else to burn down CSAM. Would Man sabotage his own laboratory and property and try to frame one of you? He strikes me as the vindictive and unstable type.

Tell Jeff I wouldn't gloat so much about this if I were him. For one thing, it looks suspicious. For another, CSAM shutting down will accelerate the transfer of any remaining lab specimens to new and potentially more hazardous facilities. That's nothing to celebrate.

However, like you, I'm mainly worried that whoever committed this vandalism might brand the Friends of Smithy with a reputation for violence through association. You've commanded public sympathy so far, but these recent uprisings coming so close to the conclusion of the trial threaten to detonate that positive image—along with any sympathy the judge might have for your cause. Even if whoever's behind this isn't formally affiliated with you, if they're acting from the belief that they're serving your interests, it could look the same to Borley and the public. Maybe whoever did this doesn't realize they're sabotaging themselves and your cause. Then again, maybe they're trying to do just that. First the zoo, now CSAM.

Again, see my note above re Man. Really, Ruby, this possibility is more likely than a ghost trying to blow up the lab.

Have you considered going back to Scranton after your depo for an extended visit with your parents, or even until the baby comes? It sounds like the boys are mainly running the show without your input anyway. Just think: you'd be closer to me, and I could visit. I'm sure the old neighborhood would be a safer and less stressful environment for you.

It sounds like you have human shenanigans enough without adding conspiracies and hauntings to the mix. I never know what I'm going to hear next about this trial. If it were televised regularly, the ratings would surpass any soap opera.

I'm impressed with Tina Rausch. She's concocted the Grand Unified Field Theory of the haunting, deftly combining the legend of the murdered servant and the myth of the suicidal teacher into one compelling spirit message. Now Trevor Hall seems destined to become the next Winchester House. Perhaps it will rival Disneyland's Haunted Mansion as the best retirement home for spirits . . .

EXCERPT FROM PRIVATE INTERVIEW
BETWEEN REID BENNET AND SAMANTHA
STONE, ESQ., CIRCA 2000

Samantha Stone: Wouldn't you know Ruby recognized this weird woman from the photo in the article? It seems that several years earlier, she had visited a fortune teller downtown, a Madame Jeannie or something, to seek advice about the ghost that nobody was yet sure actually existed. Anyhow, this kid had been the psychic's receptionist.

Reid Bennet: Small world!

SS: Suspiciously small. I might have doubted the identification, but Ruby had a freakishly good memory. Even though she'd only met with the girl for a few minutes, Hegge and I believed her. She was also very reluctant to admit how she knew this woman; it wasn't a declarative accusation. When Ruby told her story, she sounded embarrassed about what she'd done. It was even news to Jeff. He was more annoyed that she'd kept it from him than that she'd gone in the first place. Ruby swore she'd said nothing explicit to the psychic about any phantom. The psychic didn't mention any ghost, either, during their session. But she or her assistant must have recognized Ruby from the news, assembled the pieces, and decided to profit from the trial.

I researched the business and found out Madame Jeannie had retired at the start of the year, just as the trial was getting underway. The younger girl, Tina Rausch, tried to make a go of things herself; she must have thought she could use Smithy to elevate her reputation. She started selling talismans and spells for repelling ghosts, in case anyone wanted protection from the Dark Woman.

RB: Did your team consider going public with her pre-existing connection to Ruby and the case? It seems that would have shut the movement down.

SS: Oh, Ruby wanted to expose her. We told her there was no harm in going along with the story, or at least in not contradicting it, but she insisted innocent people *could* be harmed. People were apt to be swindled, people might be genuinely frightened by the ghostly claims, or warring factions might come to violence. There had been a break-in at CSAM and disturbances at the zoo by that point.

Hegge told her, "These people are grown adults." Though, granted, some of them were very young adults. "They have the freedom to make bad choices. They can throw their money away if they want." But she remained agitated. The boys and I had our work cut out trying to reign her in.

I remember Brad arguing that even if the older medium was a fraud, the girl might have really had a vision. He thought we should team up with Rausch, see if she had suggestions for helping Smithy. Ruby didn't like that idea, and Hegge didn't want us to be seen openly fraternizing with the newest act at the circus. He thought coexistence and quiet tolerance were preferable. So, we let her and her group have their meetings and their marches. And we let her tell her version of the ghost story of Trevor Hall.

The ghost angle was always a long shot. We didn't really expect the judge to go for it, but we had to try everything to get him to keep an open mind for Smithy's sake. Just then, it looked like our gamble was paying off hugely, at least where the public was concerned. Rausch fueled a movement—on both coasts. Hegge thought it was a coup: publicity we didn't have to generate or feed. It gathered its own momentum. Rausch made Smithy arguably more popular than he had ever been. Naturally, Hegge wanted to let it ride. Let the crowds go wild. Let them tell stories about the vengeful ghost and the kindly ape trying to protect us all from her wrath.

RB: What did Hegge believe about Smithy's abilities?

SS: Hegge believed in succeeding. He believed in going big. I think he admired Smithy. He thought the chimp really was as smart as people said. Maybe smarter.

He once told me, "If Smithy really knows what's good for him, he'll keep this ghost act going just to keep everyone guessing."

RB: This ghost "act"?

SS: The behavior. Not that it was faked necessarily. I don't know what Hegge thought about it, really. We didn't talk about it. *Really*. I didn't even spend much time thinking about the ghost stuff myself. All that I'd seen Smithy do in the way of communicating and interacting was impressive enough for my standards. The ghost angle was a means to an end.

Though for all we knew, it could have been true . . .

NOTES LEFT FOR SMITHY
AT THE DISCIPLES OF SMITHY SHRINE

Circa May — June, 1979

Dear Smithy,

My doggy Lionel had to be put to sleep last month. He was old, almost fifteen, and my parents said we needed to do it because he was suffering. He was having a hard time standing and wasn't eating very much. They said it was for the best, and I didn't want him to be in pain, but I still feel really bad about it. He looked so sad when we left him with the vet. I just want to know he's OK now and he's not mad at me for what we did. We loved him and we thought it was the right thing to do. I would never hurt him otherwise. Can you please tell Lionel I'm sorry? And I miss him and love him very much. He's a big Chow dog with a lot of fur around his head like a lion's mane. That's why we called him Lionel.

I asked my Sunday school teacher Miss June if I'd see Lionel in heaven, but she said animals don't go to heaven because they don't have souls. I don't believe that. I'm sure you don't, either. If you can see people ghosts, you can probably see dog and cat ghosts, too. Right?

Please give my love to Lionel. Thank you very much.

Susie, age 11

*

My daughter died unexpectedly two years ago.
I thought it was the end of my world. Friends told
me I would see her again, that she was in a better
place, but I never believed them. I didn't believe
in an afterlife. I'd always thought religion was a
crock, even before it was fashionable to question
authority. But thanks to you, my mind is open. I
listened to the testimony about what happened in
Rhode Island, and I believe you did see something
in that house.

Animals are innocent. Unlike people, an animal
would have no reason to lie. You don't need money.
You don't need to control the masses. I believe you
said you saw a dark spirit because you actually
did see it. If that spirit can exist, then maybe
my daughter still exists, too, somewhere. Maybe I
really will see her again, someday. I never had
that hope before.

I feel happier now in my daily life. Little
things don't trouble me like they used to. I'm not
as worried about getting older because I dare
to think that when I die, it won't be the end.
Perhaps it will be another adventure.

Thank you for your messages. Thank you for
making me believe.

*

Please tell your ghost friend we know the
newspapers and the radio lady got it wrong about
who she is. We know she's not a vengeful spirit.
We know she's seeking peace. Please don't let her
be mad at us for this mischaracterization. My
people will do our best to correct the record and
clear her name.

*

Smithy, your awesome. Thank you for telling
us the Good Word. Even when your all locked up
don't let the man keep you down. Remember Jesus
was prosecuted too. Keep preaching the Gospel.

*

Please keep telling us the news from the other
side. We believe. We're eager for your news.

*

God bless you, Smithy.

*

We love you, Smithy!

*

We believe in you, Smithy.

LETTER FROM RUBY DALTON
TO TAMMY STEINMETZ

May 30, 1979

. . . It's not funny! If you lived here, if this were your life, you'd be mortified. This nuttiness keeps getting worse—worse than I ever imagined.

The sole, small blessing is that these "Disciples" hijinks aren't affecting the trial. No witness has mentioned Smithy's newest followers, and Hegge isn't planning to put any of them on the stand.

This "Grand Unified Theory," as you call it, is ridiculous. The ghost doesn't care about the house. She wants <u>Smithy</u>. None of this was ever about Trevor Hall. That may be the place where we encountered Her, but She moved on from it long ago, as current events should make clear. Tina Rausch is creatively starved if she's resorting to the stereotype of a ghost possessing a house. I can't believe anyone would place any relevance on that at this point.

I'm so sick of these hucksters trying to elevate their own reputations by standing on Smithy. The true believers are hard enough to face. Their hopes are <u>so</u> high, and they're <u>so</u> earnest. They act as if Smithy were the Chosen One. They sincerely believe he has the power to do incredible things: to bridge the gap between worlds, to know the future, and to work wonders. When some creep tries to take advantage of them, it makes my blood pressure spike. But it didn't work long for Marianne, and I expect Tina's scheme to fall apart any minute now. I only hope she doesn't dupe anyone too severely in the meantime.

The newest development is that the Disciples have set up a kind of shrine to Smithy by the big water tower. People leave notes or icons and light candles and gather to sing and pray. It's created a big traffic snarl, but Hegge insists it's great publicity. Anything that keeps Smithy in the public eye in a positive light is bound to help us, even indirectly.

I was curious to see what the scene was like and to get a sense of what people are saying and feeling, so I visited yesterday. I considered wearing a disguise to prevent anyone from recognizing me, but I couldn't work up enough energy to put one together. As I made my way downtown, I felt so <u>sneaky</u>. The closer I got, the sleazier I felt, like I was trespassing or spying, forcing myself into a space where I didn't belong, even though I had every right to walk down the street and observe. Because I am an outsider. Even though I'm one of Smithy's advocates, I don't carry the inner light of faith in him. My presence sullied their adoration.

In the end, I didn't even get close to the shrine. When I was about three blocks away, I stopped and just hovered, rubbernecking at the gathering of people from a distance, along with the other pedestrians and tourists cruising through town. The assembled acolytes seemed upbeat despite their mourning garb. They waved at people driving by and spun their signs like jugglers. I could barely read them, but I gathered they're supportive of Smithy. Hegge's right about that being a plus. If you read the local papers, you'd see that some people in town would like to lynch our poor baby just to be done with him already. I only wish these groupies supported Smithy as an ape who deserves humane treatment and not as a would-be religious figurehead.

Is it strange I've never thought of Smithy as someone magical or holy? When we first developed an inkling that he might be using his signs to communicate with forces beyond mere mortal comprehension, I felt awed. I was anxious about the implications and the consequences to us, but I was also excited and proud of him. Still, I considered his ability something cool that he could do, not something intrinsic to his character. I believed Smithy was gifted, the same as an athlete who can run a mile in under four minutes, or an eight-year-old prodigy who can write an opera. I was sure he was special; I never considered that he was divine.

Am I short-sighted? Am I missing a bigger point that's obvious to everyone else? Did <u>you</u> ever think Smithy could be magical? Maybe that's hard to do since you had to change his diapers.

What if these people are right that he's the harbinger of some New Age, and all along I've been griping about him and failing to appreciate his magnificence? Should I be struck down for my disbelief?

If Smithy really were a Chosen One, then all my suffering would be in service to a greater cause. All would be justified. It's appealing to believe that. It lures me toward feeling victorious and self-satisfied, but I don't dare give in, lest I become as gullible as all those kids on the corner.

Still, it's a beautiful thing to imagine. Far, far better than to contemplate him being yet another of nature's gifts about to be sacrificed on the altar of science . . .

EXCERPT FROM "TRESPASSERS SEEK NEW GHOST AT TREVOR HALL"
by Patricia Hartigan-Hendricks

The Newport Daily News, **May 31, 1979**

Police last night responded to a call from the notorious Trevor Hall. Caretakers Salvatore and Regina Scolari heard strange noises from the first floor and instead of assuming they belonged to spooks, the Scolaris reported intruders. Officers subsequently rounded up three teenage trespassers whose names have been withheld due to their ages.

The intruders confessed they had been inspired by testimony in the ongoing Smithy trial to break into the house to contact the spirit of Eric Kaninchen, a former researcher under Piers Preis-Herald who was killed in an automobile accident in 1976. Kaninchen allegedly conducted occult rituals in the pantry during his stay in the mansion. Filled with holiday revelry and illicit alcohol, the trespassers forced their way into the same pantry to attempt to communicate with Kaninchen's spirit . . .

DIARY OF RUBY DALTON

May 31, 1979

. . . *Tammy's voice was choked with tears again, just like the day she called to tell me Eric had died, but beneath her words I heard anger, not sorrow.*

"How dare they! How dare those hooligans try to turn him into a bogeyman! Another ghost story for Trevor Hall! Eric's not some legend, Ruby, he was our friend! And what's this crap about 'occult rituals'? It was <u>one</u> séance that didn't amount to anything."

I murmured soothing things, but I, too, felt angry at these ignorant, disrespectful brats for abusing my friend's memory. I'm also resentful they created this mess the night before I testify, as if I didn't have enough on my mind.

Above all, I'm surprised. Eric's only been gone three years. (He would have graduated by now!) How can he be a ghost story already? I thought ghosts belonged to dusty history, to the shadows of rumor and gossip. I thought they were forgotten figures whose identities had become so tattered they could be stitched into something new and terrifying. Eric isn't that far gone. Jeff, Tammy, and I still remember him. And his poor mother! How must she feel through all this?

Does she believe her son is earthbound and lurking in Trevor Hall's kitchen, waiting for vandals to call him up?

Disgusting!

And yet, our ghost must have started out this way, too, with plans for Her future and a family who loved Her and missed Her when She died. What would they have thought of us kids huddling in the library, speculating about their daughter's romantic entanglements and whether Her end was natural, digging into Her life, trying to contact Her? Is that all it takes to start a ghost story? One dead person and a lot of imagination?

I mentioned my thoughts to Tammy, but she was more practical. "This is all Trish's doing, trying to stay in the spotlight. The next time I go to Newport, I'm going to march into her office and break her nose!"

DEPOSITION TRANSCRIPT
OF RUBY DALTON

June 1, 1979

Latimer: Were you wary of Webster after he attacked you?

Dalton: Not really. I figured Smithy reacted as he did because I'd spooked him or hurt his feelings by pushing him away. I felt guilty about it, actually. Besides, he apologized to me. The next day, after I'd had the night to calm down, Jeff took me to Smithy's room and he signed, "Sorry."

Latimer: Had Jeff told him to do that?

Dalton: Jeff arranged it, but he didn't coach Smithy. Jeff said after I was taken out of my room that night, Smithy was signing "Sorry," so I believe Smithy honestly regretted his actions. He knew they were wrong.

Latimer: By that point, hadn't Webster also attacked Eric Kaninchen and threatened the animals?

Dalton: That was out of character. Smithy was under stress.

Latimer: Was he under stress when he attacked Wanda?

Dalton: I couldn't understand that. Smithy loved Wanda. She was one of his first teachers. I decided

Smithy had lost his temper and just wasn't aware of his own strength or the damage he could do.

Latimer: What I hear you saying, Mrs. Dalton, is that you were repeatedly astonished by the chimp's increasing violence. You didn't anticipate it, yet you remained unconcerned in its aftermath.

Dalton: Not . . . I didn't expect trouble. I was devastated for my friends, but those were three incidents over a year. From day to day, Smithy was sweet. It was easy to get comfortable around him. Besides, I thought once we got Smithy out of that house, he'd go back to normal.

Latimer: You blamed the house for his behavior?

Dalton: Yes.

Latimer: Why?

Dalton: I . . . thought it was an insalubrious environment, that something about the house was affecting his behavior. Like mold or asbestos. Smithy scratched up the walls sometimes. He could have opened a pocket of some harmful substance that affected his mind or senses. I thought a change of environment would help. He always behaved well when visiting the Meyer School or staying with Sarah McMann.

Latimer: If you believed the house affected the chimp's behavior and disturbed the other animals, did you ever think of leaving?

Dalton: No.

Latimer: Why not, if you believed it was a dangerous and haunted place?

Dalton: I didn't know if it *was* haunted. That was the problem. I didn't know if I was going crazy, or if Smithy was, or if there really was a ghost. It was the not knowing that upset me, not fear of Smithy. I was tormented by thoughts of what might be going on around me unseen, or whether I might be cracking up. I didn't know which option was worse. Still, I stayed, because even though I didn't know if there was a ghost inside Trevor Hall, I *did* know there was a recession going on outside it. I saw that with my own eyes back in Scranton. And I decided to take my chances with the ghost.

Latimer: Who was this ghost?

Dalton: I've no idea. There were rumors about her being a servant, but no specifics. Whoever she may have been, the world has forgotten her name by now. Oh, but it will never forget Smithy's! (*Laughter*)

Latimer: Let's move on. When you brought Webster to CSAM, did you think the location would offer him a fresh start?

Dalton: No. I was uneasy about his prospects.

Latimer: Why? Were the facilities inadequate?

Dalton: No. In fact, the chimpanzees' living quarters were larger than I'd anticipated. It was Man who worried me. He was abrasive and insensitive.

Latimer: He refused to coddle your prized chimpanzee.

Dalton: No, he didn't show *any* concern for Smithy. I knew Man had outbid other buyers and I assumed he had big plans for Smithy, but he didn't seem to care about him at all. Not about his health or his comfort or his language abilities. He was disdainful. And he carried a cattle prod everywhere. We never used such things in Newport.

Latimer: Perhaps that's why the chimp was able to hurt your friends.

Dalton: I don't think violence is an appropriate way to deal with any situation, whether with people or animals. As we spoke to the other employees and learned more about how the animals were treated—and how some of them had died—Jeff and I became more fearful . . .

[Cut]

Latimer: Did you see anything at CSAM that you thought was ghostly or weird?

Dalton: I-I saw the chimps reacting to something unseen. It happened during our gambling study and even when they were simply in their outdoor cages. They acted terrified and went into a frenzy, but I couldn't see what had upset them. Nobody did.

Latimer: Did Webster display the same fear and agitation during these incidents that he showed at Trevor Hall?

Silence.

Latimer: Ms. Dalton? I asked you, did Webster also act fearful?

Dalton: I'm thinking! No. No, *he* wasn't afraid. The others were.

Latimer: Why should Webster's behavior toward this supposed ghost change at CSAM? According to you, he was terrified of this spook before.

Dalton: For one thing, the ghost never attacked him with a cattle prod. There was worse to fear at CSAM. For another, he may have learned to tolerate her. She's been the only real constant in his life through all he's endured. Jeff and I usually weren't allowed to see Smithy. Even Brad wasn't allowed in the isolation ward. But *she* could always find him. Maybe he developed some misplaced affection for her—like what happened with Patty Hearst or Jim Jones! Smithy was all alone in a strange place, and she was something familiar he could depend on, even something not quite right . . .

[Cut]

Latimer: Was it ever your intention to undermine or malign Manfred Teague?

Dalton: No. On the contrary! Working for him, I was always anxious about possibly doing something wrong that might reflect badly on CSAM or get me fired. I was very careful in my work. I didn't want to give him any reason to criticize me or let me go.

Latimer: Did you enjoy working for CSAM then, since you wanted to hold on to your job so desperately?

Dalton: No, I was miserable. Every day when I woke up, I felt like crying because I knew I had to go into that office. I never knew what awaited me, but it was bound to be something bad.

Latimer: Why not seek other employment?

Dalton: Do you know how hard it is for a married woman to find a job? Most employers don't want to hire women anyway, but when they find out you're married, they'll say things like, *What are you doing here? Go on home, sweetie, and let your husband take care of you.* Or worse, *Why are you trying to take a job away from a man who needs it?*

Latimer: Was that Dr. Teague's attitude?

Dalton: No. He had other faults, but he never gave me that attitude. I encountered it elsewhere. Even though I despised working for him, I knew I was lucky Dr. Teague was willing to employ me.

Latimer: Did your husband influence you to remain at CSAM?

Dalton: Well, I—we both—chose to watch over Smithy and make sure he would be safe in his new environment. Chimps are sensitive to changes. Smithy had never been around other chimps before. I don't think he knew what they were. It was a major adjustment. We also wanted to make sure his language skills weren't forgotten. At first, our plan was to stay for a few months, maybe a year, to provide some continuity to help Smithy transition. Afterward, I thought we would go back east, finish school, and embark on our own careers. But Jeff wouldn't think about leaving. He was personally invested. He thought of Smithy as his responsibility, his child. So, we've been here ever since. I've supported Jeff in helping Smithy and the other chimps.

Latimer: Do you believe you're helping Webster and the chimps with this lawsuit?

Dalton: I hope so. With all it's costing us, it had better count for something.

Latimer: Are you aware that animals have been sold, and funding to care for those remaining is tight?

Dalton: Yes. That wasn't our intention. And yet . . . I can't say I'm fully sorry. Those animals are probably better off than with Man. He tormented them. He terrified them. I saw it in their eyes and their gait. Wherever they're going next, for however much time is left for them, I hope they won't fear anything or anybody like that again.

Latimer: Mrs. Dalton, you've devoted four years to CSAM both to satisfy your husband and to protect your favorite chimp; how has that strategy worked out?

Dalton: I think we kept Smithy in one piece longer than he might otherwise have lasted. Man was horribly aggressive toward him in the beginning, but we've protected Smithy and even continued his language lessons informally.

Latimer: But now you're in court. Your actions have threatened CSAM's ability to care for all its animals. In putting Man Teague on trial, you've also put Webster on trial. Now the world is hearing about his bad behavior. Is that what you wanted?

Dalton: Those outcomes are incidental. We had to protect Smithy, and this was the only way. I wish it hadn't come to this. I wish things were easier. But I have to hope that by the end of the hearing, he'll be saved, and we'll be vindicated.

Latimer: Is that all, Mrs. Dalton? Didn't you initiate these proceedings because you wanted to shake up the status quo? Didn't you want to make a name for yourself?

Dalton: No.

Latimer: Are you sure? Because that was your goal when you joined Dr. Preis-Herald's project in Newport. I can play the film for you to refresh your memory.

Dalton: That was different! I was speaking as a scientist involved in research then. This suit now is solely for Smithy's benefit.

Latimer: You don't benefit at all? This suit has the potential to change the standing of non-human primates everywhere. Isn't that worth boasting about, Mrs. Dalton? Isn't the real reason you're involved in this trial because you want to advance your own ends through Webster?

Dalton: No! I wanted nothing to do with this trial! I hate it! I hate seeing my name in the papers. I hate seeing my bloated, distorted image on TV. I hate breathing legal arguments and testimony day after day. I hate that my husband is never around. I hate that reporters call at all hours of the day and night, even though we've changed our number four times. If this is what fame is like, I want no part of it! I'm about to have a baby, and I want to give my child a normal life. A quiet life. At this point, I'd like nothing better than to go home and be a housewife for the next eighteen years. I've tasted excitement, and it's not for me.

Latimer: Why not do that Mrs. Dalton? Why not drop the suit and move on with your life?

Dalton: I can't. It's not my decision to make. The trial is bigger than I am.

She laughs.

Dalton: I used to say I wanted to be a part of something big. Oh, be careful what you wish for! This isn't about me; it's about Smithy. It's all about him. Always has been! I'm just caught in the tide. I'm trapped just like he is. He's in the cage, but I'm a prisoner, too. I can't stop even if I want to. And I do! I wish it were all over. I wish we were both free . . .

LETTERS TO THE EDITOR
OF *THE FRESNO GAZETTE*

June 3, 1979

I started subscribing to the *Gazette* when the Smithy trial began because I was so interested in the proceedings. After reading last Tuesday's article, I'm in shock. These cult members all sound deranged! They should be put into an asylum before they kill somebody. One young woman believes the ape is communicating with her telepathically? That's what Son of Sam said. Somebody ought to put that ape down for society's sake before he stirs up more insanity.

Anna McGill
Brooklyn, NY

*

As I read Dan Ross's article, my emotions vacillated between amusement and demoralization. It's clear the young people involved in this new "movement" are trying to get attention any way they can. I don't know what role the adults like Mr. Sharp have to play. Are they merely misguided? Or do they have ulterior motivations for joining the next revolution? I feel inexpressibly sad for the next generation trying so desperately and creatively to fill their empty lives, and also for the hapless chimp caught in their "movement." I'm sympathetic to the general effort to protect Smithy, and I wouldn't like to see this unusual and fascinating creature harmed. Yet, I'm astounded by how the public's aspirations for the ape have grown ever more elaborate. First, he had the ability to communicate, then he was a medium, and now he's a prophet. Where will it end? Won't somebody please intervene before tragedy strikes?

Fred Bowe
Solvang, CA

Another cult! "It could only happen in California." That's what people will say about us. This new Church of Smithy will only end badly. Look what happened at Jonestown! If the ape tells them (telepathically, through the TV) to commit suicide so they can enjoy the glorious afterlife he's already told them so much about, what will they do? What will *we* do when we realize we could have and should have stepped in sooner to stop the madness?

Louis Maddox
Concord, CA

*

The Bible is clear:

"Do not listen to the words of prophets who prophesy to you, filling you with vain hopes. They speak a vision of their own heart, not from the mouth of the Lord."

"The prophets prophesy lies in my name. I sent them not, neither have I commanded them, nor spoken to them; they prophesy to you a false vision and divination, a worthless thing, and the deceit of their heart."

"False prophets will appear and they will provide great signs and wonders, so as to deceive, if possible, even the elect."

These fools have been deceived because they don't know Jesus. They will sell themselves to the false prophet and be damned for their sins. We must return to teaching the Bible in our schools so our children will learn right from wrong and live godly lives and not bow down before monsters again.

Lauren Greene
Harrisburg, PA

*

This new cult of personality is merely a distraction from the real question of what's to be done about the chimp's welfare. I wouldn't be surprised if Manfred Teague and his legal team had paid these so-called Disciples to put on their show and seduce the media away from reporting about the case itself. Don't fall for it, Fresno!

M.J. Harper
Fresno, CA

HOME VIDEO FOOTAGE

Date: June 4, 1979
Location: Daltons' Kitchenette

Brad and Jeff sit at the dining table in the Daltons' apartment. Their hands are spread flat on the table. Jeff looks at the camera and says, "It's June 2nd. This is our fourth attempt to reach out to any spirits that might be watching and listening and might be able to help us help Smithy. We humbly ask—"

Brad interrupts. "Hey, before we start, can I say something? I thought maybe we could try something different."

"Go for it," Jeff says.

"OK." Brad clears his throat. "When I was a kid, my older brother had this book of ghost stories—"

"I didn't know you had a big brother," Jeff interrupts.

Brad wrinkles his nose. "He's not important. What is important is he read this one story aloud to me and his friends. See, in the story, this guy, who was a radio host, wanted to do a ghost hunt show for Halloween. He set up his equipment in this old spooky house to do a live broadcast and told his listeners stories about all the things that had happened there, what the ghost had done, and what it was supposed to look like. He said that when it got to be midnight, everybody listening at home should concentrate on this ghost and wish for it to appear. He said the power of all the people working together would be able to summon it, and then he could tell them what was happening live on the air."

"OK." Jeff sits back in the chair, crossing his arms and frowning.

"The thing is, the radio guy was full of it. The house wasn't haunted, it was just some old house that had been empty a long time. The ghost story was just made up for entertainment. This guy was going to fake a haunting using sound effects and stuff. Except the people listening at home *did* manage to summon a ghost. He was right: the power of everybody focusing and visualizing the spirit at the same time actually brought it to life. And it attacked and killed the guy in the story. Creepy, huh? My brother scared himself while he was reading it, but I thought it was a neat idea. I started to think maybe I could make stuff appear if I tried hard enough, so I started wishing for things, like my parents winning the lottery, or me finding a magic lamp—"

Jeff says, "Brad, that was a cool story and all, and it kind of reminds me of the one that Claire lady told us, but otherwise, I'm not sure what your point is."

"Look," Brad continues, "if we get a bunch of people together to think about making contact with the ghost, maybe then it would appear. We'd have more energy than just us two can produce."

Jeff cocks his head. "I get you, man. That's an idea! It would take a lot of organization. How would we get all these people together?"

"We wouldn't." Brad grins. "They could do it from home, just like in the story. We'd just pick a date and time when we want to communicate with the spirit and tell everybody, *Hey, concentrate at this time*. Kind of like mass meditation."

Jeff nods. "OK, but we'd still need to notify vast numbers of people to perform this visualization at a set time. We'd have to print out flyers or put an ad in the paper or on a billboard or something." He chuckles. "Maybe we'd have to get our own radio show."

Brad grins. "Nah, *we* wouldn't. I know somebody who already has a radio show . . ."

PRIVATE INTERVIEW BETWEEN
REID BENNET AND CELIA ARMENDARIZ,
CIRCA 1989

Reid Bennet: *Do you feel you bear any responsibility for the extreme reactions some people displayed toward Smithy and the unrest they caused during the trial?*

Celia Armendariz: Not at all. I just disseminated information, same as any other news organization. If people don't like what they hear, that's their problem. People are responsible for their own actions.

RB: *But surely you must acknowledge that your show served as a vector for—*

CA: —the riots?

RB: *I wouldn't categorize them that way. Although the New SLA demonstration wasn't exactly peaceful, it wasn't a riot. The second mobilization, however, was more fraught. The organizer specifically cited "Whispers in the Dark." Do you remember what might have upset him so much?*

CA: I'd be surprised if he actually listened to the show. More likely, he just accepted whatever other people who also hadn't listened to it presumed it was about. It's too bad that broadcast doesn't exist anymore.

She chuckles.

Immediately after we finished recording, the tape got stuck in the machine and melted. It just happened that one time. Didn't you know a guy who recorded the show on reel-to-reel?

RB: *He hasn't got a copy, either. He doesn't remember why.*

CA: Interesting. Well, if some force doesn't want people to listen to that broadcast again, I can't imagine what it's trying to hide. I don't remember saying anything particularly controversial.

RB: *What do you remember?*

CA: Brad Vollmer contacted me—I knew of him from friends of friends, Fresno was a small enough town—and he asked if he could come on the show. Of course, I said yes. Brad was a major figure in the case, so it was real coup to have him. He talked about his relationship with Smithy, told us about Smithy's favorite foods and what he liked to do for fun. He really humanized him, you know; made people feel a connection to him. It was great PR. Brad wanted to talk in more detail about the sign language, but frankly, that wasn't as juicy as the other stuff, and so much of it was being covered in the trial already that I asked him to step away from it and get back to the ghost.

Brad told me he was actually with Smithy when he saw the Dark Woman one day. Brad didn't see anything for himself and didn't realize anything was wrong until Smithy signed to him. That surprised me. I always thought people had a sixth sense about ghosts, that they'd get goosebumps on their neck or their hair would stand on end. But Brad just took Smithy out of the room, and that was the end of it. The ghost didn't come after them, and nobody who used that room afterward reported anything strange.

We talked a little bit about the trial. He couldn't talk in detail about the strategy, of course, but he mentioned how it was important to make the world understand how special Smithy was and how much we'd be losing if anything happened to him. He said that's why they were talking about ghosts at the trial, even though ghosts were "out there."

He and Jeff Dalton were researching ghosts at the time, talking to mediums and channelers like I was, and reading actual case histories from the Society for Psychical Research to learn more about how hauntings work. Brad said they'd even had a couple séances to communicate with the researcher who'd died and ask him for his help, to act like a guardian spirit for Smithy during the trial. I asked if they'd tried to contact the Dark Woman. Brad said they weren't sure how to reach her. It's important when you're summoning a spirit to know its name, and of course, nobody did. But he said everybody listening to the show could help: if we all concentrated on the Dark Woman at the same time during the trial, we could summon her through our collective force of will, make her appear so that others could see her talking to Smithy. He asked us all to think about her at the next court date, starting from the time the judge gaveled the hearing in, and to send good vibes so she would help us. Maybe that was the kicker: trying to get listeners at home to "contact to the dead." At the time, it seemed innocuous, even childish, like, "Clap your hands if you believe in fairies." But I was all for trying anything that might do Smithy some good.

Brad talked for the entire show. We didn't have any time to take questions. I was going to have him back the next night so we could talk to some callers, but in the meantime, the second demonstration went down, and when I heard about it, I didn't think it was such a good idea to bring Brad back in case we stirred up more trouble . . .

KHJ-TV NEWS BROADCAST

June 8, 1979
In the Newsroom

Esther Cox sits behind the desk, looking solemnly at the camera.

"For the second time, a mob of vigilantes has descended on the Fresno Family Zoo where Smithy, the chimpanzee who is the focus of a major court action, is temporarily housed. Last night, a crowd of fifty to seventy persons, some of them armed, amassed in front of the zoo."

Her voiceover plays over footage of people milling around an entrance gate. Some men hold rifles; several hold torches. Women stand in the crowd holding signs: "Thou shalt not suffer a witch to live." "Get thee behind me, Satan!" "Kill the beast." A man with a torch looks directly at the camera, realizes he's being filmed, and steps forward, scowling and gesturing to move the camera aside.

The film cuts away to a paunchy man with sideburns wearing a pale blue leisure suit who stands in the flatbed of a pickup truck. One foot rests atop a pile of firewood.

Cox's voiceover continues: "The mob consisted largely of members from the Ministry of Truth and Life, led by the self-styled Reverend Jeremiah Trask of Sunnyvale. Trask says he was called upon to preach at the age of fifteen. He started his ministry three years ago."

Trask raises a fist to the sky and declaims, "The Bible warned us the Great Beast would come to seduce the faithful and denounce the Lord. We just didn't know its words wouldn't be spoken aloud." An off-screen crowd shouts and whistles to punctuate his every sentence. "Now the Beast is in our midst, enticing our neighbors to commit violence in his name. Encouraging our children to consort with unnatural spirits! To raise the dead! We say, 'Enough! We won't have it!' Go back to the pit that spawned you, Satan, and take your devilish hijinks with you! Leave our community and our innocent babes alone!"

The crowd screams and a torch flares up in front of the camera, washing out the picture.

The footage cuts away and the camera again shows Esther Cox facing the audience soberly. She says, "Police responded quickly and dispersed the crowd without firing a shot or making any arrests. Reverend Trask was admonished to secure a permit the next time he wishes to assemble, and to remain two hundred yards away from the perimeter of the zoo."

ILLUSTRATED FLYER

Circa June 1979

A screaming ape with sharp fangs, dark, inverted eyebrows, and a sinuous tail ending in a point stands atop a blazing fire. Within the flames are screaming people; some, by their size and attire, including a beanie and a hair bow, are meant to represent children.

The text above reads: "And the beast was given a mouth to utter proud words to blaspheme God and to slander his name and his dwelling place and those who live in heaven."

DIARY OF RUBY DALTON

June 10, 1979

I'm so angry, my hand is shaking and my handwriting looks like I'm in a taxicab. This is so, so wrong! Where do I even begin?

This cartoon is over the top. And stupid! Chimps don't have even have tails! Trask is an idiot! I wish I could leave it at that, but I know too many people are actually listening to him and believing what he says. That fills me with despair. And fear. I'm afraid for Smithy. The mob last night intended to <u>kill him</u>! They had torches and firewood. They wanted to burn him at the stake like a witch! I feel sick thinking about it.

Do Trask's people honestly think Smithy's a monster? Or do they just want an excuse to hurt and destroy? Smithy's an animal—a clever, spirited animal, sure, but a creature of natural instinct. He doesn't know right from wrong or good from bad in a moral sense. He's intelligent, but he doesn't have the kind of agency to be evil.

My God, what madness! I hope Celia Armendariz is proud of herself. I hope Brad and Jeff are proud, too.

I feel terrible for Mr. McDonald. He's tried to be kind by taking in Smithy. He doesn't deserve this trouble, and neither do his other animals. Now they're all targets. This trial has too much collateral damage: first, the other chimps from CSAM, now these poor animals that were never even part of CSAM or the language study. Enough is enough.

What will become of Smithy if McDonald doesn't want to keep housing him? He's agreed to let him stay for now, but if anything else should occur, Smithy could end up somewhere with a much poorer standard of care, to say the least.

God, I wish this trial were already over.

DIARY OF RUBY DALTON

... *I savored my evening with Jeff. He was unusually tender, patting my aching tummy and stroking the side of my neck in the place that always makes me tremble.*

He told me, "We're almost there, sweetie. A little while longer, and we'll have it all made."

I knew he was feeling good about the trial, but I wished he was feeling good about me.

We've got two more witnesses and closing arguments to go. It's been quiet all week, blissfully so. I should feel relieved, but I can't shake my worry that this calm is a trick. Latimer will spring a surprise in court, or the nutcases will pull something ugly at the last minute. Even though Latimer went easier on me than I'd expected in my deposition, I don't think it was from kindness. More likely, I didn't have whatever information he wanted. As much as I want everything to wrap up peacefully before I deliver, I don't think this last stretch will be as easy as Jeff thinks.

I hated to spoil our happy, intimate moment, but I had to ask: "What if we don't get the result we want?"

He kissed me and said, "Think positive, honey!"

I pressed. "I know you don't want to tempt fate, but have you prepared yourself in case Man gets the upper hand?"

"No, because I don't see how that'll happen. Latimer didn't convince anybody that Man is a humanitarian. Wanda didn't support his case. He hasn't been able to shake anyone's testimony except through innuendo and mockery. Unless he springs a surprise witness—and there isn't anyone left who fits that bill—he'll have to make do with me and Brad. I've already been on the stand once, and I didn't self-destruct."

"Brad hasn't had any courtroom experience yet," I observed.

"Brad will do fine. All he has to do is tell the truth. What more is there to say?"

DIARY OF RUBY DALTON

June 21, 1979

Forty-eight minutes since my contractions began. Yet I'm sitting in the waiting room, just keeping track of time. I thought I'd be rushed to a bed, but the nurse only smiled and told me to have a seat and let her know when they start coming every five minutes. She said it could take <u>hours</u> to get to that point! God, I hope not. This isn't the way it happens in the movies.

So many things haven't happened like I expected. I thought Jeff would be with me, but he's in court, so I had to put myself in a taxi. I suppose if I really am in labor for hours, he might arrive in time for the birth. Also, Angie planned to be with me, but she's not coming for another two weeks. The baby's early. The nurse said not to worry, it's not enough time to make a difference.

There goes another one. It's ten times worse than menstrual cramps. My whole body squeezes. I hope this doesn't last too long.

Two hours gone. I wish I'd brought a book. There's nothing to do but look out the window, stagger up the hall, or page through the same tattered magazine for the tenth time. I've heard of labor pains, but I didn't know how much of that suffering would be waiting.

~ ~ ~

Hour 5: Another nurse just came by to check on me. That makes six. They're all polite—Joyce, Tina, Sandra, Betty, etc. They all look down at their clipboards. "Ruby Dalton? How close are the contractions? How are you feeling? Can I get you anything? Doctor will see you later."

As soon as one leaves, I hear whispering in the hall, and a little while later, another comes in.

By now, is it more likely that every nurse on this floor has a copy of my chart? Or that they've recognized me from the news coverage, and they're gossiping about a celebrity in their midst?

Please don't let any tabloid reporters come looking for me! I couldn't bear it.

Suspicions confirmed. Nurse Sandra finally came and told me quietly there was a TV in the nurse's break room and that I could watch highlights from the hearing on the afternoon news. Watching the trial usually upsets me—but being alone, bored, and miserable is worse.

Now I'm ensconced with the nurses instead of on public display. They smile at me and go back to their knitting or their magazines or their soft gossip, but I can feel them watching me when I'm not looking directly at them. As soon as I do, their heads snap back, and they play dumb. Luckily, only two or three are here at a time.

Here's a candy striper. Bet she wonders what I'm doing here. Wonder who'll enlighten her.

Five more minutes until Smithy news. I've never watched the updates with an audience before.

Contraction! At least I'll have plenty of attention when I need it.

Local headlines. Here we go!

We're done for.

TELEVISION BROADCAST
COURTESY OF KFSN

JUNE 21, 1979

A man wearing a checkered suit and sideburns stands in the foreground; the courthouse is in the background behind him.

He says to the camera, "This is Rob Mannheim reporting from the Fresno County Courthouse where testimony in the Smithy trial is shortly expected to conclude. A lively crowd has already gathered."

The camera cuts to a cadre of middle-aged men and women singing "Onward Christian Soldiers" and holding signs reading "Jesus Loves You!" "Get behind me, Satan," and "Honk if you love Jesus." Then it pans to a nearby group of youths in jeans and T-shirts who march in a circle as they sing "We Shall Overcome" and wave signs reading "Free Smithy!" "Save Our Smithy," and "Honk for Smithy." Every time a horn honks, both groups cheer.

The camera returns to Mannheim, who says, "This trial has stirred strong feelings and desperate acts in the community, sometimes in favor of the ape's freedom and sometimes in support of its destruction. As you can see, there is tremendous community interest in the court proceedings. I haven't seen a crowd like this since the Stones came to town." His head snaps to the side as a white panel truck turns into the parking lot in the background. "It appears the ape in question has just arrived."

Behind Mannheim, the students notice the truck and stop walking. They applaud and cheer. Further behind them, the religious demonstrators cry out and run toward the truck, brandishing their signs and shouting, "Down with Satan! Kill the Beast!" The students rush to block them, and they jostle.

Mannheim runs toward the melee as the camera closes in on the action. Someone in the crowd swings a sign and cracks it over another person's head.[13] Instantly, the warring groups start to push and swat with their signs. A bearded young man advances on a heavier balding man, brandishing his sign as though it were a sword. The balding man responds in kind. They joust, clashing their signs.

At that moment, a line of people dressed in black charges up the steps and into the middle of the fight. The members of the group whoop loudly and wave their hands. The woman leading the charge bellows, "Defend the prophet!" The newcomers try to position themselves between the battling pairs. With no signs or weapons of their own, they holler and wave their hands as if to create a distraction. The bald man smacks the woman in black across the face with his sign. She immediately covers her nose and starts howling in pain. The young man puts a hand on her shoulder; she starts pummeling him with her fists.

In the distance, police whistles shrill over the war whoops and shouting. A line of officers descends the courthouse steps to break up the fighting.

Mannheim, flushed, faces the camera and smiles. "Would you look at that! Court isn't even in session yet! Who knows what will happen next?"

---

13 The camera cannot discern who struck the first blow; the aggressor's identity remains unknown.

COURT TRANSCRIPT

Testimony of Bradley Vollmer
June 21, 1979

Latimer: Please state your full name for the record.

Vollmer: Bradley J. Vollmer.

Latimer: What is your middle name?

Vollmer: Jay.

Latimer: What does that stand for?

Vollmer: Uh, jay. J-A-Y, like the bird.

Laughter in court.

Hon. N. Borley: Order, please!

Latimer: Thank you, Mr. Vollmer. When did you begin working for Manfred Teague?

Vollmer: That was, oh . . . around December '73.

Latimer: What was your role when you were hired?

Vollmer: I applied to be the janitor. The ad said facility manager, but I knew what that meant. I was supposed to be on hand at all times to help with technical difficulties, clean-up, and care of the animals. I fed and watered them, cleaned their cages, and made sure they were healthy and didn't hurt each other. That was the coolest part of the job. I'd never seen any chimps, or even monkeys, before, not even in a zoo or at a circus. I thought getting to work with them sounded neat.

Latimer: Where had you worked previously?

Vollmer: I traveled around and did odd jobs.

Latimer: Did you have references?

Vollmer: No, but Man didn't ask for any.

Latimer: Really? No history of working with primates, nobody to vouch for your character, and he gave you a job and a place to live anyway?

Vollmer: He didn't pick me out of a hat. I met with him and did an interview. He had to have liked something he saw.

Latimer: In fact, Dr. Teague eventually promoted you, correct?

Vollmer: Ah . . .I didn't get any raise, if that's what you mean. It's been minimum wage the whole time, and no Christmas bonus.

Latimer: Did Dr. Teague broaden your responsibilities?

Vollmer: Oh, yeah! I got to help with the studies and work with the chimps instead of just being their keeper. At the end, I was on a research team and turning in reports just like the college students.

Latimer: Bailiff, would you please escort the chimp into the courtroom? Shall we see how Webster communicates, Mr. Vollmer?

Vollmer: Absolutely! I haven't seen him in weeks!

Latimer: Please refrain from initiating conversation. Let's see how he spontaneously reacts to you.

The bailiff leads the animal into court on a chain. Upon seeing the witness, the chimp becomes excited and attempts to run to him. The bailiff restrains him and escorts him into his cage. The animal gestures.

Latimer: What do those signs mean?

Vollmer: "Brad play. Let me out."

Latimer: Well, I'm afraid we can't do that. Are those the most common signs Webster uses with you?

Vollmer: He can have a full conversation. He's just excited to see me. And he doesn't like to be locked up.

Latimer: He's not repeating a ritual? Performing actions that have previously rewarded him with his desired outcome?

Vollmer: I could talk to him if you'd let me and prove he understands. I can ask him questions or give him directions.

Latimer: No, not right now. Let's return to your experiences at CSAM. Dr. Teague trusted you, didn't he? Isn't that why he elevated your position?

Vollmer: I don't know about that. Between you and me and the courtroom, I think he did it so he wouldn't have to pay another researcher. He already had me under his roof, why not get more work out of me for the same pay? Ol' Man likes to watch the bottom line.

Latimer: How did you and Dr. Teague get along? Did you argue?

Vollmer: Not until Smithy. Mostly, I kept my head down and focused on my work. I was there for the animals, not to get in a fight. Man blew his stack all the time, but I didn't take it personally if he was mad at me. I knew he'd get mad at somebody else sooner or later. And sure enough, if he had any complaints about me, he'd forget about them by the next day.

Chimpanzee hits the bars and signs, "Out."

Latimer: He's insistent. How frequently did you take this chimp out, Mr. Vollmer?

Vollmer: As often as I could. When he first came, I took him from his cage every day. We took walks around CSAM. It's a big place. Lots of trees and open space. I wish the animals could have lived free in the open instead of in enclosures. Sometimes I brought Smithy to my place to chill out. Later, when he started doing trials, we didn't have as much freedom. I'd get him out once a week if I could. When he was in solitary, I couldn't see him at all. Then, only Man had access to him.

Latimer: Was taking the animals out part of your job?

Vollmer: Sort of . . . .

Latimer: Care to explain?

Vollmer: OK. On my first day, when Man told me to make sure the animals were healthy, I joked with him. "You mean, make sure they get their exercise?" And he went, "Yeah, make sure they stay in good shape. Make sure they're eating." So I took that to mean I could take them out if they needed a run and some fresh air. A lot of times, the animals would get real uptight. They'd cry or sit and rock for hours. They wouldn't eat. I'd take them out to play to cheer them up.

Latimer: Did you ask Dr. Teague's permission? Or would you just say, "I'm going to take Bobo out for a run?"

Vollmer: Neither. I just did it.

Latimer: You didn't advertise it?

Vollmer: No. I mean, I knew he'd find out if he watched the cameras, but I didn't make a big deal about it.

Latimer: Was that because you suspected what you were doing was wrong and Dr. Teague would disapprove?

Vollmer: No. Well, I thought maybe he'd think I didn't need to take them out as often as I did. But *I* thought it was necessary. I watched them and I knew what they needed. If my job was making sure everybody ate properly, then I needed to take them out of their cages to persuade them to eat.

Latimer: Did you ever feed the animals unapproved food substances?

Chimpanzee signs, "Chips, burger. Give Smithy chips Oreos."

Latimer: What was that?

Vollmer: Ah, yeah, I did. He's asking me for snacks right now. See? He understood you.

Latimer: What sort of foods did you serve that were not on the approved dietary list?

Vollmer: Just regular food. The same stuff I would eat. I cooked them scrambled eggs and bacon, toast, pancakes, burgers. I gave them popcorn or cookies or ice cream. Whatever they wanted.

Chimpanzee signs, "Good. Give Smithy."

Vollmer: We're making him hungry!

Latimer: Was that good for their health?

Vollmer: I told you, I ate the same stuff. And it wasn't like I fed them buckets of lard every day. It was for special occasions. That slop they got wasn't appetizing. I had to make sure they ate something. When they got scared and worked up—and the poor things were always stressed out and losing their hair—they'd lose weight. I had to fatten them up to keep them healthy. But I'd take them out for exercise, too.

Chimpanzee whines and signs, "Brad out."

Vollmer: You see, it all balanced out. Anyway, they deserved a treat after what they went through in those experiments.

Latimer: Did you object to the tests the animals underwent?

Vollmer: Not all the tests. Some were straight-forward physical ability tests. I didn't like what the medical tests did to them. I hated to see the animals get sick, but it had to happen before we could test the cures. That was hard to deal with. Not knowing which ones would pull through. And I couldn't help those apes. I couldn't feed them extras or break them out for some fun because that would have thrown off the results, and I knew better than to tamper with any experiment. All I could do was keep them company. Sit by their cages and talk kindly to them or bring a radio so they could hear music.

But some of the animals that weren't part of any study got pushed around an awful lot. Man would hit them with his cattle prod randomly, just to show he was boss. And they were petrified of him. They went around hunched over, always looking over their shoulders. I hated that. So, I did what I could to make up for their suffering. I was extra nice to them, so they'd know not everyone at CSAM was a hard case. I wanted them to know they had one friend they could trust. I thought of the apes as friends. When I couldn't make their situation better, I could at least help them feel better.

Latimer: Do you believe your actions were in line with your job, or in opposition to your orders?

Vollmer: My orders were to take care of the animals. That's how I took care of them.

Latimer: Calm down, Mr. Vollmer. There's no need to get excited.

Vollmer: I'm calm, Mr. Latimer. I'm just dandy.

Latimer: Your arms are crossed.

Vollmer: Yeah, well, I do that sometimes.

Latimer: From your body language, I assumed you were upset. Especially since we're discussing the disconnect between your assignment to provide for the basic needs of the animals and your attempts to befriend the animals, which were the property of CSAM and not your pets.

Vollmer: I don't know what you mean. I don't see any disconnect. I told you, I was taking care of their health. Their whole health. These are living, feeling creatures. Man and the other scientists were treating them like . . . like I treated my toys when I was a kid. When I was done playing with my army men, I threw them back in the toy box until next time. But you can't do that with an animal. You can't keep locking them up and forgetting them until you decide you need them for a project. They're still there whether you're using them or not. They still have needs and wants. They need attention and respect. That's what I gave them. That's what Man overlooked.

Chimpanzee signs, "Quiet."
Vollmer signs, "OK."

Latimer: Mr. Vollmer, I asked you not to address the chimp.

Vollmer: Why'd you bring him out here then? Besides, I was just giving him the high sign. He wants me to calm down. I guess he thinks I'm upset, too.

Latimer: I had the bailiff bring the chimp here so I could observe his behavior and see what sort of alleged communication he initiates with you, his closest caretaker. I must say, it's equally instructive to watch you. I see you disregarding my instructions and doing what you think best, just as you ignored the spirit of Dr. Teague's orders and manipulated his words to suit your own desires. You established your own status quo, positioning yourself as the animals' savior at a facility where you worked as an entry-level employee, effectively betraying the man who invited you into CSAM on faith alone and gave you abundant opportunities. Wasn't that your intent all along? To overthrow Dr. Teague? To supplant his approved experiments, experiments you hated because you believed they harmed the animals, with studies of your own choosing?

Vollmer: That's ridiculous! I'm not the one who betrayed the IRB. I'm a pretty mellow guy usually, but I'll call BS when I hear it.

Chimpanzee forms his fingers into a circle and touches them to his pursed lips.

Latimer: Mr. Vollmer, Webster made that gesture when Dr. Preis-Herald was on the stand, and he didn't recognize it. We also saw that gesture, a circle placed next to his lips, in some of the recent video footage. Can you tell us what that gesture signifies?

Witness's reply is inaudible.

Latimer: I'm sorry, Mr. Vollmer, I didn't catch that. Could you please repeat your answer so we all can hear it?

Vollmer: He wants to toke.

Latimer: To talk? Isn't that what Webster allegedly does all the time?

Vollmer: No, ah, he wants a roach.

Latimer: You mean that the ape enjoys eating insects?

Vollmer: No, he wants to-to smoke a joint. Grass. Weed.

Latimer: Are you referring to *marijuana,* Mr. Vollmer?

Vollmer: Yes.

Latimer: How would a chimpanzee come to make such a request? How could he possibly have any experience with marijuana?

Vollmer: I, ah . . . I've smoked with him before.

Latimer: The two of you together have smoked marijuana? You and Webster?

Vollmer: Yes.

Latimer: When was this?

Vollmer: During his time at the facility.

Latimer: When, precisely?

Vollmer: Off and on.

Latimer: Pray, tell us why?

Vollmer: I just wanted to help him out. Smithy was so lonely and upset when he came to us. He hadn't been around other apes before and most of his people were gone. The Daltons weren't allowed to see him much. He wasn't adjusting well. I wanted to make him more comfortable, to help him feel like one of the guys. So, when I took him out for walks or to play, if I lit up, I'd share it with him. He wanted it. He'd ask for it, so I gave it to him. We'd pass the joint back and forth. We shared, and that's how we got to be friends. Smithy liked smoking. It calmed him down, mellowed him out.

Latimer: For the record, Mr. Vollmer, are you admitting to us that you consciously gave an illegal, controlled substance to a valuable lab animal belonging to CSAM?

Vollmer: I did.

Latimer: This is an animal for which you claim to have deep affection and concern, yet you had no qualms about jeopardizing its well-being with a potentially harmful chemical substance.

Vollmer: I didn't hurt him! Nothing bad happened to Smithy from a little smoking. I would never hurt him!

Latimer: How can you be sure? Maybe the violent behavior we've heard described is the result of cannabis eating away at the chimp's brain.

Vollmer: You're talking like someone who's seen *Reefer Madness* too many times. I didn't poison Smithy! I smoked the stuff, too, and I wouldn't have done that if I thought anything was wrong with it. I didn't give him anything I wouldn't take myself. Neither of us got hurt.

Latimer: Did your supervisors at the facility know you and the chimp smoked joints together?

Vollmer: Of course not!

Latimer: No, because if Manfred Teague had discovered you were abusing drugs while on the job and giving them to his animals, he would have fired you immediately, isn't that so?

Vollmer: But you're making it sound like that was all we ever did together, and that's not true! We didn't smoke all that much.

Latimer: And yet it must have happened frequently enough because Webster has a sign for it. A sign he associates with you. When was the last time you used marijuana?

Vollmer: Not for a long time.

Latimer: Please define "a long time" for us.

Vollmer: Um, about six months ago. It was at my buddy's birthday party, like, right before the Super Bowl.

Latimer: The Super Bowl was approximately *four* months ago. Is that the last occasion when you smoked marijuana?

Vollmer: Yes, sir.

Latimer: Is four months ago a "long time" in your estimation?

Vollmer: No. It just seemed a lot longer.

Latimer: Perhaps your perception of time has been negatively affected by your habit. Certainly, your judgment has suffered.

Hegge: Objection! Your Honor, Counsel is badgering the witness. These are statements, not questions.

Hon. N. Borley: Sustained.

Latimer: Nothing further, Your Honor. Bailiff, will you please remove the chimp?

COURT TRANSCRIPT

Testimony of Jeffrey Adam Dalton
June 21, 1979

Latimer: You worked closely with Mr. Vollmer, didn't you, Mr. Dalton?

Dalton: Not really. We were friends, but Brad didn't participate in the experiments until about a year ago.

Latimer: I see. How often did you share in his drug use?

Dalton: I don't smoke. My wife doesn't like the smell.

Latimer: Come now, Mr. Dalton. You're under oath.

Dalton: All right, I did it once, to be polite, so I could legitimately tell Brad I didn't like it. He never pushed it on me. He didn't push it on Smithy, either. You made him sound like a drug fiend. It was never like that. Brad used recreationally. He wasn't trying to corrupt the animals with marijuana. He used it to positive ends. It had a medicinal effect on Smithy. You can sneer, but I saw what it accomplished.

Latimer: Then you approved of Mr. Vollmer's actions?

Dalton: Not at first. I was furious when I found out he was giving Smithy drugs. I was like you; I thought it would harm him. But it helped. Smoking calmed him and gave him back his appetite. I would have done anything to comfort Smithy. It never occurred to me to give him grass, but that worked, so I tolerated it.

Latimer: Was Webster the only chimp who used marijuana?

Dalton: You'd better call Brad back to the stand if you want to ask that.

Latimer: I don't need your advice, Mr. Dalton. My concern is the health of the apes. If Mr. Vollmer provided illicit substances to the subjects, wasn't he jeopardizing CSAM's research? Many of its studies pertained to drug treatments or to the animals' physical and cognitive abilities, correct?·

Dalton: That's right. I started with a study on the reaction time of macaques. However, I sincerely doubt anything Brad gave the animals would have affected any studies. He wasn't distributing blunts willy-nilly. Smithy was the only chimp I ever saw smoke—which wasn't as often as you're making it sound—and anyway, he was never part of any drug trial. The gambling study never reached the phase where drugs were administered.

Latimer: Webster participated in a nutritional supplement trial.

Dalton: He did, but during that time, his food intake was regulated. Brad didn't overfeed any chimps whose diets were monitored for medical purposes. Marijuana might make you hungrier, but it doesn't impact your ability to retain weight if you're given fixed portions. Besides, the amount of marijuana he used was so small as to have a negligible effect.

Latimer: Are you speaking as an expert?

Dalton: No, I'm not an expert, but I've read about the drug. Small amounts, scattered over time, don't cause lasting damage. Brad smoked more than any animal and he functions fine. The drug didn't damage his cognition in the long term. He's smarter than many of the people I've known in my life.

Latimer: Are you certain the drugs Mr. Vollmer administered without permission or supervision didn't harm any of the apes? Or impact any of the studies? Can you swear to that?

Dalton: I cannot . . . but I have great confidence.

Latimer: If the drug use did adversely affect the research, then CSAM would be deeply disadvantaged, correct?

Dalton: An experiment is designed to wash out any nuisance effects. Any possible artefact from the drugs would get canceled out in the statistical analyses.

Latimer: Are you sure, Mr. Dalton? Or did you and Mr. Vollmer collude to sabotage Dr. Teague's work by tainting his subject pool?

Dalton: We did no such thing. I wouldn't want to screw up Man's research. I wanted everything to go off without a hitch. I worked hard to do a good job so I could build my credibility as a contributor. I wanted to prove my worth so the higher-ups would listen to me and take my research proposals seriously.

Latimer: Ah, yes, we return to the language studies. You petitioned four times within your first year to start an ape language program, didn't you?

Dalton: Yes, I did. I believe studying primate language is important. Learning about other species also teaches us about ourselves. We can learn when humans start to acquire language, and better ways of teaching language, even new techniques like facilitated communication. That's why I never gave up on introducing such a program to CSAM.

Latimer: Yes. It's a pity all your efforts ultimately failed.

Dalton: I don't consider them a failure at all.

Latimer: Did you have much objective success in teaching the other chimps—apart from Webster—to sign?

Dalton: Not at the same rate we did with Smithy, but circumstances were different. The other chimps were much older when they began to sign, and they lacked Smithy's discipline. Every moment in his formative years was geared toward language mastery. For only six hours a week, our other subjects made encouraging strides—enough to justify continuing the program.

Latimer: Really? I've read your reports, Mr. Dalton. We saw portions of the videos you made during training. I'm not impressed. Webster is supposed to be your biggest success story, the fruit of your communal labors, and he doesn't make much sense. We've observed his behavior in this courtroom. Given the opportunity to interact with Dr. Preis-Herald, he failed to do so. When he did sign, it was gibberish. Foul gibberish, too.

Dalton: If you review the transcript of Dr. Preis-Herald's testimony, you'll see he referred to the *president* of Yale just before Smithy signed. Smithy may have interpreted that to mean the President of the United States. If he believed Nixon was responsible for selling him out to Man Teague, it's understandable he would say *Fuck him*. I would, too, if I were in Smithy's position.

Latimer: Does he *say* these things?

Dalton: Yes, he does. We've given you all kinds of supporting evidence. Most of this trial has been people testifying that they've conversed with Smithy. You've watched hours of film of him. In the last video, I asked him, "What do you want for lunch?" and he signed, "I want to eat a roast beef sandwich and Jell-O." He named the items himself; I didn't offer him options.

Latimer: But did he say all of that? In the transcript prepared by the translator, the only words that could be identified were his name sign, "eat," "sandwich," "hot" and an unknown sign that the research team claimed was the chimp's own term for "Jell-O." These words weren't assembled according to traditional rules of syntax. All we have is a bare bones, *Me Tarzan, You Jane* expression onto which the ape's handlers have imposed a message of deeper significance. How can we be sure that message is what the ape intended to communicate? Half the message is a third party's interpretation of it.

Dalton: Wanda already told you: sign language doesn't translate one-to-one to English. There are words and a prescribed word order, but most of it's based on kinesics and facial expressions. Besides, all language is open to interpretation. We can never be one hundred percent sure of what another human being intends to say. Speech often comes out garbled or inelegant, but we can still discern the central meaning. Look, do you have any children?

Latimer: Mr. Dalton—

Dalton: Do you have small children in your life? Have you ever cared for anyone else's small children?

Latimer: Mr. Dalton, I ask the questions here.

Dalton: Have you ever conversed with a toddler?

Latimer: Your Honor, the witness is out of line.

Hon. Nathaniel Borley: Mr. Dalton, please answer counsel's questions and refrain from asking your own.

Dalton: Your Honor, I'm using a hypothetical situation to explain my argument. Listen, if you've ever talked to a toddler, you've noticed they don't use proper grammar. They spit out broken pidgin like, "bed now" or "cookie Mommy" or "walk park" to convey, "Please give me a cookie, Mommy, and then let's go for a walk in the park." You can't expect fully sophisticated speech at that age. Well, Smithy is at the level of a human toddler.

Latimer: I'm surprised you referenced Wanda Karlewicz in your defense. According to a Declaration from Dr. Preis-Herald, you once accused him of selecting his assistants based on how well they filled out a miniskirt. Given those qualifications, how do you value Wanda Karlewicz's alleged expertise?

Dalton: Wanda's smart. She's extremely capable. In fact, I think Piers took advantage of her capability and hired bimbos to round out his lab because he knew Wanda was able to do so much on her own. She was pretty, too, but I never doubted her skills. And I know what you're trying to do. You're trying to change the subject so you can use an *ad hominem* attack on me like you did to Brad, but it's not going to work.

Latimer: Calm down, Mr. Dalton. I'm only addressing your own testimony. You brought up your wife a moment ago. Did she go to work at CSAM willingly?

Dalton: She wanted to be near Smithy, as I did. She didn't like working at CSAM, though. There were times when she wished she could quit, but we all stuck it out.

Latimer: Did you pressure her to remain in her job when she was unhappy?

Dalton: I coaxed her to stay on because I didn't want her to let Man get the best of her, and because I wanted us to remain a team. I felt we were stronger working together. We didn't get to collaborate on any projects and our work hours didn't often overlap, but we had the same goals and we kept each other going.

Latimer: That doesn't sound much like teamwork to me. I'm aware you weren't assigned to work on the same projects, but you didn't include Ruby in your language side project, either. Why not?

Dalton: I already told you: our schedules didn't align. I had to work on that project in my spare time, and my days off and her days off weren't always congruent.

Latimer: Mr. Dalton, I have here Exhibit Q, the work schedule for CSAM's third quarter last year. It shows you and Ruby each had Sundays off, as well as alternate Thursdays. And you both worked a seven-to-five shift Mondays and Wednesdays. How often did you have dinner together?

Dalton: Maybe once a week?

Latimer: That often? Were you trying to avoid each other.

Dalton: Of course not! The project was demanding. We wanted to get enough evidence to satisfy—

Latimer: We? Are you referring to yourself and Ruby or yourself and Mr. Vollmer?

Dalton: All three of us. We were all invested in Smithy's success. That took time away from Ruby, but she understood it was necessary.

Latimer: Once again, Mr. Dalton: Did your wife tell you she wanted to quit CSAM?

Dalton: We discussed it from time to time.

Latimer: She told you she wanted to quit, and you talked her out of it, correct? And when she told you *the ghost* wanted her to quit, how did you respond?

Dalton: W-what? Where did you hear that?

Latimer: I'll ask the questions, Mr. Dalton. Once you and Ruby both left CSAM, did you spend more time together?

Dalton: We met with the lawyers and we attended this hearing together until her condition became too uncomfortable, but we didn't exactly go out on the town.

Latimer: What is "her condition?"

Dalton: She's expecting.

Latimer: Ah! Your first?

Dalton: Yes.

Latimer: How far along is she?

Dalton: She's due later this month.

Latimer: She's about to deliver your first child any day now? Why aren't you with her?

Dalton: I had to testify today. You subpoenaed me!

Latimer: But you've been here in court every day. Why are you here and not with your family?

Dalton: What's your point?

Latimer: Mr. Dalton, you've been acting as if you were fighting a crusade: devoting every minute to proving the credibility of your beloved chimp, promoting sloppy research as a great discovery, endorsing highly questionable and potentially harmful interventions—all at the expense of your family. If you're not a man obsessed, then what kind of husband and father-to-be are you?

Dalton: You know what? Fuck you, Mr. Latimer.

Hegge: Objection!

Hon. N. Borley: Order in the court!

Latimer: Are you objecting to your own client?

Dalton: First you refuse to see what's right in front of you, then you see things that don't exist!

Hegge: I'm objecting to this line of questioning. Your Honor, counselor is deliberately trying to provoke this witness! These questions and insinuations—insulting insinuations—have nothing to do with the well-being or abilities of the chimpanzee. And that's why we're here, not to dissect my clients' personal lives. This is highly inappropriate!

Latimer: I'll withdraw the last question. Plaintiff's witness.

Hegge: No! No questions.

Hon. N. Borley: Then that concludes testimony. Court is in recess!

EXCERPT FROM
SMITHY: THE MILLENNIUM COMPENDIUM
BY REID BENNET, PHD

Jeff Dalton gave the last courtroom testimony, but during the recess, Judge Borley agreed to accept testimony from Smithy in a closed-door session. The transcript of that interview, mediated by the court interpreter and attended by Lance Latimer for the respondent and Conrad Hegge for the plaintiff, has never before been released . . .

COURT TRANSCRIPT

Testimony of Webster AKA "Smithy"
June 21, 1979

Q: What is your name?

No response.

Q: What is your name?

No response.

Q: Who are you?

No response.

Hegge: Your Honor, may I propose Smithy be interviewed by a familiar face? The presence of so many strangers in an unusual location is clearly having an adverse effect on his desire to communicate.

Latimer: Objection! It would be impossible to separate the chimpanzee's actual ability from any coaching his handlers may provide. If this creature can indeed communicate, he should be able to communicate with anybody.

Hon. N. Borley: Sustained. Mr. Hegge, we've already reviewed why your clients cannot be present.

Hegge: May I point out that unwillingness to communicate with a stranger doesn't signify inability to communicate? Many toddlers are shy around new people and won't speak to them when addressed.

Hon. N. Borley: Noted, counselor, but surely you must appreciate our dilemma.

Hegge: Try asking him something else to draw him out. Ask him what foods he likes. Ask, "Do you like c-o-o-k-i-e-s?" and such.

Q: What do you like to eat? Do you like cookies? Do you like candy?

Chimp signs, "Give Smithy cookie please. Love cookie. Good."

Latimer: Now he's begging for treats . . .

Q: Do you like bananas? Do you like soda? What do you like to eat?

Smithy: Smithy like cookie, soda, hamburger, Jell-O please eat.

Q: Who is Smithy?

Smithy: Me. Smithy me.

Hon. N. Borley: Well, that's a start.

Interpreter arranges a set of photos on the table.

Q: Who is that?

Smithy: Jeff.

Q: Who is this?

Smithy: Ruby.

Q: Who is this? This one? This one?

Smithy: Sarah. Piers. Isaac.

Q: What is that?

Smithy: Smithy big house. Home back.

Hon. N. Borley: Please ask if he ever saw anything strange or unusual at this house.

Q: Did you see anything funny here? Did you see anything strange?

Smithy: TV. Watch TV.

Hegge: That's a legitimate answer. Once again, he's demonstrating a childlike, literal interpretation. You may have to ask him more directly about what he's seen.

Latimer: Shall we ask flat out if he's seen a ghost? Put words in his—hands? Ridiculous!

Hon. N. Borley: Ask him these.

Judge writes a series of questions and hands the paper to the interpreter.

Q: Have you seen a black woman?

Smithy: Taniesha.

Q: Did you see a black woman at this house?

Smithy: Cages Taniesha black.

Latimer: This isn't going anywhere.

Interpreter: Your Honor?

Hon. N. Borley: Move on to the next question, please.

Q: Wanda is hurt. Why did you hurt Wanda?

Smithy: Bad woman.

Q: Who is bad?

Smithy: Bad. Angry.

Hegge: Ask if it was Wanda or the ghost.

Q: Who is bad? Wanda bad? Black woman bad?

Smithy: Bad and bad again.

Q: You pushed Gail. Why hurt Gail?

Smithy: Bad woman. No more. Go away.

Interpreter: He doesn't mean me, does he?

Latimer: Did he push Gail to make her go away?

Hegge: Ask if he saw the bad woman that night.

Latimer: Which woman is bad? His keeper? The "ghost?"

Q: Is Gail bad?

The chimpanzee does not respond. The interpreter shows the photos of Gail and Wanda.

Q: Did you hurt them?

Chimp covers his eyes.

Hegge: Let the record show the chimp is covering his eyes! That's his sign for the ghost!

Latimer: Or it's a sign he doesn't want to face his actions. Or it means nothing. This is an exercise in frustration, Your Honor. The responses are too open to interpretation.

Hon. N. Borley: Repeat the question, please.

Q: Did you hurt them?

The question is repeated numerous times, but the chimp does not respond for several minutes. The interpreter displays a picture of Manfred Teague. Smithy recoils and snarls.

Q: Are you afraid of Man?

Smithy: Smithy want to go home. Take Smithy home.

Hegge: Where is "home" to him? CSAM? Trevor Hall.

Smithy: Give Smithy hamburger and soda please.

Hegge: Your Honor, Smithy is agitated. May we take a brief recess and resume questioning after a meal break?

Hon. N. Borley: No, counselor, I've seen enough.

COURT TRANSCRIPT

Closing Statement of Conrad Hegge
(Plaintiff)
June 21, 1979

This trial has covered considerable uncharted territory. In olden days, a map would denote unknown territory with the words, "Here there be dragons." But besides dragons, one may also find hills of gold.

Over the past three months, we have explored the boundaries of science: primate language, animal ethics, and life beyond death. You have heard experienced researchers in their respective fields discuss Smithy's abilities. You have heard from the people who know Smithy best, those who lived with and taught him. All the testimony agrees that Smithy's rare talents ought to be further explored through scientific investigation, not destroyed in a petty power grab.

Some of the testimony has covered challenging concepts. I could find only two other historical examples of a ghost figuring into courtroom testimony. The testimony in this case was given by witnesses who had nothing to gain by making their statements, and who, in fact, had much to lose. Yet, they testified because they swore to tell the truth.

At times, their testimony may have seemed unsatisfactory or incomplete because the witnesses could not fully explain what they experienced. It would be more convenient to tie up such accounts with an explanatory bow, to tag them with a motive and embellish them with a how and a why. Yet, very little is known about these phenomena. It may be tempting to doubt the assertions made on Smithy's behalf, given their novelty and controversial nature, but if testimony concerning the supernatural aspects of this case lacks fine detail, that *supports* its veracity. It's not a detriment. Someday, we may be able to fill in all the gaps in our understanding. With Smithy's help, I believe that possibility is more likely than not.

Smithy has demonstrated to multiple witnesses, across time and across locations, that he can understand and produce conversation. In impartial film footage, you have seen him engage other apes to sign with him, showing that he is able to perpetuate language. Finally, he has innovated language by developing signs of his own for novel words and concepts.

Moreover, Smithy has demonstrated his ability to participate in community life. As part of the household at Trevor Hall, he shared the responsibilities of cleaning and cooking. He obeyed his teachers at the Meyer School for the Deaf and achieved progress concomitant with a young human student. In many ways, Smithy has shown he is something more than an animal, even if he is not quite human. Who knows what further progress he can make? Please don't foreclose further investigation by sentencing Smithy to a living death.

As a subject in Manfred Teague's neural trauma study, the best parts of Smithy's character, the best qualities he has to offer the world, will be obliterated. This magnificent being, a being of intelligence and curiosity, a being of artistic sensibility, a being of compassion, will be destroyed. Is any potential scientific gain worth that cost?

Your Honor, I ask you to weigh the evidence and to weigh the potential good against the potential evil that might result from each outcome. Furthermore, I ask you to reserve judgment for Smithy himself and not for any of his caregivers. Regardless of how some of the witnesses may have behaved during these hearings and whether or not their lifestyle choices meet with your approval, please consider how their testimony and expertise bears on Smithy himself and his right to life, liberty, and happiness.

No less a personage than Gandhi reminds us that, "A nation's greatness is measured by how it treats its weakest members." If we as a nation wish to serve as an example to the rest of the world of what freedom and equality look like, we must hold a reckoning of how we treat our society's most vulnerable members, a description that surely fits Smithy.

Having been a pawn in the designs of one human after another since his infancy, Smithy now has the opportunity to claim a degree of personal sovereignty for the first time. He has the potential to establish a new precedence for other sentient non-humans seeking freedom in the future. This is the moment to chart new territory.

Your Honor, the Plaintiff rests.

COURT TRANSCRIPT

Closing Statement of Lance Latimer
(Defendant)
June 21, 1979

This trial has covered many diverse topics, but the guiding force has always been science. Science, we were told, is the means by which the plaintiff's case will be proven. It is for the sake of science that the chimpanzee must be set free. Science will support this action. Science will turn the tide.

Science is not like a courtroom. You don't have to prove a claim beyond a reasonable doubt. Scientists have to prove a claim is likely beyond chance. They must establish probability that findings are due to the proposed cause and not to any other factor.

In this case, the plaintiffs have simply failed to establish that the animal's purported language "skills" are due to an inherent understanding and not to misunderstanding, chance, or coaching—even unintentional coaching. In claiming their evidence is conclusive of anything out of the ordinary, they are blowing smoke in your eyes.

As for their paranormal claims, the plaintiffs again fail to demonstrate supportive evidence. Their star expert, Dr. Ohrbach, by his own admission, does not study ghosts, nor has he ever investigated this chimpanzee. Instead, Dr. Ohrbach merely alluded to some fascinating research he claims has the potential to broaden our understanding of the human mind. All he has done is extend the hope of "Something More."

His testimony is completely irrelevant to the defendant's premise.

The testimony from those claiming to have seen the ghost is equally insubstantial. What you've heard were frightened, puzzled, imaginative young people who allowed the power of suggestion—and the desire for "Something More"—to override their common sense. It's caused them to see spirits in the shadows of a darkened stairway, or even in a well-lighted courtroom.

I, too, want to believe in "Something More," something remarkable beyond this day-to-day grind. All the while, I've been challenging the plaintiffs' evidence, I've been hoping, deep down, that something would stick. I acquiesced to the plaintiffs' request to bring the ape into court because I hoped doing so might somehow reveal untold insights: that animals can converse with humans, or even that life after death exists. Unfortunately, all that resulted was more grandstanding. It's all smoke and mirrors.

Yet, I don't believe the plaintiffs are duplicitous. Rather, they may be victims of self-deception, as their former mentor, Dr. Preis-Herald, believes. For that reason, Dr. Teague wishes to drop his counterclaim for damages against these well-meaning but misguided young people.

Instead, we request a restraining order that will prohibit any of the parties—Bradley Vollmer, Jeffrey Dalton, Ruby Dalton, Samantha Stone, and Conrad Hegge—from coming within one hundred yards of the chimpanzee, Webster. We again ask that the custody matter be dismissed.

We've been subjected to a wide range of testimony—most of it tangential to the questions at hand—and to some highly unconventional arguments, but we have not received evidence to substantiate that the chimpanzee deserves any kind of special status or protections. Webster is not a wordsmith. He is not a missing link. He is not the hope for mankind's future. He is a common animal with an uncommon history and an uncommonly devoted following, but that is not sufficient or necessary criteria. Scientific evidence must be both.

Your Honor, the defense rests.

DIARY OF RUBY DALTON

June 22, 1979

Everything's over now.

After fifteen hours, I'm finally a mommy! And it's no wonder I feel so sore: Brian Alexander Dalton, Mama's "B.A.D." boy, is eight pounds, six ounces, and thirteen inches long. He's the perfect comfort for me. And for his daddy.

Jeff arrived in time to hold my hand while the anesthesiologist shot me up with drugs, but he waited outside until the messy part was over. He came back to hold the baby and watch his fingerprinting and foot-printing. He kept looking from our son to me and back again. He'd seemed frazzled after court, but then he looked wall-eyed, almost like a little boy at Disneyland who's not sure which marvel to see first.

When the nurse and the doctor finally left us alone, Jeff sat by my bedside and started kissing my face. Gently, up one side and down the other, even though I was sweaty and red and bloated.

He whispered, "Thank you, Ruby. Thank you for being so strong. For putting up with—everything. Thank you for everything you've done. And thank you for our son. Thank you, sweetie."

EXCERPT FROM "BORLEY'S VERDICT"
by F. C. Howe

The Fresno Bee, **June 22, 1979**

Pens scratched frantically as the Hon. Nathaniel
Borley delivered his long-awaited verdict in the
Smithy trial. Despite the length of the hearing
and its wide-ranging testimony, Judge Borley
delivered a focused rendering, concentrating on
the questions at hand in the petition and ignoring
the personal foibles and wilder accusations
displayed during testimony.

He addressed each point in sequence, beginning
with the claims about Smithy's special nature:

*"This court has heard ample testimony regarding
the chimp's value as a scientific resource.
Numerous authorities have spoken in support of
his capacity to use and understand language. I
find this testimony credible. I believe Webster has
the potential to contribute to further cognitive
research. However, based on the precedents cited
by Dr. La Fontaine, I don't believe Webster is
crucial to such research. Other apes have also
demonstrated language skills and could serve
equally well as subjects. Further, we have heard
that Smithy was able to teach other chimpanzees
in his facility how to sign. These were garden-
variety chimpanzees with no special upbringing or
intensive training. If they were able to develop
this ability, then I am confident any other ape
could do so, too.*

*"As for the testimony concerning the
chimpanzee's other abilities, his alleged
power to interface with supernatural beings is*

beyond the jurisdiction of this court. Although parapsychology is a recognized science, its evidentiary standards are protean and difficult to define. Many of the topics parapsychology covers, including the possibility of life after death, are matters of faith rather than science. Therefore, the court cannot make a ruling in support of Webster's indispensability to parapsychological research."

Regarding the requests made on Smithy's behalf:

"The plaintiff has requested a form of modified emancipation for the chimpanzee, Webster, asking that he be elevated to the autonomous status of a United States citizen, with limited rights including freedom from search and seizure and protection from cruel and unusual punishment. The latter would encompass protection from Dr. Teague's proposed neurological study. This request is dismissed with prejudice. Insufficient evidence exists to support personhood for the chimpanzee. Webster cannot enjoy the rights of citizenship because he lacks its concomitant responsibilities. He does not contribute to society or uphold its laws. He lacks the intellectual capacity to understand the structure or obligations of human society. Although he has enjoyed the society of human beings, he is not a part of that society, and so he must remain apart from it.

"Consequently, I cannot grant the motion for physical liberation. Webster is incapable of living on his own and providing for his needs and must remain dependent on humans for care. The plaintiff claims his current legal caregiver, Manfred Teague, is an inappropriate provider and asks that Webster be permanently removed from his care. The only alternative would be to transfer him to another, similar facility, where he would again lack physical freedom and self-determination. I see no value in taking this step.

"Moreover, both the plaintiff's own and neutral experts concur that the quality of the facilities at the Center for the Scientific Advancement of Man and the nutrition Webster received there surpass the national standard and are appropriate for a chimpanzee of his age and size.

"The main point of contention remains Dr. Teague's proposal to vivisect the animal's brain. I find that the defendant has furnished insufficient evidence to demonstrate the necessity or value of such treatment. Furthermore, I find that the proposed surgery fits the definition of cruelty to animals. It is reminiscent of the shameful lobotomies once inflicted as a matter of course on our mentally ill citizens. Society should indeed be judged by the way it treats its vulnerable members. Therefore, I uphold the original injunction prohibiting any surgical or physical modification of the animal."

The final ruling:

"In sum, I find that the research chimpanzee Webster, AKA, Smithy, remains the property of Manfred Teague and CSAM. Judgment for the defendant . . . "

DIARY OF RUBY DALTON

(CONTINUED)

June 22, 1979

. . . *By 8:30, court was back in session and Judge Borley read the verdict.
We watched the live coverage on TV as I nursed our baby for the first
time. I didn't want that bad news (I knew it was bound to be bad)
interfering with our time together, but Jeff insisted. I'd hoped Jeff would
rather see and hold his little boy, but it was like he couldn't help himself,
like he was under a spell and compelled to pay attention to Smithy.*

*Of course, Jeff raged over the verdict. He backtalked to the television
as though Judge Borley might hear him (or care): "You're kidding me!
We proved Smithy can teach language and that renders him obsolete?!?!
'Any old chimp can learn to sign.' OK, you black-robed bastard, but how
many can spontaneously transmit it, huh?*

*"How can he claim Smithy has no responsibilities? He did chores! He
did homework! I didn't do my homework when I was in kindergarten,
and I almost had to repeat a grade. Does that make me an un-person?*

*"'Intellectual capacity?' What about the millions of people who lack
'capacity'? Do we throw them all away now? We specifically mentioned
Eugenie! She lacked capacity, and even Piers said Smithy was more developed than her, dammit!!!*

*"One facility is not the same as another! If Smithy were a patient in
Bedlam, Borley'd transfer him to a more humane hospital. Why won't he
do it for a chimp?*

"Back to Teague!?!?!? Shit, shit, shiiiit!!!"

Jeff stood in the corner and banged his head against the wall.

*"Why did we bother with a trial? Why did Borley let us go on week
after week presenting our evidence and bringing in experts and showing*

548

our videos if he was never even going to consider any of it? If he thought the parapsychology stuff was bull, why let us admit it into evidence? I thought he was keeping an open mind. He was making fools out of us! Did he just like the publicity then? All the cameras in the courtroom?"

Jeff tottered back to us and sank onto the edge of the bed. He moved like an old man, and I wondered if he'd given himself a concussion.

"I thought we were onto something, Ruby! I didn't think he'd give Smithy citizenship, but I thought he'd remand him to a facility where he could keep studying language. I never thought we'd go right back to where we started." His fists pummeled the sides of his head.

All the while, I kept silent, biting my lip to keep from yelling, "Shut up and stop hitting yourself! I told you this would happen! You're going to scare the baby. You're scaring me!"

I worried if I started to yell, I wouldn't be able to stop. Brian may be too young to understand language, but emotions are clear; I didn't want our baby's first experience of this world to be ire. So, I held Brian snug against my chest. One of us has to act like a grown-up, now that we're parents.

Jeff didn't speak anymore, but he breathed funny: rapid grunts punctuated by deep hitching. I eyed him closely, lest he start throwing a fit again, and angled my body to shield Brian from him.

I tried to burp him, but the baby started to cry. Jeff jerked like he'd been startled out of a dream and stared at us. That's when I realized he was crying, too. His reddened, watery eyes widened, almost guilty. "Hey, Bri . . ." Jeff reached out and tweaked his little foot. "It'll be OK. Don't cry. We'll figure something out. All is not lost."

I couldn't hold back then. "He's not crying about the trial. He's hurting. I can't burp him right." Eureka! Jeff reached out. I hesitated before passing Brian over, but I thought maybe his daddy knew something I didn't. Sure enough, Jeff got him to belch and didn't mind the mess running down his shirt collar. His voice, harsh and angry moments before, became light and dreamy for our baby. And he smiled. That's what I wanted to see! I wanted Jeff to enjoy being a father. I wanted him to forget about Smithy and all the pain he entailed.

Never mind that all the time Jeff spent feeding and burping Baby Smithy gave him the experience he needed to care for Brian.

"All better now." Jeff kissed Brian's forehead and put him back in my arms. "I'm sorry, Ruby. I shouldn't have lost it like that. Or yesterday, either. All this is my fault. But I'll fix it."

"No," I told him.

"Yes, it is. I screwed up, but I'll do better on the next round." He stood up. "I'll call Hegge. And Brad. No, he and Brad are probably together, so just the one call." His hand jingled loose change in his pocket—change I put there by working long hours at Gottschalks and writing plaintive letters to my parents and in-laws. "I'll be right back, sweetie." Jeff stroked my hair and started to leave.

"No." I kept my voice even by staring at the linoleum floor. Cold, hard, smooth, steady. "Don't call. Don't do anything else."

"Huh?" He had no clue.

"We've done enough. We've spent the past five years doing our damnedest for Smithy. We got as far as we could. He's not going to be freed, but he's not going to be lobotomized. We got people to pay attention and open their minds. That's enough. It's time we moved on with our own lives. Let someone else help Smithy. Someone who has more resources and fresher ideas."

"But it was your idea to go to court!" Jeff protested.

"For the injunction, not the trial! I never wanted this circus to take over our life. Our whole life together has been about Smithy, Smithy, Smithy. I've had enough! I'm satisfied with the verdict. I don't want to relive the past year hoping for a different outcome. That's insanity. We've done all we can to help him." Then I added, spitefully, "You weren't exactly helping him with your outbursts, were you?"

Jeff flinched. "Ruby, honey, this doesn't sound like you. You just had a baby, and that—"

I sensed where he was leading and wanted to slap him. Instead, I told him everything I've been longing to say for the past nine months, everything I've been mentally rehearsing while standing behind the register, all the words chasing round in my head during labor.

"I'm not drowning in hormones, if that's what you mean! I'm telling you, Brian needs us more than Smithy does. Both of us! We brought him into this world, and we owe him our full attention and love. Maybe you don't feel that way. You haven't been around much. All through my *pregnancy, I was working and you were at court or with Hegge. Or Sam. You never came to any of my appointments. I had to get myself to the hospital yesterday, Jeff! I thought you were going to miss the birth! I don't want you to miss the rest of Brian's life.*

"*And even before then, you've missed most of our marriage. What did we do on our anniversary last year? We didn't spend it together. You were working with Smithy and the other apes on the language project.*

"*I've done things your way, Jeff, meaning I've done things alone. If I have to raise a baby by myself, too—it will be on my terms.*"

He blanched and reeled back when I said that. I wasn't expecting it, either. It just popped out.

"*Ruby . . .*" *His eyelids fluttered as he tried to process my meaning.* "*Look . . . Smithy is the first real responsibility I ever had. He's the first thing that ever depended on me. He's like a son to me. What kind of father would I be if I abandoned him? How can I take care of Brian if it turns out I couldn't take care of Smithy?*" *The pain in his eyes glittered fiercely through tears.* "*I have to save him! I have to prove to myself I can keep him safe, or I'll never trust myself to take care of anyone else.*"

"*Jeff,*" *I said,* "*you've done everything possible for Smithy. You saved him from being destroyed a little piece at a time. What happens now isn't up to you. And Smithy is not your son.* Here *is your son. I care for Smithy, too, and I gave him all I could, but I have nothing left for him.*

"*I've spent too much of my life trying to make other people happy. I thought sticking it out at CSAM meant I was strong. It didn't. It meant I was stupid. I made myself suffer; I'm not doing that again. I don't have to live my life to impress my dad or Man or even you. It's time I did what will make me happy. I have that freedom, and I'm not going to waste it.*

"*I can still do great things, even without Smithy. I can raise a family, finish my education, have my own career someday.*

"*I want all those things. I want to start over, Jeff. I want to leave Fresno. I want to leave Smithy. I want out.*

"*One way or another, I want out.*"

He looked at me in silence, his face as pale and stiff as the walls around us.

"*Ruby . . . did you really see the ghost?*"

June 22, 1979
Location: The Courthouse Steps

Sam and Brad stand before the courthouse doors,
addressing a crowd of reporters and cameramen.
Sam looks composed, but Brad is red-faced and
agitated.

A reporter asks, "Brad, what's your reaction
to the verdict?"

Brad yells, "What the hell do you think?" Sam
squeezes his shoulder, but he shakes her off. "I'm
furious! I can't believe this! Everybody gave me
grief for toking, but I think that judge must be
smoking something if he thinks Manfred Teague is
fit to take care of Smithy!"

Sam grabs his forearm and whispers in his ear.
Brad pulls away and says, "No! I'm not listening
to you anymore. You said you'd help us! You said
you'd help Smithy! What good did you do?"

John Bell asks, "What about the injunction?
That guarantees him protection."

Brad makes a rude noise and says, "Yeah, he
doesn't get a lobotomy. Praise be! He's still
going back in that hellhole. We've already told
you how bad things are there! Man can't cut
Smithy open, but he can still terrorize him.
If you don't think Man's going to punish Smithy
after what's happened here, I've got a bridge for
you to buy. He won't have any kind of good life
there. Without me looking out for him, he's too
vulnerable. Even if I can't keep him myself, I

want Smithy somewhere safe where he'll get good care."

Rob Mannheim asks, "What's your next move?"

Brad says, "I'm not letting Smithy go back to CSAM without a fight! I'll chain myself to the zoo's front gate to keep Man from getting to him if I have to. And then we'll see about a new petition and—"

Mannheim says, "But he's already taken Smithy back into custody."

Brad's head swivels to follow the reporter's voice; he asks, "What?"

Mannheim says, "Man went straight to the zoo after court was dismissed."

Brad shouts, "No!" He looks at Sam, his face pale and full of disbelief. She looks back at him sadly. Brad asks, "Why?"

Sam says, "We thought it best to avoid a scene. To keep him away from the fanatics."

Brad demands, "Why didn't you tell me? I thought we had time! I thought it wouldn't happen 'till tomorrow!"

Sam argues, "Brad, it wouldn't have done any good."

Brad asks, "Is that why you scheduled this press conference? To distract me? I thought you were on our side! You were supposed to be working for us!" He runs forward as if to shoulder his way through the cluster of cameras. Sam grabs for him again. Brad yells, "Leave me alone! Smithy! Buddy!"

Brad cranes his neck, staring anxiously into the crowd. His face searches the camera lenses, as if looking for Smithy. Brad says, "If you're watching this . . . If you can hear me right now, I . . . I'll think of something. Don't give up! I won't leave you there, buddy! I won't, I—" He pulls his arm away from Sam and wipes it across his face. "Go away! I . . . Smithy, please don't be mad! I swear, I didn't know! I did the best I could! I'll fix it, I promise. I . . . I . . . "

Brad's voice chokes away and his face contorts. He breaks down sobbing and circles his hand over his chest and stomach, repeatedly signing "I'm sorry."

LETTER FROM RUBY DALTON
TO TAMMY STEINMETZ

June 29, 1979

Do you believe in angels? How about angels with muscled abs, perfect teeth, and an ear-splitting yodel?

I refer to Clifford Stanhope, former Hollywood heartthrob and star of such gripping dramas as "Tarzan and the Lost City of Z," "Tarzan v. the Mole People," and, inexplicably, "Tarzan Conquers the Nazi Menace," in which Lord Greystoke goes up against an enclave of Third Reich refugees, including Josef Mengele, who have enslaved a native village for use in their nefarious experiments.

It seems after working alongside various exotic animals, Mr. Stanhope became interested in conservation. He converted numerous acres in San Diego County into a preserve for former show animals and other endangered species. He regularly donates to People for Primates. He also followed Smithy's case closely and was moved to help him out—to the tune of I-don't-know-how-many-thousands-of-dollars that he's offered Man to purchase Smithy!

Hegge arrived with the scoop just as Brad dropped by with a stuffed monkey for Brian. ("It was the closest thing I could find to a chimp," he said. "And since chimps are some of my best friends, I thought he'd make a good buddy for your little guy." It was a sweet thought. I didn't have the heart to tell him I want nothing more to do with chimps for the rest of my life).

I feared Hegge and Brad would come to blows; Brad's so angry that Hegge didn't cross-examine him or Jeff, though after the ridiculous things they said, I'm sure Hegge wanted them off the stand post-haste. However, Brad simply glowered and squeezed his hands into fists.

Jeff started badgering Hegge about an appeal, but Hegge promptly shut him down. "You can't appeal a verdict because you don't like the outcome. I told you up-front, this entire venture was a long shot. The most important thing was to spare Smithy from harm, and there we succeeded."

"He's still in harm's way with Man," Brad objected, his voice rising.

"He may not remain with Man for long," Hegge countered. "I happen to know many good offers have come in to buy Smithy from CSAM."

"Man will never sell him," Jeff despaired.

"You might be surprised. Man didn't want to sell Smithy to _you_. That doesn't mean he wants to keep him. You've always said he never liked the chimp, and that's even truer now. Man has endured months of bad publicity, legal fees, and few partnerships. He needs money; I believe he will let Smithy go for the right price."

"Yeah? What price is that and who's gonna pay it?" Brad groused.

Hegge told us.

On the surface, it looks good. Stanhope can swing in and play the hero again by giving Smithy a fairy-tale ending. Life as the pet of a spoiled movie star is much better than what Man had in store for him. But that future still falls short of what we wanted for Smithy. Stanhope acted with Sambo the orangutan for ten years, so he thinks he's an expert on apes. Never mind that a chimp's needs and disposition are far different from an orangutan's.

Brad pointed out that Stanhope's nature preserve is designed for big animals to roam: elephants, zebras, gazelles. But Smithy won't be able to run free. He's going to live out his days in a cage.

Alone.

Alone, but for the crowds of tourists who want to gawk and goad him. Stanhope doesn't own any other apes, only a few capuchin monkeys. The solitude could destroy Smithy just as much as Man's experiment in butchery.

"Before, his brain was in danger. Now it's his mind," Brad argued. "You didn't see him in solitary. It was ugly. Smithy won't think, 'Whoop-de-do! I get to live with Tarzan!' He'll be wondering, 'Where is everybody? What did I do to deserve this? When will somebody let me out to play?'

"And it's not like Stanhope lives there anyway. He'll drive down to—where the hell is it again? Escondido?—for a weekend here and there, but he won't be involved in Smithy's life. He doesn't really care about Smithy, either. Smithy needs someone to put him first for a change."

"Eden is better than any outcome we could have hoped for," Hegge promised. "Deep down you know that, Brad."

Brad put his face in his hands and sighed. It sounded like air rushing out of a balloon. It was the sound of hope deflating.

"Is it a done deal already?"

Hegge nodded.

"Can I at least talk to him before the transfer? Stanhope, I mean? You say he cares about animals and wants to do right by Smithy, but the problem is, he doesn't know how. Let me tell him what to do so he can give Smithy the right care. All I want is for my friend to be happy."

Hegge gave him a pitying look. "I'll see what I can do, but Mr. Stanhope is a very private man when the cameras aren't rolling."

"Please tell him I just want to talk. If he doesn't want to talk to me, I'll write him a letter. I don't want anything from him. I just want things to work out for Smithy."

OUTTAKE FOOTAGE

MORNING TALK WITH CELIA ARMENDARIZ
Courtesy of KHJ-TV
Broadcast Date: October 18, 1991

Tammy Steinmetz sits in a chair, fiddling with the purple paisley shawl wrapped around her neck.

Off-screen, Celia comments, "That's a lovely shawl."

Tammy says, "Thank you."

Celia remarks, "I've noticed you wearing it in other interviews. Is that shawl lucky?"

Tammy laughs. "It was a gift. From Wanda. I try to wear it any time I do an interview about our study, on the off chance she's watching. Maybe she'll see it, and she'll know . . . " Tammy shrugs. "No hard feelings."

LETTER FROM TAMMY STEINMETZ
TO RUBY DALTON

May 20, 1988

. . . Because I'm a public figure, my contact information is readily available. Reid's written to my home and office addresses and called my office twice. His calls were cordial and old-times-sake friendly. Yes, he wanted to talk about Smithy, and yes, he asked about you.

I told him you're happy with your current life and you don't even like to think about those days, let alone discuss them. I let him know money wouldn't change your feelings and you'd be grateful if he dropped the subject. I don't imagine he got anything out of Wanda, either, but her role, though dramatic, was more limited than yours. Besides, everyone already knows her story.

I'll stave him off as long as you want me to, but if you don't mind some big sisterly advice, I think you could ditch him more successfully if you threw him a bone. It needn't be anything major; just let him know it's an exclusive. I think he craves novelty more than sensationalism. He needs a tagline for his book: something along the lines of, "Never before told . . . " And of course, he's crying about needing to "get the word out before the tenth anniversary." He's probably badgering you so much because his clock is ticking.

If he can get a nibble, I'm sure he'll back off. Playing hard to get is what intrigues him. He's imagining you're hiding fabulous secrets.

I could act as your intermediary, so you don't have to speak to him directly. I've always believed transparency is the best way to set the record straight. I want to do my part to foreground the truth and rein in some of the more outrageous perceptions. Reid has his quirks, but I believe he can accomplish those purposes.

Of course, it's easier for me to talk; Smithy didn't rule my life. I know how you feel about that "sinkhole" in time, but Ruby, you've come so far since those days. My goodness, you're den mother to a whole generation who's never even heard of Smithy . . .

LETTER FROM RUBY DALTON
TO TAMMY STEINMETZ

June 6, 1988

*. . . "Badgering" doesn't come close! Our phone number's still unlisted,
but he got our address somehow; I have six letters, each sent three weeks
apart, to prove it. Fortunately, he hasn't gone as far as to show up on our
doorstep, but I keep expecting it.*

*I still get the creeps when I think about him waiting for me out-
side the boys' school with that lame excuse about visiting a colleague in
the neighborhood just as school happened to let out. Evidently, my failure
to invite him for dinner or a drink didn't faze him.*

*Maybe he's not exactly stalking us, but he's obnoxiously persistent.
Rather than keep fending off his advances, I'm taking your advice. In
this box, you'll find every scrap I could collect about the trial, CSAM,
and Trevor Hall. I never realized how prolific a diarist I was. I've also
thrown in some letters you wrote to me, and I even asked Vinny to dredge
up whatever he kept from me in those days.*

*I bequeath to you my entire trove of items about Smithy. Use them
at your discretion. Send the whole lot to Reid or parse it for whatever
you feel is most relevant. I trust your judgment. In any case, I want it
understood this is my sole contribution to the conversation. Reid is not to
contact Jeff's school or mine, nor send any more letters to our house, nor
loiter in front of our children's school, nor is he to contact anyone from
our extended families. I will not give interviews or answer any questions.
I will not provide any personal details about my current life.*

*Smithy didn't just consume my twenties. He's still with us to this
day. Though Jeff doesn't talk about him openly anymore, I catch a wist-
ful look on his face from time to time. It happens in relation to random
things: the kids eating Jell-O, a broadcast of "Sesame Street," an ape on*

the television. We still haven't taken our kids to a zoo. Jeff can't bear to see any monkeys or apes in a cage, and I can't bear to see them at all.

I've always worried that Jeff blames me. He's been a perfectly involved father and husband these last ten years, and he claims to enjoy teaching, but I wonder how often he thinks about the life he could have had if he'd stuck with Brad in trying to rescue Smithy. Is presenting science to third and fourth graders more fulfilling than blazing trails across the scientific and legal fields? Do our three children make up for the first child he lost and worries he betrayed?

I ask myself these things from time to time, but, Tammy, I don't want to find out. I could strangle Reid for raising the topic between us again. No more! I wash my hands of the whole business. Tell Reid this is all I have and all he's going to get. Make him listen. He's always liked you.

VIDEO FOOTAGE

A *CURRENT AFFAIR*
Broadcast Date: September 29, 1987

Brad Vollmer sits on a soundstage decorated to look like a living room. He faces the camera and an off-screen interviewer.

Brad, at one time, Smithy's fate was precarious, but he's no longer in jeopardy. In fact, his arch-nemesis recently passed away[14]. Yet, you continue, in your own words, to raise hell. Some folks think you're a sore loser because you didn't get to keep Smithy.

That's bogus! Listen, people think we won the case. All we did was help Smithy go from the fire to the frying pan and die a slow, sad death instead of being horribly mutilated over several months. He is dying inside, slowly. And I can't reach him! I can't do a damn thing to help him.

All Smithy's fans and "disciples" forgot about him once the trial ended, and Smithy didn't make a miracle or raise the dead or do whatever they expected. People would tell me, "Brad, shut up and go home! Smithy's not going to get his brain chopped up, he's going to a nice big farm where he can run and play with other animals. He's famous now. He's got it made." They don't care that Smithy's all alone. For chimps, that's torture. Solitary confinement is what the worst

14 Manfred Teague died of cirrhosis in June 1987.

of criminals in prison get. Smithy's been alone for *years*! I've tried to warn Stanhope chimps are social animals. They need company. Stanhope's got Smithy locked in a cage all by himself. For privacy! Just 'cause Stanhope likes his privacy and wants a great big mansion all to himself, he assumes a chimp will like it, too. Chimps go crazy when they're isolated. Some waste away. It's put down as heart disease or failure to thrive, but they die of loneliness.

Is publicly name-calling Cliff Stanhope and confronting him at autograph shows the best way to help Smithy?

I've tried doing things the "nice" way, believe me. Right after Stanhope bought Smithy, I wrote him letters thanking him for helping Smithy. I said I knew he'd want to do right by Smithy, so I told him what chimpanzees are like and what Smithy likes. Stanhope totally blew me off. I thought at first he wasn't getting my letters, like, his agent was screening his mail or something, so I drove down to Hollywood and hung out in Bronson Canyon where he was filming. I just wanted to talk to him during a break, but he had his bodyguards run me off. Then his lawyers sent me cease-and-desist letters saying I wasn't even allowed to write to him anymore. So I had my lawyer, Sam Stone, write letters, too. And the word came back that Mr. Stanhope didn't "desire any congress with Mr. Vollmer or his representatives."

I went down to Eden last Christmas and tried to go inside with the big crowd. I thought that place was a public zoo, but it's Stanhope's private menagerie. He only lets the *hoi polloi* in on certain holidays: Christmas, New Year's, July 4th, his birthday, and whatnot. Well, someone at

the gate recognized me and threw me out. They've
got my picture at the entrance with a big line
drawn through it! Maybe they've got pictures of
Jeff and Ruby, too; I don't know.

How are Jeff and Ruby? Why haven't we heard from
them lately?

Oh, after the trial and all the publicity, Ruby
was done. I couldn't blame her. She went through
a lot. All the time Jeff and I were working on our
strategy, she was working retail to pay the rent.
When we gave interviews, she was dodging reporters.
She never liked the limelight. After the trial,
she convinced Jeff to move north, nearer to his
folks. They're both teachers now. Well, Ruby's
subbing part-time. They've got two more kids,
and she wanted to be home while they're young. It
wouldn't have been fair to talk them into staying
in the fight with me. The kids should come first.
Smithy's *my* kid, and I'm not going to give up on
him. I swore I'd help him. Judge Borley and Cliff
Stanhope have tried to make a liar out of me, but
I won't let Smithy down!

Exactly what do you want from Cliff Stanhope?
Maybe he's watching tonight. What would you like
to say to him if he is?

All I want is what's best for Smithy. Sure, I
want to see him again. I miss him! He was the best
friend I ever had. But I'm not trying to take him,
just talk to him. I worry about him. Stanhope's
not sadistic like Man, but that doesn't mean he's
a good caregiver. Tonight, I'll show the world
what I mean.

What have you got for us, Brad?

I've hired a private eye, a former green beret from 'Nam who's a master at getting in and out of situations without anyone hearing him breathe. He's slipped past Stanhope's guards plenty of times to do surveillance for me. He's brought back photos and video of how Smithy lives.

Let's look at a sample.

The video cuts to a camcorder recording on night vision. The image is in grainy black and white, the exterior of a thirty-by-fifty-foot cage. Within the cage are small shrubs and two banyan trees. Interlocking rings hang from one tree; a swing hangs from the other. A structure of overlapping platforms stands in one corner of the cage. Toys, including building blocks, a rubber ball, a teddy bear, a toy car, a miniature piano keyboard, a Rubik's cube, and various picture books are scattered on the floor and on the platforms. A large chimpanzee knuckle-walks back and forth in a tight circle. Periodically he shakes his head and snorts.

The video cuts to a split-screen of surveillance footage on the left and Brad's reaction-shot on the right.

See all that stuff he has? All kinds of toys but nobody to play with. Company's what Smithy really wants. Can you see how bored he is, the way he keeps moving around?

Have you watched this already?

No, I've been afraid to.

The surveillance camera zooms in on the chimp. Smithy glances backward, toward the platforms, as he paces. He growls.

He's in a bad mood. This is a typical tantrum. I've got hours of him pacing or kicking the bars of his cage, or worse, hitting his head against the bars.

Abruptly, Smithy pauses and stares at the platforms. Then he wiggles his fists, thumbs and pinkies out.

What's he doing now?

Brad frowns.

Huh. That means "play."

Smithy stands upright and wiggles his hands again.

What do you want to play, buddy? Who are you gonna play with?

A ball that had been stationary on the platform about eight feet off the ground rolls off and bounces toward Smithy. He screeches and spins in a circle.

What was that? Is someone in there with him?

No, he's alone. He's always alone.

Smithy knocks the ball back toward the platforms. It bounces out of the frame and rebounds toward Smithy. He signs, "play," and hits the ball again. In the reaction pane, Brad, frowning, tracks the ball as it bounces back and forth twice. The surveillance camera pans back, showing a full

view of the cage. Smithy is the only occupant.
The ball bounces in the center of the cage once,
twice, then rolls away. Smithy whines and signs,
"play," again, pauses a beat, then trudges to the
corner away from the platforms and sits with his
back to both platforms and ball.

He's lonely . . . He's signing so he doesn't
forget what it's like—

—*to have someone?*

Yeah.

*So, he's talking to himself? Like a bum on the
subway?*

Brad scowls.

Don't say that, Celia. It makes him sound too far
gone. I've got to get him out of there!

The filmed footage goes black and the split screen
becomes a single image of Brad.

How can we help?

Write letters. Public disapproval helped get
Smithy away from Man Teague. Let Cliff Stanhope
know you don't approve of the way he's letting this
precious animal waste away. If he loves animals
as much as he claims, he'll transfer Smithy to
a proper sanctuary or bring in more chimps, so
Smithy has someone to play with. Smithy still
needs your help. Don't give up on him!

*Thank you, Brad. Cliff Stanhope declined to be
interviewed for this segment, but we'll be keeping
our eyes on Smithy just the same.*

VIDEO FOOTAGE

MORNING TALK WITH CELIA ARMENDARIZ
Courtesy of KHJ-TV
Broadcast Date: October 18, 1991

Tammy reclines in an easy chair, speaking to Celia off-screen. A purple paisley shawl is wrapped around her shoulder.

. . . No matter what I accomplish in my career, I'll always be in Smithy's shadow. I encounter reminders of him under the most unexpected circumstances.

Such as?

About two weeks ago, I had a speaking engagement at a PTA chapter in Queens. After it ended, I remained behind, conversing with the members. One woman asked if I had children, and when I said no, she looked *very* disapproving. Unfortunately, I experience that sort of reaction a lot. I explained to this lady that I'd already helped raise five younger sisters and a chimpanzee, so I felt no need to raise a baby of my own. Her eyebrows went up, and I fully expected her to lay into me about being selfish and irresponsible. People seem to think if a woman isn't a mother and has no interest in being one, she must be a monster. Instead, she wanted to hear more about the chimpanzee.

Celia laughs.

Once I mentioned Smithy's name, she grew excited and spent the next fifteen minutes pressing me about what Smithy was like and whether I believed he could talk—and whether I believed in the ghost, of course.

How has your experience with Smithy impacted your life?

The Smithy Experiment definitively steered me toward a career in education, first as a teacher and now on the schoolboard, but teaching language skills to a chimpanzee wasn't the most formative experience I had in Newport. Trevor Hall provided robust training for challenges I would have encountered no matter what career I might have chosen.

What were some of the lessons you learned?

I learned how people can work together in pursuit of a shared aim—and how they can oppose each other in spite of their common goals. That prepared me for politics. I also encountered an unseemly trend our society has spent the past twenty years fighting: namely, misogyny in the workplace. Professor Hill is currently raising awareness of sexual harassment, an issue that deserves our attention and demands change. We must also consider the simple, daily nastiness women face while trying to earn their daily bread. The snide remarks. The casual dismissal. The skepticism. The resentment. From men and women both.

I witnessed all the above at Trevor Hall. I participated in it, too. I was privileged to work alongside brilliant women, one of whom acted as our de facto director of operations. I could have learned from Wanda Karlewicz, but too often, I helped undermine her by actively speaking and acting in opposition to her or by passively allowing others to do so unchecked.

Why?

I convinced myself Wanda deserved it because she was pushy and difficult. My colleagues and I frequently complained about the things that made her a strong leader: her unyielding vision, her commitment, her drive. We held Wanda accountable to society's feminine stereotype—the friendly, sensitive, nurturing angel in the home—and blamed her for not conforming. In truth, I was jealous of her. I was so certain I knew what was best for Smithy, and I resented that my accomplishments weren't recognized as readily as hers. Also, even though Wanda was a brilliant and dedicated researcher, a dark part of me attributed her position to her special relationship with Dr. Preis-Herald. Instead of considering that he was drawn to her because of her intelligence and efficiency, I chose to be uncharitable. The oppression at Trevor Hall was mild compared to what my poor colleague, Ruby Dalton, later encountered at CSAM, but to the extent that misogyny did exist, it existed because I enabled it. I regret that immensely. To Wanda, I wish to say, *I'm sorry.*

EXCERPT FROM PIERS PREIS-HERALD'S ADDRESS TO THE COMMITTEE FOR THE SCIENTIFIC INVESTIGATION OF CLAIMS OF THE PARANORMAL CSICON, 1998

A recent Gallup Poll showed seventy-five percent of Americans believe in an afterlife or a supreme being. Matters of faith may inspire and make the world more magical and exciting, but unsupported, unscientific beliefs can also cause devastating harm.

Consider what befell poor Georgia McMasters right here in LA. Because one of her students suffered nightmares after sneaking a peek at a horror movie, the child's mother and her friends became convinced—in the absence of any physical evidence—that he was being molested by Satanists at preschool. Half the instructors were driven to accuse the other half of devil worship, cannibalism, and child abuse for fear they might be arrested next.

To this day, thousands still believe a secret labyrinth lies somewhere beneath the old school building. Never mind that Long Beach was once a swamp and it would be physically impossible to construct a basement under the school, let alone a network of tunnels! Good people lost their jobs and reputations. McMasters lost her home and her family business and was ultimately run out of town.

Consider, likewise, the Emerson family. A respected police chief in a middle-class Oregon suburb, married twenty years, devoted to his family and community, became a monster overnight when his bipolar teenager accused him and his colleagues of using her in sexual rituals. Within a month, most of the town's police officers were sitting in their own jail cells. Newspapers called it "The Second Salem Witch Trial."

In both cases, plaintiffs were represented by Samantha Stone, who, while in law school, assisted in the sideshow known as *Friends of Smithy v. CSAM*. Since then, her name has been merged with the incredible. Stone became one of the foremost lawyers in the country by riding the wave of the "Satanic Panic" to notoriety. Her cases made headlines because of how insane they sounded. But instead of repelling the public, her ludicrous claims fired them up and ultimately destroyed lives.

It's tempting to paint Stone as a publicity hound, but I think she sincerely believes in bunkum. That's why she's so skilled at persuading others to believe it. Connie Emerson's stories were so vivid and Sam Stone's advocacy so persistent, some of the accused even believed they *had* committed the awful deeds and then repressed the memories. It sounds bloody mad now, but these stories were so detailed, they persuaded many people at the time to accept them.

Those details are hallmarks of False Memory Syndrome. If someone told you to think of a pink elephant, your imagination would supply details of how such an elephant might look. You might focus on details like the exact shade of pink of the elephant's hide. And are its eyes also pink or are they blue? Likewise, if someone asked you to remember sacrificing a baby to Satan, your imagination could also propose a detailed scenario for how that might look. It might be so detailed, it seems like something that really happened instead of a legend you created.

It's fascinating—and frightening and disheartening—to see how easily the most intelligent people will subvert their rational judgment in favor of the most absurd things, especially when such weirdness brings them comfort.

My own erstwhile assistant, Jeff Dalton, was a bright and clear thinker when I knew him, yet he became a proponent of facilitated communication, a fraudulent tool of self-deception. Why? Because empirical evidence supported this technique? No; because the idea that a being might wish to communicate but need accommodation to do so satisfied Jeff's ongoing need to believe Webster was a great communicator.

What most shocked me when I began to speak publicly about Webster is how he's primarily identified with spiritualism. People don't even consider his role in primate language studies, or if they do, they erroneously believe my study supported primate communication and Webster's so-called mediumship bears this out. So many of the books written about the case focus on its most sensationalistic elements, and those are what now dominate the public mind. A young girl, no older than ten or twelve, who attended my program in Philadelphia last week, brought with her a children's book that included a chapter called "The Chimp Who Talked to Ghosts."[15] Presenting such farce to impressionable young minds should be a criminal offense. However, adult literature doesn't fare much better. The biggest bestseller, *Speaker for the Dead*,[16] was penned by the same New York tabloid reporter who capitalized on the so-called Long Island Horror, a tale that has been discredited by numerous media outlets.

Just yesterday, I received a letter from an infamous collector of random Webster-centric trivia, whose hodgepodge of mind-numbing detail over the past quarter-century purports to be the "definitive" true story of the case, inviting me to contribute my research notes "to make the scientific import of the story better known." In the interest of preserving public sanity, I will retain my records for my own use.

The importance of teaching skepticism to help inoculate the public against the pitfalls of believing in unsubstantiated things cannot be understated.

15 *Ghostly Animals: Ten Truly Haunting Tales* by Bryce Crosby and Ellen Zola
16 Preis-Herald appears to be confusing *Speaker for the Dead*, Llewellyn Press's award-winning history of spiritualism, with *Speak No Evil* by Ray Hanson.

VIDEO FOOTAGE:
THE ELIOT GUTHRIE HOUR

Broadcast Date: July 7, 2000
Location: Talk-show studio

A middle-aged black man in a blazer and glasses crosses the stage amid applause, shaking hands with members of the audience as theme music plays.

Guthrie says, "Thank you, folks! I'm so glad you could join us. Today, we'll conclude our week-long trip back to the 1970s by revisiting a phenomenon that dominated headlines: Smithy the "talking" chimpanzee.

The camera cuts to the audience for reaction shots. Some people look questioning. Others nod in recognition.

The camera returns to Guthrie, who continues. "Today, Smithy lives in Eden, actor Clifford Stanhope's private animal sanctuary in Southern California. But here's what he was up to twenty-five years ago . . .

A montage plays clips of Preis-Herald's 1972 interview; the research team at Trevor Hall; stock footage from Smithy's birthday party; stock footage from CSAM; newspaper headlines from the trial; stock footage of Smithy in court; the verdict; Brad's tearful interview; Brad leading a protest outside Eden.

The reel fades out and the camera zooms in on Guthrie standing in front of two easy chairs. He says, "Please welcome the man who has chronicled all the events you just saw: historian and author Dr. Reid Bennet!

Reid enters stage left wearing glasses, a bowtie, and a jacket with patches on the elbows. He blinks in the bright lights and waves before shaking hands and sitting beside Guthrie. He says, "Thank you, Eliot! It's my pleasure."

Guthrie says, "We're glad to have you. You've written the book on Smithy—literally." He holds up a hardcover copy of *Smithy: A 20-Year Compendium*, weighing it in his hands. "Look at all that detail!" Guthrie flips to pages at random, marveling. "Photos, interviews, reprinted articles . . . "

Reid says, "I tried to be thorough."

Guthrie asks, "How long did you spend writing this?"

Reid says, "I spent six years gathering all the material and another three years getting from first draft to publication. I reached out to the principals involved—you know, I knew the Yale research team personally when I was younger. For a time, I even dated the charming and brilliant Tammy Cohen."

Guthrie says, "That's what makes this book so interesting. You include your own memories of what was happening at the time, before the trial, before the controversy. In this age of the tell-all memoir, no one else from the Newport days has written an account."

Reid says, "Well, the Daltons have retired from the public eye, but Ruby generously provided me with her diaries, both from Trevor Hall and the CSAM years. This book includes her insider's view of the experiment, the media notoriety, the trial, and more.

Now, my *new* book, *Smithy: The Millennium Compendium*, includes never-before-seen photos and documents. For instance, Ruby Dalton's roommate and pen-pal in Scranton shared with me letters Ruby had written her from Trevor Hall describing the study and some of the more bizarre events *as they occurred*. It's a pure, unadulterated view of what the researchers thought about what was going on and what would happen next. That's gold to a historian. Or a Smithyphile."

Guthrie says, "Why write another book now? Will you be releasing a new Smithy book every five years?"

Reid laughs and says, "I felt the time was right. As we move into the next millennium, we're seeing an upsurge of interest in unusual topics. People are rediscovering Nostradamus's prophecies and delving into New Age mysticism. Interest in Smithy and his alleged powers has revived, too. Moreover, we've seen recent advances in primate studies. Eric Kaninchen once suggested language research should continue with bonobos. Now scientists are teaching bonobos to communicate through pictorial keyboards. Allegedly, some can even write! Then there's Smithy's impact on popular culture, like the recent sitcom, *Chumps*.[17]

Guthrie says, "I wouldn't think *that* merited a book . . . But, Dr. Bennet, why write about Smithy in the first place? You have a doctorate in history; you're part of the Newport Preservation Society; and now you're a tour guide at Trevor Hall. Isn't that right?"

Reid says, "Yes. After the Society acquired Trevor Hall in 1984 and restored it to its former glory—a lengthy endeavor, since the previous tenants, Sal and Regina Scolari, were poor caretakers—the house was opened to the public in 1994. I don't believe my academic qualifications bar me from writing about this subject matter. On the contrary, I'm able to apply my curatorial

17 The show, a riff on *Friends*, followed the zany misadventures of a group of twenty-somethings who respond to a want-ad that requires them to live together in a Manhattan townhouse and teach a chimpanzee how to act like a human. The title refers to a typographical error in the ad. "Chumps" was canceled four episodes into its thirteen-week run.

standards to a topic of great interest that hasn't always been treated respectably. I believe my own small involvement in the story grants me privileged insight into the case. Further, my unique assembly of exclusive primary sources from those intimately familiar with the case—"

Guthrie interrupts, "How much cooperation did you get from Piers Pries-Herald?"

Reid frowns and says, "None, but I didn't need to speak with him. His publications are readily available, as is that found-footage tape he hawks on his website. Dr. Preis-Herald is an important source, but one that's been mined dry over the years."

Guthrie says, "You've got one piece of material from Dr. Preis-Herald that few people have seen before . . . "

"Yes." Reid extracts a manila envelope from his coat and opens it. He holds a letter up to the camera, making the Yale letterhead visible.

Guthrie asks, "What is it?"

Reid says, "Essentially, it's an informal cease-and-desist letter. You see, Dr. Preis-Herald didn't care for the interview I gave *The Newport Daily News*. First, he called my office to abuse my secretary, then he sent me this lovely missive." He reads, "Keep your damned 'opinions' to yourself and your bloody nose out of my affairs. Above all, keep my name out of anything you write in the future. If you continue to malign me or my work, my attorney will give you cause to regret it, and I'll gladly hammer the point home myself."

Guthrie says, "Wow! What did you say to annoy him so much?"

Reid says, "I merely spoke to the paper about the historical evidence for a ghost at Trevor Hall, of which little to none exists, and provided an analysis of why such stories persist. I noted Dr. Preis-Herald cited the rumored ghost as a reason he cut short his experiment, though he pooh-poohed the idea back when he was still hoping to break ground with Smithy. He accused me of putting words in his mouth and misrepresenting his research, but I did nothing of the kind."

Guthrie says, "But Preis-Herald isn't the only one who's made such a claim. During your first year with the Newport Preservation Society, weren't you disciplined because you were, quote, 'embellishing' during a tour?"

Reid's eyes narrow. "No, that's not true at all. I've never been disciplined, and I've never told untruths to my patrons. Not intentionally. History is always changing as we discover new facts to alter our previous understanding of a situation. Hence, the tours I give may change from one season to another. Perhaps someone overheard new, unfamiliar information and thought I was, er, improvising. Or possibly someone was jealous of my superior knowledge and wanted to cause me trouble. I try to avoid imposing my own perception of an event onto others. I prefer to share all available details and possible interpretations and trust my listeners to discern which are best substantiated."

Guthrie asks, "Dr. Bennet, what was your purpose in telling Dr. Preis-Herald's students about the legends surrounding Trevor Hall? Were you trying to frighten them?"

Reid says, "No. I never imagined any of them would believe in ghost stories. These were graduate students. They seemed solid and intelligent. I never credited the tales myself."

Guthrie asks, "Why mention them at all?"

Reid says, "Eliot, when I know something interesting about a place or a person, I'm compelled to talk about it. That's a fine trait for a lecturer, but it didn't make me popular with my peers in my youth. I simply wanted to

share the lore I'd acquired through my studies of
Trevor Hall. I thought the students would like
to learn more about where they were living . . .
and I thought I might impress some of the girls."

Guthrie asks, "Do you believe Imogene Rockwell
haunts Trevor Hall?"

Reid says, "No. By all accounts, Mrs. Rockwell
died a natural, peaceful death. There's no reason
to associate her with the Dark Lady."

Guthrie asks, "So why has she been identified
as the ghost?"

Reid says, "That's a fascinating question!
The answer lies in the history and psychology
of Newport itself. There's something frightening
and transgressive about the idea of a servant
dominating a mansion long after its rightful owners
have departed. The Newport elite are supposed
to be in charge, but by entering the realm of
the spirits, the servant acquires greater power.
People in the community probably remembered
Imogene Rockwell had died in the house, even
though the circumstances of her death have been
transmuted over time and multiple retellings.
Perhaps there was even a grain of truth to stories
about a rivalry between Mrs. Rockwell and another
servant, or rumors that she had been involved
with Master Trevor. Thus, Imogene Rockwell was
condemned by subsequent generations to haunt
Trevor Hall. But this is folklore! Local color!"

Guthrie asks, "Have you ever seen a ghost or
witnessed anything at the house that you couldn't
explain?"

Reid says, "Never!"

Guthrie suggests, "Isn't that consistent with
the Daltons' claim that the ghost followed Smithy
to his new home at CSAM?"

Reid answers, "It's consistent with a ghost
never having been in the house in the first place."

Guthrie says, "I still don't understand why you pressed your collected 'folklore' about a haunted Trevor Hall on an impressionable and naïve audience. Were you hoping to entertain them, or were you trying to influence them with your stories?"

Reid raises his hands and says, "You've got me, Eliot! I cleverly planted the story of a haunting to make Trevor Hall uninhabitable so that someday, decades in the future, I could have unfettered access to the property I'd always admired."

Guthrie says, "You've written a popular book about the case and you're the consultant for a forthcoming documentary about Smithy produced by TV personality Celia Armendariz-Huerta. You're benefiting."

Reid says, "So are you. You've granted Celia permission to use footage from today's show; she'll compensate you, and you'll broaden your audience."

Guthrie says, "A Mrs. Belancourt from Herbert Terrace, the nearest property to Trevor Hall, once called police to report a suspicious character skulking around the estate; when police arrived, they arrested *you*. What was that about?"

Reid laughs. "That was a misunderstanding. It happened my first day on the job. My supervisor had given me the wrong key and I couldn't unlock the front gate. I walked around, looking for another entry or a weak spot in the hedges to squeeze through. Mrs. Belancourt happened to be walking her dog and spotted me running around. I don't doubt I looked suspicious. But my supervisor verified my credentials to the police, and afterward, I went to Herbert Terrace and introduced myself to the Belancourts. We've since become good friends and we often joke about my dark past as a housebreaker."

Guthrie quietly flips through Reid's book. "What would you say to readers who might accuse you of trying to control the narrative and have the final word on the Smithy matter?"

Reid says, "First, I'd say they didn't read my book closely. I worked carefully to capture the total environment in which the experiment took place by not restricting myself to reports of the study. Instead, I included the researchers' impressions about the house, the town, and their goals for the study, so my readers can evaluate how likely it was that the team became victims of mass hysterics, or if their claims of a haunting were credible. I've maintained a level of personal objectivity. If you'll note, Eliot, I didn't burnish myself anywhere in the text. In fact, you'll find some unflattering remarks from the principals. My duty as a historian is to preserve the whole truth, and nothing but the truth, for posterity."

Guthrie asks, "Why insert yourself into the narrative at all?"

Reid says, "Unfortunately, most books about this case have been written by people who had no ties whatsoever to anyone with firsthand involvement in these matters. These *hacks* simply attempted to capitalize on a popular story and profit from a gullible public, often by manufacturing details wholesale. Their works have perpetuated some of the worst misconceptions that pervade popular culture. I *was* there, Eliot. When I write about my dinner with Tammy or share a letter I received from Dr. Preis-Herald, I'm showing you my bona fides. I'm telling you why you can trust me."

Guthrie says, "When we return, we'll hear another perspective on Smithy. Stay tuned to see who'll be joining our retrospective next!"

The camera fades out, then fades back in on a solemn Guthrie. He says, "If you're just joining us now, we've been revisiting the famous case of Smithy the chimpanzee. Smithy's story took a dark turn on July 4th, 1975. The events of that night were recreated for television in the clip you're about to see."

A clip plays from *Unsolved Mysteries*. A silhouetted image of a woman falls backward from a rooftop in slow motion. She reaches up to grasp the parapet and hangs from it.

Tammy's voice-over says, "I had just turned my back when I heard Gail scream. That scream froze my blood. I spun around. And—I couldn't see Gail! I heard Gail scream again and I started running toward the sound. Gail was hanging off the roof! Her little fingers were hooked over the parapet, but her body was dangling in the air. Her legs were kicking but there was nothing under her!"

The scene cuts to an image of Tammy, seated, talking to the camera. She says, "I was sure I was about to watch Gail fall to her death."

The image freezes and the camera pulls back to show the studio. Guthrie and Reid sit at a round table in the middle of the stage, along with a newcomer. The camera zooms in on Guthrie.

Guthrie says, "We're joined now by Gail Beveridge, one of Smithy's original instructors at Trevor Hall." He turns and shake hands with a stylish blonde woman in a teal sweater and dangling turquoise earrings. A caption below her smiling face identifies her as "Gail (Ehrlich) Beveridge."

Gail says, "Hello, Eliot." Reid starts to rise and extends his hand across the table. Gail nods at him, and adds, "Reid." He sits down.

Guthrie says, "I know what we saw just now was a reenactment, but it felt so real. I'm relieved to see you here in one piece. What was it like for you to watch that and experience it again vicariously? Do you remember hanging from the roof like that?"

Gail says, "Not really. When I think about it, it's like a bad dream. The medics said I was in shock. I don't remember anything after Smithy launched himself at me. I felt the impact when he hit me"—Gail folds her hands over her chest—"and how terrified I felt when I started to go backward. A part of my mind knew I was falling, and I couldn't do anything about it. I could hear screaming from a distance. It was me screaming, but it didn't feel like me."

Guthrie nods, his brow creased sympathetically. Reid leans forward, his chin on his tented hands, his eyes fixed on Gail.

Gail continues. "All I knew was my arms were getting tired and sore, but it was like they were stuck in place. I didn't dare move. Thank God Eric—rest his soul—was there. I don't think Tammy could have rescued me on her own. I know she would have tried. I'm so grateful she was able to get help."

Guthrie says, "So are we."

Gail says, "Thanks to her, I'm still here—and I'm *here* now—but I don't remember much. I couldn't tell *Unsolved Mysteries* anything, so they ended up having Tammy narrate. Hearing other people talk about it, or watching something like that, terrifies me, but it fascinates me, too. Because I'm sort of experiencing it for the first time, just like your audience, even though I was there."

Guthrie says, "Thank you for that descriptive—and harrowing—explanation. If I may say, you handle trauma graciously." Gail laughs and looks away from the camera. Guthrie continues, "You didn't let the trauma beat you. That you're able to talk about it is impressive. You even went to the hearing and testified of your own accord. Was that hard? The memories were fresher then, I imagine."

Gail says, "Yes. That was the first time I'd talked about Smithy—not just in public but with anyone. I used to pretend nothing had happened."

Guthrie asks, "Did it help to get those memories in the open?"

Gail says, "Yes. Now I've gone over it so often, it doesn't bother me anymore."

Guthrie says, "Good. And what about the ghost? Does it still bother you? Have you seen anything like that since?"

Gail's face turns stony and her eyes lower to the tabletop. She says softly, "No."

Guthrie says, "That was a terrible trick! I was proud of you when you went back to court the next day and didn't let them intimidate you."

Gail smiles at Guthrie and sits up straighter. "Thank you."

Guthrie asks, "What are you doing now? Did you stick with psychology?"

Gail says, "No. For the past fifteen years, I've been a mommy and a homemaker. My husband, Alan, and I have four beautiful children."

Guthrie says, "Congratulations!" Gail beams. "And you've continued to follow Smithy?"

Gail purses her lips and says, "Yes."

Guthrie says, "In fact, you saw him again recently, didn't you?" Reid sits up straighter.

Gail nods. "In the summer of 1989, my family took a vacation to California."

The camera shows a photo montage: a family of six standing in front of Sleeping Beauty's castle; posing with Frankenstein's monster; three children playing on a beach; an Orca jumping out of the water. Gail's voiceover narrates. "We went to several theme parks. And we visited Eden."

The final photo shows each member of the Beveridge family holding a tiny American flag, posed in front of open bronze gates, ornate with a motif of vines, leaves, flowers, and fruits.

Gail's voiceover continues. "We were in San Diego over the July fourth weekend, so we got to go inside. My kids were excited because I'd told them about Smithy. The good stories about my friend Smithy, the talking chimpanzee, nothing about what you just saw. I read to them from the picture book[18] and showed them some old Polaroids. They couldn't wait to meet him for themselves."

The camera cuts to the table. Guthrie asks, "How did you feel about seeing Smithy again after so long, and on the anniversary of your attack?"

Gail says, "I had mixed feelings. I was curious to see how he was doing—I'd heard so many different things in the media, and from Brad's newsletters for the Friends of Smithy—but I was terribly nervous."

Guthrie asks, "That he might attack you?"

Gail says, "No. It was the kind of feeling I get before a confrontation. Like, when I knew my parents were going to ground me. I was half-afraid and half-ashamed to meet him. Even though I knew he was going to be behind bars. So, I stayed in the very back of the crowd with my youngest, Clay. I held him in my arms so he could see. He was happy. I remember he kept singing that little song about the monkeys jumping on the bed. He couldn't discriminate between apes and monkeys. He pointed at the cage and said, "Look, Mommy! A monkey!"

Smithy was crouched up on a platform in his enclosure with a blanket pulled up almost over his head. It looked like he was trying to hide, like he was scared. And I felt sorry for him. I thought all the noise and excitement might be overwhelming. As people gathered around his cage, they yelled and called out to him. Everyone knew how famous he was."

18 *Smithy Can Sign* written and illustrated by Alejandra DaVinci

Reid asks, "Do you have any home video or photos of how he looked during your visit?"

Gail frowns and says, "No, we brought our video camera, but the guards at the gate told us we couldn't use it. I didn't end up taking any pictures. Anyway, my two oldest kids, David and Diana, who were twelve and ten at that time, pushed their way to the front of the crowd. I'd taught them to sign—not fluently, but some basic signs—so when they called to Smithy, they also signed, 'Hi, Smithy! How are you? I love you,' and told him their names.

"Well, Smithy just peeked out of his blanket for a while, but then he noticed my kids, and came to life. He bounded down from his platform and made a beeline for them. Everyone gasped when they saw him move. Then he signed, 'Let me out,' 'Let's play,' 'Got ice cream?'

"My younger daughter, Carrie, worked her way up to join her brother and sister. Smithy pointed at her—she's blonde, like me—and signed, 'Pretty.'"

Guthrie says, "Wow! Your kids were talking to the chimp that you taught."

Gail says, "It was amazing! But the guard posted by Smithy's cage came over right away and told my kids to leave. He said they needed to stay back for their safety, and that they couldn't talk to Smithy anymore. So, they started to walk away. And Smithy began bleating! He was, literally, like, crying out to them. And he signed to them—by name! 'Diana, please let me out' and 'David, help me, please!'

"He *noticed* them sign their names and he *remembered*! He was still so sharp! Even after all that time alone, he was still learning, still trying to communicate. And he remembered to say 'please!'"

Gail's voice hitches and Guthrie passes her a box of tissues; she takes one and blots at her eyes. The camera zooms in on her. Gail continues. "My kids were so upset because Smithy was begging them for help, and they couldn't help him. They were crying. They wanted to leave Eden. They didn't even want to stay and see the lions and tigers. Or the fireworks. It was terrible! A theme park isn't supposed to make you miserable."

Guthrie says, "Most theme parks don't have animals in cages."

Gail says, "We'd been to the zoo before, but none of the animals there asked us to help get them out. My kids felt sorry for their friend. They thought of Smithy as a friend, you see, because they'd grown up hearing and reading about him. I felt so helpless."

Guthrie pats her shoulder, then looks into the camera and says, "We're going to take a little break."

The camera fades out and back up on Guthrie and his guests. He says, "Joining us now is animal rights activist, Brad Vollmer, one-time researcher at CSAM and Smithy's self-proclaimed champion."

Brad enters stage right, waving to the audience. He has shoulder-length, graying hair, a goatee, and wears a T-shirt screened with a large picture of Smithy's face and the words "Remember Me."

Guthrie says, "Welcome, Brad. Thank you for joining us."

Brad says, "Thanks, Eliot. Afternoon, everybody."

Guthrie says, "Please tell us briefly what you've been up to lately."

Brad says, "Fighting the good fight for Smithy and as many animals as I can. I'm working with People for Primates, PETA, the World Wildlife Federation, and any other group that wants to improve conditions for animals in captivity and increase rights for sentient animals."

Guthrie asks, "Aren't all animals sentient?"

Brad says, "Yeah, of course, all animals feel pain and have intelligence to a degree, but . . . "

Guthrie finishes, "All animals are equal, but some are more equal than others?"

Brad smiles and says, "That's it." He alternates his responses between Guthrie and the camera. "All animals deserve respect, but some—apes, elephants, dolphins—deserve additional consideration because they're more highly developed. A dog . . . Look, I love dogs. Dogs are loyal—but they're dumb. You can kick a dog or beat it or leave it outside in the rain or disappear for days at a time and not feed it, and that dog will still love you. They don't judge you. They love unconditionally. But chimps have standards. They discriminate. If a chimp likes you, it means something! You're special. You've arrived."

Guthrie says, "Speaking of chimps, tell us about Smithy."

Brad says, "I haven't given up on him—I never will—but if I focused only on what I've accomplished for Smithy, I'd be very depressed, Eliot. Happily, I've been able to help some of our other animal friends. Perdita the Orca was a big victory. She was a two-year-old killer whale, a big girl, who was brought to Ocean Harbor for rehabilitation after she was injured by a freighter. But the park kept her as an attraction in the equivalent of a tiny wading pool. It was awful. She barely had space to turn around. After a five-year campaign, Born Free put enough public pressure on Ocean Harbor to release her back into the wild."

Guthrie says, "I read about that. Wasn't Perdita later killed by Alaskan natives during a sanctioned ritual hunt?"

Brad flushes and says, "Yeah . . . but at least she got to enjoy a few months of freedom before that happened. I haven't had as much luck with any of the gorillas or chimpanzees I've tried to help. The Friends of Smithy have brought amicus briefs in five lawsuits to date asking for legal remedies for research apes in New York, sideshow apes in Ohio, and privately owned and abused apes in Tennessee."

Guthrie asks, "What relief are you seeking?"

Brad says, "We want the animals transferred out of abusive and neglectful environments to places where they'll be treated with dignity, preferably a sanctuary like Bob La Fontaine's."

Guthrie says, "You're not seeking emancipation?"

Brad frowns and says, "No, nothing that progressive. But even with what little we're asking, judges still turn us down. Most of them use Borley's decision as a precedent. They say it makes no difference where an ape lives 'cause it'll still be in captivity. They've been saying that for twenty years with no consideration of how that decision's impacted Smithy!

I keep trying, with letter campaigns, the courts, and public calls for action, to get Cliff Stanhope to sit down with me, or if not with me, with anyone from People for Primates or another organization that can speak on Smithy's behalf. He wants nothing to do with us."

Brad turns to Gail. "Stanhope may be helping out big game animals, but Eden's no paradise for Smithy. He needs companionship and intellectual stimulation, and he's not getting it there. Stanhope's never added any other apes to his sanctuary and you're telling us he doesn't let Smithy interact with human visitors, either."

Gail says, "That was ten years ago."

Brad says, "Then or now, there's no excuse! He wants to communicate!"

Gail nods vigorously and says, "He does! Even though the noise and crowds startled him, he reached out. He called my children by name. He wanted to talk to them."

Guthrie asks, "How do you respond to people who call you a fanatic?"

Brad asks, "You mean people who think I want to ban pets and let apes vote and hold office?" He runs a hand through his hair. "Hey, I've got nothing against pets. I don't even mind zoos, as long as they treat the animals with dignity. Nothing like being chained up in a pit or confined to a tiny cage—the way Hansel and Gretel are at the Mowerbank Township Zoo!" He glares at the camera. "And I'm not trying to take away anyone's cat or dog. Big cats and alligators and chimps shouldn't be private property, but little domestic animals, I have no problem with—so long as you bring them inside when it's cold and don't leave them chained up all day."

Guthrie says, "That's good to know. Brad, what have you got for us today?"

Brad says, "I've got surveillance photos from Eden." He reaches under the table and picks up a manila folder. He opens it and begins fanning photographs over the table. "My PI is still on the loose. Stanhope's guards have never caught him—and never will. He's too good for them, and after years of watching Smithy suffer, he's down for the cause, too." Brad says to Reid, "You can have these for your book."

Reid nods and leans forward, looking eager. He asks, "What have we got?"

Brad says, "It's Smithy's home for the past two decades."

Gail picks up a photo, nods and says, "That's how it looked when I saw it."

Brad says, "Then nothing's changed since 1989. See how the cage is exposed on all four sides? And the trees aren't thick enough to provide full coverage? Smithy has nowhere to go if he wants privacy. Unless he hides under a blanket. He's doing that in this picture."

Brad passes a photo to Guthrie, who studies it and then passes it to Reid and Gail. An image of the photo is projected onto a screen above the table.

Brad continues. "All these pictures are time-stamped. They were shot within a three-hour span. It's a fair sample of how my poor old buddy spends every day. He lies around, lethargic. Then he sits and stares out the bars, at nothing, for hours."

Brad holds up a set of five pictures and cycles through them as the camera zooms in. All show Smithy seated in the middle of his cage, staring to the right.

Brad says, "These were all taken fifteen minutes apart. He didn't move a muscle."

Gail says, "It's almost like he's meditating."

Guthrie asks, "What's this?" and holds up a photo of Smithy motioning with his hands.

"It looks like he's signing."

Brad says, "Yes. That's the sign for 'fly.' He wants to leave, spread his wings and be free. I've got video of him signing, too."

Reid asks, "Might you be projecting your own meaning onto his actions? Could his gestures be random?"

Brad glowers and rises from his chair. Guthrie holds up both hands, placating, and says, "Gentlemen, please leave the fights to Jerry Springer." Brad sits down again, still scowling.

Reid says brightly, "At least Smithy's well-fed. He has space to move around and toys for enrichment. It looks like he finds ways to play, even when he's by himself." He passes a photo to Guthrie, who shows it to the camera. The image depicts Smithy sitting in a stationary swing in his enclosure; his feet hang down and his hands lie in his lap. Gail picks up a stack of photos, studies one, then shuffles it to the back and looks at the next.

Brad says, "This is the most verbal ape of our time, and he's had no one to talk to for *decades*! He's starving for companionship! Denying him that is like denying him food or water."

Reid asks, "If Stanhope brought in a playmate for Smithy, would you be satisfied?"

Guthrie asks, "What sort of companion would be appropriate for him? Would you be satisfied with any other chimp, or insist that Smithy be paired with one who could sign?"

Brad says, "Look, if I could talk to Smithy for five minutes and ask him, 'Are you happy? What do you want?' and if he told me he's OK being alone—"

Gail screams and throws the stack of photos on the table. She clutches her hands in front of her face as if they've been burned. Her mouth hangs open and her eyes bulge.

Guthrie asks, "Gail, are you all right?"

Gail says softly, "He's not alone."

Reid asks, "What?"

Gail repeats, "He's not alone." She points. "Look!"

Guthrie picks up the photo on top of the stack and examines it, impassive. Reid peers over Guthrie's shoulder to look at the photo and whistles. Brad glances between Gail and the men, confused. Finally, Guthrie turns the photo toward the camera and asks, "Can we get a close-up?"

The camera zooms in on an image of Smithy sitting in the swing. His lips purse in a hooting motion and his hands form the sign for "play." The angle of his body and the shadow on the ground indicate the swing is in motion. Guthrie runs his index finger over a section of the image and says, "Back here."

The camera zooms closer to a patch of shadow behind the swing and follows the path of Guthrie's finger. The shadow immediately behind the swing is thick and forms the hemline of a dress. The entire outline of a woman's figure is visible, including sleeves and hands positioned behind Smithy's shoulders. The camera pans up from skirt to shoulder; in place of the figure's face, only blackness is visible.

EXCERPT FROM
SMITHY: THE MILLENNIUM COMPENDIUM
BY REID BENNET, PHD

The photograph and its negative have been closely examined by many world-class labs, including the FBI's forensics department. None has found any evidence of digital enhancement or other tampering. The female's image appears in only one photo in the series. The time stamps on the photos before and after it indicate a lapse of only five minutes for the series and no point of entry or exit for any human.

And so, the twentieth century's biggest controversy about words closed with an image.

Smithy still lives in Eden. He has the cage to himself, as far as the naked eye can see. But few people—aside from Dr. Preis-Herald—believe any longer that he is alone.

Nor that we are alone in this world—or the next.

ACKNOWLEDGMENTS

Smithy started life just over eight years ago as a fleeting "What if . . ." that crossed my mind while reading a book over lunch. It's so gratifying to see what I initially thought was a semi-silly idea that only I might find entertaining finally come to fruition through the publication of this second book in the duology.

I owe much to all the people who helped bring me to the close of this journey, starting with my first readers Janice Burdick, Patrick McCann, Keith Darrell, and Katherine Kerestman, who gave me their time and their feedback. Special thanks and much love to Matt Stedman for all his support and encouragement.

I'm much obliged to Lawrence Ramirez for a crash course in linguistic anthropology that provided background for Book 1.

While attending my first Stokercon in 2017, I was fortunate to meet writer and freelance editor Stephen Provost whose input greatly helped refine this book. Thank you, Stephen!

I'm grateful to the Inkshares team--Adam Gomolin, Noah Broyles, Avalon Radys, Kurt Mueller, and Pam McElroy--for giving me the chance to tell my story, not once but twice, and for guiding me in bringing Smithy's story to life. Thank you for believing in me.

Many thanks to all of my supporters including my friends, my relatives, my extended Collins family, my co-workers, the North Torrance Mystery Book Club, and all of my readers for believing in Smithy.

Finally, throughout this book, I've taken certain artistic liberties, including (but not limited to) where the legal system and primate behavior are concerned. Though I tried to maintain historical and factual accuracy as much as possible, sometimes concessions were needed to advance the story. Thank you, readers, for indulging me.

INKSHARES

INKSHARES is a community, publisher, and producer for debut writers. Our books are selected not just by a group of editors, but also by readers worldwide. Our aim is to find and develop the most captivating and intelligent new voices in fiction. We have no genre—our genre is debut.

Previously unknown Inkshares authors have received starred reviews in every trade publication. They have been featured in every major review, including on the front page of the *New York Times*. Their books are on the front tables of booksellers worldwide, topping bestseller lists. They have been translated in major markets by the world's biggest publishers. And they are being adapted at the biggest studios and networks.

Interested in making your own story a reality? Visit Inkshares.com to start your own project, connect with other writers, and find other great books.

Printed in the USA
CPSIA information can be obtained
at www.ICGtesting.com
JSHW032218150424
61207JS00010B/213